THE HAND BEFORE THE EYE

Donald Friedman

Mid-List Press
Minneapolis

FIRST SERIES: NOVEL

Printed in the United States
First Edition
03 02 01 00   5 4 3 2 1

Chapter one, "Jewing," originally appeared in a slightly different form in *Tikkun*.

Library of Congress Cataloging-in-Publication Data
Friedman, Donald, 1943-
    The hand before the eye / Donald Friedman.
       p. cm.
    "First series—novel."
    ISBN 0-922811-42-3 (alk. paper)
    1. Jews—New York (State)—New York—Fiction. I. Title.
    PS3556.R5185 H3 1999
    813'.54—dc21
                               99-046568
                                   CIP

To my parents, Sylvia and Bert,
and my sister, Phyllis, who never got to read this,
and to my wife, Lisa Palmer,
who eased their dying and who midwifed the writer in me

Just as the hand, held before the eye, can hide the tallest mountain,
so the routine of everyday life can keep us from seeing
the vast radiance of and the secret wonders that fill the world.

—Eighteenth-century, Hasidic

I

A FROG IN THE WELL

JEWING

Lawyer Farbman had no time. Always, he calculated the shortest route: from home to office, seat to door, from a to b. He engineered his way through the noise and soot of Forty-Second Street, avoiding the human debris like a missile sensing obstacles. All the while his mind raced ahead, charting critical paths through the day, the week, the year.

With only hours to catch a plane and two day's worth of work to do before then, Farbman had been forced to take his banker, Worrad, out for one of the leisurely, expense-account lunches the man demanded along with first-run theater tickets and four-hundred-dollar cases of single malt scotch delivered discreetly to his Pound Ridge home at Christmas. It wasn't the usual baksheesh but a real problem. The examiners had come in. Farbman sat, so stunned he stopped glancing at his watch, incredulous at the annihilating message delivered between the throat clearings.

It was regrettable, but there hadn't been a payment on his firm's credit line in over two years. Even the interest wasn't current. But they wouldn't just yank the rug out? They would. Farbman's cherished tenet, that when you are in deep you tell the bank what to do, had somehow escaped his friend at the Chase.

Muscles constricting behind his vest, Farbman considered whether the same sentence would have been passed on a Hoyt or a Kellogg, if a club tie and braces would have made a difference. One week to produce six months of vigorish and a major reduction in the balance. With no concession for the funeral Farbman had explained he had to attend the next day in Mt. Pisgah, Illinois. Mt. Pisgah, Illinois, for Chrissakes, not Queens. It would take two days.

Farbman signaled for the check. "There has to be something ..."

Worrad dusted off the last sip of his Manhattan and stood. "Do a Chinese cleanup."

"How? You've got everything we own. No other bank would lend us a dime."

Worrad shrugged and, explaining he had an appointment, exited as the waiter returned to inform Farbman his credit card had been rejected.

Returning to his office, anxious as he was, Farbman had a determined beat to his stride which gave him an attractive purposefulness. He paused and accepted the photocopied handout from an earnest young Hasid only because he had been unbalanced by the bold question, "Are you Jewish?" In fact, Farbman thought his straight blond hair and blue eyes would have protected him from such an intrusion. The barely legible message, "The Meaning of Havdalah," of the Lubovitcher Rebbe—the mystic pope to the Jews of Eastern Parkway—with local Sabbath candle-lighting times, was shoved into his coat pocket. There it made its presence felt and prompted him, as he ascended in the Art Deco elevator cage, to try, for a moment before his floor, to riddle his Jewishness.

Certainly Farbman was a Jew. He knew some dialect jokes which he told poorly. He had been circumcised, become bar mitzvah; had joined a temple, supported the U.J.A., married a shiksa. But what about ritual observance? The proselytizing Hasidim with the van downstairs were inviting Jewish passersby to put on tefillin, to wrap the leather phylacteries around arm and head as the orthodox did every morning of their lives, and Farbman admitted he wasn't even sure what tefillin were, what was in the little boxes attached to the straps. The closest he had come to them was a display case in the lobby of his Reform temple, and an ugly black tangle in a Baggie that had belonged to his grandfather.

Did an abbreviated, English-version seder count? A political lecture or a book review from the rabbi on his annual High Holy Day appearance? How would those pasty-faced diamond merchants in their beards and earlocks and old world clothes account him? Would they, like their infamous persecutors, take his ethnicity as a genetic fact, as binding and as no more or less significant than eye color and the size of his feet? Farbman rejected such a notion: Jewishness was a philosophic decision, not programmed into strands of DNA. Yet his swarthy, kinky-haired doctor friend, Harold, who *had* put on tefillin, insisted that he was what a real Jew looked like. Sitting behind the wheel of his targa Porsche one day, Harold had twisted the mirror so Farbman could look at his blondness, his prominent cheekbones. "You are an aberrant form; the result of some Cossack rape."

The elevator doors opened to Farbman's floor, to reality. He was too busy for such musings. His life, even without the Damoclean threat of his bankers, was deadlines: court filings, statutes of limitation, and trial dates organized around constantly changing calendars crosschecked by all too fallible humans and machines and supported by the indefinite, uncertain cash flow of contingent fee cases. The spending always outstripped the judicial alchemy that turned lost limbs and mangled bodies into cash. Farbman's entire operation was tied to the banks by the about-to-be-severed umbilical cord of interwoven, overdue notes.

Marucci, his partner, was waiting for him, sitting behind Farbman's desk, chewing his fingers. Farbman broke the bad news.

"Jesus God." Marucci blanched. "What are we going to do?"

"Shake the trees," Farbman said. "Get the new bills out today. What's for trial or settlement, besides Alvarez? What about the kid with the hand off?"

Marucci shook his head. "It got carried. The die manufacturer's expert had a scheduling problem. What's-his-name, the cervical quad, should be reached in two or three weeks, but right now Alvarez is it. There's been some talk of 'nuisance value' on the incomplete abortion.

Maybe I can squeeze a little more."

Alvarez was the unpromising double leg-off. Farbman had sued every deep pocket they could think of but had yet to dream up a viable theory of liability against any of them. The problem was that Alvarez was simply a drunk who had wandered into a warehouse one night and fallen asleep under a truck that, the next morning, had backed over him. Alvarez hobbled in once a week or so to hit them up for an "advance," a few bucks to keep him in wine.

"He'll be in this afternoon," said Marucci. "I'll see if I can at least get him in shape for his courtroom debut."

"Look, I know this funeral is really badly timed, and I'm going to cancel it," said Farbman.

"No you're not. You can't change anything here anyway. Go. Relax a little. Get laid maybe."

"At a funeral, Marucci? In Mt. Pisgah, Illinois?"

"Where else will you find the time?"

"Not that I couldn't use it." Farbman remembered the reality of his life with Ann Marie.

Marucci put a hand on Farbman's shoulder. "Don't look so grim. It's just the pressure."

"I don't know," said Farbman.

There was a moment of silence for Farbman's dead sex life.

"Okay, let's get some money in here." Farbman waved good-bye to Marucci and buzzed his secretary, instructing her to keep the most pestering calls off his back. "Especially Ida and Janet, and their suicide threats."

"Ida called while you were at lunch. She says Janet's right on the edge. Ida's hidden her medication. She gives her one allergy pill at a time."

"Spare me."

Ida was the seventy-five-year-old mother of the obese, regressed fifty-year-old Janet Sodowick, a divorce client who telephoned or had her family telephone a dozen times a day or more when she was off her medication. Since an attorney could not withdraw from a matrimonial case once the retainer was spent, Farbman was stuck with Janet and the rest of her relay team: a widowed mother and two maiden sisters—fat, wheezing viragos with identical faces of thick, white make-up and hair thinned by years of chemicals to bleached-out wisps and strands.

Farbman was trying to cajole money in an intense but affectedly casual dialogue with his speaker phone when his door opened without a knock. His nineteen-year-old secretary, Joy, stuck her trendy mane of striped hair inside. Held frozen in place by Farbman's opened palm, she whispered: "Ida's on oh-three and your daughter's on oh-eight."

"Arnie, do what you can for me. My kid's on the other line. I'll get back to you Monday."

He pushed the appropriate button and asked worriedly: "Jennifer, you okay?"

"Guess what, Daddy?"

"Jennifer, are you all right?"

"Yes, Daddy. Now guess what."

"I can't. Listen, Jennifer, your dad's really busy right now—so if you want me to know, you've got to just tell me."

"Mom took me and Jason to the doctor, to Harold, and we've got something, I forgot what, but we can't touch anyone and we don't have to go to school tomorrow."

"Jennifer, put Mom on right now."

"Daddy, it's like bugs or something."

"Jennifer, where is your mother?"

"I'll get her. When are you coming home, Daddy?"

"Jennifer, get Mom," ordered Farbman, putting as much authority as he could into his voice while staying well short of the tone he used to terrorize his associates. He heard the crash of the receiver being dropped on hand-cut Mexican tile and his daughter calling shrilly for her mother.

Joy opened the door again. "Come in," said Farbman. "I'm just holding."

Farbman was of several minds about his secretary. Did she know she was making a spectacle of herself in her tight jeans and pumps? Was it for him? If it were some faddish new abandon in dress codes, it had no place in a law office, and he would have one of the older secretaries speak to her. On the other hand, if it were intended for him alone …

Farbman thrust his palm toward Joy again as his wife began to speak. Indifferent to the gesture, his secretary blurted: "Ida says she must talk to you. Janet slashed her wrists." She turned to leave the room.

"Wait!" Farbman yelled. "Sorry, hold on, Hon, will you? No. Just a minute…. Two seconds…. Will you please find out, as I asked you, whether she has actually cut them or is just threatening?… Ann Marie? What's going on with the kids?"

"They have scabies."

"Am I supposed to know what that is?"

"Listen, save that tone for your staff."

"Okay. The question is withdrawn. I'll reframe it. What is scabies? Would you please tell me if you know?"

"I want to strangle you when you talk to me like that."

"Look, all I want to know is the state of my children's health, for Chrissake. Can't we for once just focus on the topic instead of getting lost in another battle about how we discuss it?"

"You're too much. Scabies is like lice. It's a parasite that gets under the skin and lays eggs that keep hatching and spreading all over the body. That's what those red curvy lines are that the kids have been scratching for the past week."

"My God! Is it contagious?"

"Harold says it's highly contagious, at least through direct physical contact—which means we're safe from each other—if not from the children."

Her reminder poked him sharply in the gut. He had self-righteously endured about three years of enforced celibacy, three years of sexless sniping. It had begun so far back he could not even recall the first prideful withdrawal, or which of them had decided that that time the other would have to make the effort.

"But it's contagious even during months of incubation so you can be spreading the disease as a carrier and not even know you have it."

"Oh, my God. So you and I could have it, too?" Farbman was suddenly aware that he was itching under his sleeves, then under his socks.

"Yup. To get rid of it you use the same stuff you use on crabs. Just cover the body from head to foot, every crack and crease. Leave it on for ten hours—but no more or it soaks in too deep."

"What stuff for crabs?"

"You never had crabs?"

"No, I haven't had crabs. You've really got some image of me."

"Well, I have."

Farbman paused to let the idea register.

"What are you saying to me? You picked up crabs in your convent school dormitory?"

"No, in a Fort Lauderdale motel room on a spring break with four other girls from Sorrows."

Joy appeared suddenly again in an ersatz fur jacket, carrying her purse and more papers for Farbman. She did not wait for him to interrupt his call. "Here's your letters. Ida's still on hold. She says Janet really cut them. Mr. Hagan called. He says he's going to the judge in the morning unless you call him within a half hour and agree that Mr. Lardiano can take the children to ski Copper Mountain. Marilyn says she can't finish the bills because the computer's broke and should she type them. Mr. Alvarez—the double leg-off—is waiting out there for you. Here are your other messages. Oh, and your father just called. Says he needs your help with a legal problem. I've got to run, it's five ten and someone's been waiting for me." She turned to leave, then added: "Oh yeah. I made your reservations to Chicago. You pick up your ticket at the airport."

Ann Marie finished up: "Look, I'm staying home with the children tomorrow and taking the treatment. Harold says it's optional for you and me. But we could keep reinfecting each other. You can decide what you want to do when you get back from the funeral. The kids are screaming."

"Wait," said Farbman.

"Can't. Have a good trip. Give my condolences to Michael and his father."

Farbman punched Ida's blinking light. Her whining, hectoring voice actually caused his ears to hurt.

"She didn't get the check again and that louse is driving in a new Porsche automobile with the woman—"

"Ida, did she cut her wrists or didn't she?"

"The girl is absolutely suicidal. I swear she'll kill herself if she isn't divorced in a month."

"She didn't cut them, did she, Ida?"

"She had the razor in her hands."

"Good-bye, Ida. *In her hands* is not cutting."

As Farbman returned his father's call, Joy's words reverberated. *Your father needs your help with a legal problem.* Farbman had been waiting his entire life for such recognition. Like any Jewish son he understood that he could never please the man. That he would never overcome the stigma of being a failed premed. But after a decade of journeyman lawyering, Farbman figured his father might have judged him competent enough to stop turning all of his well-paying work over to others. Now, it appeared his moment had arrived.

Farbman's father was a dentist who owned, in various partnerships, a dental laboratory and a half dozen commercial real estate parcels including a medical building, three gas stations, a strip mall, and a free-standing Pizza Hut. These enterprises not only generated transactional work—the paper drafting for leases and acquisitions, the applications and approval processes—but choice litigation. Over the years Farbman's father had been embroiled in construction disputes, claims of professional negligence against engineers and architects, zoning and planning board appeals, partnership breakups, and actions for breach of contract—stuff that Farbman handled for others—and every last bit of it he had sent to competing lawyers.

Megan, his father's spinster office manager, asked after Ann Marie and his children.

"Everyone's just great, just great," said Farbman.

"Your father's with a patient, but I know he wants to speak to you."

Farbman was placed on hold and forced to endure easy-listening music. Eventually, his father came on line. "Hi. Thanks for calling. Bite, honey. Again."

"Hi. I just got your message. I'm hurrying to get to Michael's mother's funeral."

"I heard. Terrible. Bite. Again. Again. Release. When will you be back?"

In the background Farbman heard the spine-shuddering whine of the drill. "Right away. I've got a lot of office pressure at the moment."

"Side to side now. Open. Could you stop by the house on your way to the airport? I need a legal opinion on something and I'd rather not wait if you can do it. Spit, dear."

Noting the sun dying over New Jersey, an elated Farbman checked his watch and realized the Masada limo had been waiting twenty minutes already. He told his father he was on his way. He grabbed his coat and bolted for the door, almost colliding in the reception area with his only hope, the hopeless, red-rimmed Alvarez.

"We go to court for money, jess?"

Farbman nodded as he put a couple of bills into the man's hand, thinking to himself, Alvarez, you really don't have a leg to stand on.

As Farbman pushed through the revolving door, a blast of arctic wind almost knocked him over. He flipped up the collar on his overcoat and waved when he spotted the Lincoln parked behind the IRT entrance at the corner. The flow of people moving behind the police barricade toward the subway was obstructed by a grotesquely fat woman wearing dancer warm-ups over blue jeans and a mantilla of filthy blanket pieces over her head and shoulders. She held her left arm in a circle as if cradling a basket. With her right arm she seemed to be strewing imaginary petals before the processionary crowd that divided around her.

"Saturdays," she cried, "Sundays, here. Wednesdays. Here, Mondays."

Farbman, holding his breath against her effluvium, squeezed around her and through the crowd, into the well-padded back seat of the Town Car. He shuddered, chilled from just that brief exposure to the cold. Farbman remarked to the driver, who gave his name as Ariel, how early it was to be so dark, and he thought about how much Ann Marie hated the winter.

"It's not only the cold and the dark of it, but the silence," she would say. "Listen: Nothing. No bugs, no birds, no sound." Then she would inevitably rhapsodize about summer and most especially about the humid, barefoot summers of her Ohio childhood, about her memories of riding the neighbor's horse, of tubing down the river, the cicadas perpetually droning in the background, and when the seventeen-year locusts emerged and blanketed everything—fields, trees, lawn, house— so you couldn't take a step outside without crunching them underfoot, her Jack Russell terrier scooting about, devouring them by the mouthful. This, while the boy Farbman in Brooklyn, on another planet, was discovering a thousand and one uses for concrete and asphalt; rollerskating and hopscotching, playing stickball and stoopball, biking in the alleys. Then the two of them collegiately meeting in late adolescence and finding pleasure in the slap and thump of the tumescent muscular Jew against her bony Irish back.

Harold, when he wasn't just being dismissive, calling Ann Marie "the white woman," suggested Farbman's attraction was more a matter of oedipal inevitability than natural selection, and Farbman—joking she was better than oedipal, she was table grade—could accept the hypothesis without needing to spend a sports car's worth of hours on somebody's couch testing it out.

But he often wondered what could have drawn a girl reared on white bread to the eater of lox and chicken schmaltz? Was there some analogous Electral charge produced by the chortling drunk in grass-green golf pants she called Dad? Perhaps it was the satisfaction she received by more direct expressions of Jewish orality.

Or used to receive. Sex was so far back in their connubial history they no longer even discussed it. Instead, each day they carped and verbally ambushed each other. That morning Farbman couldn't find the dark suit he wanted to wear at the funeral and was told it was still at the cleaners. And his favorite gray sport shirt was still in the laundry. When he pointed out to Ann Marie that it was more than a week for both of them, she said Opal had had a problem with her son and missed a day going to his school and there was not time for the woman to get the laundry in with all the other housework. "You said we can afford help two days a week and that's it. If you don't like the way I direct Opal, you do it from now on. In fact, why don't you take over managing the household, and I'll criticize you."

Farbman would love to have written off his wife's irritability to the temperature drop and an inadequate number of lumens hitting her retina, but she was just as miserable at their beach house during the summer solstice. He closed his eyes and saw Ann Marie standing at the sink, rinsing and stacking bowls and pots from dinner on a dishtowel, her wine glass topped off with the remains of the bottle she had drunk by herself. She was singing a snatch of something he couldn't quite make out except for the words "curtain" and "lady" and "night."

Something glittered in her hair, which, when he stepped closer, was revealed to be an iridescent green insect.

"Hey," he said, "there's something in your hair, a bug I think," and she replied, "The little green guy? He's been with me since I got back from my walk."

Farbman smiled. "I'll get him, just hold still."

"No. Just leave him." Ann Marie backed away, raising her dripping hands in defense against him. "He's grown attached to me. I take him around."

"Are you nuts?" said Farbman, still smiling. "Let me get it off."

He reached again and Ann Marie slapped his hand, hard. "I told you 'no' and I mean it. Leave him alone, just leave him alone," she shouted, then started crying. "He appreciates me. That means something to me. And stop looking at me like I'm crazy and get away."

Out the limo window, Farbman saw a man crawling into his tiny, cardboard home—one of a dozen lining the sidewalk of the Midtown Tunnel entrance. What we have all come to, Farbman thought. And what trouble had his father come to that he needed his son's help? Farbman's mind ricocheted among the possibilities: mob threats on a construction job, tax fraud, a malpractice suit. The limo dispatcher called to report that there was plenty of room on later flights but no cheap fares left, so he'd have to pay full coach. Farbman said he hoped he could avoid that, and Ariel, who had been as suicidally aggressive as the name Masada Limo promised, honking and weaving his way through the lethargic Expressway traffic, immediately pulled on to the shoulder to end-run the next clot of cars. Farbman, hearing the accelerating wheels on the gravel, relaxed and made a mental note to add a ten to his normal gratuity.

He returned to speculating on his father's predicament for a while, then clicked on the little gooseneck lamp over his shoulder and read a law journal until they reached the winding suburban streets of his parents' neighborhood. He instructed Ariel to wait in front of the Tudor house where Farbman had once lived but where he was now required to ring the bell.

Dr. Farbman opened the door, took his son's hand, and squeezed it firmly with fingers conditioned by forty years of manual labor. "I see you're still too good for a taxi. Wish I had your money. Don't take your coat off. I want you to come out in the yard. But say hello to your mother first."

Farbman walked into the kitchen, kissed his mother, and failed his personal test of adulthood by immediately opening the refrigerator, as he did every time he entered his parents' home. He told his mother that Ann Marie and the children were wonderful and that he couldn't stay for dinner, then slid open the patio door to join his father. It must be serious business if they had to speak outside. Did he think the house was bugged? Farbman followed his father across the floodlit lawn to the spot where Farbman's childhood swing set once stood. It probably wasn't professional negligence since the dentist could just turn the claim over to his insurance carrier. Unless it involved a complaint to the State Board.... His father gestured toward the neighbor's property. "You see this?"

"What?"

"The big tree limb here."

"Yes."

"So, what do you think?"

"What do I think about what?"

"Can I just cut it or do I have to ask McDonough first? I know it's his tree, but I'd prefer not to deal with the anti-Semitic bastard at all."

For a long moment Farbman just stood there, dumb, unwilling to comprehend; then he mumbled that he'd have to research it. His father shook his head in disbelief. "This is so complicated?"

Farbman said he was late for his plane, and walked off hurriedly to the car, making a big thing of looking at his watch, which told him he'd already missed it.

Approaching death ... thought Farbman as the plane turned onto final approach for the landing at O'Hare. Approaching death from the sky, eating almonds. Then he made a game of it. Traveling through the dark, over endless flat land, he thought: Approaching death in debt, in a rented car.

Michael's mother and father were holocaust survivors. While they were in the camps, Michael and his brother had lived with gentiles. Somehow the family was reunited after the war and found their way to a poultry farm in Illinois. Farbman had warm memories from his college days of Michael's big bosomed mother and her lavish dinners. He knew from Michael that she had died at home, her body returned once again to the skeletal weight of the camps.

At the Mt. Pisgah Motor Inn—fifteen wooden units with a small square swimming pool fenced off in the asphalt lot—Farbman found a green linoleum floor and a blinding, buzzing florescent light. The inhospitality of the place contrasted starkly with his past visits: Michael's mother pressing food on him, insisting he sample three desserts and always "mit shlag." Then, sitting on her clumsy furniture, draped with antimacassars, she'd put Mozart on her Victrola and, when a bored Michael left the room, tell stories about her girlhood before the war, when her worries were music lessons and homework and boys, and what it was like when things began to change. Farbman, climbing into his sagging bed, recalled how he would follow her up to the guest room so she could personally demonstrate the light switch, open the window, give him a towel and an extra blanket—even tuck him in if he'd asked. Imagining he had, he slipped into the cowl of sleep.

Farbman slept through the alarm on his runner's watch. When he finally got to the funeral home there was a line of cars waiting to park. He tried to steer to a spot near the entrance, away from the rest of the traffic, but an attendant trotted over to send him back with the others. Farbman pointed out the obvious bottleneck the attendant was creating, but the man couldn't be reasoned with. "All right," said Farbman, "it's your funeral."

Taking a pointed, too small yarmulke from the usher, Farbman tried to balance it on his head, feeling like a child as he entered the overflowing chapel. The funeral home was clearly unprepared for the number of mourners. Conscious of his blondness among the dark Jewish faces of Eastern Europe, Farbman gave his condolences to Michael and his family. Then he stood against the wall among the farmers and tradesmen who nodded in recognition or solemnly clasped their rough peasant hands.

The rabbi said Michael's mother was a woman who lived, who *was*, her past. Forced to leave her family in hiding, she had survived to bring them forth to thrive. She was, he said, independent, courageous. A Jew who was nagged always by the question of her family's and her people's sufferings but who, nonetheless, lived always devoutly, honestly, courageously.

"Our ranks," he said, "are depleted."

Waiting in the car for the funeral procession to unsnarl, Farbman was transfixed by the sight of a long-legged woman with pronounced cheekbones and a full sensuous mouth, exiting the funeral home. Michael, smiling, led her straight to Farbman, and introduced her through the window.

"This is my cousin Leah, the ectress," Michael crudely mimicked the Yiddish dialect. "Can you give her a ride to the cemetery?"

Farbman was already leaning over to open the door. "Of course, Michael. Can I take anyone else?" he added for Leah's benefit as she slid in.

"Hello, I'm Leah Stein." Cool, firm grip. A mouth that made Farbman's blood course. "And it's 'aspiring' actress at the moment. I pay the bills with voice-over."

The voice that supported the body was deeply pitched and slightly raspy. Farbman found it so intoxicating that his brain seemed to dull as she spoke.

"Where are you from?"

She told him that she'd driven from Chicago the day before and stayed at Michael's parents' home.

"How was it?"

"Heavy scene with the rabbi till real late. Did you stay here last night?"

"Yes."

"Don't tell me you stayed at the Anthony Perkins Memorial Motel? Next to Mickey D's?"

"You're not kidding. I wouldn't even consider a shower until morning."

They both laughed. The shared humor felt good, but Farbman wondered if he could trust it, whether her openness was a reaction to her bereavement or to him.

"What kind of scene with the rabbi?" he asked, engaging the gears and taking his place in the procession.

"He came by to discuss the eulogy and started right in on the survival stuff."

"Is that so bad?"

"It is for kids whose parents, like mine, never let them forget it." She turned to look out the window. "We just didn't want that crap. We don't see them as heroic, you see, just people who'd simply been altered forever by their pasts. 'Scarred' doesn't do it. Maybe 'raped,' like someone who was raped as a child, who could never take full pleasure in life again."

"But isn't it still a giant, unignorable fact?"

"Of course; it's just not the part of our parents that we care to dwell on, or even remember."

"I thought the rabbi came across as someone who knew and cared about your aunt."

"Well, he didn't."

"Are you going to stay with the family for a while?"

"You know," Leah said, "I actually had planned to be down this weekend anyway, for a sort of retreat in the state park. With an Hasidic rabbi coming all the way from the Pacific Northwest, of all places. It will be my first orthodox shabbos. I mean my mother lit candles and stuff, but we never really got into it."

"I never did, either. But a day of rest sounds like a great idea." The picture of himself in some lonely rustic setting with this woman made Farbman delirious.

"Well, Heschel and Buber say the idea is not so much to rest, but to try not to impose oneself on a world of things. To create a place in time, outside the temporal world, for one day. To experience the joy of that spiritual, timeless place. You can't mourn on the Sabbath, so my aunt's death will be an additional burden to deal with."

"Who is this rabbi?"

"His name is Sholem—Avram Sholem. He was invited to visit by a local Reform congregation. The woods was his idea. A compromise, I guess—a neutral meeting ground. Sholem is a famous mystic who sat at the right hand of the Lubovitcher Rebbe and who was sent out by the Rebbe years ago to proselytize. You know anything about the Lubovitchers?"

Farbman, catching a dubious look on her face, groped in his pockets for the Rebbe's 'Thought of the Week.' Producing the paper for Leah, he thought: At last, manifest proof of God's existence.

"I'm no expert," Farbman said, "but I've always been fascinated by Lubovitch."

"Far out," said Leah, reading about Havdalah, which Farbman had not read far enough to learn was the concluding service on the Sabbath. "You'd like Rabbi Sholem. He's a remarkable man."

"You've met him before?"

"Just once, years ago, at a Reform Jewish summer camp. Instead of serving up the usual Ethical Culture-type moral instruction, Sholem became our spiritual leader—our rebbe as the expression goes. He just appeared one day in his shtetl costume and, without introducing himself, led us outdoors where he had arranged a circle of chairs." The husky laugh again. "Beware of his circles."

"I'll remember that," said Farbman as he pulled into the cemetery.

The cemetery was demarcated from the flat desolate landscape by a six-foot, chainlink fence. Farbman and Leah stood behind Michael and his family, who stood under a canopy over the open grave. Nearby the indifferent gravediggers lounged and gawked. A little farther away a backhoe chugged as it dug another grave. It beeped as it backed, louder than the rabbi's words, and ground its gears when it moved forward. But the stunning, echoing sound of the first shovelful of dirt on the coffin cut through all the noise. Farbman felt Leah grasp his arm. She cried softly next to him as the shovel was passed from Michael to his brother. Farbman's pulse thudded in his ears. He tried to draw comfort from the bewildering Hebrew, to ignore Leah's casual appropriation of his supporting shoulder and his discomfiture at the guilty awareness that they stood as a couple. The yarmulke blew off his head, and Leah was forced to release Farbman's arm as he went to retrieve it. She did not take it again, and they did not speak as they left the cemetery.

At the farmhouse, Farbman paused on the porch to pour the ablution water from the pitcher over Leah's hands, then his own. Inside, as they lifted their paper plates with each forkful of smoked fish and potato salad, Leah continued her description of Rabbi Sholem's camp visit while Farbman stared into her eyes.

"Remember the circle?" Leah continued.

"Beware," said Farbman.

"Right," she smiled, and explained how Sholem, addressing everyone, including the counselors and other rabbis as "kinderloch," had astonished them by announcing that they were going to pray; or rather, that he was going to pray and that everyone else should feel free but not obliged. "He sat down, took off his glasses, and closed his eyes." Leah mimed the removal of the glasses and pressed her fingers to her eyes. "Then, he opened them again. He asked us to ignore what he called 'idiosyncrasies'—his tendency to rock back and forth and to pray aloud. 'Pay no attention,' he said. In a few minutes he began to dovin, to chant and to rock, back and forth."

Mesmerized by her full, sharply defined lips and enveloping voice, Farbman began to marshal his explanations to Ann Marie for a delayed return.

Leah continued. "Well, the kids exchanged looks and squirmed and smiled and whispered and felt very uncomfortable. In what I remember as a very brief time, the undertone of whispering and squirming began to recede and his chanting began to dominate and possess me. I felt a lump in my throat. Another girl was the first to start crying, but she was soon followed by everyone else. Rabbis, counselors, kids.

"When everyone was weeping and sobbing, Sholem opened his eyes and looked at the havoc he'd wrought. Then, he smiled, and grabbed the hands of the two people closest to him and shouted 'Kinderloch, let's dance!' And he broke into some wild Hasidic melody, leading the entire camp, singing and dancing and holding hands, through the woods and fields."

"How soon do we leave?" asked Farbman.

"Any time," said Leah, "just so we're settled in before sundown."

Farbman got Ann Marie on the telephone and easily convinced her that he ought to spend another day with Michael, and maybe he should take a little religious retreat himself.

"Stay as long as you like," she offered. "We wouldn't talk this much if you were home."

He felt more guilty giving the same explanation to the children. Jason, however, was enthusiastic: "Great, Dad. I'm going on a trip, too, with my Hebrew School class tomorrow. To Ellis Island, and then to the lower East Side to see where your grandparents came in and how they lived and everything."

"Okay," said Farbman, "we'll compare notes when I get back."

Farbman had no difficulty getting a room in the state lodge on that cold Friday night. The place was dead. The only guests were the Reform congregants who appeared unsettled at having had to travel to the woods as a precondition to their religious experience. They chatted sociably among themselves as they entered the room in which the chairs had already been placed in a circle.

Rabbi Sholem appeared in the doorway: huge and forbidding in his black clothes and beard—exactly as Farbman had expected him to look.

"Gut Shabbos, kinderloch," he greeted them. Quickly appraising the people, he took their hands and separated couples from each other, putting Farbman just far enough from Leah that he couldn't see her.

There were immediate, anxious efforts to regain control: "We are so glad you could come," began one of the wives. "Why don't you tell us a little about yourself," suggested a physician.

Sholem said, "No, kinderloch," in a paternal tone, although he was no older than most of those in the group. "Let's sing a song."

"We don't know Hebrew," they protested. "We don't know any Hebrew songs."

"You all know the hymn 'Goin' Home?'" Sholem inquired, without a trace of irony. When they nodded yes, he began to sing and everyone joined him.

Go-in home.

Go-in home.

Go-in home to God.

Farbman noticed that Sholem's mournful voice subsumed the others and colored the melody with Hebraic lamentation, with the hint of a wail. It imparted an immediacy that made Farbman's mind run to images of grief, to the graveside at the burial of Michael's mother. He started to wish her well, and the realization struck that she was gone. Beginning to cry, he wondered whether his kind, directionless thoughts were what was meant by "prayer."

When the song ended, Farbman could hear snuffling and nose blowing. He looked up into Sholem's eyes, and it seemed that the rabbi spoke directly to him.

"I recently discussed prayer with another clergyman who told me that when he prayed he saw 'a gray shape, sort of rectangular or oblong.'" Sholem laughed as he described it, and by the shake of his head acknowledged with what sadness he viewed the silly idea. "When I pray," said Sholem, smiling, "I see a white-bearded old man on a throne, probably the angel Gabriel."

Several people shook their heads angrily, and a Honda dealer and his friend, a liquor wholesaler, rolled their eyes. Sholem took note but continued, unperturbed. With songs and food and talk, he had his "kinderloch" recall the odors of their mothers' kitchens.

Farbman smelled potato latkes and kreplach and noodle kugel. Hidden melodies were drawn out of him—tastes and sounds that returned to him the simple pleasures of childhood, the feeling of having his loving Eastern European grandparents just in the other room.

Rabbi Sholem called it the game of "Jewing." It was the mystification of the ordinary. "When you play this game," Sholem said, "you transform the familiar, and you, the player, and others around you, experience life in a way that enriches and nourishes the players. You do this by hallowing the everyday."

Instead of criticizing Reform practices for their deviations from traditional ritual, or for the incorporation of Christian ceremony, the rabbi focused on the apparent lack of satisfaction in the Reform congregants. His objection to the organ in the temple was not that it was Protestant but that it was depressing.

"If you want music," he suggested, "why not a brass ensemble, or a string quartet?" He began to hum possible arrangements of familiar liturgical tunes as they might be played by such instruments.

Farbman asked why Sholem played the specific game that he called "Jewing." Did the rabbi think there was some qualitative difference among the possibilities of mystic experience promised by the Buddha, Saint John of the Cross, or the Baal Shem Tov? He did not. Sholem spoke only of "the fact of particularization." Farbman had been acculturated as he was. The smells of his mother's kitchen. Farbman could not intellectually justify the fun of this game, and Rabbi Sholem didn't want to: he went out of his way to discourage profound talk.

As it grew late and people began to drift off to their rooms, Sholem intercepted and embraced each one. He would whisper in an ear or perhaps kiss a cheek, Farbman couldn't be sure; but all of them, even the eye-rollers and head-shakers, hugged back and one of them—the eye-rolling Honda dealer—to Farbman's astonishment, jammed his face in Sholem's frock and wept like a child.

Farbman continued to focus on sensory perceptions and discovered that this engrossing play kept him in the moment and, wonderfully, that the immediacy of his experience brought release from anxiety. His breathing deepened and he relaxed into a timeless present.

So involved was Farbman in the game that he only gradually became aware that everyone, including Leah, had gone, leaving him alone with the rabbi. Together they walked through the chill dark to their cabins. Haunted by images of Ann Marie, Farbman struggled with guilt, suddenly recognizing that, like himself, she was who she was; not the object he had made her, but another person, another source of holiness. "All this is nice," said Farbman to the rabbi, "but what about right behavior? What about sin?"

The rabbi paused and looked up at the endless constellations. "Above us and with us right now there is past and future, all we have done and all we will do. You must do today what you do on Yom Kippur, that sacred day of atonement—be here, in the present, acting in this world. Saying the word differently, you must strive for 'at-one-ment,' to be at one with that past and future."

The grinning shaman hugged Farbman hard into his black coat and turned him loose.

"For true repentance there must be change. Remember when it comes—the flash, the insight—that it's only the beginning. To become a baal teshuvah takes more."

"A what 'chuva'?"

"Never mind. That's for another day. Shabbat shalom," he said and went inside.

Farbman awoke and was out the door with the first light. For hours he walked over the dead land, through cold gray woods, over hoar-frosted fields, branches snapping underfoot. When was the last time he'd seen the sky from horizon to horizon? When had he breathed such air? He felt his body open, his mind unfurl. He wandered without aim or direction.

Following bright glints of sunlight, Farbman came to a lake. By its edge stood the hulking black figure of Sholem and next to him, Leah. Farbman's feet smashed through the snow crust as he approached to greet them. They smiled at each other and said, "Gut Shabbos," their breath visible spirits. Leah searched Farbman's eyes, and he flushed.

Flanked by his two friends, Farbman felt the cold empty woods as he walked. He felt his body feel the cold and the ancient pine woods, and the flow of affection from the people next to him. They were connected to him, as he realized he was to the barren oak and birch, to the birds wheeling overhead, to his wife and his family, even to the family in Europe he'd never met, distanced by death and years.

Farbman returned alone to his cabin and sat on a wooden chair by the window in the warming sun. A deer appeared briefly at the wood's edge, then disappeared. Farbman did not know the time and did not care. He was hungry but did not want to leave his little patch of sunlight. He hoped the deer would return.

A knock: Leah with some bread and cheese, the meal she was afraid he would miss. "You're a life saver," said Farbman. There was only one chair so they pulled the bed by the window to eat in the sun.

While they ate they shared nothing but silence and shy smiles, Leah leaning back luxuriating in the heat that poured through the window. Their eyes met and locked. Leah made a low purring noise and lifted her sweater over her head. She wore long cotton knit underwear, buttoned down the front. It was white with a pattern of tiny indistinct violets and it clung to her torso outlining her breasts.

As he reached for her she leapt at him. She sucked the breath out of him as they crushed, made crumbs of the bread, yanked at their clothes. They kissed, bit, licked, and scratched, spun around like magnetic toy dogs. He threw her legs over his shoulders and she grasped him by the scrotum and, grunting, pulled him repeatedly into her.

In his mind's eye they stood now at the burial over the open grave while the rabbi and the mourners intoned Kaddish and they pumped in the rhythm of the prayer. He was, by turns, a Yeshiva student sneaking out of his dirt-floored study hall in Poland for a tryst with a forbidden thick-muscled farm girl and, flipping her to her knees, a Polish peasant catching and subduing an aloof Jewess in the leaves. Farbman took her like an animal in rut, held her in place with a fistful of hair, the slippery fingers of his other hand kneading and thrumming, while she screamed and clawed at his buttocks.

They laughed and sweated and the room stank to heaven with their juices and their come. Then Leah noticed the dusk and exclaimed, "The Havdalah service," and they covered themselves to rejoin the others.

For his last transformation, Rabbi Sholem, the shaman, illusionist, and champion game player—eschewing the wine, the candles and the aromatic herbs—performed the concluding service of the Sabbath with a transporting can of Coke, a ladies' compact, and a match. Farbman had never felt more at peace.

That night Farbman dreamed of Michael's mother's funeral, but it was Alvarez in the grave. He was in an open coffin only half-filled, his prostheses misplaced. The backhoe began to move, to fill the grave, while Farbman shouted, "Wait, let's find his legs." But as the machine backed and beeped its warning, Alvarez opened his eyes and cried for help. Farbman clambered into the grave and pulled him out by his arms just as the dirt avalanched in. "You must stop sleeping in such dangerous places," Farbman admonished. "Suppose you hadn't heard the horn."

Farbman awoke with itching bumps and welts on his hands and chest and groin. He thought first of the worn-out mattresses he'd been using, and then he remembered the scabies. He sat on the edge of the bed scratching and cursing his luck while considering what he would say to Leah.

He didn't realize what the dream meant until he was halfway through his shave. He raced to get Marucci on the phone.

"If that truck had had a standard backup warning on it, Alvarez might still have his legs." Huzzahs. Money in the bank.

Before he could call Leah, he found a note from her shoved under the door. *Sorry to leave without goodbye. Remember the Sabbath day and keep it holy.*

Farbman resolved to do just that. Next week he would make his own Shabbat, create his own timeless world, perhaps renew his vows with Ann Marie.

But driving back to his plane, Farbman remembered he would have to get the cervical quad ready for trial the following Monday. He would lose a day to the scabies cure. And he had promised to go to Jason's Saturday soccer game. Maybe the week after....

Sitting that night on his son's bed, he asked Jason about the excursion to Ellis Island, his connection with his heritage.

"It was great, Dad. The bus broke down and we missed the boat, but they gave each kid two dollars and they told us to pretend we were immigrants and to bargain with the shopkeepers like it was all the money we had. Then we went to this awesome delicatessen, Katz's, and there was this old sign on the wall that said 'Send a salami to your boy in the army.'"

Farbman kissed and hugged his child good-night and, after a moment's reflection, said, "I'm glad it was fun."

A CROW AMONG PIGEONS

Farbman couldn't believe it: Like the frog in the well in the high school algebra problem, he'd climbed up two feet only to slide most of the way back. The Alvarez money had pacified Worrad and the bank and brought his and Marucci's mortgages current, but it hadn't eroded the mountain of trade payables. The cervical quad was no-caused by a jury unsympathetic to a showoff drunk doing a jackknife off a No Diving sign into a shallow lake. Nothing was settling; no one was paying. Farbman scowled at his stained list of aged receivables, then stabbed his associate's intercom button. "Reilly, we got the judgment against Munro eight months ago. Why hasn't it been collected?"

"No assets," Reilly responded. "He ignored two subpoenas and a court order for supplemental proceedings. When I made the contempt application, he finally showed and answered 'no' to every question except liabilities. He's got no house, no car, no cash, no collections, no expectancies—just his paycheck from counseling at the state rehab center—but there are several wage executions ahead of us."

"What about the leg?"

"What about it?"

"Did he wear it to court or did he come in on crutches?"

"He was wearing it."

"So why didn't you grab it?"

"Are you kidding? Just start yanking on his leg in the courtroom? We don't even have a writ yet."

"We don't need one. Read the file. The security agreements and financing statement give an express right to repossess the liened chattel."

"Liened chattel? It's his leg, for Chrissake—"

"It's our client's leg until it's paid for, and it's a damned expensive one. I remember this Munro. One of those prove-it super-handicapped. He had six or seven thousand in custom hydraulics installed to improve his marathon times. Never paid a nickel on account, no defenses, no offer of a payout, just took the merchandise and ran. Get Constable Wolchensko. He'll do anything; just don't complicate it when you talk to him. There's only one strap holding it on with a simple release—call the client for the particulars." Farbman slammed down the phone and was instantly aware of his neck heating with shame.

It was little more than a month since his retreat, since his return as a visionary, when he had stunned Marucci and their staff by recalling their law school idealism, their Legal Service apprenticeships, the time when they had conceived themselves to be instruments of social justice. When they worked with a higher purpose.

"Remember, Marucci," Farbman had rhapsodized, "the pleasure of thwarting evictions? Of enjoining utilities?"

They'd laughed and reminisced about their efforts to untangle the cross-collateralized lives of people who had defaulted on shoddy time-payment appliances and found their homes foreclosed upon.

"Yeah," his partner had observed wistfully, "the days of no overhead and no wives." Marucci then informed Farbman that he would be thrilled to hear that they had been referred the worthless case of an elderly, dependent-less black woman who had frozen to death in Queens after Con Ed cut off her heat. Found under a dripping pipe, firemen had to chip her free of her worn-out barcalounger. While Marucci conceded this gave the case an appealing gruesomeness, it had little value because there was no one to claim a resultant pecuniary loss and because medical opinion was divided on how painful it is to freeze to death. "Who knows, your average juror may think it's really pleasant—like the story of 'The Little Match Girl.'"

"That's not the point. Those jurors are also the conscience of the community. Con Ed is a *public* utility, Marucci, answerable to the people. Is this why you fought and died in Viet Nam? There'll be a million in punitives."

But only a few creditor-pressed weeks later, Farbman was referring to the dead woman as his "Fudgsicle" and wondering if he could squeeze maybe twenty, twenty-five thousand and close it out. Once again he was scuttling and scavenging. Inner peace had given way to anxiety and urgency. Each day he hurried to a gobbled lunch, searching for pick plays in the crowd, dodging the flotsam and dross of Forty-Second Street. The sudden clarity he had experienced in those Illinois woods—seeing the landscape on the return trip as though it had been washed, the normally dull winter tones enhanced, the snow and dark trees, the patches of bark, the ochres and umbers vibrating—was gone. He had forgotten the season. He no longer noticed the sky.

The surprise of having encountered clerks and ticket-takers and of recognizing them as harried *people*—as concerned as he with paying the rent, with their children's small successes, their spousal estrangements—and of having smiled and been smiled back upon, had been replaced by the familiar vision of others as obstacles in his mental flow chart. For an instant, they had all—the rabbi and porters, Leah and his wife and the airport counter girl ladling his soup, his clients and creditors—been wellsprings of holiness, sparks from the fire of the Divine. Now, again, people were merely problems to be solved or circumvented, seduced or run over.

Ann Marie, who for the first time in years had been briefly visible, was again a car-pooling wraith, an idea in his head. Flush with his new-found truths he had enthusiastically related an edited version of his experience in the woods which she received with a singular guilt-inducing equanimity. He shared his epiphany like Jason or Jennifer with their day's school work. As Ann Marie emptied the dishwasher, he had pressed for more, to exact some recognition. "Well?" he insisted.

"How nice for you," she had acknowledged, finally, over the clatter of stacking plates, "to have noticed the world. Who knows, perhaps on your next trip you'll discover your children and, in time, even your wife." Then, turning to scour the sink, she pulled the faucet lever until talk was impossible.

Inspired on his return to attempt sex with his wife, Farbman, concerned about the risk to her, put off trying until he could depose Harold on the incubation periods of all known venereal afflictions. He had confided his story in the steam after their sacred, uncancellable Friday night racquetball game. Harold, like Ann Marie, was unmoved by suggestions of transcendence.

"I'm glad you got laid but why do you have to make it into something mystical? It was a funeral fuck," the doctor had pronounced, making his slippery gym-hardened muscles jump under his hands. "What people do when they get close to death. You were in the right place, that's all."

Farbman was devastated to hear that assuming he passed an AIDS test, to clear the latest strains of gonorrhea and chlamydia he'd have to allow two to three weeks, and for genital herpes and the cervical cancer-causing warts, six months to a year. There was no way Farbman could explain using a condom.

Although he still clung to her in the night, without his passion Ann Marie faded, once again, along with his perspectives on law and humanity and his revelations about time and the universe, into the background of his daily grubbing. Unable to have either protected or unprotected sex with her, unable to bear the pain of her accusatory silences, of watching her resigned labors, Farbman withdrew.

The memory of sex with Leah, however, did not recede. The sensations engendered in that desolate cabin seemed imprinted in the very tissues of his body. At his desk, worrying his recalcitrant clients or crafting an argument, the pleasure would return, to twitch his loins and bring disrupting pictures into consciousness. After three neutered years, Farbman felt as though he had just emerged above ground.

He considered an assignation with Leah in Chicago. Her number was unlisted and by the time he'd dreamt up an excuse to get Michael to track her down and Farbman got her on the line, more than a week had gone by. When he mentioned that he'd come down with scabies after their encounter, Leah happily had no idea what he was talking about. Unhappily, however, she didn't want to make conversation beyond asking why he was calling. Her distance left him scrambling for a response.

"That last night the rabbi said something to me I didn't understand and he wouldn't explain. I thought maybe you could help."

"Doubt it, but try me."

"He predicted I would have a big moment out there—and I certainly did—but he said it would just be a start. That I was a long way from what sounded like 'chuva.' You have any idea—?"

"Baal teshuvah."

"Exactly, what is that?"

"You really have no idea?"

"Should I?"

"You should if you're Jewish. It means, literally, 'master of the turning,' which probably doesn't help you. However, I can't really do this now, I'm late for an audition. You'll have to read a book or take it up with your rabbi."

Farbman wanted to make sense of his transcendental experience, and to educate himself as Leah suggested, but other needs pushed to the fore. And while he was sure that something more had awakened in him than carnality, he definitely had sex on his mind. In addition to Leah, he had considered and rejected dalliances with his now crewcut secretary, Joy, and with one trial and one appellate judicial law clerk. For three consecutive evenings that week he had stayed late after work eating dinner alone at the Alibi, the local lawyers' hangout, and decided, finally, to move the leggy waitress, a garrulous part-time business student named Deborah Must. He'd done nothing really to signify desire, only asked a few foundation questions—to relax the witness, establish rapport—which was all it took to uncork breathless, free-associative, intimately detailed disquisitions on her aspirations and entanglements. Before she'd written bluefish and home fries on her pad, Farbman learned she'd been "tricked" into seeing a married man for whom she was now "over the edge"; that she'd been getting lousy pap smears that had something to do with venereal warts some other guy, this bastard psychiatrist, had given to her who she found out knew all along he'd had them. Pausing to place an ambiguously reassuring hand on Farbman's arm, Deborah reported that they were all gone—that she'd asked her doctor repeatedly because we're talking about an innocent third party here—and (her hand warming his flesh through his jacket and shirt) she was absolutely not contagious.

Now, his intercom buzzed. It was Joy reminding him he had a case management conference with Judge Boyle at Manhattan Supreme. She brought the file and placed it on his desk, then stood jotting last minute instructions, the tulip grace of her body as she shifted weight holding Farbman despite his need to go.

Then, at the subway stand, squeezed next to a pair of stocking heads, bolting a hot dog and a papaya juice, Farbman felt a strange, premonitory vulnerability. At first he thought it was just his forced posture—stretching his neck to avoid dripping on his tie, squeezing his briefcase between his calves—perhaps the press of the crowd behind him. But, as a new graffiti-proof express was pulling in and Farbman began taking the stairs two at a time, his mind was tricked by the sensation of flight into a sudden registration of fear. He looked but saw nothing in that dank miasma to alarm: the accustomed homeless with their bottles and bulging shopping bags, advertisements for designer jeans and hit shows posted on walls dripping with excretions. He thought back to his encounter in the woods. Unable to marshal evidence of his own transformation, he nonetheless felt the stage had been set for some life-altering event. Slipping between the closing doors, he began to search everywhere with his eyes, although he didn't know for what. Was he hoping for some omen or apparition? A cross in the sky over Brooklyn? A bush burning in Central Park? A crow scratching among the pigeons? Hurtling toward Foley Square, the lights of the stations flashing by, Farbman reflected on the silliness of looking outside himself for a sign that he had changed.

Yet there was a new look to the old courthouse that he could not ascribe to anything beyond his own perceptions. And that surprising awareness he was feeling of a common humanity, this time with an immigrant family begging Farbman's assistance with a crumpled court notice, and a sense of estrangement from other lawyers.

Sitting in chambers surrounded by a pack of gray or navy chalk-striped, three-piece suits, Farbman thought *vested interests, legal suits.* At the head of the conference table presided the very short, shirt-sleeved Judge Boyle, who still retained the bedside charm of his years as a ward-healer. Beirce was right, thought Farbman. A judge is just a lawyer who knew a governor. But how much better to have a street-savvy hack like Boyle than most other judges he could think of: white-cuffed former general counsels who had spent their lives representing ideas—like corporations, governments, and agencies—rather than people. He thought about the father of the family in the hallway behaving as though he could not distinguish the marble columns of this justice building from those of a Pinochet or Duvalier. Soon, however, he'd learn about American redistribution of wealth through personal injury, find his way to a storefront shyster, and maybe damage his back just enough to capitalize a small business or send his kids to college.

The case on which Farbman was appearing involved the head-on collision of several cars and a bus. There were dozens of plaintiffs in the case—including all the bus passengers—and when the realization hit that there might not be enough insurance to cover them all, the toll of defendants began to rise as well. To keep things manageable the judge called for a committee of plaintiffs' counsel and one for defendants, and a leader for each.

"We need two chairmen—chair*persons*," the Court hastily corrected itself as it noted the bespectacled blond associate sitting across from Farbman and a few seats down. Farbman contemplated a crack about lawyerettes—but recognizing the humorless Grace Pittipaldi, decided to bite his tongue before he found himself staring down the wrong end of a federal civil rights suit.

Pittipaldi had averted her eyes when he glanced her way, still embarrassed, he deduced, about her breakdown during the Blocker case, an interminable divorce made so by Farbman's religiously scrupled client. Several times Farbman had cornered Pittipaldi procedurally, humiliated her when he'd found substantive areas in which she was unknowledgeable, and, by patronizing her with an affected impatience, wrung concessions unfairly. Previously smug in the belief that she deserved it for her unsmiling, rigid professionalism, for her decision to work in this very hot, very masculine kitchen, Farbman, suddenly realizing that he was staring at her breasts, began to recognize another possible source for his legal aggressiveness.

"Tommy," the judge continued, "you got the bus so you be defense chairperson." Tommy McMahon, recovering alcoholic—recovering, that is, from the night before—nodded slowly, his watery eyes half-closed, whether wincing from the title or the morning light, Farbman couldn't be sure.

Boyle then asked that the lawyer with the heaviest plaintiff, meaning the largest claim for damages, identify himself. The plaintiffs' lawyers shrugged and looked at each other. Unlike the defense attorneys who could bill for their time, no one on the contingency side of the case wanted the plaintiffs' chairpersonage since it would mean hours of uncompensated paperwork and administrative bullshit.

"Any stiffs?" the judge asked.

"I have one, but he was decapitated instantly and there's only a weak dependency," muttered a lawyer Farbman couldn't see in the second row.

Tommy McMahon, then spoke, with effort, his eyes still unfocused: "Somebody answered rogs with a 'lacerated liver.'"

"That's me," allowed a solo practitioner. He showed obvious distress at the prospect of having drawn the short straw.

Then, from the other side of the room came a new voice. "I've got a faciotomy and possible osteotomy—they're going in to break bone. There's two hundred thousand in medical bills so far and still climbing."

The others shook their heads in an admixture of relief and envy and made appreciative blowing sounds. The face of the enthusiastic young man who had spoken turned ruddy.

"Okay," said Judge Boyle, "You're it. Who you with, son?"

The young man identified a large Bronx plaintiff's firm, a negligence mill clever enough to have nailed down the telephone number, which it used to exhort the barrio to fulfill the American dream by dialing a–b–o–g–a–d–o.

The court shook its head. "Tell Lester congratulations, he's now plaintiffs' chairperson. Write this down. He and Tommy McMahon will work out an agreed pattern of discovery once all the plaintiffs decide what they want. Defendants will agree on who's going to do the examinations so we don't have plaintiffs made ill and injured from being subjected to too many doctors. Now, what defendants aren't in the case yet? Whose road was it?"

The face of the young man from the Bronx mill lit up, and he waved his hand. "It was designed by the state and maintained by the county and one town, Yonkers. Yonkers was responsible for the ramp where the soda truck entered. Of course, the state is probably immune from just design defects, but state-controlled repair work was going on in one lane and somebody third-partied the subcontractor doing the concrete work. But we haven't amended yet."

"How about the tour guide?" asked a portly, white-haired lawyer unplugging his ear with a paper clip. "My client says she asked the driver to pass the microphone just prior to the accident. She may have distracted him."

The white-haired lawyer looked confused at the collective moan from the other plaintiffs' lawyers at the table.

Judge Boyle was solicitous. "I meant defendants with money, Fred. I don't think you want to let the target defendants start finger-pointing at some poor tour guide."

"There was an A & P on the hill with a flashing sign," Farbman offered, "maybe it was responsible." There was a pause while the others—Pittipaldi included, he was pleased to note—stared at him, considering whether he was serious.

ONE FLESH

Three weeks after the bus accident conference, Farbman and Pittipaldi met again. She had summoned him to her office in order to take the deposition of Elmo Blocker in the divorce case that had become her nemesis. For the second time in the course of *Blocker v. Blocker,* Pittipaldi appeared about to burst into tears. Elmo Blocker was a Catholic zealot with a borderline personality disorder and a childlike literalness who claimed that he did not understand virtually every question posed to him and, when provided with clarification, the explanation as well. Farbman believed that much of Blocker's obtuseness was morally inspired: Blocker loved his wife and did not accept the idea that their contract before God was subject to temporal dissolution.

"Where were you working during the year before you separated?" asked Pittipaldi.

"Well, that's a trick question I can't really answer."

"Mr. Blocker, I assure you there is no intention on my part to trick you in any way. As I've advised you repeatedly before, you have only to tell me when you don't understand a question and I'll rephrase it. Now, what don't you understand?"

"First off, you know full well, and your client sitting beside you, full well knows that we were married under sacrament and we were never and will never be asundered in the eyes of God or the Church or mine. And I would suspect your eyes, too, unless you've really left the communion, which is none of my business. Second off, I don't know what you mean by 'working'—"

"How can you not know what 'where you were working' means? What do you think it means?"

Farbman was, regretfully, constrained to object here since it did appear that the form of the question was unclear to his client. He also reminded Pittipaldi that it was her responsibility, not the deponent's, to make sure that the questions were clearly understood, for, as she had instructed him at the outset, he was under oath and his answers would be used against him at trial.

"What could possibly be unclear about where he was working?" she asked.

"Well, I suspect that Mr. Blocker is uncertain whether you are referring to traditional, salaried employment, or whether you include entrepreneurial efforts, which may have been part-time and may have failed or been minimally remunerative, or whether you include charitable and other volunteered undertakings." Farbman paused, satisfied that Blocker was now sufficiently cued so that he would spend the next hour in earnest ramblings about every church committee on which he served, his avocational tract writing, and a half-dozen hare-brained business schemes. He could see that Pittipaldi knew it too; the color was out of her face and she was shuffling aimlessly through her notes.

"I also have a problem with 'where,'" added Blocker.

Trying unsuccessfully for hours to pry a usable answer from Blocker fractured Pittipaldi's equipoise, and turned her customarily crisp interrogatories into stammered fragments or overlong convolutions. Still, the lovely lawyer forged ahead—bravely, Farbman thought, even as he tilted his chair back and began a campaign of objections requiring her to reframe each successfully constructed question.

When he was convinced that her eyes were misting, and that she was heading for another breakdown, Farbman suggested a recess, asking if they might confer privately. Pittipaldi, who had reached reflexively for her cigarettes a dozen times (Farbman had threatened to walk out if she smoked), agreed but warned him that she intended to light the cigarette she'd been holding for the past quarter hour whether he liked it or not.

Farbman stood in her office, reading her walls while Pittipaldi retreated behind her desk to her executive recliner. There were framed prayers amid Mother Seton and Fordham Law diplomas. On the desk a large paperweight Pope with his ring extended tottered on a stack of pleadings.

Farbman fingered the unbalanced Pope and watched Pittipaldi strike the match with the cigarette held primly away from her mouth. He tried, exactly as he had on first meeting Ann Marie, to conjure up an image of opposing counsel in a parochial school skirt and knee socks.

"How dare he contribute five thousand dollars to the parish church when his family didn't even have an air conditioner?" Pittipaldi exhaled a furious, smoke-filled breath.

Farbman pulled his eyes from the shapely Calvary on which her cross rested. "You have something against the Church?"

"I'm Catholic," she explained.

"No kidding—your wall is bleeding." He gestured at the prayers.

"Are you this glib about your own faith?"

"About most things actually."

"And this mean to everyone?" There was a catch in her voice.

"Mean?" Farbman moved to the window and looked out. A man hawked umbrellas from behind a table on the sidewalk. He stood in the cold drizzle, with his own umbrella resting on a shoulder, making change with a customer. Farbman pitied the man. But attempting a self-congratulatory comparison of the man's daily, cop-evading hustle with his own profession proved uncomfortable, and he abandoned it.

"Don't play the innocent," Pittipaldi went on. "The way you humiliated me when you quashed my subpoenas and returned my interrogatories—"

"It was your second set and they were way out of time—"

Her face was blotched and he could tell she was about to weep.

"It was the way you did it. You wouldn't have sent that sardonic letter to a man." She yanked a tissue from the box on her desk, dabbed under each lens, then honked her nose. "I'm not going to let you do this to me again. You've been a perfect shit in that deposition—don't deny it."

Farbman moved to comfort and reassure her. He placed his left hand on the top of her chair and bent to apologize, to engage her eye to eye. She stared straight ahead sniffling, while Farbman squinted painfully through the smoke. "I'm sorry—" Farbman began, moving his hand from the chair back to her near shoulder.

"Don't you touch me!" Pittipaldi leaped from her seat. "That's assault, Farbman!"

"No, unconsented-to touching is a battery; you remember, an assault is the offer to do bodily harm. There was no assault and that was no more a battery than being nudged on a subway."

He moved around her chair, and brazened right up until she was backed against her credenza and they were face to face. "This is a battery," said Farbman, inclining his head and placing his lips against his adversary's.

Pittipaldi pulled away, stared him straight in the eyes, and spoke with a studied composure. "I'm going to give you exactly one opportunity to avoid criminal and ethical complaints."

"Okay, okay," said Farbman. He straightened, queasy, realizing he had gone too far. "I'm sorry. What do you want?"

"This case ended. We're going to abort this grotesque examination and, with your on-the-record consent, adjourn for ten days. That will give you time to talk settlement with that mental deficient, and me time to draft the charges against you. We'll exchange unfiled charges for what I'm certain will be a more than equitable proposal."

The idea was unthinkable. Not only did his client's principled opposition to divorce constitute a desperately needed, overhead-paying annuity, but Elmo Blocker had engaged Farbman on the explicit premise that there would be no compromise of his scruples. If Farbman did anything but litigate his case to a court adjudication Blocker would be screaming for a refund and probably have him up on charges as well.

"Be reasonable, Grace—" Farbman began, thinking surely somebody with that name could be swayed.

"I am. I was going to give you two days."

A nervous Farbman made a quick pass of his palm over his secretary Joy's skunk-striped brush of hair as she bent over her message pad. Sopping wet in a laughably wrinkled suit—his umbrella having blown irremediably inside out shortly before a crashing deluge—he noted how quickly his chill was chased by desire.

Joy asked if he liked the cut, and Farbman said he did. She smiled. Scott, her boyfriend, whose hair was shoulder-length, was ambivalent, she said, and she'd had second thoughts. She said that she had placed all Farbman's calls on his desk, except for the last, which was from his wife, who only said she needed to speak with him. Then, pointing to the mound of dark wet fabric on Farbman's side chair, she asked if he'd like it dropped at the cleaners downstairs.

Farbman was astonished and thanked her profusely. No personal errands—which meant he and his clients got their own coffee—was the polestar of Joy's employment. He reached for the telephone to call Ann Marie, then remembered one last thing: Could Joy possibly make some after-hours, mutually convenient time available for him? Among other things he wanted to teach her how to prep a file. Of course, not that very evening, Farbman (who had arranged his first date with Deborah Must on her only weekday night off) considerately observed. Perhaps Sunday, Joy thought, if it were for pay and didn't conflict with her New Age music concert at St. John the Divine.

"This Sunday is the Purim Carnival," Ann Marie reminded Farbman when he returned her call.

"I'm going to try—"

"Spare me. This will make the third Purim without you. Frankly I've had it. I've changed too many diapers to eat prune Hamantashen; and the R.C. in me is convinced God must be angry watching the rabbi doing cartwheels in his Buffalo Bob outfit—"

"Hold on, Hon, will you? My light's flashing—"

It was his secretary. "Mrs. Fleischman, the new matrimonial, is here.

I'll show her where the coffee is and try to find some water for her dog."
Joy was off before Farbman could ask, "Dog?"

Ann Marie continued: "I've been running around shopping for material and assembling Jennifer's Queen Esther costume for three days.
Jason will be working a hang Haman booth, and they are both looking
forward to your being there."

"And I've been running around assembling the money so you could
do your shopping."

"Okay, I've told you."

"And I've told you," Farbman informed the dial tone.

Mrs. Fleischman, engulfed in the pelts of a protected specie, entered
Farbman's office followed by a small beribboned mop and Farbman's secretary tightrope-walking with an overfilled plastic container that she
settled on the floor by the dog.

"We'll have to be brief," said Mrs. Fleischman. "I'd forgotten about
MeTu's haircut—but at least we have this chance to meet."

Farbman was sympathetic, charming, and businesslike as he fished
for a retainer large enough to meet the week's still uncovered payroll,
but knowing all the while that he was the real fish and hoping against
reason as he swallowed the bait that this wife would be different, that
he wouldn't be listening to her demands without compensation for the
next two years. Farbman received her confession of infidelity. He counseled the need for discretion, and when she looked blank, he instructed,
"Screw in the afternoon."

She brightened at the advice. "Thanks," she said.

On hearing that Mr. Fleischman's valve business generated a lot of
cash and that he'd once told her "something about two sets of books,"
Farbman interrupted the interview to call Turk Horowitz, his accoun-
tancy-trained private investigator, with instructions to get a truck and
collect Mr. Fleischman's office garbage for the next two months. "But
bring it to me without the coffee grounds and Big Mac wrappers, okay,
Turk?" Farbman and Mrs. Fleischman shared a smile. He explained con-
cepts of marital fault and encouraged her to think of some examples
from her own coverture.

Joy put through a call from Grace Pittipaldi. "I told her you were in conference, but she said it was urgent."

"Urgent," repeated Farbman to Mrs. Fleischman, who nodded understandingly. His stomach churned as he relived his disastrous tilt with Pittipaldi. Since there was no possibility of overcoming Blocker's obdurate morality, Farbman's only recourse was somehow to dissuade the woman.

"I've changed my mind."

Farbman could feel the tension release in his gut. "I'm so glad." He saw his smile reflected on Mrs. Fleischman's face. Perhaps he had not misjudged Pittipaldi after all. Their passionate antagonism, her signals of marital discord, her teary revelations of vulnerability—all pointed to an incipient fire, a lust that, once ignited, might consume them both. He envisioned them rolling on her floor amid the toppled Pope and papers.

"I found when I checked my calendar that I won't have time to review the proposal next week, so I'll have to have it by Friday."

"Come on now, I can't—" His smile left Mrs. Fleischman's face.

"Friday's it."

"I'll telephone my client as soon as I've completed this conference."

Farbman apologized for the interruption and returned his attention to Mrs. Fleischman and to her initially tentative then snowballing litany of spousal abuse: his indifference to her emotional and physical needs, his absorption in business and sports ("He telephones his children good, night from the office.")—in short, Farbman reflected, the cruelty grounds of any happy marriage that has persisted more than five years. He marveled at the compression of history in her anger; how two-year-old slights, forgotten anniversaries, the accumulated dross of the relationship were all held at the ready in some mental pouch to be recited at a lawyer's request for a list of "specific grievances."

"Don't misunderstand," Mrs. Fleischman paused, pen poised, the enamel of her nails glistening over the signature line of her check, "I only want what's fair."

"It's not nearly enough," Marucci despaired. "Assuming we forget a fortune in payables—" he began checking off the chewed fingers of his left hand, "—there's payroll, there's the quarterly taxes, last month's rent, interest on the renewal note—and remember we both have installments due for camp tuitions." Marucci paused to chew on his cuticles. "I'm telling you this is worse than the mortar at Lang Ming Mang."

Marucci's wartime allusions were sometimes jocular, sometimes deadly earnest; but, despite a relationship more brotherly than businesslike, Farbman occasionally mistook a literal intention as ironic and, as he did now, provoked his partner by responding with what he erroneously thought was a similar joviality. "Only Jews send their kids away for the summer, Marucci. Christians are supposed to keep their children around for lawn mowing and family excursions."

"I've been assimilated like everyone else—Christ, I just read where Geronimo's great-great-grandson was bar mitzvahed at the Wailing Wall."

Marucci really had become Jewish, Farbman reflected. The same man who at eighteen had worked and thieved to have his punctured eardrums repaired so he could get in the army now believed his son needed a BMW when he got his license.

"Are you sure—Geronimo?"

"Yeah, I'm sure. What are we going to do?"

"For some reason I thought it was Sitting Bull."

"Fuck you." Marucci started for the door.

"Hey, wait."

"Listen to me. Listen to me." Marucci clutched his stomach. "I don't know how much more my ulcer can take, dodging collection agency phone calls, trying to explain to secretaries why supplies weren't delivered, or why we're being sued by our experts, trying to practice law while you're off seeking a piece of the true cross—or, let's be honest, just a piece."

Farbman, stunned at his partner's vehemence, rushed around his desk to try and set things right. "Hey, you were serious about Lang Mang—?"

"Lang Ming Mang."

"Well, don't worry, Marco, none of these mortar shells has your name on it."

"I'm alive," Marucci looked deep into Farbman's eyes, "because I always worried about the one addressed 'to whom it may concern.'"

Farbman put a paternal hand on Marucci's shoulder. "You're worried about camp? I promise you they'll go to camp."

Marucci shook off the hand. He reached inside his jacket as if for a pistol and produced an envelope instead. Farbman's name appeared in Marucci's irregular scrawl—a fragmented combination of cursive and printed letters. "I'm withdrawing from the firm. It's all in here. We'll talk about it after you've read it."

Oh Jesus, Farbman said to himself, what have you done now, Marucci?

"Marco, just tell me what it is."

"The IRS slapped a lien on the firm account today."

Farbman's face went slack.

"I owe for two years. Don't look at me like that. We didn't have it and I couldn't ask you to borrow any more when we were in so deep—"

"You just drew for taxes."

"I lied. That was for Joslyn. She got a judgment. I was nine months behind in alimony and the bitch got a judgment."

Marucci explained that he'd been using the money that should have gone for alimony to keep one of his sisters in a private detox facility, to support an unemployed but devout brother, and to pay for a wedding for that same brother's sixteen-year-old daughter who'd been knocked up by a fellow supermarket clerk and high school classmate.

"Get me the lien," said Farbman, "and don't think about it again. I'll take care of it."

"I don't want you—"

"Don't worry. I've got a lot of resources. Mr. Big left a message, and it sounds like he's got a real problem."

There was a noticeable lightening of Marucci's expression. "Criminal?" "Criminal" meant a large up-front cash retainer.

"Don't know yet. Keep your fingers crossed. And, Marco—"

"I know. You're working, too."

"The 'piece' I'm after is spelled with an 'ea,' and it's for both of us."

Marucci left with his envelope still in his pocket on Farbman's promise to call Big right away, by which Farbman meant right after he had confirmed his plans with Deborah Must.

"I'm so glad you called," she gushed, causing an immediate sinking in Farbman. It seemed she'd caught a cold while cocktail waitressing the night before. The heat had been kept low for a big crowd but nobody showed up, and she'd made "like nothing" working until four a.m. "I mean I was shivering so bad I asked one of the kitchen guys I know to put his arms around me to warm me up. So now I've got a fever so if you don't want to see me tonight—I don't know how much fun I'll be, or really what you expect anyway."

With no alternatives Farbman warranted to Deborah that he had no expectations beyond dinner and they disconnected.

Remembering Pittipaldi's threats encouraged Farbman to introduce the concept of settlement to Elmo Blocker. Blocker quickly disabused him of such notions. "'And they twain shall be one flesh, so then they are no more twain, but one flesh,'" said Elmo, reminding his lawyer that this was God's merger.

They would discuss it again another time, suggested Farbman.

Replied Elmo: "'If they hear not Moses and the prophets, neither will they be persuaded though one rose from the dead.'"

He was at the front door turning out the lights when he remembered his children. Farbman telephoned them good-night from the receptionist's desk sitting on her little steno chair, feeling enormous in his overcoat. Where was he and guess what? cried Jennifer. Mommy let them have dinner in the living room in front of the fire! Would he hurry home to see her costume and the 'A' she got in social studies? Jason had scored three runs in kick ball. They would save him some marshmallows. Farbman felt a yank in his chest, a longing for his wife, and for what their one flesh had wrought; and, with profound regret that he could not be with them, he exited for his quest to find another, less complicated solace, into a bitter wind that immediately made his eyes well up with tears.

HOMELESS

Deborah had proposed her nothing-much neighborhood Italian place, considering that it was late and a work night and how she was feeling and all. They walked from her apartment, Farbman stopping three times to give money to beggars. "Why do you do that?" asked Deborah. Farbman paused to consider. "I guess I'm afraid not to."

"Well, I work too hard for my money to give it to a crazy alcoholic too dumb or lazy to find his way to a shelter. Or better to Florida."

Farbman told her that was his partner, Marucci's, view and, as they were seated among the plastic greenery, that he thought both he and Deborah would make sensible derelicts. On the wall, an electric sign like that reporting headline news in Times Square, reiterated the specials of the day and advertised the restaurant's catering services.

Except for the two of them and a few regulars perched on barstools flashing white cotton socks above their pointy black shoes, the place was empty. Farbman could hear Deborah getting sicker, losing the l's and s's in her monologues, despite her attempts to clear her head with three double Absoluts on the rocks. Then, she changed tack and fed her cold with oversized orders of mussels, veal, and pasta and, since

Farbman didn't drink, her own half bottle of Bardolino. But, although her voice got clearer, Farbman heard little of Deborah's dinner talk—a continuing sniffling inquiry into the nature of men, or as she termed them, "potentials"—which Farbman, picking at his putanesca, prodded along with therapist-like nods and rhetorical repetitions of her own words. He was having a hard time getting his mind around the idea that Marucci had again engaged in a childlike concealment from him and had thereby exacerbated his otherwise manageable financial problem to the point of jeopardizing their partnership.

"Messy?" Farbman, aware that Deborah had paused, repeated her last word, prompting her to elaborate on her concern about what some potential might think of her after seeing her apartment, and enabling Farbman to return to the problem of Marucci's tax lien. He'd have to open a new account in the morning, get a list of outstanding checks, and, before they bounced, telephone the payees with some story. He figured he would have enough to cover the checks with Mrs. Fleischman's retainer and whatever he could get out of Mr. Big.

"Don't get me wrong," said Deborah, putting her hand on his arm. Farbman's fork was stopped in midair, and he looked up. "I'm not scattered when it comes to work and school." Farbman nodded and refocused. He'd blown off his familial and professional responsibilities to score points with this great pair of legs and if he didn't pay some attention he'd blow that as well. So when Deborah started to relate her discovery of how you get guys to switch from beers to scotch, Farbman asked why you'd want to do that. Better tips, said Deborah, explaining that hard drinks were three seventy-five so they give you a five and then usually take the quarter and put the buck back. "I expect a buck; but if it's beer it's three twenty-five so you get seventy-five cents and you get gypped. Anyway, so the secret I discovered? You say, 'Hey boys, why don't we have some shots?' and they always go for it."

Farbman shook his head admiringly. "Doesn't that interfere with your functioning?"

"No, I drink a lot, but it doesn't show. I mean, how many did I have tonight?"

"I wasn't counting."

"Me, neither. Can you believe it, I took six aspirins today and my throat is still really sore." She asked for another shot of Absolut, and Farbman signaled the waiter.

Huddled, shoulders bumping, heads bowed into the wind, they hurried back to Deborah's place past heaps of plastic bags and dented trash cans with lids chained to railings.

Deborah made Farbman wait outside while she straightened. The hallway was filled with vaguely rancid dinner odors—cabbage, pan-fried meat. He'd forgotten to call Mr. Big. He felt sweaty and a little nauseated. Farbman leaned his head against the wall and was surprised by a burst of acid in his throat. Big began his day at 5:30 at his Hunts Point meat plant. Farbman could set his alarm and try to call him there. He'd better not blow it. Mr. Big didn't appreciate waiting more than twenty-four hours for a return call. He expected service and got it. Mr Big was an annuity. He was either making a deal or trying to get out of one. He'd always been involved in regulated businesses that required endless compliance efforts and invited regular investigations and frequent charges. Farbman had earned many thousands of dollars drafting and then successfully litigating his way out of contracts for Bigonocco's enterprises. For the last four years, veal had been Mr. Big's business. Twice Farbman had gotten him acquitted on charges of injecting unapproved drugs into the calves. He had gotten three separate animal rights suits dismissed. But Farbman had lost the last hearing on the issue of sanitation in the packing plant and Big had been forced to turn in his U.S.D.A. stamp for six months.

Deborah opened the door. Farbman took note of a thickly painted-over mezuzah and entered a large, linoleum-floored studio with a kitchenette and island on one side, a desk and a personal computer on the other. In between were a worn velour couch, a Danish coffee table, and some chairs. Deborah pressed on him some pretty good creeper dope, which she shared, wincing with each drag, free hand to her throat. As Farbman loosened his tie and reached for the joint, he began to script his early morning call to Big, only to be interrupted by Deborah.

"Guys buy me a lot of drinks now. There's this drink, the Orgasm, a lot of guys will order and ask if I want one, you know—'Hey, you want an orgasm?' and I always say, 'I never turn one down.'" Deborah's skirt hiked up her thighs as she leaned forward to pass the joint.

"You date these guys?" Farbman asked, thinking if he left then and didn't get lost trying to find the L.I.E., he might get four hours sleep.

"I never accept invites from customers. You know how many times I hear there's a limo outside waiting to take us anywhere? I meet guys at clubs, or on the beach in the summer. All my doctors ask me out." She passed the roach by pressing finger to finger, the pad of her finger rolling submissively under Farbman's.

"Is that the married one, the doctor?"

"I forgot I told you about him. No. That's the guy I've really lost it for. I mean he's got everything. I told you I didn't know he was married, right? Darlene, my girlfriend fixed me up on a blind date. I said I'd go as long as he wasn't married or had a girl. When I saw him I said, this is a blind date? He is about six four and could be in GQ except he's maybe a little rugged, which I like—built like a bull if you know what I mean—and we were totally compatible and I knew it instantly. You know how it works, like it's on or it's off. It's my test. I have this light bulb in my head; it's either on or off. Like the way it was with my doctor—I had an earache and I just got his name from the hospital—I mean, when I met him in the office I thought, wow, this is my doctor?—older, about thirty, with unbelievably long eyelashes and big shoulders—so I said yes. But he was all over me from the beginning of the evening, and the switch just went from on to off. When that happens, there's nothing you can do to repair it.

"So, anyway, the switch was totally on with this blind date. I mean I couldn't believe how well it was going. We even played games right away—you know, pretended we didn't like each other? He was with another guy, and I was with Darlene, and we'd told them we had appointments later, we had to meet other people no matter what, so we could get out of there, you know. So we left and they followed us to the club. I couldn't believe it. It was so romantic. It turned out he has his own masonry business with about twenty guys working for him, and this unbelievable truck with huge tires and all this chrome. Well, I was totally over the edge for this guy, so I decided I absolutely wouldn't sleep with him on the first date. I told him I was going to bed and if he was too drunk to drive he could sleep on the couch."

Well, could you believe it, he undressed her in her sleep and looked at her body. (Farbman allowed as he could.) The next morning she found the guy sitting on the chair next to her bed, saying, "I've got something to tell you. I'm married." "Get out, just get out of here," she'd screamed at him. So he left, but they kept having lunches together, and it turned out when his wife got pregnant she gained all this weight and never lost it. And it seemed he's got this thing for how women look and so he'd been sleeping on the couch for, like, four years.

"I couldn't believe it. If I were his wife, I'd work out for him. I'd pump iron twelve hours a day for him. So we kept having these lunches and we got to the point where we weren't even talking about anything, just flirting, talking about how it would be if we did it and then we just stopped even speaking sentences, I literally tore his shirt off, we were *so* hot when we did it.

"I've really lost it for him, and I just don't know what to do. I'm fed up with doing everything at his convenience. Last time I blew off a date with a doctor."

"The psychiatrist with the warts?" asked Farbman.

Deborah shook her head 'no' as she inhaled.

"The one with the long eyelashes?" Farbman guessed again. He noticed a magazine advertisement thumbtacked into a corkboard above her desk. He had seen the ad before. In it a young woman in a short skirt carried an attaché case in one hand and patted her Wall Street-type boyfriend on the ass with the other as they walked along.

"No, this was the plastic surgeon who did my implants. Took all of my savings. I've got *nothing* in my account. But they came out pretty good. I mean I've got real good proportions now, and, like, guys never looked at my chest before and now they look all the time. I think my tips went up about twenty percent, so I should break even in about two years. You should see what it's like when me and Darlene get dressed and go out to do the bars. We are so bad. There are guys all over us. Other women hate us. You can see them reeling their guys back in."

"Question?" Farbman interrupted.

"No, I won't let you look now. When I first got it done, I was really blatant. I only wore my guinea tees, and, once when I was driving right after, when I saw this friend of mine in his car, I flashed him right in the middle of traffic on Queens Boulevard in broad daylight."

"Question?" Farbman repeated.

"No, you can't see," Deborah giggled. "Now I'm really used to them. I can sleep face down, which I couldn't for months. I mean they're really a part of me. I like this one better because it's mushier; the other one is too hard. And there's no loss of nipple sensation, which I'd been told might happen."

"Question?" Farbman tried again.

Deborah paused and studied his face for a moment. "If I show you, you've got to promise not to touch."

Farbman smiled.

"I mean it, say you promise. You know what it means if you break your promise, right?" Deborah cautioned as she unbuttoned her blouse.

"I'll end up in the nether place?"

"Huh?"

"You know," said Farbman, "nether-nether land?"

"Okay, there's one bad part: the scars came out really bad." She tossed the blouse at a chair and it fell just short and hung off the arm. "See, they're wide and dark and bumpy. They weren't so bad at first, but he tried to fix them. Lucky Darlene just has a hairline and you can't see it at all. My doctor said it just happens like that with dark-skinned people."

"He shouldn't have tried to fix them," said Farbman, a sudden interest in his voice. "You call me and I'll check it out with some plastic experts I use. I think you've got a case."

"You really think so? You can't tell when I'm not holding them up—when I'm like this you can't, can you? How about if I were doing like Penthouse poses?"

Diffidently tossing what remained of her clothes alongside Farbman on the couch, the now sniffling Deborah, on a small hook rug, moved through a series of poses, unconsciously replicating in life the untouchable two-dimensionality of a studio-arranged centerfold. She spread and stretched to reveal herself with medical clarity.

Farbman couldn't decide for whom she thought she was performing. He blamed himself that her efforts were without effect on him. He considered how a younger or older or less jaded man might more willingly suspend disbelief. Her eyes were so lighted with fever that they shone through all her drinks and fatigue. He appreciated her wonderfully smooth, olive-toned muscularity, the way she had worked to reshape her body and her life—however much informed by fashion—into her ideal image. Unlike Farbman, she had taken her vision and done something with it. But his middle-aged lawyer's eye continued its pragmatic dissection, and he was finally rendered impotent by the combination of the TV laugh track he could hear in the next apartment, the iconic posters of scruffy nihilistic rock stars on the wall, the marketing textbooks that shared a shelf with stuffed animals, and by the thought of all who had come before him and all who would follow.

"I must go," he said, pretending reluctance, willing conflict into his face. He helped her to her feet and held her, pitying them both for whatever had drawn them together, then released her and was out the door before discovering whether she'd protest.

THE LAUGHING COW

Still fretting that he hadn't yet contacted Mr. Big, Farbman fell asleep alongside a pile of covers in which he assumed his wife was cocooned. A pack of howling creditors, led by a naked Deborah Must yelling "I changed *my*self," pursued him through his dreams. The tormented, tossing Farbman reached out several times to anchor himself with the mound of blankets. He awoke minutes before the alarm was set to go off.

Farbman tiptoed through his dark, cold home, images from sleep slowly subsiding from consciousness. He paused in the living room, redolent with the smell of damp ashes, to examine an odd shape on the coffee table by the fireplace. A half-filled bag of marshmallows. A single skewer left for him. Ann Marie's pointed gesture. Farbman knelt and felt around for the damper and closed it. Then he went and sat at the desk in the den to call Bigonocco at the meat plant. Muting his voice in the early morning quiet, Farbman forced Big to shout at his workers to keep it down so's he could hear. Once again Big wanted out of a contract—a contract which Farbman reminded him he'd just made.

"It don't matter," Big responded. "I've gotta get the veal heads back.

It's worth a lot to me if I can bone those heads."

"Boning, packaging, that's U.S.D.A. business. How you gonna pack meat without a federal stamp?"

"Schwartz'll bone them for me under his number."

"But his operation is kosher, and who knows what the rabbis will let him do. Besides, what's in it for him?"

"I dunno. Maybe he likes me. Maybe in return for my not making a telephone call, heh, heh, heh. Anyway it only costs a buck a head, and I'm just going to take trimmings he can't use. You can get four, five pounds out of the tongue, cheeks, backs of the ears."

"So what's the deal?"

"I got places I can push the stuff out in Iowa and Illinois for kielbasy and hot dogs." Big pronounced the 's' in Illinois. Farbman decided he'd eaten his last hot dog.

"Hey, Big," began Farbman, resolving to inject a little levity before he attempted the close, "you hear about the guy walks in a store, asks for a kielbasy? Store owner says you must be Polish. Guy says, why do you say that? Suppose I asked for a bagel? Would that make me Jewish? Or pasta—would that make me Italian?"

"It's a hardware store, I heard it. But it's good. Look, I want you to get on this today. See if they'll let me out for something reasonable."

"You got a reason they should?"

"You think of one. If not, I'll just keep the heads and we can go to court for a couple of years and settle later."

"You know what it will cost you to tie them up while you do your business?"

"Whatever, I'll still make five, ten times what it costs me."

Out of the corner of his eye Farbman caught himself reflected in a darkened window and for an instant thought there was a stranger there and was frightened.

"I'll drop money off by you today," said Big. "Fifteen do it?"

"That'll be fine," said Farbman.

Saved. Farbman took a deep breath. Unless Marucci was holding back some other bad news, Big's fifteen thousand should take care of his partner's tax lien, the firm's overdrafts, and the week's payroll. Of course,

Farbman realized, he would just be trading one debt for another, since he would end up owing Mr. Big a lot of hours. Farbman tried not to think about a future of working off already spent retainer money, a future he'd already hocked to twenty other clients. At least Marucci wouldn't bolt now. He was generally okay when he could be left alone to practice law—his version of Freud's "ordinary unhappiness"—which he repeatedly declared was all he asked. He just couldn't deal with this management stuff, stuff which he regularly reminded Farbman was for Jewish heads. Marucci's own financial affairs, he confessed, had been a disaster since the Army had stopped controlling his paychecks.

After detouring to stroke each of his children's heads as they slept, Farbman returned to his bedroom struggling to devise a strategy for making sexual reparations to Ann Marie. He forced his mind back to their courtship, to remember the happy, freckled apostate he'd run off with. He raised an image of her playing sorority softball—green-eyed, straw-haired, his shiksa dream girl—talking it up around the infield, pounding her mitt, flexing shapely, tanned, sports-hardened legs. Farbman stood, chilled by the breeze from the open window, staring down at the bed covers. That straw-haired girl was in there—the gutsy kid who had turned her back on her social class, community, faith, family, and friends to throw her lot in with him, with Farbman of Brooklyn, lately of Rockville Centre. Surely, the least he could do for the mother of his beautiful children, his general contractor and social secretary, his helpmeet and rib, was make the first overture. Farbman peeled off his undershirt and shorts in the freezing air and let them fall to the floor beside the bed. He gingerly approached the lifeless mound—he guessed from the rear—trying to keep the picture of the coed in focus. He paused for a moment attempting to locate her breath sounds under the hum of the air conditioner that Ann Marie required year round as a sleeping aid, along with waxy earplugs and eyeshades, to see if he could calculate where her face might be. He began gently to loosen the covers, and in a few moments had freed enough slack to reveal the top of her head.

Leaning on one arm, his head bent over his wife's, Farbman continued tugging until her head was fully uncovered, at which point he encountered resistance. The sheet clenched under her chin would not pull free. Farbman pulled the hair back from the side of her face, trying to ignore the wax stoppel that protruded from her ear, and began with two delicate fingers to lift the eyeshade. Ann Marie emitted a guttural protest and swatted hard at his fingers. As the blow caught him square-ly on the mouth, cutting his lip with a tooth, Farbman inhaled a snoot-ful of digestive odors so putrid it made his stomach churn.

In the daylight, standing next to Ann Marie at their side-by-side sinks, Farbman examined his swollen lip, filled with self-righteousness for his spurned effort. "I closed the fireplace damper during the night when I went downstairs to make a business call," he announced as he manipu-lated his lip in the mirror.

"You did that? Took the time to close the damper, busy as you are with all your nighttime business. Wow. Thank you."

"That's not the point, is it?"

"It's not? Well, I guess I'm so stupid I missed it. Why don't you explain it so someone as stupid as your wife can get it."

"The point is," Farbman enunciated each word slowly, with convic-tion, "that we had better do something to fix this before it's unfixable."

Ann Marie threw her lipstick so hard into the sink that it bounced out broken and left peach smears in three places on the black marble. "You pay no attention to me for months on end, then you come in one night, in the middle of the night, when I'm sound asleep, motivated by your own guilt, or a skin book, or god only knows what fantasy, and approach me like it's your mitzvah for the month, and you expect me to wake up and roll over dripping and panting. Well, forget it. You hear me?" Ann Marie's voice rose to such volume and intensity that the "hear me" was an almost indecipherable shriek that brought Jason and Jennifer running. They tapped repeatedly on the bathroom door and in fright-ened voices asked: "Are you all right, Mommy?"

As Ann Marie reassured the children, Farbman exited, feeling like a chastened child. He told himself that is what he got for trying—then, that he deserved worse and she, better.

Farbman strode through the front entrance of his office instead of using his politician's back door, and was brought up short by a crowd of katzenjammers. Waiting for him were Janet Sodowick's mother, Ida, looking, with her cornstarched face, like a deranged Kabuki actor, describing her daughter's latest suicide attempt to the rapt receptionist and to Elmo Blocker, who was holding one of her hands and shaking his head supportively; two men holding "contact letters"—form notices sent periodically to bodily-injury clients to update their files or reaffirm the attorney-client relationship—their eyes riveted to an expanse of stockinged thigh on, of all people, Deborah Must; a process server delivering news of a suit brought against the firm by an attorney alleging that Marucci had stiffed him on a forwarding fee; and finally, Farbman's only scheduled appointment, Rhonda Pond, a new matrimonial, in to work on her divorce complaint and, hopefully, to drop off the second installment of her retainer.

Farbman thanked the process server, accepting his papers as though they were just another delivery, assured everyone else he'd be right with them, and fled to his office, Joy rising to follow with a handful of messages as he passed her desk. Marucci was waiting for him, seated in Farbman's chair as he entered. "Couple of nice looking customers waiting out there. Need any help?" Farbman tossed the new lawsuit to Marucci. "How about getting on the phone and making this go away? Oh yes, and how would you feel about letting me sit down and go to work?"

Marucci moved to a side chair, and Farbman took his place at the command console. He explained to Joy that he'd just run the gauntlet of his petitioners and asked if she knew what Blocker, Ida, and Deborah wanted. "Ms. Must," read Joy from her pad, "says she has a malpractice case she discussed with you."

"Okay, Marco," said Farbman. "A present. But first you've got to promise to close out the Fudgsicle today." Marucci made an 'X' over his heart, and Farbman went on. "The one with the great legs and the runny nose—a waitress at the Alibi. Had an augmentation mammoplasty; ended up with a slight keloid formation which the surgeon worsened by removal. Also a possible products case. There are substantial variations in the implants." Farbman reached for the telephone. "I'll see if Harold can give us a quick briefing and some references."

Farbman asked Harold's nurse if she could interrupt his examinations for a quick question. Joy continued: "Ida says she's got to speak to you before Janet kills herself, and Mr. Blocker says he's got some money for you and he'd like to arrange a meeting so you can talk to his priest. Turk Horowitz called. He's collected the garbage on Lomax and will start collecting Fleischman's this week, but he'd like a payment on account. There are two messages from Mr. Worrad at the bank—he wants you to call as soon as you get in. Also your wife just called and I didn't have time to write it up but anyway she forgot to tell you she's going out to look at summer rentals in Amagansett today and she'll wait if you want to go but you have to leave now."

Harold picked up then, and Farbman thanked him for taking the call. "I've got a problem. What do you know about implants?"

"Considering you're a nonsmoker, and don't have diabetes, arterial disease, or a spinal injury, I'd assume your difficulty is psychological—probably a result of all those religious attitudes you've picked up recently. I suggest you forget about an implant all together. Maybe try injecting papaverine into your Johnson, but only after you've given therapy a shot."

Farbman assured Harold that any fears of impotency were entirely projective on his part, and after getting the name of a plastic surgeon Harold felt would educate the lawyers but never testify against a fellow doctor, confirmed their Friday racquetball game and said good-bye. Joy declared that she was not going to the concert that Sunday and would be available to meet Farbman. Farbman saw Marucci's eyes widen, felt his own face flush. "I'm sorry, Joy. My kids are in a Purim—uh, a play—this Sunday. Just found out yesterday. I'll try and get you started if we can catch a free moment during the work week, okay?" Joy shrugged and left. Farbman turned to Marucci: "Promised to teach her how to prep a file."

"You don't need to explain anything to me," said Marucci.

"Maybe just something about damage control, and about trusting your partner. Ask the bookkeeper, will you, for a list of our unpaid checks so we can see what has to be covered."

"Hey, I heard the same story about Joy you did—probably half the office did."

"What story?" asked Farbman.

Marucci, on his way out, closed the door and held his hand on the knob behind him. "Both Karen and the receptionist heard her masturbating in the ladies' room. She told them she does it sometimes twice a day to relax. C'mon, like you didn't know." He opened the door and left.

Returning his banker's call, Farbman learned that so far two small items had come in for payment and that, with the IRS lien, there were insufficient funds to cover them. Farbman assured the man that all outstanding drafts would be covered and that he, personally, would be over as soon as he finished up some uncancellable appointments. Farbman wanted to call Big to find out when his lifesaving infusion would arrive, but Rhonda Pond, the new matrimonial, had already been waiting a half hour. And, since Blocker had brought money, Farbman decided to squeeze him in next.

Blocker had exhausted his savings, withdrawn his pension, and used up his credit in a futile effort to thwart his wife's suit for dissolution and to maintain the fiction that he still had an intact family. While Farbman certainly appreciated Blocker's contributions to the firm's cash flow, he had, as a matter of conscience, several times attempted to get his client to see things more realistically. On the last occasion that Farbman had tactfully suggested to Elmo that he may have misperceived the role that either scripture or canonical law would play in the proceedings, Blocker had smiled and inquired jesuitically if Farbman knew the difference between perception and reality. "No," Farbman had answered truthfully, "tell me."

"Perception," replied Blocker, "is real."

Blocker had taken twenty-five hundred in cash advances on his bank credit cards, borrowing at rates which, if charged by people more ethnic than David Rockefeller, would be called usury. With that money Blocker hoped to rescue his teenage son from a mother who allowed the boy to display pictures of naked women on his wall and who blinked at the boy's frequent truancies from Sunday Mass. It was the kind of parenting, Blocker suggested, one might expect from a person who is not "a woman of her word."

Farbman nodded, thinking that Pittipaldi was definitely a woman of her word and that his reckoning with her was at hand.

"I understand, Elmo, but the courts don't intervene in matters of day-to-day child-rearing." He added that there were some psychologists around who would say that the adolescent's behavior was normal, even healthy.

Farbman was, in turn, advised by Blocker that "Jesus spoke of the judge which feared not God" and that he didn't have to be told about psychology. He'd read it. He'd heard the filth that poured out of Dr. Ruth's mouth, he knew those high priests of hedonism who purveyed moral decay in the name of mental health, who blessed pornography and perversion, and if the court wouldn't correct the situation then he wanted his son with him so that he could. So Farbman had to explain that with teenagers the court followed the "gorilla rule" of child custody—as in "Where does the gorilla sleep in the forest? Wherever he damn pleases"—and he intimated that Blocker would get more control, more time with his son, more of a say in his upbringing, if he had his mother's support, which Blocker might secure more easily, and certainly more economically, by making a deal rather than litigating. Farbman added that he was willing to talk to Blocker's priest and, as he had with other clients, assist in procuring an annulment. Meanwhile, would it not make sense to try to reach some peaceful accommodation with his wife and children?

"'The father,'" answered Blocker resignedly, "'shall be divided against his family.'"

"Who said that?" Farbman wanted to know.

"Who said that? Jesus said that. 'A man's foes shall be they of his own household.'"

"Really?" Farbman was genuinely surprised. "Who said he said that?"

"Matthew. 'He that loveth son or daughter more than me is not worthy of me.' And in Luke it's written, 'If any man come to me and hate not his father, mother, wife and children he cannot be my disciple.'"

Farbman paused to turn that idea around in his head for a minute. "I was taught," Farbman said, "that to bring peace to your household is to bring peace to the world." He considered the family photos on his desk, the morning's exchange with Ann Marie, and how few familial ploughshares he'd hammered recently.

"Who said that?" asked Blocker.

"Don't recall. Someone."

"Maybe you did," suggested Blocker, rising.

"I definitely did," said Farbman.

Blocker paused and stared Farbman in the eyes. "We are at war. Fight on, Mr. Farbman."

Pittipaldi's avenging sword gleamed in Farbman's mind. "Didn't Jesus preach turn the other cheek, and that his kingdom was not of this world?"

"It is okay to be a soldier and a Christian. There are acceptable, even transcendent, channels for violence. The Crusades were blessed. It was a new way of earning salvation. You may find it interesting to know my birthday is November 27."

"I know that day is important," said Farbman, "I'm just not connecting it with a year."

"1095. November 27, 1095."

"Of course," said Farbman, "the uh—"

"The start of the First Crusade."

"Onward Christian soldiers," said Farbman, taking Blocker's money. He promised to call Pittipaldi before the day was out and demand the torching of the centerfolds, and asked Joy to usher in Rhonda Pond. While he was waiting, he buzzed Marucci on the intercom and told him he was in a little mess he'd tell him about later. Meanwhile, could he do him a favor and run over to the public library, see if you can find some medieval Christian authority—a pope or a saint, maybe—who preached love and reconciliation, particularly among family members.

"You're nuts. Both of us have more important things to do."

"Fine, I'll do it myself."

Rhonda, a handsome three-year veteran of the nuptial bed, fiddled with her belt, a dun chunk of hair falling over one eye, as she ticked off the acts of abuse Farbman had explained to her were prerequisite to emancipation from the relationship neither she nor her husband wanted to continue. "He promised we'd have kids before we were married, then wouldn't ...," she recited into her lap.

Farbman, playing amanuensis, observed how the black patent leather belt gave a subtle accent to the soft black fabric of her clinging dress. "'Refusal to have uncontracepted relations,' is what we call that," he explained, as he jotted down what became grievance '(f)' on his yellow pad.

"No, that's not right," Rhonda replied, brushing the slant of hair from her eye, then looking down again to pull the belt tighter through the buckle.

"What's not right?" asked Farbman.

Rhonda looked confused.

"Did your husband use a contraceptive?" asked Farbman.

Rhonda had tightened the belt past the available holes so she loosened it until a hole appeared, inserted the tongue, and closed it. "No," she replied.

"He insisted that you use one?"

"No."

Farbman paused. "Why don't you just describe sexual relations with your husband in your own words."

"Well ..." Rhonda flushed and began tugging on her belt again. "He always pulls out early and he masturbates mainly."

"Could you elaborate a bit?"

"I dunno. Three or four times a day that I'm aware of. Have you ever heard of anything like that?"

"You'd be amazed," said Farbman. "He does this in front of you?"

"No. Well, sometimes, and a lot—like at night and in the morning—when he thinks I'm asleep. Sometimes when I come home from work I catch him with his pants down, or he'll just be coming out of the bedroom with a sheepish look on his face and I'll see that the Nivea cream jar is out. He uses *a lot* of my Nivea cream, most of which I end up paying for."

Farbman flipped through his notes. "What sort of work does your husband do again?"

"He teaches introductory philosophy at the community college—part-time, because he's been working on a novel."

Joy's voice interrupted over the intercom. It was Mr. Big. He had a crisis—how to fire a huge, odor-emitting clerk by the end of the day before his entire bookkeeping department quit—and he wouldn't stop by, but would put the check in the mail.

"Big, listen to me." Farbman spoke with real urgency. "Don't do a thing until we map it out. It's lucky you called. I can't go through it all with you now—someone's sitting with me—but listen, if she's really obese—"

"Two fifty, easy," Big interjected.

"Okay, she's obese, and—listen to me—the obesity qualifies her as handicapped. And the smell suggests to me you're being set up for either a discrimination or a wrongful discharge suit, or both."

"I don't think I can wait. The girls working on each side of her have been scattering mothballs around their desks and chairs, like some kind of shield or somethin'. They tell everyone it's because it keeps the mice away, but we all know what's goin' on."

"Big, listen to me, this is serious. We better meet."

Big said he'd be in after lunch, and Farbman hung up, releasing a giant exhalation.

"It's a science fiction book," Rhonda went on. "About units of time and what exists between them. His main character discovers another dimension with whole other worlds between each tiny time unit. I don't think it's going anywhere and I don't want any part of it—royalties or whatever. He can keep it all."

Farbman hurried Rhonda through her litany of Mr. Pond's transgressions, assured Rhonda that she could, despite her husband's vigorous objections, hold on to his name (which she said she found more euphonious than her maiden name, Schtrunken), gratefully folded her check into Blocker's and Amber Fleischman's, and mentally calculated the shortfall as he went to collect Marucci for lunch.

Farbman found his partner in the hallway bidding Deborah Must what Farbman considered a rather unctuous good-bye—Marucci's hand gripping Deborah's arm above the elbow. Irritated, Farbman said nothing except that they deserved a good meal, and they agreed on the Oyster Bar. Joy caught Farbman as they were about to get on the elevator to tell him his friend Michael was calling and it sounded important. *Leah* was Farbman's thought as he returned to his office and pushed the blinking light on the phone. Farbman had spoken to Michael several times since the funeral. He tried to figure how to bring Leah's name into the conversation and missed his friend's opening comments. He heard Michael say he had a "situation." A "real moneymaker." That there were "only one or two units left." Farbman had enough presence of mind to ask what kind of customer they'd be suited for.

"I was thinking of you," said Michael. "Somebody who's serious, who wants to make real money, not some eight percenter. This is an incredible deal. We're looking at three times your investment. Company is private now, but not for long. The guys here are fighting to get the last few units, and I held one out for you."

"Thanks," said Farbman, explaining that he was "not real liquid" at the moment.

"Hey, who has a hundred grand in uninvested cash? You can do it on a letter of credit. Just call your banker, and you and Marucci can share the unit because you're already a partnership."

"Unfortunately I've drawn down my credit lines."

Michael wanted Farbman to understand that he wasn't interested in the sale, that Farbman was his friend, that they were talking a lifetime relationship. "I want you buying years from now. I just wanted to give you a shot at a situation usually only the big hitters get to see." Farbman said thanks, again, and asked whether there was any chance Michael would be coming this way soon, and how was his father doing and, he was curious had he heard anything from his cousin Leah.

"Not really. She called once after I'd given you her number to say she was disappointed about not getting in some theater group in Chicago—wolf, something wolf, I think—and was moving to New York, although there was a possibility in L.A. She said she'd call with her new number. Listen, I'll hold this unit for a couple of hours, say three your time. Give you a chance to talk to Marucci and your banker. Okay?"

"No kidding—New York. Did she get a part or something?"

"I dunno. Three o'clock, okay?"

"Listen, this city can be a little overwhelming, so tell her to call me, and I'll help any way I can."

"Sure. I told you you can do this on a letter of credit, right?"

En route to lunch Farbman told Marucci about the investment opportunity. Marucci said he knew nothing about investments but thought it was a great idea if Farbman could figure out how to buy in without any money. They visited Worrad to hand over the Fleischman, Blocker, and Pond retainers, along with a modest receivable that had arrived in the mail. And with a promise that Mr. Big's ten would be deposited by the close of business, Farbman persuaded Worrad to issue an immediate credit to their account. As they were leaving, Farbman mentioned that they were looking at an investment and wondered what they would need to get a letter of credit for, say, a hundred thousand. Worrad told them that with the firm's furnishings, equipment, checking accounts, and receivables already assigned to the bank, they'd have to offer some personal collateral. Second mortgages on their homes, assuming there was sufficient equity, should do it. Since Marucci had lost his house in his divorce, Worrad gave Farbman an application to take, with the reminder that his wife would have to cosign.

The two partners joined the lunch hour crowd on Lexington Avenue, then entered the Calcutta of Grand Central to get to the Oyster Bar inside. Farbman handed singles to women pushing their worldly possessions in shopping carts, or dragging them in boxes, adding to the din that bounced around the tiled passageways and carried into the restaurant. Joy had reserved a table in the back room and they were quickly seated. Marucci ordered a glass of Chablis. Farbman ordered seltzer and lime, and asked if Marucci should really be ordering wine, with his ulcer. Marucci said he needed something to wash down his Tagamet. Farbman sighed and proposed that Marucci, instead of ordering by the glass, take a look at what was probably the most extensive domestic wine list in New York.

"Thanks, Dad," said Marucci, "but the glass will be fine."

"But you never order a single glass," Farbman chided.

Marucci explained his drinking was genetic, adding: "Just pray I don't have the old man's extra chromosome and rip you off."

The maitre d' took the one-page menu from the scowling Marucci and turned it to reveal the wine list on the back.

"Fine. I'll take a bottle of this." Marucci pointed with his index finger.

"An excellent choice. One of the best of the California boutiques. Their Fume is also nice."

Marucci asked the man if he had crabs and, before Farbman could make the obvious joke, was apologetically informed they were not in season. Marucci told Farbman they weren't the kind he wanted anyway, you couldn't get them in a restaurant.

Marucci wanted crabs like his father used to bring home when he was a kid. Hardshells covered with paprika.

Farbman asked Marucci if he knew Grace Pittipaldi. Marucci couldn't place her.

"An associate at Sommer and Darcy. Blond, glasses, nice body, kind of dour?"

"Sorry, no bells."

"Well, I kissed her."

Marucci clapped both hands to his chest. "Be still my beating heart," he said.

A waiter returned with the wine, a bucket, and a bottle of mineral water. Farbman explained he'd ordered seltzer, that he preferred larger bubbles, that Marucci only wanted a half bottle. The waiter said that the wine Marucci had selected didn't come in half bottles and that they didn't have seltzer, but that he'd bring club soda. Marucci told the waiter not to worry about it, he'd only drink half. Farbman said he'd rather not have the sodium and settled on New York City tap.

"You don't get it," said Farbman. He lowered his voice and leaned over the table. "She's threatened to file an ethics complaint and maybe criminal charges."

Marucci swallowed his first glass and began to refill it. He clutched the bottle by the neck as he poured, oblivious to the water that dripped onto the tablecloth and his place setting. "Who'd ever guess you'd be such a lousy kisser."

The waiter interrupted again to take their orders. Marucci complained about their not having crabs, then ordered a tuna steak. Farbman told him he was killing the Pacific dolphin by supporting the tuna industry and Marucci said he was only eating tuna because he didn't see dolphin on the menu. Farbman ordered a lobster salad, and Marucci told him that the lobster was the cockroach of the sea. The waiter hurried away with the menus.

Farbman said, "Marucci, you know the climate today. An off-color joke in the workplace means your job and six-figure damages for the victim. What do you suppose they'd do to a lawyer?"

"Lift your ticket for sure. Maybe a caning."

"I can't survive if I can't practice law."

"Poverty isn't so bad. You get to appreciate simple things. Like crabs, for instance." Marucci refilled his glass.

"This woman is really out to get me."

A different waiter brought their food and asked who got what. Farbman told him.

Marucci told Farbman to lighten up. He clutched his fork with an overhand grip, thumbed his rice onto the tines, shoveled his food into his mouth and chewed it with his mouth open. Two kernels of rice were stuck in the corner of his mouth. Farbman pointed to the same corner of his own mouth. Marucci told Farbman to leave him the fuck alone.

Outside the restaurant doors a stringy-haired derelict in a soiled camouflage suit stopped Farbman and Marucci. He had a cardboard sign reading "Viet Nam Vet" hanging from a piece of twine around his neck and held a styrofoam cup from the Greek diner on Forty-Second Street. A picture of the Acropolis was printed in blue on the cup. Farbman reflexively pulled a single out of his pocket and Marucci snatched it from his hand. Eyes burning, Marucci shoved the bill in the man's face and asked if he'd lie down and let him step on him for the dollar. "Come on, Marucci." Farbman hooked his arm and tried to pull him away. The contracted biceps felt like a frozen slab of beef. Farbman paused, awed by his partner's strength. This was muscle formed by loading trucks, by street fighting, and by humping a mortar tube through Asian rain forests. Not by circuit training at the health club.

They were standing under the low arched ceiling of a dreary, loud Grand Central corridor. It was one hallway in what Farbman had christened "the corridors of powerlessness."

"Fuck you, man, what's your problem," said the Vet.

"Marucci," Farbman pleaded.

Marucci, his arm in Farbman's, allowed himself to be led along, and in a bit Farbman returned to his problem with Pittipaldi. Marucci said Farbman was overreacting. Farbman decided to record their next conversation so Marucci could hear the malevolence in her voice. Then, to help cheer them up, he returned to their favorite topic: The Way Out. A shared fantasy, it was to be Farbman's ultimate gift for Marucci, against which all else would pale.

Every lawyer Farbman knew had the same dream: to find another way of earning a living. Farbman told Marucci they'd start by buying into Michael's "moneymaker"—a mixed-use residential/shopping/restaurant/recreational complex in booming Texas oil country. That way, as Michael had put it, they'd not only get shelter and a good return but assure the preservation of their capital. Safety first.

Farbman decided he would bring the second mortgage papers home for Ann Marie to cosign that weekend. He knew she'd resist; he could picture her face all pinched with doubt. He'd have to explain to her that they wouldn't really be borrowing, it would just be collateral. Maybe Michael could fax some pictures or overnight some brochures so she could see what it looked like. Farbman would remind her of shopping in the Bourse in Philadelphia, and how much she liked Manhattan's South Street Seaport. Farbman recalled the frustration of getting his wife to understand that when you put twenty thousand down on a hundred thousand dollar house and its value increases to a hundred and twenty thousand, your return isn't twenty percent, it's a hundred percent.

Marucci removed his arm from Farbman's and reminded him about his idea to market unstainable neckties. Then, when Farbman sighed, asked, "What do you want me to do?"

"Nothing," said Farbman, "I'll take care of it. Just close out the Fudgsicle."

"I'd kiss you," Marucci said with a smile, "if you weren't so homophobic."

Mr. Big got off the adjacent elevator almost at the same moment as Farbman and Marucci stepped off theirs. Farbman took Big directly to his office, just glancing at the top message in the pile Joy lifted off the spike and handed to him as he walked by. Ann Marie had called from the Realtor's. She'd narrowed the selections to two places—one twenty-five thousand, the other twenty-two thousand and she wanted his help with the decision. Also she'd left the exact dates for her family reunion, and Joy had cleared his schedule and ordered their plane tickets, and which credit card did Farbman want them charged to? Farbman, trying to calculate which card had enough credit left to cover the tickets and how he would come up with the deposit on the summer house, started to tell Joy to tell Ann Marie to use her own judgment, then decided he better speak to her himself. He asked Big if it would be all right if he returned his wife's call, and Big smiled and waved as if to convey a shared masculine understanding about the importance of pacifying wives. Farbman dialed the Realtor's number on the message and asked for Ann Marie, all the while studying the way Joy shifted her body as she turned to leave. Impulsively, with his hand over the receiver, Farbman called to Joy and matter-of-factly mentioned that he'd checked and the Purim play was earlier than he'd thought so he could keep their Sunday afternoon appointment after all.

Ann Marie got on and told Farbman that the house for twenty-five thousand wasn't as modern as the one for twenty-two thousand, nor were the furnishings as nice, and that the cheaper one also had an extra toilet and shower on the deck, but that the one for twenty-five was just behind the dunes, maybe fifty yards from the beach, and was really private. Farbman said for the three grand he'd rather have the proximity to the ocean, and Ann Marie said that's how she felt too, but she knew that money was tight and she didn't want to make the decision without talking to him first. Had Joy given him the dates of the Jamison reunion? He confirmed that it was all set, and cut off her profuse thanks, saying it meant a lot to him, too. She added one important thing she had forgotten to mention: This Friday night Jason and

Jennifer's Sunday school assignment was to have a traditional Sabbath meal. They had learned the Shabbat blessings, over the candles and the wine and bread, and were dividing them up. They also had some songs they were practicing.

"That's wonderful," said Farbman, the word "Shabbat" immediately calling to mind a cabin in snow-covered woods; Rabbi Sholem; the clear cold sky; Leah's body, her thick brown hair, her deep voice. Her. Death, and the weight of her breast in his hand. Shabbat was a place Farbman visited when he allowed himself a respite. His own little cabin in time.

Ann Marie warned him not to dawdle with Harold at racquetball. Sundown was early this time of year, and the kids had been given the exact candle-lighting times.

Farbman was remembering a weathered old man chopping ice at the edge of a pond near the lodge, to give the ducks a margin of safety. He thought: I want to stand on spread legs in the snow, breaking ice in the sun of a winter day. To save ducks. He saw himself pounding ice, swinging a sledge at a post.

Ann Marie said she would use her silver and a white linen tablecloth. She'd get a challah and make something special.

Big started pointing to his watch, and Farbman got off. Big said he'd made the deal with Schwartz. "He'll bone the heads for a buck a piece. You start working on it yet?" asked Big, laying his check on Farbman's desk. The check bore the imprint of Bigonocco Veal: the name arced over a cartoon drawing of a smiling cow's face. It had, over the years, inspired in Farbman the same confidence in its negotiability as the picture of Hamilton on the twenty.

When Farbman told Big that he believed there might be some contractual ambiguities, Big chuckled. He liked hearing about ambiguities in statutes and case law and agreements. It was as reassuring to him as his cow-faced drafts were to Farbman. Big was philosophical about the impediments to agreement-breaking. "Contracts," he said, "should be like marriage—you just break 'em whenever one party wants out."

"Now what do I do about this smelly cow in my back office?" asked Big.

Farbman counseled Big to take her aside and promise his full support if she were physically afflicted, offering not only the benefits of his corporate medical plan, but reimbursement for the costs of uncovered treatment; but, at the same time, to warn her that if this is merely a matter of hygiene, she'd better get it together, it being more than her co-employees could bear.

Big rose as if to leave, but, as Farbman stood with him, Big said there was one more thing. He hesitated, fixing for a moment on something outside Farbman's window. "You know Sal, my stepson, he's got a nose problem." Big reached into his pants pocket and pulled out a business card which he handed to Farbman. It was Marucci's Farbman & Marucci Attorneys-at-Law card. On the back, Marucci's scrawl had receipted Big for ten thousand dollars in cash about three months earlier. Farbman sat back down, weak in the knees, suddenly aware of his motile stomach, of lobster salad fermenting.

"Anyways," Big continued, "Sal got busted in Queens and pled out with some dumb ass Legal Aid lawyer, and they were going to send him away since it was his second time and a sale. I figured that's what should happen to him, but his mother got real upset, and so I called to see if you could do anything on this sentence. You weren't around so I spoke to Marucci. He said he knew some people in Queens and might be able to reach the judge, get him like, say, two years of weekends. You know—weeding vegetables, peeing in a bottle once a week."

No! Farbman shouted to himself. Not this. Not the old half-for-me-half-for-the-judge scam. This was a con Farbman had only heard about in courthouse gossip, plied by the sleaziest of the marginal practitioners, the guys who lived out of their hats, picking up trade outside municipal court. The judge was never contacted, the lawyer just kept what was supposed to be the judge's half as a bonus if he happened to get the result.

"The deal, Marucci told me," said Big, "was five for you guys and five for the judge if you could reach him. If not, I get the judge's five back. Sal got time, and I've called Marucci for the five back and he's ducking my calls."

Farbman was in the midst of his apology when he heard voices raised in the outer office, then what sounded, even muffled through the door, like squeals. He excused himself and hurried out. All the secretaries and two associates were grouped around Joy's desk. Joy turned as Farbman approached. Behind her, leaning on her monitor, was a leg. Farbman picked it up, telling everyone to go back to work.

"It's Mr. Munro's. Constable Wolchensko gave it to Reilly in court, and he just brought it back," said Joy. "Reilly borrowed ten dollars from me for a cab, which I need you to give me back because I'm out."

"Why didn't he take the subway?" asked Farbman. "You know we don't pay for cabs."

"I guess he didn't want to carry it in the crowd. It's creepy. It gives me the willies."

The leg was wearing an argyle sock held up by a thumbtack in the shin. It gave Farbman the willies. He asked if Reilly had said anything else, if there'd been any problems. "No," said Joy, "just that he quit."

Farbman took the leg to the exhibit room where key evidence was stored and unlocked the door. Between themselves, Farbman and Marucci referred to it as "the vault," and sometimes as "the comfort room," for they would, at times of financial stress, stand amid the defective products, the death and injury-dealing instrumentalities, and contemplate the security of their future. Warehoused on the gray metal shelving was an intrauterine device that caused sterility; a bagel cutter that had sliced off Mrs. Schwartz's fingertip; a pair of lead-lined gloves that had leaked and caused a radiologist to develop bone cancer; a paper cutter that had fallen off a stationary store display and knocked a customer in the head severely enough to cause seizures; an exercise bicycle with a faulty seat that had sodomized an exerciser. Farbman inhaled and was calmed by the certain value of these things.

He leaned the leg against the wall, wedging it behind the snowblower that had chopped three right fingers off Mr. Kearny, then decided it should be less obvious and laid it on its side behind a cataract-inducing microwave oven.

Farbman locked the door as Joy ran up to inform him that Ida had called from Long Island Jewish Hospital. Janet had overdosed and was in intensive care. Also Mr. Blocker called and wanted him to read a portion of Corinthians and to copy it and send it to Pittipaldi and the judge.

Mr. Big had left, said he'd call later. Mr. Worrad called from the bank and asked when the deposit was coming over. Also Ms. Pittipaldi called sounding angry, and before Farbman returned the call, did he want her to get a Bible so he could fax the passage to her? And which credit card did he want to use for his family reunion tickets? If he didn't buy them today he'd lose the cheap fare.

Farbman, figuring they'd probably let him run over his credit limit, said VISA. Forget the Bible, he told Joy, tell Worrad the money will be there in an hour, that the next time Ida called to put her through, that he wanted Pittipaldi's number, and that she should call Michael and ask him to hold the unit until tomorrow. And to find Michael's cousin Leah's new phone number.

Farbman returned to his office and dialed Pittipaldi. When the receptionist answered "Sommer and Darcy," Farbman remembered he wanted to record the conversation and began fishing in his desk drawer for the hookup. He tugged the microphone wire out from under a stack of folders and began stalling for time to connect it to the handset. "Gosh," he said, "I just forgot who I was calling." There was an understanding laugh on the other end. "Wait, wait—no, I called him, and then what's-his-name called me and … I've got it—Grace Pittipaldi. Is she in?"

"Who's calling?"

"No, you'll think I'm an idiot forever. Is Grace in?"

"May I ask who is calling, please?"

"All right, go ahead and ask." Farbman licked the rubber suction cup, stuck it to the receiver, and inserted the plug end into his dictating machine.

"Who is this?" Exasperated now. Farbman pressed the RECORD and PLAY buttons, checked to see that the tape was rolling. "Tell her it's Farbman."

Pittipaldi picked up after a long pause and began by suggesting it was one thing to mistreat attorneys but abusing her staff was surely beneath even him. Farbman explained it was just banter, and that he was sorry if it were misconstrued.

"Well, let me make sure I'm not misconstrued. You will deliver me your client's generous proposal by this Friday, or by next Monday I'll file charges that will ruin you professionally, if not personally as well."

"My God, Grace. Just because I kissed you?"

"You assaulted me."

"I kissed you. And how would you prove it anyway?"

"I told my husband and he can corroborate under the 'fresh complaint' hearsay exception."

"What are you trying to turn this into, a rape case?"

"That is precisely my point. And my husband will attest to the devastating emotional impact this has had on me—depression, sleep interruption, sudden episodes of free-floating anxiety. Just look under Post Traumatic Stress Disorder in the D.S.M.—for which, by the way, I am about to begin treatment with those eminent plaintiffs' physicians, Prakeesh and Livermore."

"Those charlatans."

"Really? I never heard you describe them as such when offering their opinions on the psychic injuries sustained by your client in the bus accident."

"Your head didn't go through a luggage rack; you were kissed. Besides, what you're demanding isn't compensation from me but from Blocker. What it comes down to is you're trying to force me to sell my client out. And he is, in any case, completely unsalable. He keeps telling me that it's okay to kill everyone including your own family for Jesus. That he was born on November 27."

"I'm not going to get involved in a comparison of our respective tactics in this case or who was the first to take any advantage that offered itself, no matter how unfair. As they say in the vernacular, 'What goes around, comes around.' And all I expect is that he'll waive his demand that the house be sold and divided and deed it over to her, which I think is fair."

"But Grace, nothing I did was outside the rules."

"Staying within the rules is not a defense here. Friday, Farbman." The line went dead. Farbman depressed the STOP button and hung up the phone.

Joy came in. Michael had left Leah's new phone number for him. Worrad had called again for the money. Farbman pulled out Mr. Big's check to give to Joy to take to the bank. He paused for an instant reflecting on the logo, on his lost associate and his partner's scamming, and with a sudden empathy told himself this cow's got nothing to laugh about.

FRICTIVE LOVE

Farbman admitted to Harold that things weren't going so well. The two men were sitting in the sacred steam after their Friday night racquetball game. Harold had once described it as a mechanized Navaho sweat lodge. Farbman had lost three straight and felt as weak as if he were coming down with the flu.

"You wonder why your life is a mess?" Harold said. "Look at you." He slid the fingers of both hands caressingly over his washboard abdominals. Dark thatches of hair grew on the backs of his hands and fingers and on the tops of his long bony toes. "You've got no home life, no relationship with your wife, you spend no time with your kids. You work like a dog and spend more than you make without even enjoying it. You've put yourself so deep in hock you'll be on a walker before you get out from under."

"Thanks," said Farbman. "You folks in the healing professions have a knack for making a body feel better." Boiling drops of condensate dripped from the ceiling and landed in little fiery bursts on his scalp. A hidden engine came to life, and a blast of steam scalded his feet. Farbman climbed to a higher bench where he was forced to stoop below the cloud of trapped heat that pressed down from the ceiling. "Anything else, Doctor?"

"Well," said Harold, "I don't want to alarm you, but you looked so uncoordinated on the racquetball court tonight, I was thinking of referring you for a brain scan."

The flow of steam at his feet stopped, and Farbman descended to the lower bench. "I don't believe this. I've come to the devil for help. Why don't you just tell me to kill myself."

"Inconsistent with my Hippocratic oath. I mean, as your friend I might be tempted."

"Fuck you, Harold."

"I'm sorry." He sat up and put his hand on Farbman's shoulder. "What is it? You and Ann Marie?"

Farbman allowed himself to be consoled. He wanted to talk about finding a simpler, rural way of life, but he knew how ridiculous the idea sounded.

"We're having more friction than usual."

"Love is friction. I take it, though, you do not refer to the resistance of two bodies against each other, but to those daily unpleasantries by which marrieds reassure each other of their devotion?"

"Yes," said Farbman, "just everyday frictive love."

"I don't think that's a word—frictive."

"No?"

"No. Fricative, yes," said the physician, "but that refers to breath sounds."

"Do you think it would have been better if I'd married a Jewish girl? Not that I could have. For some reason I've only been attracted to non-Jews."

"'For some reason?' Of course you're only attracted to shiksas. That way you stay faithful to Mom. People with low self-esteem usually seek opposites. Given your feelings of worthlessness—"

"Oh, listen to Sigmund fucking Freud."

"Look, I'm just saying—"

Farbman stood. "I've had enough." He pushed open the door and Harold followed, the two not speaking. A moment later, a sulking

Farbman asked to borrow Harold's shampoo.

Harold handed the tube to Farbman and said, "Can I give you one more bit of advice?"

"What?" said Farbman petulantly.

"Wash. Rinse. Repeat," said Harold.

Harold approached as Farbman was toweling off. "What about you?" Farbman asked.

"What about me?"

"You and women." Farbman said.

"How about I tell you over dinner? Unless Ann Marie's waiting for you."

"Women," Harold began, as the waitress in her red obi poured tea, "are a matter of sex or kids. Everything else is more fun with a man. As you know I've never been interested in kids. So the point of what I'm doing with women is sex, not relationship. The relationships I get into develop over about two weeks and plateau right there."

He paused over the selection of sushi. Harold ordered in Japanese, stumbling only on the word for quail eggs. He wanted them raw on pureed sea urchins.

"But," asked Farbman, "what do you say to the women?"

"I explain it straight up. Doing that, I've learned, gets you the best sexual response." The doctor probed his cold spinach appetizer for bonito flakes, which he licked off the ends of his chopsticks. "Mind you, I'm not looking for a whole lot of depth in a partner. I like them young, still anabolic. You know—bodies still synthesizing tissues, building bones, preferably without wisdom teeth. Not yet breaking down, stiffening up, getting smaller. Not yet people. I wouldn't know what to do with a real person, someone like Ann Marie."

"And that's fulfilling?"

"It's a matter of tradeoffs. Being single is great sex maybe twenty, thirty times a year. Getting hard-ons so big the skin on your face stretches. Orgasms so intense your teeth hurt.

"For this you give up warm experiences around the holidays. Sharing relationships. Yesterday I took this twenty-three-year-old nurse to a couple of clubs, then home for a night of gymnastics that was worth a year."

Farbman vibrated with envy. He longed for such sex, to make manifest the sin that until Leah he'd committed only in his heart. He checked his watch and realized if he didn't call right away the children would be in bed soon.

He'd missed the whole Shabbat meal. They'd waited and hadn't even lit the candles at sundown. His daughter asked if he'd wake her up when he came in. She wanted to show him how she looked as Queen Esther. Could she light the candles again so he could hear her say the prayer and then just blow them out? His son asked if he could help make the roof removable on his model Sumerian house.

When Ann Marie got on, the shelling started.

Farbman stood reading the graffiti on the pay phone wall until she finished and slammed down the receiver.

A man's foes shall be they of his own household. Farbman heard Blocker's voice through the dial tone.

Farbman returned to a half-melted bowl of green tea ice cream Harold had ordered for him. Harold, who had already consumed a box of hot sake, a beer, and his complimentary plum wine, picked up Farbman's, expressing his appreciation for Farbman's abstemiousness. "Just don't let it extend to your sex life. As you start aging, you can't afford long periods without fucking. It's a medical fact. Use it or lose it."

They said good-bye in the parking lot. Harold floored the Porsche, and Farbman, whose cell phone was low, headed for a booth on the street. He pulled out his book of phone numbers, found Leah's newly inscribed number, quickly punched it in, and then hung up before the first ring. What did he want from her? He dialed again, panic fluttering in his chest.

When she answered, Farbman tried for lightheartedness. "You shouldn't be answering your phone on Shabbat."

"Jerry?"

"My god, how soon they forget."

"Mel? Who is this? Say some more." She laughed.

Dropping his voice to parody a radio announcer, Farbman said: "We met in another world. In another time. We were united in a sacred ceremony of unspoken vows, witnessed by pines."

"I know who this is." He heard her sigh. "Listen, what we did was no more than affirm we were alive, and whether sacred or profane I'm not prepared to say. I do know that it had meaning only in that context."

"A funeral fuck."

"Exactly. So, how can I help you?"

"I never found out what teshuvah is."

"I told you—turning. As in away from sin and back to the faith. Repentance. It means changing who you are. How you think. What you do."

"What a coincidence. I've been thinking a lot lately about changing my life," said Farbman.

"You have something in mind?"

"No. In the woods with Rabbi Sholem I experienced … I don't know. Whatever it was, it was brief. I definitely don't have a word for it. Maybe it was living in the present for a moment or two. No big deal, I guess, but …"

"Oh, that was just God."

"You're making fun of me."

"It's Heschel."

"Why would Heschel make fun of me?"

"The present, said Heschel, is the presence of God. Sensing the present is sensing God. Bravo, Farbman. It seems you saw *the* light. Now what?"

"It got dark again."

"It usually does."

"How could it be otherwise? Who's got time for Sholem's games once you're back in reality, loaded with responsibilities, with the lives we've been saddled with?"

"What do you expect? To pick a persona as an actor gets a part? Jump from Hyde to Jekyll and stay there? You got a start—what happened in the woods was teshuvah. But whether you decide to play a different game is another matter."

A homeless man hovering outside Farbman's booth suddenly put his face to the glass. Farbman opened the door and said he was almost done, but the man didn't back off.

"Where are you calling from?" Leah asked.

"A pay phone."

"Say good-bye," said Leah, "and go home." With those words the shade came down on Farbman's memory of the two of them amid trees and snow, sunlight and birdsong.

"Good-bye, I will," said Farbman. And hanging up, and having nowhere else to go, he did.

LOX AND MOUSSE
AND THE WHOLE MEGILLAH

It was Sunday and Purim, and Farbman was determined to invest the day with meaning. Sundays were, of course, the traditional day for confrontation and outpourings of rage. In his childhood, before the weekly altercations by which his parents molded his experience of family, there would be big plates of scrambled lox, eggs, and onions, bagels with cream cheese, white fish, kippered salmon and sturgeon, and herring in sour cream. In his adolescence Farbman would be the focus of the hostility, his father excoriating him for lack of effort in school or around the house, for his failure to appreciate how hard his father worked (or really, as Farbman came later to understand, how much his father detested his work). After the fights, and sometimes during, relatives and friends would visit and in the evenings there were trips over the bridge from Brooklyn, to Lee's walk-up Cantonese place on Pell Street, then back home in time for the Ed Sullivan Show and perhaps a little schoolwork before bed.

With Ann Marie, Sundays were more dilute. There were bagels and low fat cream cheese, but eggs had been out of the question for years. The family never sat down together anymore because the kids went off to Sunday school like little gentiles: the Jewish holy Sabbath, observed for thousands of years on Saturdays, fought for in United States' courts—died for in Europe—had been willingly abandoned in the free air of Rockville Centre to accommodate Little League games and soccer practices. And while relationships were tense on Sundays, avoidance rather than outright skirmishing was the norm. Farbman jogged. Ann Marie car-pooled. Early on in their marriage there were softball and touch football games. More recently they'd joined tennis and health clubs. Hours were passed plowing through the *Times*. Not infrequently Farbman drove to his office so he could clear his desk, get some work done without the damn telephone, prepare for a trial, or have a partners meeting with Marucci.

Today, though, Farbman was going to celebrate with his family. Make amends for Friday night. Focus on the children. As soon as he heard them coming down the stairs, he put aside the rest of the Sunday *Times Book Review.*

Jennifer raced up, flaunting her cardboard-and-glitter Queen Esther crown. "Do you like it, Daddy? I made it myself."

"You did not, you liar. Mom did most of it." Jason hung back, a somewhat reluctant Mordecai in an old bathrobe and a mop beard.

Jennifer climbed into her father's lap. "She didn't, she only helped with the scissors," said Jennifer.

Farbman effusively praised both of their costumes and then asked if they could tell him what Purim was all about. "You know all I can remember are the games and the food at the carnival. Can you guys tell me who Esther and Mordecai were?"

"I'll tell it," said Jennifer, beginning, "Once upon a time there was this evil king." She was immediately corrected by Jason. "It was his minister, Haman, who was evil." Jennifer continued to plug along, ignoring Jason's harsh corrections. What emerged was the simple childhood tale Farbman recalled: Haman's plot to have all the Jews killed and the reversal of the king's decree through the efforts of Esther, his beautiful bride, and her cousin Mordecai.

When the children had had enough of their father's attention and run off to their rooms, Farbman, curiosity aroused, began to search for

a Bible. There was nothing on the bookshelves, and he was soon ran-
sacking the attic cartons of college texts for a paperback King James version he'd used in a lit. course. After two sneezing fits and ten minutes of
crouching under the eaves, he yelled to Ann Marie for help. She
thought she'd left a Bible in the dining room sideboard with the
Passover Haggadahs and some other "religious stuff." This seemed
appropriate enough to Farbman, considering the contemporary cultural
reduction of their religious observances to large family meals.

In the large drawer next to the sterling service, amid stacks of
chocolate company Haggadahs and half-filled boxes of Hanukkah candles, were a plastic sandwich bag containing his grandfather's phylacteries and a steel dreidel he'd brought from Russia. A small velvet tallis
bag from Farbman's childhood—a gift from the same grandfather—lay
on top of two leather-bound volumes, the Pentateuch and Haftorah, a
gift from the Temple Board on his bar mitzvah. They had not been
opened then or in the twenty-three years after.

Farbman toyed with the tefillin and decided it was time he knew
what phylacteries were. He found a dictionary and after finally trying
ph instead of f, and y instead of i, found the word listed between two
other frequently used words: phylacobiosis (an arrangement in which
ants live and work alongside termites) and phylactocarp (a branch of a
plumularian hydroid). According to Webster, inside the leather boxes
were parchment slips inscribed in Hebrew with these passages—
Deuteronomy 6:4-9 and 11:13-21 and Exodus 13:1-10 and 11-16.

Returning to his search for a Bible, the penny suddenly dropped,
and Farbman opened the Pentateuch to the appropriate sections. Apart
from reiterated injunctions to love the one God with all one's heart,
might, and soul and to keep those words ever-present—bound to one's
hand and between one's eyes, written on doorposts and gates; and to
remember, teach and celebrate the story of the Exodus—what Farbman
found was this promise: that if he harkened diligently to the Lord's com-
mandments he would be given the rain of the land in due season and
could gather in his corn, wine, and oil, and Farbman's cattle would have
grass in their fields. And there was this warning: that if he turned aside
and served other gods, the Lord's wrath would be kindled against him,

heaven would be shut up, there would be no rain, and the land would not yield its fruit, and Farbman could expect to perish quickly from off the good land the Lord had given him.

Farbman stared out the window at his front lawn. It was brown and lifeless, and the yard looked dead in the cold winter light. He knew he'd been worshipping the wrong gods; but he also knew that spring rains would come and that the contract chemical company and old Mr. Antonelli would return and his grass would be green again.

The kids, who had begun yelling to go, got in the car with Ann Marie. Farbman paused holding the driver's door open, then stuck his head in to ask if it wouldn't be a good idea to include his parents, make it a real family Sunday. He left everyone sitting and ran inside to call. His mother answered. "I never dreamt of having an affair before last night," she said. "Forty-two years I'm married."

"What? You're telling me you're going to have an affair, Mom?"

"What are you talking? Are you crazy? I said it was a dream. You were in it."

"That's funny," said Farbman, "I don't remember anything about an affair."

"It was with the actor Rex Barker. Do you remember him?"

Farbman heard the volume drop as an extension was picked up.

"Sure, he played Tarzan. But it's *Lex* Barker."

"No," said Farbman's father, "it's Fess Parker."

"No," said Farbman, "that's Davy Crockett."

"Listen, I was just going to call you, I need your help with a legal question. I thought of calling Morrie, but nowadays he only deals with big stuff. You know he's representing all the General Electric employees who are buying that subsidiary upstate. I also thought of Alvin, but he's really given up the practice, he's so busy running the steel company. My God, is he making money."

"Dad, I left Ann Marie and the kids sitting in the car."

"That Nazi machine. Be careful."

"I know, Dad." Farbman's father had never gotten over his son's purchase of a German car. He'd been warning ever since the first time he saw the Mercedes that it was designed so that if Jews sat in it the doors locked and gas came out of the speakers.

"All right," said his father, "I'll make it quick."

"I'll get off," said his mother. "Annie and the children are good?"

"Great, Mom."

"Send them my love and to her family. I understand you're going to her reunion next week."

"Two weeks. Why don't you come over to the Temple to the Purim Carnival, see the kids in their costumes. Then we'll go into the city, get some Chinese. Like old times."

"Thank you, Darling, but I don't think so. What do you think, Buddy?" She pronounced his father's name with a long 'u,' as in Judy."

"Bea, I thought you were getting off," he said to Farbman's mother who hung up without another word. "Do I want to go to a Purim Carnival? No thanks. I've done my Purim duty. Now it's your turn. Maybe we'll have dinner with you, but I'm not driving into the city. If you want to stay local, maybe."

"Okay, Dad. I'll call you later."

"Wait. You didn't answer my question." Farbman sighed. "You know our friend, Albie Laub?" his father asked. "A lovely man. Originally an accountant, made a fortune in chemicals? Anyway, Albie and his wife, Rhoda, a lovely lady, unfortunately with osteoporosis, keeps breaking foot bones, decided to go spend a week in Esztergon, Hungary, on a trip. Hungary? I asked. But they've been already and they know it and they say it's wonderful, very historic, good restaurants, and so on, his favorite country and the man travels everywhere in the world with his chemicals. Anyway, their flight from Kennedy to Budapest is all set for Wednesday, and something came up, I don't know, but he can't go on Wednesday. His tickets are non-refundable, non-changeable, non-nothing." Farbman started to interrupt, but his father cut him off. "I know what you're going to say. What about trip insurance? He didn't get any.

"So he asked if I could write him some kind of note. So I want you to listen to what I wrote and tell me if I could get in any trouble for this." The last part of the sentence was rendered almost completely inaudible by the voltage drop when Jason and Jennifer picked up two other extension phones. Farbman let them say a quick hello and told them they'd see their grandparents later for dinner. "Please not Chinese," Jennifer immediately interjected. "Yes, Chinese," said Jason.

Farbman got them off by ordering them outside to tell their mother what he was doing.

"'Dear Trans World Airlines,'" his father read, "'This is to certify that Albert Laub had a periapical abscess on the left second molar, maxillary'—I made it in the back top" he interrupted himself to explain, "so it would be very difficult to check—'this evening and he will need to complete the root canal procedure this Wednesday, the 18th. I would very much appreciate it if Trans World Airlines would accommodate Mr. Laub's health needs. Yours respectfully.'"

Farbman told his father that he would likely end up in the bowels of the Bastille for conspiring to commit this kind of fraud, that he'd call later about Chinese, and ran out the door. Whatever the kids had said had obviously not assuaged Ann Marie, who did not even respond when Farbman apologized. He stomped the pedal and was well on his way when he realized he had never found the Purim story, that he still didn't know the moral instruction of the day.

"Guess what, Daddy?" Jennifer asked from the back seat. "What?" Farbman responded quickly, ready for play.

"No, guess."

"Can I have a hint?"

"There are people living at the Temple."

"Sure, the caretakers, Althear and Maude."

"Nope, other people. And Jason, don't you tell."

Farbman entered the Temple with Jennifer clutching his hand and shouting to her friends, her cornsilk tresses and green eyes making her a radiant Queen Esther. Jason walked with Ann Marie. He sported a buzzed hair-do—short precisely where Jewish scriptural law exhorted long.

Before the games and food, there was a brief, song-filled service during which the rabbi, in his leather-fringed cowboy outfit, did several of his famous cartwheels. Afterward, Jennifer pulled on her father's arm and entreated him to come to the basement to see the homeless. "They're called 'guests,' Jennifer," Jason corrected, "and you'd better ask the rabbi for permission."

The rabbi explained that there were three families living in the Youth Group lounge and meeting rooms: three mothers with five children who were tutored and looked after by Temple youth while their mothers searched all day for apartments. Congregation members donated time, linens, and food, and in return, learned about the skills and courage it took to survive homelessness. How to tell a safe heating grate from one that gives off poisonous gas. Who will let you use a bathroom. Farbman was about to ask for the answers when the rabbi gestured that they should follow him.

They passed through halls plastered with crayon and construction paper scenes of the Purim story, then down a stairwell littered with laundry. Outside the guests' quarters were jerry-rigged clotheslines. On a set of sheets hung to separate living areas, Farbman recognized the tropical pattern Ann Marie had selected for their bed. The rabbi rapped on a door buck and called hello. No one responded, so he lifted the sheet. Farbman held Jennifer back, peered over the rabbi's shoulder, into an empty room, where a mass was being offered on the TV. The celebrants lined up to drink the communion wine, the priest wiping the rim of the chalice with a folded cloth after each person drank. On a wobbly wooden table were a Dumas cake box and paper plates with the remains of raspberry tortes and a white chocolate mousse.

"Nobody home," said the rabbi.

"By definition," said Farbman.

"They're probably shooting baskets," said Jennifer.

Father and daughter went off holding hands and met up with Jason and Ann Marie. Farbman bought the children hot dogs and greasy french fries. Jason pulled his father to a booth to watch him knock down Haman with softballs. The children gave him their prizes and food to hold. Jason made his father promise not to eat anything. Jennifer said he could have whatever he wanted of hers. Farbman caught Ann Marie looking on approvingly.

"What do adults do to celebrate?" Farbman asked the rabbi.

"Read the Megillah. Have fun. Get drunk. So drunk, enjoins The Talmud, that one can't tell the difference between Haman and

Mordecai."

"The Megillah?"

"The Book of Esther. We read it through twice on Purim."

"The whole Megillah?" asked Farbman. Then, as the rabbi smiled, he asked if there were someplace he could find a copy.

"You never noticed the Bibles interspersed with the prayer books in the sanctuary?"

"I'm not a very observant Jew," said Farbman.

The story of Esther began with King Ahasuerus—who reigned "from India even unto Ethiopia"—throwing a feast at which, when his heart was "merry with wine," he commanded that Vashti, his queen, appear before him and display her beauty to all. Because the order came by messenger, Vashti refused, and the King went nuts. He not only stripped her of her royal estate but got the word out to the empire so that all wives who might have been inspired by Vashti's example would, henceforth, give to their husbands honor, both great and small. Then the King's servants began a quest for "fair young virgins" to replace Vashti, and Esther was picked and crowned.

Thereafter, Haman hatched his plot to destroy all the Jews because Mordecai wouldn't bow to him. Esther, at the direction of Mordecai, agreed to go uninvited before the King to plead the Jews' cause, although to appear unbidden before the King meant certain death, unless "the King shall hold out the golden scepter, that he may live."

Farbman considered the likelihood that Esther would not get the scepteral nod, considering that the King had just selected her as the choicest virgin in the empire and that they hadn't even been married thirty days. He concluded the odds were with her and was not surprised to learn that when the King saw Esther standing in the court she obtained favor in his sight.

Farbman skimmed through the familiar parts about Haman's hanging and about Mordecai being set over the house of Haman, too impatient for even one reading of the Megillah, until he reached the ending, which was new to him. Mordecai was empowered to command in the King's name where the Jews were concerned, and he authorized Jews in every city and province to kill anyone who the Jews thought hated them. Horrified, Farbman read how the Jews began slaughtering hundreds and then thousands, and how Esther asked and got the King's consent to hang Haman's ten sons.

"And the other Jews that were in the King's provinces ... slew of them that hated them seventy and five thousand—but on the spoil they laid not their hand." Then they rested and made it a day of feasting and gladness.

Farbman hadn't been taught that all this revelry was to honor a massacre. At least the Jews hadn't looted and that was something, although Farbman thought the brag inordinately prideful under the circumstances.

On the way home Farbman asked his family if anyone had given any thought to the difference between Esther and Vashti and what the Purim message was regarding a proper wife's role.

"The message," responded Ann Marie so immediately and forcefully that the children stopped bickering and faced forward to listen, "is that a woman does not cease to be a person in her own right, with her own convictions, just because she is married. And that no matter how powerful her husband, and no matter how dire the consequences she may face in expressing her views, she must be true to who she is."

"Esther faced death by going before the King unbidden," said Jennifer.

"Yes," said Farbman, "but remember she only went because Mordecai made her. And who thinks the King would really have been so crazy as to kill his brand new wife, the prettiest woman in the kingdom?"

"So what's your point?" demanded Farbman's queen. "What is Farbman's message to his women?"

"Forget it. I should have known better than—"

"Yes, you should have."

After a silence, Farbman said, "I've got to run in to the office for a couple of hours."

Ann Marie sniffed loudly. In the rearview mirror Jennifer and Jason looked resignedly in different directions, aware that their latest dose of quality time had just ended. The sudden droop in the children's expressions were made even more poignant to Farbman by their now disheveled, food-stained costumes, Jennifer's broken crown, the cheap plastic prizes each clutched. Farbman tried not to picture Joy's body as he explained that there was stuff he just had to get ready for Monday morning but he'd be back to take them all for Chinese. Jennifer suddenly twirled her noisemaker, and Farbman felt as though he'd been rapped in the head. He said nothing all the way into their garage, except, as he scrunched into his own Mercedes, that he'd see them later.

Joy was on the telephone as Farbman arrived, sitting on her desk, wearing blue jeans and a low cut jersey. Farbman suggested they move into his office and get started. She told the person on the phone she had to get off, her boss was there.

They sat side by side on Farbman's couch, a file spread out on the floor next to them. Farbman explained how it should be organized for trial.

He heard the reception door open, recognized Marucci's footfalls—the slight click one of his ankles made—heard his door close, and saw one of the telephone lines light up. The lights were on and Farbman's door was open, Marucci must have heard their voices. Why hadn't he stopped by? Was he really rushing to make the call or, as Farbman believed, avoiding him? When the telephone light went out, Farbman excused himself and headed down the hall.

Marucci was in his dark glasses sorting papers into various piles on his desk.

"Hey," said Farbman.

"Look, I'm really fed up and I don't feel like discussing it with you."

"Tired of the professional life?"

"Tired of thieving."

"Meaning?"

"We steal from insurance companies—shit, from any cash source we can find—and we use the mangled poor to do it. We're only 'professional' because we've got a license to do it. And I think a professional would know better than to eat where he shits."

"Jesus Christ, Marucci, I'm showing her how to prep a file."

"It's none of my business."

They sat in silence. Marucci stared at his papers. Farbman fiddled with photos of Marucci's kids.

"We redistribute the wealth, Marucci. When I was doing that medieval research this week, I learned that in the Middle Ages, Jews were forced by the Church and the nobility to soak up whatever the peasants had and then have it wrung out into their coffers. The Jews were used as sponges. Convenient buffers because we could be scapegoated as heretics whenever the masses were ready to revolt. Now we do it the other way. We work in the service of the poor who no longer yell 'get the Jew,' but 'get a good Jew lawyer.'"

"Maybe," said Marucci, "but whoever's getting it, you're still just a sponge."

"Yeah, well, I want the decision whether to be a sponge to be mine, not Pittipaldi's." He retrieved the tape of their call and shoved it into Marucci's dictator. When it had run through, Marucci looked up at Farbman. "It's extortion."

"No shit."

"No, you idiot, I'm talking real extortion. Legal, not metaphoric." Marucci shook his head. "The statute says that a person extorts if he threatens to accuse someone of an offense or to expose something about the person which would hurt them. It doesn't matter whether it's true or false."

Farbman retrieved the statute from the library. "You're right. I've got her dead." He was thrilled. "I'll send her a copy and a duplicate tape tomorrow, and that should end this." Farbman followed Marucci back to his office, gleefully pounding his right fist into his left as he contemplated his next conversation with Pittipaldi.

"Listen," said Farbman, "there's something else bothering me you can help with."

Farbman showed Marucci Mr. Big's business card receipt. Marucci took a key ring from his pant's pocket and unlocked the bottom drawer of his desk. He pulled out an envelope and tossed it to Farbman.

"Count it," he said. "It's all there. The five to give back to Big and twenty-five hundred—half of the other five—for you."

"Don't be ridiculous," said Farbman, "I trust you."

"Don't," said Marucci.

Joy stuck her head in the door and said she had to go. She'd been there for two hours and that was all the time she'd planned on spending. Marucci offered to give her a lift and left, giving Farbman a cold glance.

Farbman went to the bookkeeper's office and scanned the check register where he found exactly what he feared: Marucci's handwriting drawing a check to himself on Friday for twenty-five hundred. It should have overdrawn the account, but there was a positive balance of a few hundred dollars. It took only a minute to find the answer: the check for the employees' withholding taxes and social security never made it to the bank but was in a pocket in the back of the register with a little stick-on instruction in Marucci's scrawl saying, "Hold out."

Farbman's heart sank. Needing to talk, he called Harold and immediately regretted it when Harold began, "Let me tell you about last night's. I had to pull the sheets and the mattress cover this morning and use a hair dryer on the mattress."

The phone flashed an incoming call, and Farbman said good-bye to Harold.

It was Deborah Must, asking for Marucci. Farbman said she'd just missed him. "Are you sure?" she asked. "He just called me a little while ago. Well, never mind, hopefully he's on his way." They were supposed to have dinner and she just wanted an idea how dressy she should get. Also, she was having a problem with her implants.

Deborah said that her podiatrist, whom she was dating, had a mean streak. He had gotten mad at her for making some suggestions during sex, yanked out, and punched her hard in her breast, and then put his clothes on and left without a word.

"I'm scared. The implant must have broken."

"Have you been to the doctor?"

"I'm afraid to. I've had fevers and a rash all over my body and these rock hard lumps."

"Are you in pain?"

"A lot. Do you think it's related?"

"See your doctor right away. Then get back to Marucci with all the details."

That night, after the Chinese meal with his parents at a strip mall, Farbman showed Ann Marie the brochures Michael had sent and explained the investment memorandum. Thinking to shelter her, he did not mention that part of their borrowings were needed for the Amagansett rental and to cover Marucci's theft. Ann Marie looked at the charts, listened to Farbman's pitch, and asked if it didn't really come down to a question of trust, not numbers. Farbman nodded, said he'd known Michael a long time but had made his own analysis. Ann Marie was silent for a moment, then she surprised Farbman by signing, encumbering the last bit of equity in their house.

THE GRAPEFRUIT

Farbman assured Ann Marie again and again that her over-iterated thank-yous for his willingness to make the trip were unnecessary. He held no grudges because her parents had boycotted their wedding, because her family never remembered the children's birthdays, didn't send even a card with, say, a five dollar bill at Christmas. It was good for Jason and Jennifer to meet the cousins on their mother's side, hang out for a while with relatives who didn't squabble and shout each other down at seder dinners and Yom Kippur break-fasts.

No, the trip was definitely a good idea; but that did not mean Farbman's antennae were not out, his paranoid pores not open. Indeed, the welcoming at the airport made him wonder whether Ann Marie didn't in fact owe him one after all.

Her brother Luke, a Lincolnesque former piste racer, who had limped up as they filed off the plane, hefted Ann Marie like a dance partner. After shaking hands solemnly with each child, he offered Farbman a leathern flask and couldn't wait to tell him the winter'd been so cold the lawyers had their hands in their own pockets. Then he guffawed, slapped Farbman's shoulder while Ann Marie pushed his. The children smiled and looked confused. In his last race, in Palma de Majorca, Luke had been run over by several motorcycles and their tailing draft-drawn bicycles before he rolled clear. Now he had a business that ran tented four-wheel-drive tours "To The Ends of the Earth," as his smudged business card read. Tours to Patagonia, to the islands off Chile, to Cape Horn.

"Don't worry." Luke grinned at Farbman's refusal of the flask, then pulled deep from it, wiped his lips on the back of his hand, and slipped it inside his jacket. "I've always got'er with me if you change your mind."

"Luke keeps a gas can of bourbon in the trunk of his Rover so he can keep refilling during the day," Ann Marie explained. "Don't suppose you have any beer, do you?"

"Does the Pope shit in the woods?"

Brother John was waiting in the Rover with a half case of Hudipohl long necks. No need to worry about John having enough beer along for a car ride, Luke reassured them. He'd lost his license so many times for DWI that it cost him about seventy-five hundred for a minimum coverage, assigned-risk policy.

Farbman excused himself to check in with his office. Luke, saying he wouldn't have Farbman's job for any amount of money, took another slug and went off with Ann Marie and the kids to collect their bags. Joy gave Farbman his messages: Turk Horowitz had an update on the Fleischman investigation; Mr. Bigonocco was leaving town that night for a few days and had to speak with Farbman before he left. Mrs. Pittipaldi got Farbman's package and thanked (thanked?) him and would he call when he got the chance.

Farbman called Big first, who said he'd fired the smelly tub of lard and, just as Farbman had predicted, she'd filed a civil rights' suit claiming she was discriminated against because of her obesity, and he'd send the papers along, but that wasn't why he'd called. He explained that he was going to Washington because a bunch of goddam do-gooders who didn't know jackshit about nothing were trying to prevent the continued drugging of the veal.

"The F.D.A.," said Big, "is threatening to bar oxytetracycline, and neomycin and maybe chloramphemical, too. Christ, do you know what kind of loss that would cost us? The calves need that shit or they could get all kinds of diseases."

"I didn't know they were that susceptible," said Farbman.

"They take the calves from the mothers at a week old before they get the immunities. They got to have antibiotics."

"Why not just leave them on mother's milk?" Farbman asked.

"Too much iron and other nutrients in the milk," explained Big, "stuff that keeps the meat from turning anemic white the way people want it. This is a market-driven product. Also, we got to get them away from their mothers and locked in those little crates you see in the anti-veal ads, or else their muscles are liable to develop."

"What can I do to help, Big?"

It seemed that Big and other veal farmers were going to meet with a bunch of congressmen and try to kill some new bills, or at least get veal cut out of the proposed farm animal protection act. The hope was that, with enough PAC money, the legislators would just concentrate on chickens and pigs where things were much worse anyway. Maybe Farbman could take a look at the bills and come up with some legal attack. Farbman said he'd try.

He disconnected by pressing the tic-tac-toe button, then dialed Turk Horowitz. Turk had scored. The garbage had yielded carbon sheets of invoices to Fleischman's customers not reflected in his record of accounts—dated calculator tapes of receipts, some of which reflected actual deposits and others which showed what had been withheld. And there was dynamite: copies of memos to Fleischman's lawyer about litigation strategy. The memos also contained references to questionable dealings with some very heavy guys Turk would prefer not to discuss on the telephone.

Alarms clanged in Farbman's head. Had he invaded the sacred province of lawyer-client privilege? Even if he were not subject to sanction—the discovery of the memos to Fleischman's lawyer was, after all, inadvertent—if he looked at the memos and the source of his knowledge were revealed, was he disqualified?

"However," added Turk, a nervous edge in his voice, "I think maybe my cover was blown on the last pickup. The regular garbage truck came early and was pulling in just as I pulled away, and I saw the driver get out and watch me drive off."

Turk said anyway he'd try one more time and if the paper was shredded they'd know.

There wasn't enough time to call Pittipaldi, so Farbman hurried to rejoin his family.

For the airport run Luke and John had thrown a half gallon of Jim Beam, a dozen bottles of beer and a small stack of plastic cups into a cooler that they had wedged between the front seats of the Land Rover. John apologized for the absence of brothers Paul and Mark. It seemed that cousin Dewey (actually DeWitt, Ann Marie interjected, identifying him as the son of uncle Dewey and Auntie Ford) had invited them all over for some stick and ball, which had turned into an opportunity for a couple of chukkers when some neighbors showed up with a stock trailer of ponies. So they stopped at Dewey's, arriving in time for the end of the match. John pulled up to park at the edge of the field so they could watch. Farbman, perched on the hood, said he thought polo looked like fun.

"Do you ride?" Luke asked. Farbman explained that, in addition to posing on a pony for a street corner photographer when he was five, he'd ridden at camp and at a dude ranch one summer where he'd been selected as assistant wrangler and trail guide.

"Forget it, Luke," said Ann Marie, "I don't want to spend the next six months nursing an invalid husband."

"C'mon, it's only stick and ball. We'll put him on old Coca Cola. You're playing, too."

"Sure," said Farbman, "but what'll I wear?"

"Can you really play, Mommy?" asked Jennifer.

"Your mom was the captain of the Jamison family team," Luke said.

While Luke and Ann Marie scrounged up equipment, Farbman went to call Pittipaldi from his in-laws' library, a grand room with two stories of mahogany bookshelves, a sliding ladder, and catwalk. The telephone was an old-fashioned black rotary dial. As he lifted the receiver he was startled by the voice of an old lady, loudly demanding to know who the hell he was. He circled the chair in front of him to confront the hatchet-faced ninety-seven-year-old matriarch, Grannie Cabot Kipreyer, legendary solo sailor of the Atlantic, sidesaddle Master of the Hunt, Republican benefactor, social scion, and an infamously vocal detester of politicians, physicians, lawyers, easterners, blacks, and Jews. Farbman, remembering how many noxious criteria he satisfied, identified himself merely as Ann Marie's husband.

"If those damned idiots hadn't locked up Shadow and Blitzer, you'd be lying there with your throat ripped out. I thought you were another one of those damn doctors who keep breezing by to bother me, then leave all the work to the nurses. Help me up, I want to watch the polo."

Lifting the old lady by an arm and elbow, Farbman was surprised by her frailty, the same surprise he'd felt holding a bird or picking up a long-haired cat. They had barely made it to the doorway when a handsome, earnest-looking young woman wearing pinned-back hair and a white uniform appeared. She took over from Farbman, and the old lady admonished him to pay for his own long-distance calls and not to think she didn't check her bills.

Pittipaldi denied she ever intended to make good on any of her threats. She was just trying to teach Farbman a lesson. She'd gotten somewhat carried away in her efforts to be convincing, she realized. She'd had some family stress. Her husband's business had been dead for more than a year, and his inability to earn a living seemed to have affected his feelings about himself. He'd finally taken a job that kept him on the road sometimes four or five days a week, often for weeks on end, and with all the stress things, frankly, hadn't been so great when he was home either. Well, this was really none of Farbman's business, but she felt she owed him some explanation. How about they call the slate clean, have a drink sometime, no hard feelings. She'd buy.

"Sure, Grace, only I'll buy," said Farbman.

They had rustled up an old pair of Cousin Dewey's boots which fit and a pair of Uncle Dewey's polo pants which didn't. Farbman studied himself in the mirror as Ann Marie and Luke opened the door to collect him.

"How's our number one?" asked Luke, flask in his right hand, mallets and whips in his left.

"Feeling like a number one fool," Farbman replied, declining a proffered drink.

"He doesn't drink, Luke," said Ann Marie, "I keep telling you that."

"Right. I keep forgetting. Well, that's great, you can be our designated rider." Luke laughed and hit Farbman in the shoulder.

Farbman looked down. "These pants are so tight everyone's going to know I'm Jewish even before I get on a horse."

Luke measured Farbman for a mallet and showed him how to grip it. Farbman declined a whip, asserting that he would not think of coercing the horse into any speed faster than he cared to go naturally.

They walked down to the field where the horses were tacked up and waiting, tied to the stock trailer. Jason and Jennifer and a couple of other kids were running from horse to horse, petting them. They stopped to exclaim at their oddly costumed parents. Farbman ordered them to the far side of the playing field. He saw several things he did not like. Foremost was the absence of anything to hold on to. The saddle not only was missing the horn, but the pommel was barely there at all. Even the horse's mane had been roached to a crewcut. There were four instead of two reins which he was somehow expected to control with his left hand only, since his right was busy with the mallet. Farbman congratulated himself on having had the presence of mind to refuse the whip, which he figured he would have had to carry between his teeth. That is, until he put on the helmet and discovered that the face mask not only blocked his mouth but restricted his vision.

"The face mask," said Luke, "is a nuisance. Interferes with your ability to follow the action. None of the top players use them. On the other hand they also spend a lot of money on reconstructive surgery." Luke made a huge barking sound which Farbman deduced from the hit on his back was intended as a laugh.

Luke gave Farbman a leg up, boosting him into the saddle, which Farbman found was just as flat and hard and uncomfortable as it looked. Luke showed Farbman how to place his feet home in the stirrups instead of leaving them under the balls of his feet as Farbman had been taught. Then Luke added that it was really Farbman's choice: While it was easier to maneuver in the saddle with his feet all the way in the stirrup, if he fell off, the risk of getting a foot caught and being dragged was considerably higher. Farbman, sweat dripping in unreachable places under his helmet, elected unhesitatingly to sacrifice maneuverability.

Next, Luke instructed Farbman to hold the mallet either straight up or resting on his shoulder but not pointed out like a spear. He placed the reins in the fingers of Farbman's left hand, and stepped back a few steps. Farbman's stomach registered panic as he realized he was adrift and on his own.

"Follow us," said Luke, hopping effortlessly off his good leg onto his horse, organizing his gear as he trotted off, Ann Marie close behind. They both posted smoothly to the horses' movement, their rhythm so natural Farbman immediately recognized it as being as genetic as freckles. He gave the gentlest squeeze he could with his legs, and his horse moved right out behind the others. Farbman was bouncing hard in the saddle, feeling foolish and very insecure. His hands were both so greased with sweat that the reins slid between his fingers and out of his control.

Traversing the field with his head and arms jerking spastically as if pulled by marionette strings, Farbman wondered whether this really was the image he wanted the children to have of their father. The last time Farbman had been on a horse was a trail ride at a Catskill dude ranch. A couple of hours of walking through the woods and one breathless stretch when they let the horses run. So long ago Jennifer wasn't even born.

One of Farbman's eyes closed involuntarily from the stinging sweat that ran into it. His shirt was soaked through. If only he could get out of this bone-jarring, saddle-banging counterpoint. To do that he would either have to slow to a walk or speed up to a canter. While a canter made sense since he needed to catch up to the others, he couldn't bring himself to actually urge the horse on. Instead Farbman said "whoa" and pulled way back on the now slack reins, which brought him to a full stop. Which wasn't so bad. Farbman took a breath—for the first time, he realized, since he'd mounted the horse. Convinced that all of the spectators standing by the sidelines were focused on him, he made exaggerated gestures of adjusting equipment, resetting his helmet, bending over as if checking the saddle girth. He thought of his parents—if Buddy and Bea could see him on a polo pony.

Farbman looked around for his wife and brother-in-law and saw that they had reached a practice field and were cantering around hitting balls back and forth to each other. He could see Jason and Jennifer standing by the sidelines watching their mother with some folks he couldn't make out. He took a deep breath and got his horse moving in a walk. He decided to remain at a walk until he got on to the field with Ann Marie and Luke, then trot up and make a big show of hitting a ball. When he considered himself in range of a ball, Farbman raised his mallet in what he figured was a reasonable approximation of what he saw Luke doing and gave his horse a little jab with his heels. The horse leapt into a canter, straight for the ball. "Okay," yelled Farbman, and swung with all his might at the white spot in the grass. The mallet and Farbman went flying simultaneously. He hit the ground hard and everything went dark.

When he came to, he saw that a crowd had gathered about twenty feet away. Jason ran over as Farbman was getting to his knees, yelling, "You hit Mommy with your stick, and she's hurt."

Although Ann Marie protested it wasn't worth the bother, at Farbman's insistence she and he were driven by her brother Matthew and cousin Dewey to be checked out at Our Healing Lady, where Dewey was on the board and his company had just donated a new cardiac care unit. Ann Marie had suffered only some abrasions, and a strained neck, and a slipped IUD. But the emergency room resident was deferential when the Kipreyer men introduced themselves and their cousin and, after establishing that his uncle used to be the Whipper-in at their hunt club, made a great show of thoroughness, not only taking x-rays and fitting Ann Marie for a collar but pulling out the coil and referring her to a local gynecologist.

Ann Marie chucked the referral card, but that night at dinner Farbman and her family finally wore her down and she agreed to make an appointment with her mother's doctor. They were dining at a local highway restaurant whose main draws appeared, in order, to be portion size followed by decor, a blend of pseudo-Norman and Tudor. There were plasticine stones and styrofoam beams, red bunting on the walls on which were mounted reproduction battleaxes, a bank of electronic video games, and a wide-screen TV in the bar where you waited until your party was called over the loudspeaker. Farbman gathered that the Jamisons were frequenters of the place from the effusive greeting the proprietor gave them before they were led to their seats: "Haven't seen you folks in a while," he grinned. "Missed your money—har, har. Can I bring you something from the bar?"

Yeah, a video game for the kids and that tall blond barmaid with the lazy eye for me, thought Farbman, as the Jamison elders laughed and specified their sours, and the youngers, their brands of wine and beer, moving into their third rounds, provided you didn't count any of the stuff drunk at the house that afternoon. Of course, with Ann Marie's mother, you couldn't count. She always held a paper napkin up around the sides of her glass so you couldn't see how much she had in it, and her husband and the other considerate pourers around her never got her "another", but only "freshened."

An effeminate young man, with an inflamed pimple in the exact center of his forehead that he'd obviously been worrying, introduced himself as Ronnie and recommended the "Monte Carlo Special" or their "French Dip." The former he said, consisted of ham and swiss cheese on white bread, battered and rolled in potato chip crumbs, then deep-fried and served in a puddle of raspberry sauce for dipping. Farbman searched the cyclops's face in vain for signs that it was a put-on. When Ronnie singled Farbman out to explain that the latter was shaved roast beef on a hamburger deli roll with "a pot of old Jews for dunking," he couldn't restrain himself from asking for clarification. Ronnie repeated himself and touched the eraser end of his pencil to the italicized "pot of au jus" on Farbman's menu.

Farbman asked if he could just have a plate of vegetables. Ronnie said it wasn't on the menu. Farbman explained that vegetables were there as side dishes and that he was merely proposing consolidation. Ronnie would see what he could do. A Kipreyer wife politely inquired if this was about nutrition or was perhaps a religious thing. Farbman said he thought it was a matter of aesthetics. Flustered, she changed the subject to ask Farbman about New York City. She had been so alarmed by the homeless a few months back when she flew her children in to see 'Cats' that she hesitated now to return. Didn't he feel that they ought to be taken care of? Most definitely, Farbman assured her, but it didn't seem to be a priority of the party in power.

"But taking care of the hungry and homeless is surely not a matter of politics," she replied. "It's just the—uh, Judeo-Christian thing to do."

Her husband coughed loudly and jumped in with a joke. Had Farbman heard the one about the two lawyers standing on a corner when a hot woman walks by and one says, "Boy, I'd like to screw her and the other says out of what?" And Farbman, who had heard it, only with Jews instead of lawyers, smiled and said yes, but a slightly different version.

The next day, at the reunion, each of the two hundred odd Jamison family members received a mug and T-shirt on which the family motto, Vincere aut mori, was emblazoned under an escutcheon of medieval weaponry held in the claws of a snarling lion. "Crush 'em or die," translated Matthew. "But you probably guessed that, married to Ann Marie."

"She doesn't give in easily," Farbman agreed. Luke laughed. "It's the black Irish streak in her, the 'who cares if I'm wrong, fuck you.'"

Jason and Jennifer wanted to go swimming immediately, but Luke persuaded them to come along with their parents for a quick sightsee down the riverbank. There they all stared at a section of Kentucky unchanged since Daniel Boone's day. Just up the hill from where they stood was a flagpole marking the heights to which the river had flooded since the mid-nineteenth century. The base of the pole marked the fifty-foot flood level. The top was dated 1937. Farbman noted the sycamores towering overhead, their Banyan-like roots contorted around the base of the pole. From the trees' heights he figured they were old enough to have been submerged under the high water. How long, Farbman wondered, could they have survived it?

Eisenhower might still be president, Farbman thought as he stood before a sign declaiming "The World's Largest Indoor Re-circulating Swimming Pool." For the first time in his memory he felt relaxed in a

crowd. There were no discernible threats in the comfortable homogeneity of the family, or in the faces of the other visitors to the park—
the round, jowled German and Irish corn-feds surrounding Farbman and
his splashing nuclear family. The Republican certainties he could read in
those faces reassured him. They declared that this was the place, the
time, the way to live. The buildup of atomic arms, the extinction of fifteen thousand species a year, the loss of the rain forest, the destruction
of the ozone, the rising number of homeless and disenfranchised, the
toxification of the water and food supplies—the news had not yet
reached these people.

On the other hand there were no sprouts at the salad bar in the local
Schraft's knock-off where they'd stopped for lunch. Not even the glow-
ing sulfite-sprayed greens of a fast-food restaurant. Instead there were
pickled beets from a can and crumbled bacon, white pork—with "biscuit
dipping" gravy—and mayonnaise-buried potatoes and macaroni.
Everyone smoked. Everyone drank.

Farbman, who had made his decision for health a decade and a half
earlier, eschewing alcohol and now, despite a nagging sense of
hypocrisy at the money he earned from Bigonocco, meat, as well as the
artificial, sugared, caffeinated, and carbonated, was frankly appalled,
although he remained uncharacteristically silent. He communicated his
distress only to Ann Marie who'd been trained to hear the unspoken.
With that peculiar New York provincialism that believes the Hudson
marks the world's edge and that the rest of the universe shares its values,
Farbman was as unmoored as a science fiction time traveller.

In addition to the endless handshaking, countless lawyer jokes, and
continuous retelling of the polo story, Farbman endured potato sack
races, horseshoe pitching, and a dance where he watched Ann Marie do
the Swim and the Twist in her huge collar, to disco'd hits from the fifties.

Farbman considered how it was the essence of the Jewish experience
to be an outsider, that the Jewish face had historically been pressed
against the window of some gentile society. Of course, Farbman was
also an outsider to the Jewish experience; if exclusion was the test, he
was the Jews' Jew. He was estranged from his own time, from the land,
from physical labor and, as Harold regularly pointed out to him in the

steam, from his family, from love, sex, and meaningful work.

That night lying on his side in Ann Marie's childhood bedroom, Farbman observed his naked wife pad across the floor. He wondered at his indifference. If those curves belonged to a stranger, he'd be all over her. Then, recognizing that she was a stranger to him, he smiled at the irony.

She caught him looking at her, and he gestured to her and slid over to make room. She lay on her back, chin up, eyes fixed on the ceiling, arms to her sides. As Farbman bestowed a soft kiss on her cheek, she went rigid. Her jaws clenched. The tendons in her neck stood out. Farbman saw tension in the muscles of her legs, in the flex of her toes. He caressed her, massaged her shoulders. Her arms. Her feet. When he thought she'd begun to relax, he pressed gently between her tightly joined knees. In a sudden, mechanical action she jerked the near leg closer to him, communicating by the gesture that he had produced no more than compliance. Farbman, instantly limp and drained of desire, attempted to will himself to passion, reminding himself of his love, drawing upon memories of excited forbidden gropings in this very room years before. He stroked the inside of her thigh toward her groin in a way that had always made her mouth fall open and her breath quicken, and he saw her grimace with each pass of his hand.

"What is it?" he asked.

"Don't be angry. I just feel bad. I'm trying. Don't be angry," she repeated. Farbman had failed before, but he could not recall ever having experienced such a feeling of helplessness. He threw the covers off and after tossing a dozen stuffed animals on the floor slid into the other bed. For hours he lay there unable to sleep. How did he get into this mess, and how, dear God, would he get out?

The following morning, setting forth with his family, Luke leading them through the backyard, Farbman's spirits rose unaccountably. The sky was blue and greying into the white of a cold sun. Farbman swallowed deep draughts of clean air. He could see into the stratosphere where the only clouds were contrails with gauzy edges. The neighbor's field they marched across was ploughed and hardened into irregular ruts, covered with corn stubble that poked Farbman's rubber soles.

Farbman was thrilled to be outside. A young Labrador appeared and bounded over to them for pats, then ran away to chase a stick, then back again.

Farbman saw himself walking on the earth, located by latitude and longitude, he and his family, a fortunate distance from typhoons and slaughtering armies. They were utilizing their allotted continuum of time. Navigating around the cow pies, they crossed pasture to woods where there was a dirt road that led them through other pastures and meadows and finally back into woods again. Jason and Jennifer stuffed their pockets with fallen buckeyes and hazelnuts. The brothers laughingly recounted recent unsuccessful efforts by a developer to turn the farms and woods into a subdivision.

"But it'll go sooner or later," said Farbman. "You can see the city pushing out. The crime and garbage, decay and taxes are fueling the flight. The large estates providing all this green-space are doomed by the cost of labor—and death taxes."

"Who invited him?" Matthew shouted over his shoulder, and everyone laughed.

"Yeah, lighten up Farbman," Ann Marie urged.

"Why do they call it Indian Hollow?" asked Jason.

"Because Indians lived here," answered Luke. "They made pots from the clay. Left arrowheads all around."

"Are there Indians here now?" asked Jennifer.

"No, stupid," answered Jason, "they're extinct, right, Dad?"

"Don't call your sister 'stupid,' Jason," Farbman admonished. "I wonder where he gets that from," Ann Marie stage-whispered.

Farbman asked what that was supposed to mean. When had she ever heard him address anyone as stupid?

"You should hear yourself sometime, listen to your tone. Just because you don't use the word, doesn't change the way people feel."

"Could we do this another time?" Farbman asked, concentrating on his balance as he followed his in-laws sliding down a mud bank of blue clay into the hollow.

"Feel this," Luke demanded, and Farbman and both children complied, holding out their hands for the clumps Luke pressed on them.

"You could take it home and throw a pot right now."

"Can we, Daddy?" asked Jennifer.

"I want to find an arrowhead," said Jason.

"Let's walk upstream," said Luke, and he led the way up the stream-bed, swinging his stiff leg as he stepped from boulder to boulder. The children followed their uncle, Jason pausing periodically to look under a rock, then raise it overhead and throw it at the nearest pool of water, ignoring his father's cautionary words.

Jason complained he didn't see any arrowheads, and Luke said it was just a matter of looking long enough. God knew they took plenty out as kids.

"Perhaps that's why there's none now," Farbman muttered.

Luke continued without a beat. "Perfect ones with the notch and all, carved maybe a million years ago. Just think of it."

Farbman did and said it was highly unlikely considering that they were a long way from the Olduvai Gorge and that the first flinted tools only appeared in the most recent ice age about fifty thousand years ago.

"Give us a break," said Ann Marie.

They climbed in silence. Jason made another overhead toss as Farbman walked by and soaked his shoe. Farbman shouted at the boy— Hadn't he just warned him to watch what he was doing?—and Ann Marie told Farbman to leave him alone, he was just playing.

Luke approached carrying a flat rock and asked Farbman what he thought about it. "What is it?" asked Jason. "Let me see," said Jennifer, squeezing past her brother and pulling Luke's arm down to her eye level. "Fossils," said Luke. "Ferns. We're talking millions of years here."

"Can I have it?" asked Jason.

"I want it," said Jennifer, starting to cry. "Jason gets everything."

"No one is getting it," said Farbman. "It's being left right here where we found it. Where it belongs."

Heading home, approaching a thick stand of oak, Farbman was astonished to hear city sounds, a vibrating metallic cacophony that turned out to be a flock of blackbirds—crows or ravens maybe—hundreds on the ground and in the trees.

"Omen," said Luke.

"So what are they saying?" Farbman challenged.

"Dunno," said Luke, "but they sound serious. Don't they sound serious?"

That night, Farbman, the designated driver, drove his wife and her brothers and several friends in a rented van from one restaurant lounge and neighborhood pub to another. The brothers drank tequila, lime and salt with beer chasers, then competed in a game of ordering elaborately concocted drinks the bartenders had never heard of, each brother detailing precisely their construction while his siblings hooted and belittled his efforts.

They staggered out of the bars carrying glasses and bottles; they sang and cried as they leaned on each other's shoulders; and they peed on tires in the parking lot. Everyone shouted directions at Farbman, except for two of the brothers who argued that he should know where the hell he was going by now.

When they had gotten the last drink at the last open bar, they demanded Farbman take them for "Five Ways"—hot dogs layered with chili, spaghetti, onions, cheese, and beans—and then that he stop to allow Matthew and Mark (and, a few miles later, a friend of Mark's) to puke them up by the side of the road.

At home everyone piled out before Farbman parked. The recovered, still exuberant brothers stood in the headlights and made gestures approximating a sequencing gorilla about to attack. One after another they charged and rocked the van and pounded on the windshield with their fists so that Farbman, wearing a forced smile, felt caught like The Ugly American in a Third World mob.

Despite their contorted faces and screaming, leaping attacks, they were obviously having fun. Farbman nonetheless felt a growing alarm as their play seemed to possess them. The windshield cracked and, struck immediately again, crazed into a kaleidoscopic web through which Farbman could not distinguish among them.

Who do they think I am? Farbman wondered, struggling to release his seat belt and open the door as they began to push the van backward toward a ditch at the edge of the driveway. What are they so mad about? He leaped free just as the van crashed through a hedge and rolled down the slope, stopping with its right front tire angled in the air.

Leaving his in-laws hand-slapping and cheering with his wife, Farbman climbed the back stairs and went to bed.

The next day it was as though nothing had happened. Farbman awoke early in the quiet house, came down in his sweat clothes and sneakers for a jog, and found Ann Marie's father in his usual spot, seated at the dining room table in his grass-green golf pants reading the papers. Twenty years retired from the family toilet seat business ("Have a seat, please," a brother would say, then all the brothers would shout, "Your shit is our bread and butter."), he read all parts of all the papers— the New York Times and the Journal and the morning and evening editions of the local bugles—laying them out flat like a book, making his way down each column, turning the pages with the blackened tongue-licked thumb of his left hand. Unseen in a doorway, Farbman studied this ritualistic processing of the world's events into grey matter storage from which, based on Farbman's experience with the only laconic Jamison, the news would never be brought forth. On Sundays he would deposit the advertising supplements and coupons into a basket that held the grocery list. Afterwards, Jamison would scrub the newsprint from his hands, retrieve the list, and report to his wife, who would then tell him what to buy. Unlike Farbman's parents, who provisioned for months as if in anticipation of famine or pogroms or war, the Jamisons believed in marketing for only a day at a time and there was never any food in the house.

Farbman backed away still unseen and hurried out the kitchen door for a short run—more for a hit of outdoors than real exercise. He recalled his courtship visits. Most times Mrs. Jamison cooked on alternate days, and in the summer, when the family demanded a lot of barbecue, about one in three. Mrs. Jamison or one of the boys ran the backyard grill when it was used, but often they just drove to a black takeout place on the wrong side of town for what were called rib sandwiches: racks of pork ribs in a medium sauce laid on two pieces of white bread, wrapped in waxed paper and then in old newspaper. The family picnicked at a plank table in the gnat-filled August air.

The food didn't really matter, Farbman reflected as he reentered the kitchen after his run, squinting through the cigarette smoke at his puffing in-laws who were affably starting the day with a bit of the hair of the dog, it was just an accompaniment to the beer, the cases of Hudipohl or Bud that were used to wash it down each week.

Farbman showered and changed and, because Ann Marie was so resistant, called himself for her test results. As soon as he gave his name, the young woman who answered the phone asked him to hold for the doctor, which gave Farbman a sudden palpitation until he reminded himself that he had slipped into a time warp when doctors still made house calls, still had a bedside manner. He looked forward to hearing some folksy, midwestern, flat-toned reassurance. What he got was a very unreassuring description of the sonogram findings, which, as near as Farbman could comprehend, had revealed a grapefruit wavering around on a twisted stalk—and an immediate referral to a local surgeon. The doctor said he was sorry, and Farbman felt a cold stab of panic in his spine.

He got Harold on the line within seconds. Farbman read his notes with the calmest, most studied casualness he could command, then concluded with "So what do you think?" His friend spoke with a harsh, direct, unsettling sense of urgency. He asked who Ann Marie's gynecologist was, and, when Farbman named the fatherly counselor who had delivered both their kids, Harold just said "No, not for this." He would call Twiford Potter, a buddy from Mass General, who did a fellowship afterward at Memorial and was now at N.Y.U. "Get her home today. I'll call back with a time to bring her to the hospital."

In the kitchen Ann Marie and her family were laughing at someone's joke. No, it turned out they were laughing at half a banana Farbman had left on the counter. Ann Marie explained he did it all the time and it drove her up a wall coming in and finding little banana stubs lying around inside the blackened peels. Her brother Mark said he had a roommate once who would slice off a chunk and leave the rest and he too was Jewish and maybe it was a Jewish thing. Farbman, ordering himself to grin, said it probably had something to do with circumcision, and got Ann Marie out of the room with a request that she help him find something. He told her that he'd gotten the results—that there was some kind of growth—and had told Harold and that, while Harold was very relaxed about it, Farbman insisted that he get someone really good to check her out right away. "Harold said he has someone and would set up an appointment for our return. I told him no, I want it done now, that he should call today and we'd pack and be available tomorrow."

Ann Marie's eyes widened and searched his face for telltale messages. "Hey, Farbman, anything you're not telling me?"

"I love you, and I needed an excuse to cut this visit short."

"That I can believe," she said smiling, and stepped into his huddling arms.

In Farbman's head, colliding thoughts, the din of scrabbling black birds.

II

THE INDIVIDUAL CASE

CRAZY

Since Harold lived only a short walk from the hospital, and there was nothing Farbman could do after he'd given Ann Marie a last kiss outside the O.R., Harold told Farbman to wait at his apartment for the results of the surgery. Waiting with them was Birgitta, Harold's roommate of forty-eight hours. Birgitta, who wore only a pale blue terry cloth robe, had soft brown hair and bare feet and was, if Farbman remembered correctly, the one who liked to be tied. Twiford Potter called about six as Birgitta was transferring takeout Chinese to serving bowls. Harold nibbled on fried noodles while he listened with the mouthpiece of the receiver held near his right eye. When he got off the phone he was smiling. Great news. Ann Marie was in recovery; the tumor was indeed grapefruit-sized but a dermoid, which was benign.

"What's that mean, 'dermoid?'" Farbman asked after expelling an enormous breath, curious now that they had passed safely through the shadows of malignancy and death. Harold reached behind a machine that simulated cross-country skiing for a fat book. He read aloud to Farbman and to Birgitta who gave up trying to serve and nestled on the floor alongside Harold's chair. Her chin rested on the armrest, while

Harold petted her head. The thing removed from Ann Marie had matted hair and perhaps teeth. Sometimes even a rudimentary jaw. Also skin parts, which is why they were called dermoid.

Farbman pictured a carved and painted coconut head while Harold read on. The thing was derived from all three germ layers. Harold explained that germ layers were the primordial strata from which all the special cells of the body originated. Farbman felt relieved that he hadn't done anything to cause this, that something had gone awry in the very making of Ann Marie.

He thanked Harold, called his home where his parents were baby-sitting, and passed along the reassuring news. Then he hurried to the hospital and, when she was finally out of recovery, held Ann Marie's hand while she slept. Tubes ran into her nose from the wall and from IVs into her arm, and from under the sheet into a plastic bag of urine. Ann Marie moaned once and Farbman got the shiver one gets when touching another's wound, that queasy autonomic reaction that overwhelms no matter how innocent or accidental the contact, as reflexive as yanking a finger from a flame. Farbman considered why nature would cause us to feel physically upset when we realize we have accidentally caused another pain. Perhaps it was empathy. He would have to ask Harold, a man not given to the metaphysical. He would surely have a physiological explanation. Before Farbman left he arranged for private duty nurses and ordered flowers.

Over their bedstead and on the surrounding walls were little framed pictures that Ann Marie had drawn over the years. Farbman lay on his back staring at their family's illustrated history, too far away to be able to read the captions. He got up and moved closer. Under the rock arch at Natural Bridge, Virginia. His parents' fortieth anniversary party. Their first Amagansett rental. Five-year-old Jason attempting a two-wheeler. A Jamison reunion. Farbman remembered each event but without the feeling of having been there. Face-to-face with the evidence of his wife's desperate need to prove they had a life, he tried to force out some tears at his reflected face, but none came. Insufficiently ardent; now insufficiently sad.

Farbman slept fitfully and was awake before daylight. For breakfast he gave the kids cereal and lighthearted reassurances that their mother would be back soon. The kids showed him where the small brown bags were stored and he tossed a peanut butter sandwich, an apple and two Oreos in each one.

"Mommy always draws something on our lunch bags," said Jennifer.

"Like what?" asked Farbman.

"Like turtles," said Jennifer.

"You don't have to do anything for me." Jason wanting to let him know that he didn't need babying.

Farbman, figuring he couldn't draw a turtle any worse than any other animal, emptied the bag on the counter and smoothed it with the edge of his hand, then held his hand out as if he were a surgeon. "Crayon," he said. As he started on the turtle's shell he decided it looked like the beginning of a whale. "Can you tell what it is yet?"

Jennifer was on tiptoe peering over his arm. "A whale!" she exclaimed, obviously pleased. Farbman refilled the bag, then put a football on Jason's, telling him that way he'd know it was his.

After dropping the children at school he stopped to look in on Ann Marie. Contorted in pain she had been trying to get her Demerol shot for fifteen minutes. The floor nurses kept saying they'd get there when they could, and the private duty nurse seemed to have disappeared on a break. Farbman, shaken by his wife's pain, swallowed his anger and stood supplicatingly at the nurses' station. "She's got a private duty," said the charge nurse, closing her copy of *Bride's* magazine. She possessed a shining forehead and a scowl that did not leave her face even when she smiled. Farbman explained he didn't know where the private duty nurse was. He was assured she must be around somewhere. He returned to Ann Marie, who had tears running down her cheeks, her muscles contracted against the pain. She asked Farbman if he would try again to get someone but please not to antagonize them.

Farbman returned to the nurses' station and waited there, ignored, while the charge nurse made notes on charts. He said to himself: I see from the slowness of your comprehension that you are the unfortunate offspring of a syphilitic mother. Your resentment at being saddled with this congenital affliction is understandable. And I'm sure you're worried about meeting the payments on your new plastic-covered nuptial furniture. But if you continue to take it out on my wife I will shove that ballpoint pen up your nostril into your small reptilian brain. Aloud, he politely asked to have Twiford Potter paged. When asked why, he explained he could see she was engaged, so he could have the doctor give his wife her shot. The nurse said that wasn't necessary, she recalled his wife, the gallbladder in 4214 who always demands painkillers early, and they were only about ten minutes behind schedule. Farbman said she had the wrong patient, his wife was in 4212. The nurse said fine, go to her room and she'd be along with the shot.

For the next five minutes Farbman stood rooted at the nurses' station, staring, while the nurse finished her paperwork. Then he accompanied her until she administered the injection. After that he went to find the head of private duty nursing, a tough little spinster who introduced herself as Clancy. After Farbman told what happened, working in the fact that his wife was a Jamison, Clancy threw up her hands. What could she tell him? Things were different today. You're not talking any more about dedicated girls trained by nuns but island women with an attitude. Before they wouldn't wash your floor and now they won't wash your back. But Farbman was not to worry: Clancy would personally get someone reliable and caring for Ann Marie.

Farbman made one more stop on his way to work, at an art supply store to get a how-to-draw book that broke down animals into constituent circles, squares, and triangles which Farbman felt confident he could master. He walked into his office, book open, mentally sketching a dog and imagining the pleased faces of his children, and was confronted by a week's worth of mail. On top was a letter from Blocker.

Joy had prioritized the mail for Farbman's review. The now well-established hierarchy placed checks on top in descending magnitude and bills on the bottom just above third-class junk. Personal letters and appreciative, or at least positive, client communications were in the second tier, but desperate, lunatic, and threatening letters were sandwiched under the pleadings and over the invoices. If a Blocker epistle was Farbman's greeting, either Joy was making a point or Farbman's day was running downhill fast. Blocker wrote:

Dear Lawyer Farbman:

I'm very unhappy with the apparent lack of progress in this testimony process. To be held hostage to secure a piece of paper without spirit and moral teeth. Matrimonial vows which cannot be broken and which you must admit do supersede judges' pronouncements, even the 'decree.'

In so saying, I ask most respectfully that you disclose your plans, when you have reviewed the previously sent copies of literature. My wife has brought into the house and exposed to our children. Rabid. Subverting. Feminism. Which suggests blatantly that women should leave the communion of the Roman Church 'for the sake of their own humanity.' Because the church will not 'dialogue' with said feminists. As if sacred principles are as elastic as the arbitrary decisions of political appointees.

Can you imagine the mother of your own children willfully undermining. All you have struggled to imbue. Orthodoxy she says must prove itself. God's spirit she says is manifest in science and liberationist movements. (Next it will be God in abortion!)

And of course but not least that marriages are not indissoluble she says under Sacrament. Annulment she calls "a cruel fiction" and will have none of it.

You must tell the court Mr. Farbman. The plain truth about the evil this woman is doing in what I know to be a fashionable derangement but evil nonetheless, to our children. Meaning the pornographic pictures. Meaning the attack on the church. On our children's religion. This is our chance for custody and don't hold back. I will get the money, somehow, my children's souls are at stake. Please hurry. The slower the courts, the faster the money bleeds. Most respectfully

Farbman didn't remember receiving any literature. He buzzed the file room and asked Angel, the surly, half-stoned clerk, for Blocker's file. Through the intercom Joy said "Turk Horowitz," and Farbman got Turk direct from his hospital bed where he was being treated for snakebite.

It was a particularly toxic variety of copperhead that had been hiding in Mr. Fleischman's garbage can, a reptile not indigenous to the state, let alone to the Queens' block in which Fleischman's valve business was situate. Turk advised Farbman that he had consulted another lawyer-client of his and was suing Farbman.

"Get well soon," said Farbman.

Farbman was thinking about calling Amber Fleischman to see if she could provide some insight when Angel walked in with a slim, red, elastic-banded folder a fraction of the thickness of Blocker's file. Farbman was about to remonstrate with the young man for his carelessness when he noticed that, though the file folder did have Blocker's name and address on the label, the file number indicated that it was a bodily injury case and that Marucci had signed the client up. Farbman called to ask his partner what the story was.

"No big deal. You must have been out when he called. It was just after Christmas. Blocker got frostbite on his penis while doing double shift as a magi in a live nativity scene sponsored by his church."

"Magus," said Farbman.

"Huh?"

"Magi," said Farbman, stalling while he tried to understand why Marucci hadn't told him about the case, "is plural."

"Stay there," said Marucci. "I'll be right in."

Farbman, listening for Marucci's clicking ankle, decided he wouldn't press the issue. "She's okay. It was benign," Farbman informed Marucci as he walked through the door.

Marucci exhaled hard. "Thank you, Jesus." Marucci told Farbman just to look after Ann Marie and the kids and himself and not to worry about the office at all, that he would take care of everything. Farbman was so moved by the gesture he didn't even comment on its obvious futility, as he wouldn't if, say, Jason, overhearing his dad describe his financial crunch, were to offer his piggy bank.

Farbman thanked Marucci and said that, apart from settling the Fudgsicle, what he could do for him was to get on Deborah Must's case and approach it as more products suit than malpractice. The congressional investigation into silicone implants had led Farbman to believe they could be the next Dalkon shield, spawning thousands of suits nationally. If Farbman and Marucci got in there first they could bust into the big time overnight. "I've collected some journal articles associating silicone gel prosthesis with a bunch of collagen and corrective tissue diseases, but it's just a beginning. There are difficult causation issues even assuming we can prove liability for failure to warn, warranty breach—"

"Informed consent, misrepresentation..." recited Marucci.

"Yeah, yeah, yeah. So let's start by finding out who the key doctors are and getting Deborah worked up by them. Of course, knowing Deborah, she's liable to work them up first."

"What's that supposed to mean?" Marucci suddenly defensive. "Never mind. See if the American Trial Lawyers has established a data bank, and register us for exchanges with other implant lawyers."

Marucci saluted and left. Farbman returned to the mail. Among the usual client letters asking when the Kafkaesque dream would end, was another computer-plotted outcome scenario from Mironovic. It was the fourth Farbman could recall from this divorcing engineer. Each act of madness by his wife elicited another settlement proposal from him— always precisely detailed, always fair. And each proposal by him inspired Mrs. Mironovic to more extreme acting out. She had cut his suits to short-sleeve length, set fire to the kitchen for insurance proceeds which she spent on lavish gifts for her boyfriends and, most recently, found his second set of books and turned them over to the IRS. Mironovic asked why Farbman couldn't get a settlement when he was being so reasonable. He enclosed a proposal with comparative income streams and color bar graphs.

Big was on the telephone. He had to see Farbman immediately about new charges he was served with that morning. Supposedly he'd violated a U.S.D.A. ban on the use of plastic netting to shape the meat during the cutting. Farbman said he was confused. Why would Big be using anything to shape meat for cutting and, even if he did, how could plastic hurt meat?

Big sighed loudly. "The problem here is you don't know the operation now, and how can you defend me if you don't know the business?"

Farbman started to interrupt, but Big continued. "No, this is no good. I'm talking cooked meat, smoked meat, for chrissake, and you think I'm talking fresh." Big took a breath to control himself. "Come in here today and let me show you around. It's time you toured the place." Farbman knew he had no choice and said he'd be right there. In the meantime, maybe he could get started if Big could tell him what the problem was with the plastic. Big said it was some crap about chemicals in the netting supposedly reacting with nitrates in the processed meat to form something that caused cancer in mice.

With Reilly still not replaced, Farbman would have to use Marucci's associate, Kleegel, to run the search on the chemicals Big was referring to. Farbman used Kleegel reluctantly, and only after clearing it with Marucci who was accommodating to the point of giving succor, telling Farbman not to worry, he'd get it started immediately.

Farbman found himself getting teary and thought he must be coming apart. Joy came in to say that the secretaries were going to try the curried goat luncheon special at the new Donuts Plus on the corner and should they get some for him. Declining with a polite reminder that goats were animals, Farbman asked Joy to tell the garage to get his car up pronto, he was going to Mr. Bigonocco's plant in the Bronx. Farbman decided to try Amber Fleischman's number before he left but caught her just as she was "flying" to her nail salon. She said she would call back and hung up abruptly.

No sooner had Farbman passed under the face of the smiling calf and through the door of Bigonocco Veal than Big appeared, apologizing for having been so testy earlier. One of Big's best men had only the day before lost his right hand and a big piece of his forearm in the blades of their new hydraulic hock cutter and no one was back to normal yet. Farbman, mentally depositing the check for his piece of the man's injury, commiserated: it's horrible, it shouldn't have happened, and Farbman would have his safety engineer examine the machine and determine where the manufacturer went wrong. He got Marucci on the line right from Big's desk to make the arrangements. Farbman struggled to keep an impassive face as he inwardly exulted at his partner's gleeful praising:

"Oh you done good, Farbman. That's what I call a helping hand."

Marucci said Kleegel had already identified the chemical produced by the reaction of the netting and the nitrates—something called "dibretylnitrosamine"—and was deep into several databases gathering the literature on it.

Big supplied Farbman with an insulated coat like his own for the refrigerated tour, and as they set out Farbman reported on Kleegel's progress. Farbman told Big that when he and his experts were done with their review he wouldn't be surprised to find insufficiencies in the data and limitations in the sampling sufficient to establish the prematurity of regulatory action. Big smiled. He told Farbman he had every confidence in him.

Bigonocco was proud of his automated plant, particularly the dressing operation. He showed Farbman how the calf was skinned right on the floor. The calf's foreshanks were anchored with chains, while its hind legs were held on the overhead rail. A machine pulled it up as it reeled the skin in on a roller.

Big explained the slaughtering was all done kosher. The animals were not instantaneously killed but only knocked out and suspended on big grappling hooks while their throats were slit and they bled out. This was not because Bigonocco Veal was under rabbinic supervision but because years ago the Jewish lobby had gotten a law through requiring everyone to do kosher killing. And he heard the same was true in Jersey and other states, too.

"The animals walk right into this place, and when they exit they are vacuum-packed as boneless portions, diced stew, steaks, and roasts. Ready for retail sale." Big held up a handful of shrink-wrapped cellophane packages for Farbman's inspection. Then he called to one of the men to carry a couple of crates of assorted choice cuts flash-frozen for freezer storage out to Farbman's car. Farbman, queasy from breathing the chilled air heavy with the smell of the fresh-cut meat that was everywhere he looked, started to say something but Big told him not to be silly.

As the two men watched Farbman's trunk being loaded, Big told Farbman that he was organizing a committee with other veal producers to counteract the animal rights and environmental lobbyists, and he was going to try to get Farbman appointed counsel to the committee. Those ads, said Big, are so misleading. Like the one that shows a calf in the stall and says "Why can't he walk?—cause he only has two feet" makes it sound like we cut his feet off two at a time when he's alive. Not that he's just restricted to twenty-two inches in a crate. "You know what I mean?"

Big held the car door for Farbman and then closed it as Farbman got behind the wheel. Farbman lowered the window and Big leaned in to say he'd almost forgotten and handed him a check to get started on the chemical problem. He said to remind him next time they spoke about a matter with a pneumatic sausage stuffer and another problem with a violation notice that he'd thought he could resolve himself but it wasn't looking that way after all. He said he appreciated Farbman coming out, that he'd call him next time he went to the veal farm so Farbman could see that as well.

Although he should have been elated at picking up cash and the hand-off, Farbman, for no reason he could point to, felt bad working his way back through the South Bronx traffic. The roller skinning of the calves and the sectioned flesh were mixing up in his head with images of Ann Marie's surgery, and Farbman knew not only that he'd never eat meat again, he'd never feed meat to his family. The steaming boxes of veal in his trunk were like pieces of a corpse he was lugging around. He decided he had to dispose of it, and as he crossed into Manhattan he pulled into the parking lot of a Burger King to locate a dumpster. Then, realizing how close he was to Big's plant, thought better of it and steered back onto Lexington Avenue. Minutes later, observing homeless people in line for lunch at a soup kitchen, Farbman resolved to give the meat away. He remembered a church with a shelter on the West Side and took his first crosstown right.

Arms stretched around two of the cartons, his suit bunched up with his tie over the top one, Farbman threaded his way through the waiting crowd, trying to breathe in his mouth and out his nose, aiming for a stone gothic archway on which was a white metal sign with stenciled black letters: "Men's Shelter." The entrance was half-barred with one of its two wrought-iron gates. Farbman squeezed by the people blocking the open side. He negotiated his way down the steep stone stairs into a gloomy passage lighted with a single bare bulb under a protective grid. Leaning against the walls on either side were old mattresses, springs, and collapsed cardboard boxes. Farbman hadn't bothered to read the name of the church, and he couldn't remember whether Gothic architecture signified only Roman Catholic or whether it might not be Episcopal or some other Protestantism as well. This failure made him feel like the immigrant Jew in his father's joke who determines to make himself over so he can gain membership at the New York Athletic Club. Having changed his name to Hunt Palmer, moved to Darien, put his son in Princeton, and traded in his new Caddy for a used Ford, he reapplies. Then when asked his religion, he answers: "Vud else? A goy." Could any gentile tell where he was at a glance?

Farbman asked if someone could direct him to the kitchen. Going where the chapped, wrinkled fingers pointed, Farbman staggered across the worn linoleum, the boxes pulling on his shoulders and cutting both wrists. He pushed open the swinging door with his back to enter the warm, steamy room.

A scrawny old man was cleaning vegetables in a sink to Farbman's right; a young woman in jeans and a T-shirt was scraping stuff from a bowl into a cauldron on the stove. "I've got some meat here, to drop off." Farbman directed his words toward the stove. The woman turned, looked at him, and frowned. "What is this?" she said in a tone that implied he was obviously working some con and she had no time for it.

Farbman protested, eyes moving about now addressing everyone in the room. "It's just some meat—top grade, fresh frozen." He smiled. "Very heavy meat, that I'd like to donate." He explained that he had more in the car outside, and when no one responded, he said I've got to put these down, and did, making a show of arching his shoulders and rubbing his wrists.

"Who told you I worked here?"

"What?" Farbman returned the woman's gaze and suddenly, jogged by the husky voice, he matched her full lips and dark eyes to those of his memory, and gulped. "Oh, my God, Leah. I *didn't* know you worked here."

"Oh, you're telling me this is pure chance ..."

"I'd prefer to think of it as kismeat." Farbman saw her begin to smile. Not wanting to.

Farbman went to retrieve the remaining cartons and when he returned Leah and another woman were clearing space in a large stainless steel freezer.

Farbman said, "Look, my wife's in the hospital. I'm caretaking my kids and trying to run a law practice, so I'm somewhat pressed, but I'll call you as soon as I can." And afraid she would say don't bother, he made a hurried exit.

Farbman checked in with Joy and learned that Amber Fleischman had called back from her car only moments after he'd left, that Pittipaldi had proposed meeting for a drink as they'd discussed, and that Marucci had said to tell Farbman he didn't need to come in, he would cover Farbman's motions and was finishing an appellate brief Farbman had started.

As he entered the hospital lobby, Farbman thought, I do, I have a brother. When he reached Ann Marie's room, he kissed his wife on the forehead, showed her the latest cards from Jason and Jennifer, and taped the cards to the wall with a photo he brought of the Amagansett rental. From a shopping bag he pulled a two-pound tin of Godiva chocolates that he explained was a bribe for the floor nurses. Ann Marie nodded, and he took the tin out to the nurses' station, where he was enthusiastically thanked and told that his wife's private duty had just left for her break. Then he went to a phone and dialed his home.

Farbman's mother said the children were fine, but his father and she hoped Farbman would be coming soon, reminding him they had dinner plans. Also, that Farbman had to make other arrangements for tomorrow, they had an affair. Did Farbman remember the Klopnicks, a furrier they'd met on their China trip two years ago? Anyway, it was a surprise fortieth anniversary party, and his mother had to be at the hairdresser. Farbman said, "No problem, I'll get the kids after school." He hung up and returned to Ann Marie's bedside.

Ann Marie reminded him of Jennifer's friend's birthday on Saturday, and instructed him in buying the present. "Forget the big store on Sunrise Highway. Ask for Mrs. Greenwald at the small store on Park—

it's called Kid Kraft with a 'K'—and ask her to suggest something educational for around fifteen dollars."

Farbman asked Ann Marie how she was and what the doctors had to say, and she said everything was fine and asked him about the children. He was telling her how Jason was now copying the other boys and diving for every ball in soccer, and how Jennifer, on the other hand, invariably ended up involved in a conversation with whomever was nearest her—teammate or opponent—while the play went around them, when he noticed she had drifted off to sleep. Farbman stroked her head for a moment, then picked up his briefcase and left.

One morning, about a week later, just after Amber Fleischman had hung up on Farbman and said she'd call him right back, Harold telephoned and said he wanted to meet Farbman at Twiford Potter's office in an hour for a status report. This time, within moments, Amber did call. From her car, said Joy. The line at home was not "secure." Amber had engaged a surveillance expert who said it was definitely tapped. Since she was certain her husband was not on to her, it had to have been the work of a third party.

"You mean you haven't told him about your plan to divorce yet?"

"Absolutely not. I'm waiting until you get all the financial stuff together. He has no idea what's going on." She'd been doing it in the afternoon as Farbman had advised and, while her paramour was getting serious and kept pushing her to make a break, she knew she couldn't do anything until Farbman had the figures."Well," said Farbman, "we've run into a little snag in the collecting process." He told her about Turk Horowitz' mishap with the snake and asked if she had any thoughts. Amber said not really. But her husband was "connected" with "Big" Bigonocco. She'd once heard her husband threaten someone they'd end up in a Bigonocco sausage if they crossed him, but she didn't think it had anything to do with her getting divorced.

Maybe, Farbman suggested, he could make an indirect inquiry through Bigonocco, whom Farbman knew pretty well.

"Absolutely not. Right now Fleischman has no idea what's happening. I've got him in couples therapy, and we're spending hours on

who did what and who meant what—you know, communication techniques and homework assignments and the rest of that shit."

"Like what?" Farbman asked.

"At the moment we're working on the relationship between our
autonomous and our symbiotic behaviors. Can you believe it? Just don't
rock the boat."

Farbman found Harold already waiting in Twiford Potter's reception
room when Farbman got there. They were ushered right in. Twiford
Potter was blunt. The pathology was back. It appeared they'd been mistaken. It wasn't dermoid, it was malignant. Twif was so stunned he had
gone to the lab and demanded to examine the slides himself. He still
had questions. He wanted them looked at by some famous hotshot.
Meanwhile Farbman should know there were treatments. Additional
surgery that he would schedule within the next week or so, then possibly some chemo or radiation. He was checking around to see the latest
protocols at Memorial Sloan-Kettering, at M.D. Anderson, at Mayo;
compare efficacy. Twif said he had trained with Dr. Wesson, co-chair
with Smith (funny, huh—Smith and Wesson?) at Memorial and he'd call
him that day. Would Farbman like him to tell Ann Marie? No, Farbman
would tell her himself.

Farbman pushed through the revolving door and stopped on the
sidewalk. Outside the world made no sense. The sun was shining as
before. Cars drove by as before. But his wife had cancer. The cars, the
sun, the medical building, the trees were spinning around him. He was
supposed to walk over and tell Ann Marie that she had cancer. Where
was he? Harold appeared then. And Marucci. Where did Marucci come
from? His partner had an expression of such sadness and worry on his
face it frightened Farbman. Harold must have called him. Did Harold
think Farbman was going to fall apart? Marucci put his hand on
Farbman's shoulder. Harold, too, wore concern. Farbman feeling their
love and support wanted to reassure his friends, but he was preoccupied
figuring how exactly he was supposed to tell Ann Marie. Farbman's head
felt like it was floating away. He kept noticing that it was a nice day.
Then he realized he was crazy. It was not a nice day. His wife had cancer

today and he was on his way to tell her. Maybe he shouldn't? Would she ever forgive him if he told her? Would she ever forgive him if he withheld it? Where had their lives gone? Where had this world been hidden?

Farbman stood at the end of Ann Marie's bed. She smiled at him. She was glad to see him. He hadn't seen that smile in years. He started to speak, but couldn't because he kept choking on a sob. He told himself to get his shit together. He saw Ann Marie's eyes searching his face as he tried to regain control. "What is it?" she asked. "The pathology?" She held her arms out to Farbman. His eyes were drawn to the still-connected IV line. "It'll be all right," she murmured as she held him. After a moment he sat back and sniffled, embarrassed.

She said, "I don't want anyone to know. Okay? Promise."

"Promise."

Farbman and the kids had settled into a routine. He took care of their mornings and their bedtimes—baths, homework, and stories—and after school activities and dinner on the two or three days he couldn't get coverage. The mothers of his children's friends helped with carpooling when he had to be in court and his parents couldn't do it. Farbman reciprocated on weekends.

On this day Farbman had taken the children to school, then gone to the hospital to keep Ann Marie company before her second surgery. Now Farbman sat in the lobby outside the admitting office, with MasterCard and VISA welcoming signs plastered to its window. Ann Marie had been pushed off to surgery on the gurney an hour earlier and six hours after the operation was scheduled, shaking with drug-induced chill under the thin sheet, Farbman holding her hand as she wheeled through the corridors, down the elevator, and right up to the door of the surgical suite where the orderly paused to tell him "You can't go here," and Farbman reluctantly released her. As he kissed her she asked, "Will you call my parents?"

Farbman nodded, "Right away."

He watched the orderly shove her through the swinging doors, then went to the nearest phone booth and looked the Jamison's number up in his pocket directory. He paused to consider how he would inform these people of their daughter's illness—they who had virtually disowned her for marrying a Jew, who had ignored the births of their first grandchildren, who had yet to come to New York for a visit. Some harsh, recriminating tone was definitely in order here. But when he heard his mother-in-law pick up, he was as gently factual as he could be. "That growth," he said, "that they took out turned out to have some malignant cells, so her doctor—Twiford Potter, if you should want to talk to him—decided to take some more stuff out. She's in the O.R. now."

"Thank you, dear. It was considerate of you to call. I'll tell her father. Would you keep us posted?"

"Of course."

"Thank you again."

An old woman to Farbman's right kept telling everyone nearby she couldn't understand what was taking so long with her husband. Farbman wondered if he and Ann Marie would ever reach the pure mutuality of such elderly couples—what the Fleischmans' therapist called marital symbiosis. He took stock, saw his life for what it was: right now they were as unhealthy as a couple as she was as an individual. But sick relationships as well as physical disease could be environmentally induced; and just as certainly there were curative climates. Farbman thought about whole sections of the country that had chosen, like his in-laws, to live in the 1950s. He bet he could find spots in the nineteenth century. He thought, if they could only get out of New York. Why did they have to live at the cutting edge of the informational universe? In the center of a gigantic imaginary parabola collecting indiscriminately every random, senseless advertiser's pitch, every act of human depravity and viciousness, every act of political venality, every decadent fifteen-second fashion, along with more history, art, and culture than was absorbable in fifty lifetimes. He needed to locate his own patch of time: on a farm someplace where he could do simple physical labor close to nature and screen out Dan Quayle, and Jerry Falwell, Madonna, and just about everything on broadcast TV and in the newspaper. This, he decided, would be the salvation of his marriage.

His thoughts were interrupted by a walkie-talkie blasting from the hip of a nearby security guard. The old woman to his right asked

Farbman if he thought she ought to ask the people at the desk again about her husband since forty minutes had gone by since she'd last asked. Farbman said yes, but she said she'd wait a little longer. Everywhere workers pushed things on wheels: gurneys, wash buckets, crash carts, laundry baskets. Hand-trucks loaded with food, books, vials of blood, stacked fluorescent light bulbs, tanks of oxygen, and rolled-up carpets. The workers wore color-coded coats. These were people who knew what they were supposed to do each day and how much they would get paid for doing it. They knew what drawing blood, serving food, processing forms, or irradiating someone was worth to society and how to do it. Whether you wore the khaki and navy of the maintenance man at the bottom of the heap, the surgical greens at the top, or the pale blue, maroon, or white lab coats in between, you knew who you were, where you stood. What your budget was.

A pudgy, yellow-haired doctor appeared and sat down on the coffee table before the nervous old woman next to Farbman. "It's taking so long because we're having a little problem with the artery," he told her. "We're okay to here—" he indicated with the edge of his hand a point about three inches above his right knee—"but the leg's white below there. We can only do this part, and we're waiting for another doctor who will do the legs." When the doctor left, another woman reassured the old lady. What they do, she said, is feel for a pulse down there and then they put a pump in. They'd done it to her husband eleven years ago. He had stroked and then died. She told the old lady that she was lucky she was getting a specialist, that her husband had had to take a floor doctor.

Farbman was thinking how the clock had hardly moved since he'd last looked at it when Harold appeared and told him Ann Marie had come through fine, that Farbman couldn't see her, and that the best thing he could do for the next two hours was to go with Harold for a workout and a talk in the steam.

Without actually telling Harold that he planned to move to a farm, Farbman did say that, crazy as it seemed, inside him was a farmer. That he had always felt a deep connection with the land and had resonated with the values of such labor although neither he nor anyone in his

family had ever to his knowledge done anything even related to farming unless you counted a cousin who traded commodity futures in
Chicago. He mentioned his junior high school preference test which he
thought he had faked when, as a lark, he made it come out forestry but
through which his true soul had perhaps, unwittingly, been manifest.

Harold looked up from his forearms: he was pumping up the muscles by making little curling motions with each fist. "You are not supe-
rior to your life. You are not better than your actions and your
thoughts. Shit, Farbman, somehow I thought you were more in touch
than every other asshole car salesman, real estate agent, and dentist
running around believing that he is a poet at heart. Listen, you are not
an artist, professional soldier, or tightrope walker. You do not crusade
for the underdog or the environment. You do not build bridges or heal
people. You are not a scholar, athlete, or leader of men, or a scientist,
entrepreneur, or even an honest merchant. And you are most definitely not a man of the earth.

"What you are is a lawyer, Farbman, no matter what the fantasy you
cart around, no matter how you make the test come out. Not to hurt
your feelings, but that's how it is."

When they'd dressed, Harold called the hospital and relayed the
news that Ann Marie was out of recovery. Farbman thought, Great, and
where was I? On a goddamn racquetball court. Harold said the floor
nurses couldn't believe Ann Marie's strength: When they were shifting
her from the gurney onto the bed she told them to leave her alone. She
said, "I can do it myself."

"She's a tough monkey," Farbman agreed.

TAKING CHARGE

Leah, once he was able to raise the subject with her, did not share Harold's cynical view of Farbman's rural ambitions. Concerned that she would be bothered by his calling, Farbman had opened the conversation by launching into a description of Ann Marie's travails, and their impact on the family, as if to say, Don't hit me, I'm wearing glasses.

She remained silent while he talked about his wife's two surgeries and the still unresolved matter of cancer treatment. Then Leah surprised him by asking what no one else had.

"How are you doing?"

Farbman hadn't considered. Most of the time he felt he was going crazy, his world had altered so abruptly.

Leah said, "You're not crazy, you're in pain," and before he knew it Farbman found himself opening up about his fear of losing Ann Marie, his awful feelings of helplessness, coupled with the responsibility of having to make medical decisions for her without the training to make them, knowing that if anything went wrong he would be second-guessing himself for the rest of his life.

"The only positive part," said Farbman, "is that visitations like this make you rethink the way you're living your life." Caring for his children day-to-day had made him appreciate them in a way he never had before. The words 'family,' 'partner,' and 'friend' had taken on new meaning for him.

Farbman told her he longed for a life of simple, physical labor: that he saw himself caring for animals. He pictured lambs, innocent and energetic. He had recently taken Jason and Jennifer to a petting zoo on the North Shore and had thought about how nicely the sheep took food from him. He told Leah he was considering raising sheep or goats. And remembering the artisans who'd spun wool in historic Williamsburg, he added, not for slaughter, but for their fleece or milk. Just earn enough for necessities, you know.

"Don't get me wrong. I know this whole agrarian impulse I'm feeling has nothing to do with the grunt reality of farming, that it's all escapist, romantic fantasy. It's also obvious that I don't have to leave the city to avoid succumbing to the vapidity of urban life. Look at you. You work. You study your craft. And you still find time to give to the less fortunate."

"Are you saying there's no satisfaction in your work?"

"It's true," admitted Farbman, "that I am alive in my office. Harold confesses that he and his colleagues get turned on by pathology. Well, it's the same with clients in extremis. They present themselves with evidence piled up against them, injured with no one at fault, and I manage to find them some money, and they're thrilled. But the win feels empty. The scorekeeping isn't done in lives saved or books written, in houses built or trees planted, but only in dollars earned. So, when all is said and done, I'm living comfortably off their ill-gotten gain or the fruits of their greed and unhappiness.

"There's an ancient anecdote about two farmers struggling over the ownership of a cow. One pulls on the horns, the other on the tail, and the lawyer sits in between milking it."

"Okay, you'd rather be the farmer. Are you doing anything about it?"

Farbman told Leah what Harold thought, that Farbman was delusional, that his life as a lawyer was as immutable as that of an Indian born into a Hindu caste. "I'm sure he's right," said Farbman. "I'm a Jew. Lawyering must be in my blood. After all, we've been creating law for thousands of years. Arguing Talmud for centuries."

"Really? So your father's a lawyer?"

"A dentist, actually."

Leah said she didn't agree with Harold. She pointed out that before he'd gone to law school, Farbman hadn't known any more about torts than he did about animal husbandry. It's just that changing course was never easy. "The hardest part about changing," she said, "is that you have to change."

Farbman paused to let that sink in.

"On the other hand," Leah added, "you ought to find out what you're getting into. Did you ever talk to Michael? My parents were also chicken farmers. They spent their lives in hock to the feed companies. I put in several hours each day before school and after school, and there was never money for anything and no satisfaction in any of it. Many weeks our hired hand made more than we did. Talk to Michael."

"When I'm ready."

Farbman did not discuss Leah's contrarian views with Harold. In fact, all conversation with Harold was centered on finding a treatment for Ann Marie. The two friends sat across a table in the hospital cafeteria with symmetrical plates of cottage cheese and fruit salad, and paper cups of seltzer before them.

"Harold," said Farbman, "Twif is talking double talk."

Harold told Farbman to be calm, it just seemed that way because the pathology reports were, on their face, inconsistent with Potter's surgical diagnosis.

The matter under discussion was the kind of treatment Ann Marie should receive post-surgery. The answer, Harold had explained, depended to a large degree on establishing what stage the cancer was at—meaning, the extent to which it had metastasized.

"Who decides that?" asked Farbman.

"The surgeon is responsible for the staging. He uses criteria defined by some international federation of ob-gyns, but it is then confirmed by laboratory examination of slides at the same time the tumor cells are classified and graded. When you're trying to come up with a prognosis and a treatment, how much disease is left after cutting is real important."

A group of nurses carrying lunch trays passed by, each one saying hello to Harold, who nodded back and waved before continuing. "In Ann Marie's case everything was contained, no sign of spread, and Twif called it stage one." Harold reached inside his suit jacket and removed some folded papers. He handed Farbman two of the sheets, typewritten, with the printed heading "Report of Operation."

"This is a copy of Twif's operative summary."

Farbman glanced down and started reading:

The patient was put to sleep. Foley catheter was inserted and the vagina was prepared with Betadine. The abdomen was prepared and draped for a midline incision. This was made through all layers. Bleeding vessels were clamped and tied with #3-0 chromic catgut. The peritoneal cavity was entered. Approximately 100 to 150 c.c. of bloody fluid were noted, aspirated, and sent for cell block. General abdominal exploration was negative for tumor. The liver was smooth. Gallbladder area was normal. All gutters were normal ...

"Read it later," said Harold, sticking his hand over the page. "The bottom line is that while Twif saw nothing, tissue sampled from the omentum and appendix showed microscopic evidence of the cancer. If it metastasized there, she's a stage three. Twif says he doesn't have much faith in the pathologist and says if it's there it got there through direct extension from the original tumor—meaning it implanted because they were touching each other. This, only he would know."

"Twif is also, I recall, the man who said the tumor was just a shrunken head." Farbman added he also wanted Harold to know that he knew it was Potter's arrogant cocksuredness in not bothering to get a frozen section viewed that resulted in Ann Marie having to suffer through an otherwise needless second surgery.

Harold took a breath. "What do you want to do? File a malpractice suit?"

"I'm going to stop abdicating all responsibility to the doctors as if they were infallible and stop pretending their prescriptions are scientifically certain. I've got to learn enough to calculate odds and make my own informed guess as to the best course."

"How can I help?"

"Find out who the best pathologists are and let's get their opinions. Right now I'd like to read some up-to-date survey articles for an overview. Then I want to see comparisons of the various treatment options."

Harold said fine, he'd get someone to cover for him and they'd start immediately. When Harold left, Farbman pulled out his cell phone and called his office.

Joy said that Darlene Perpiacere, a friend of Deborah Must's, had called Farbman for an appointment. Farbman recalled Darlene as the lucky augmentation with only a hairline scar. It turned out, however, that hard, painful scar tissue had formed around her implants. "Capsular contractures," interrupted Farbman, "a known side effect described right in the warning labels." According to Darlene, when she went back to the doctor he tried to break them up by squeezing and twisting her breasts. In the process he'd ruptured both implants, and the silicone gel had entered her chest. She'd already had several surgeries to remove lumps of silicone from her breasts and armpits, with another coming up. She's really upset and scared, Joy added.

"She should be," said Farbman. "She's probably on her way to some terrible immune disorder." And, he thought, the firm of Farbman & Marucci is on its way. He decided that it was now time for the firm's first dignified solicitation for implant victims. He told Joy to get Darlene in the office today, and have Marucci sign her up. Then call the *Times* advertising department and get the best rates on a program of multiple inserts. Three columns by five inches should be about right, in the entertainment or some other section that tended to stay around during the week.

"Wait," said Joy, "there's more." Mrs. Pilcher's trial was for Tuesday. It was Mrs. Pilcher's claim that the State of New York could not reasonably expect her to continue to cohabit with a man who dominated the remote control and habitually channel-surfed on the only TV in the house. "Marucci says he'll send Kleegel to court with her if you don't care." Farbman didn't. Ms. Pittipaldi wanted to know if next Thursday after work for dinner was good for Farbman. Farbman paused. He had no interest in pursuing her but, afraid blowing her off might reignite hostilities, said tell her yes but that he would prefer the Alibi or some other nearby place since he was very tight on time. Sharon Beck, mother of Kimberly Beck, said she would pick up Jennifer and Kimberly after school this afternoon, and Farbman could get Jennifer any time, including after dinner. Mrs. Beck sent regards to Ann Marie. Mr. Blocker said this past Sunday was the Feast of the, the—something— Marilyn had taken the message and Joy couldn't make it out—a Holy Day of Obligation, and his boy was not in church, and what was Farbman going to do about it. Ida Sodowick said Janet remains in intensive care and that her first words coming out of the coma were "How much longer until I'm divorced?" There was also a lot of stuff involving Farbman's personal injury cases, but Marucci had taken it all from Joy and said he'd handle it.

Harold returned, so Farbman hung up and followed him into the medical school library. While Harold sat at the computer and searched the current literature, Farbman read the bulletin board notices. Amid the advertisements for textbooks, vacation rides, and shares in a Hampton house was an announcement of the committee meeting on biomedical ethics at which right-to-die advocates would be speaking. Farbman paused, wondering if it would come to that. He examined a display case filled with acupuncture needles, meridian diagrams, and ancient Chinese texts. The exotic procedure, legitimized by a Western medical school presentation, suggested to Farbman that he explore the unconventional. That notion, however, led him to consider the possibility of failed experiments and the prospect of running desperately against a ticking clock from one charlatan to another—spiritual healers, witches, herbalists, and homeopaths—until they ended up in some exploiting Mexican clinic with Ann Marie spending her final days eating peach pits.

Harold, looking strangely sobered, dropped a National Cancer Institute monograph and two recent issues of the *New England Journal of Medicine* on the glass in front of Farbman. With a very uncharacteristic stammer he suggested that Farbman read the relevant articles for a better abridgement than he could give. Then he took an awkward leave, saying he'd meet Farbman in two hours with the names of the pathologists.

Farbman read the summary on the cover of the monograph, and he understood instantly and completely why his friend was so uncomfortable. The five-year survival figures for those with Ann Marie's disease ranged from zero to ten percent, regardless of whether they were operated on or were radiated or took existing modes of chemotherapy. Worse, the median survival time for those getting the same drugs being recommended for Ann Marie was ten to twelve months.

Moreover, on the way to their deaths, the women suffered from the toxicities of the attempted cures. There was baldness and vomiting, of course, but also leukemia, which added a whole new dimension to the notion of side effect.

Was Farbman supposed to report to Ann Marie that her future now appeared to be a year of pain followed by an ugly death? That she would shortly be no more than a fading memory to her children? Farbman calculated how old Jason and Jennifer would be in a year and tried unsuccessfully to recall anything he'd ever learned about how children adapt to the loss of a mother at so young an age.

He pulled out Twif's operative notes and finished reading them, then read them through again, trying to glean from the anatomized version of Ann Marie some inference of the person, or of her life to this point. Of course there was nothing of her humanity; indeed, the surgeon's detached scrutiny of Ann Marie's interior did not yield even a clue as to what was broken in her. As Farbman stared at the description of her organs, her bleeding vessels and gutters, his mind rebelled. This was his wife, his children's mother. Ann Marie was a voice, a presence, a part of his life. While at times in the background of his consciousness, never could he have imagined her so dismally reduced. He stopped then, and chastised himself for being so unproductively sentimental.

On the other hand, science was providing nothing more than self-fulfilling predictions of morbidity and death. A terrifying vision of a cachexic Ann Marie appeared before him, huge eyes burning in a wasted face.

An awful pressure was building inside Farbman, and his chest ratcheted in against it. His breathing came quick and shallow. There seemed to be no air in the room. He touched his brow and was surprised that his fingers came away dry. He loosened his collar and wiped his face repeatedly with his hand.

Farbman paced the hospital corridors, and everything he saw became a vague, impressionistic background. He struggled to bring specific objects—an exit sign, a fire extinguisher, a wheelchair—into focus. He returned to the library and the articles on his desk, retrieved a legal pad from his briefcase, and began the briefing drill with which every lawyer is programmed from the first day of law school: getting the facts down—the question, the conclusion, and the rationale. By putting the information through this logic machine Farbman was able to grasp the nature of the problem and, most usefully, to appreciate the analytic limitations of someone not only medically ignorant but unskilled in scientific methodology and statistics. How could he tell, for example, whether the disease process in each of the patients in these studies was staged following the same protocols? Were the reported differences really statistically significant? In short, by the time he was finished, he had learned something of what he needed to know.

Farbman returned the journal articles to the desk. He glanced at his watch and noticed that it was the 28th of the month. The billing had to get out or there would be another cash flow catastrophe. So before going to look in on Ann Marie, he telephoned Joy.

Joy said Marilyn hadn't forgotten the bills, but she'd had a little problem. Things had been held up, but everything was fine and not to worry. There was really nothing that couldn't wait until the next time he came in the office. That Marucci not only had the bodily injury—"the B.I. cases" was what she said—under control, but had told her not to bother Farbman with any other work pressures and to give Marucci any calls or correspondence that she felt required immediate response. There were only two of these—Blocker again, and Mr. Big. Farbman would have to ask Marucci what Mr. Big wanted. As for Blocker, he was still very upset about last Sunday when the boy missed church, but now what he wanted was for Farbman to go to court that very day to have his wife jailed if he didn't get to take both of his kids to Virginia this next weekend where he had been offered some kind of a once-in-a-life-time spiritual opportunity.

"Better give me Marucci," Farbman said, adding, as he realized Marucci might really try to run the office, "and, listen, I want you to get all of the checkbooks and lock them in my desk and give no one, including Marucci, access to them unless I tell you."

Marucci answered the phone by asking how Ann Marie was.

Farbman said he hadn't seen her yet today, and explained what he'd been doing and the dismal results of his research. "It could be she won't make it a year." Then, hearing the words spoken aloud, he began to cry and had to struggle to regain control.

"Well, just forget about the office," said Marucci, the compassion clear in his tone, "and concentrate on Ann Marie and the kids and yourself." Marucci could handle just about everything that came up, and when he couldn't he could cover until Farbman was available. Marucci had returned Blocker's call and been informed that the man had indeed been offered what he considered a singular chance for transcendence. It seemed that Blocker had met a parishioner originally from Lake Ridge, Virginia, who personally knew Father Jim and his family, and who was going to arrange a private audience for Blocker and his kids.

Father Jim, in case Farbman was unaware, was the local Lake Ridge priest who made every crucifix and statue he got near start crying and who now had stigmata. So what, Farbman interjected, everyone's vision is a little blurry to one degree or another. Marucci said that the priest had recently been reported doing healings—a scoliosis, a partial blindness—and Blocker felt he might bring some healing to his family, get his son back on the path of right thinking and away from the centerfolds.

The idea suddenly touched Farbman. Not certainly the God-diminishing sideshow gimmickry of weeping statues, or whatever mishegaas could make a person's body so stressed it would spontaneously bleed, but the notion of such a powerful, transforming presence as Farbman had himself encountered in the person of Rabbi Sholem.

"He should go," said Farbman, "it's a great opportunity."

Marucci expressed astonishment both at Farbman's sentimentality and his ability to take a steady diet of Blocker and others like him.

"It's not that bad," said Farbman. "You'll see."

"No, I won't." Marucci said he'd reenlist in the Army before he'd do family law on a regular basis and that Farbman should hurry up and tell him what to do before he changed his mind about helping out.

"Call Pittipaldi," Farbman instructed. "See if she can get Blocker's wife to cooperate before you prepare anything for court. Tell her that if she gets Blocker's kid to go with him this weekend, I will get Blocker to negotiate an agreement before the case is listed for trial, which is going to happen imminently."

"Will Blocker do it?"

"The trip should soften him up, and if he reconnects with his son he won't care about the issues with his wife. And if I'm wrong, then what's the difference, right? Also tell her I'll see her a week from Thursday for dinner."

"This is the same Pittipaldi who only weeks ago wanted to remove and burn your entrails while you watched?"

"She gave up after I sent her a copy of the tape and the law on extortion, for which I thank you again. Pittipaldi and I are friends now. I think she understands that her anger was really just a disguised expression of her attraction for me. Now, what did Big want?"

"It was well-disguised," observed Marucci. He said Big had apparently been served with a violation notice from the feds some time ago and had ignored it. It was a second offense of using unapproved drugs and, in answer to Farbman's interrupting question, had nothing to do with the plastic netting violation Kleegel had researched. Big had turned the matter over to another lawyer who was supposed to be connected. Only instead of making it go away, the guy got everyone so pissed off that they're not only going to try Big on the violation, but they've started proceedings, based on his long history of problems, to revoke his U.S.D.A. license permanently and put him out of business.

"In fact our challenge to the plastic netting regulation and Big's refusal to comply when it hasn't yet been overturned was a final straw. They see him as incorrigible. The trial on the violation is on the calendar sometime in the next few weeks, which means," said Marucci, "about twenty-five grand, which we could really use. I hate to bother you at a time like this but my brother, Mickey, got busted again and flipped out. Some idiot forgot to take his shoelaces, and he tried to hang himself in the holding cell. I'm trying to get him bailed and into a private detox facility. I could try Big's case, but he says he wants you to do it. I didn't know what to tell him."

"Tell him I'll do it," said Farbman. "Tell him that I'm tied up at the moment with a personal problem, but if he'll get the file over from who-ever's got it we can start working it up right away. Let Joy know what you need for Mickey. If we don't have it in the attorney's account, I've still got some credit left on my home equity line."

"It's a good thing you're not here or I probably would kiss you."

"All right, you faggot, what's Marilyn's problem with the billing this month? I mean we can't keep doing this month after month. It's either the software or it's Marilyn, but I think one of them needs changing."

"It's nothing," said Marucci. "She broke her nail is all."

"She can't type with a broken nail?"

"You know how long her nails are. With one broken, that finger doesn't reach the keyboard."

"So why doesn't she just glue another one on?"

"She will, but it was her real nail. She was very proud of how she had grown it, and she had to find the broken part and then take it to her manicurist who works out of a nail salon in Queens."

"No more," said Farbman. "Anything happening on the Fudgsicle?"

"I'm working on it. Con Ed changed adjusters for the fifth time, and the new one's a woman who doesn't have a clue."

"Maybe it would be easier to get money out of the landlord. Did you ever track down who it is?"

"I asked Kleegel to do a search. Don't worry, I'll take care of it. Hey, I found a marketing guy who's interested in the unstainable necktie. He's already got an unfoggable shaving mirror."

"Marucci—"

"Before you say anything I just want to tell you about an old law school buddy of mine named Gannon, who met a guy in a bar with the idea of making this thing that looks like a tiny white rubber mat. About four inches wide and flat. They now spend their time on the golf course while the business cranks out millions—dollars I'm talking. So what do you suppose it is?"

"Tell me."

"Universal drain plugs. Now is that brilliant or what."

Farbman said it was indeed and that he was pleased Marucci was taking charge of their future. He looked forward to retiring off the earnings of whatever brilliant product Marucci could get people to buy.

Farbman found Ann Marie surrounded by medical students who were taking turns putting their status-symbol stethoscopes to her belly and shaking their heads. Farbman gritted his teeth and reminded himself of Harold's warning that submitting to student practitioners was a surcharge for treatment at a teaching hospital.

They were listening for sounds in her bowel. Apparently her intestines had become temporarily paralyzed as a result of being handled during the last surgery. Until they came back to life—"in a couple three days," Twif had assured them—she couldn't take anything, even water, and a plastic tube had to stay down her nose to continuously pump her stomach. "Else," said Twif in his folksiest style, "she'll just swell up like some old horny toad."

The problem was that after five days and no lubrication the plastic tube had become a razor shredding her throat. When the pain became unbearable, Ann Marie took to calling for more Demarol shots than the surgical insult itself required, and to make things worse, cellulitis developed at the injection sites.

Farbman, who had always taken his intestines for granted, remembered hearing somewhere that Orthodox Jews blessed God each time they took a dump. After a couple of days of wondering whether it was true, he tried his parents who, as he expected, knew about as many traditional Jewish blessings as Marucci. Then he called Leah, and she confirmed that it was so and read him the prayer. And while Farbman didn't actually pray, the last couple of times he'd sat on a toilet he'd pictured some bearded Hasid with his pants around his ankles, pinching off links and grunting thanks in rhythmic Hebrew to the Lord of all, who "fashioned man with wisdom, creating within him many openings and cavities such that if but one were ruptured or blocked it would be impossible to survive and stand before You and Your throne of glory."

There were prayers, Leah informed Farbman, for practically everything one encountered in life: blessings to be uttered on seeing a rainbow, a dwarf, or a fruit tree in bloom; when viewing lofty mountains or the ocean; after experiencing thunder or an earthquake or a comet; on meeting a Torah scholar or a secular scholar. Not to mention the endless preambles to each kind of food eaten and fragrance smelled—perfumes, trees, herbs, and so forth.

But none, Farbman noted to himself, for what he was encountering in his life; for what he saw each day in the hospital and in Grand Central Station, and on the street and in court. Unless you counted the very short newspaper vendor in the lobby of his building as a dwarf, Jews assumed apparently that God didn't want to hear about it when all you ran across was pain and hopelessness and people at their worst.

On the other hand, to be fair, he *had* come upon Leah.

"What," asked Farbman, "is to be said when one has encountered a beautiful woman?"

Leah, ignoring the coquetry, got the Siddur, the daily prayer book, while Farbman held on and, after some mumblings and page turnings, said, "Here it is. It's sort of generic—it covers beautiful trees and fields and such, as well as beautiful people." Blessed is the Lord our God, she read, shekaha lo baolamo, who has such in His universe.

"Shekaha lo baolamo," Farbman repeated, thinking how strange it was that, despite his dread and the ugliness which he knew surrounded him, the words felt right in his mouth and true in his heart.

Three days later he found on top of his otherwise prioritized mail a paperback copy of Paula Simmons' *Raising Sheep The Modern Way*. There was no cover letter, said Joy, and the packing envelope had no return address. Had he ordered it?

No, said Farbman.

Should she send it back?

Nah, he shrugged. Who knows, someday it might come in handy.

Yeah, right, said Joy, and moved on to the next problem listed on her steno pad.

CURRENT FASHIONS

Nine days post-op, and there were still no bubbles audible in Ann Marie's bowel, and Twif had felt constrained to cut off her Demarol. Her agony had become a palpable cloud in the room. The day before, Farbman had caught Ann Marie's new, astonishingly empathetic, private duty nurse standing at the foot of the bed with tears in her eyes. Apologetically the young woman had told Ann Marie: "I wish I could take some of your pain."

The medical students' eyes were, however, quite clear. At most they registered disappointment at not having won the listening competition. As they filed out, Farbman overheard one of the female students telling one of the men that she needed to pick up her car that afternoon with someone named "George" and that if it were okay she'd skip the hiatus hernia and the unstable angina and leave now.

Farbman kissed and stroked Ann Marie's head. He passed on regards from their friends which caused a sudden consternation in her face. "You didn't tell Sharon Beck, did you? If you tell her anything, you've told Rockville Centre."

Farbman said of course not and moved quickly to the chronicle of the children. He assured her that both were eating as poorly as ever. "I took them shopping and got them the mozzarella tubes for their lunches, but they wanted the construction-orange cheddar stuff that comes in the plastic well with crackers and a little plastic knife. I told them no, even though they swore every other kid has them for lunch. Jason slipped a can of synthetic squeeze cheese into the cart, which I returned at the checkout. On the other hand I gave in on the Red Hots and Skittles.

"I also bought a couple of cookbooks, and I have gotten them to eat something besides spaghetti. They love my *supréme de volaille milanaise,* which, to the unenlightened, appears to be just chicken in bread crumbs and parmesan, with tons of lemon slices." Ann Marie said he couldn't make her laugh, it hurt.

"The first grade took a walk in the woods, and then drew pictures to illustrate what they'd seen." Farbman pulled out Jennifer's rolled-up drawing to tape to the wall, confessing he had removed it from the hallway display. The drawing was appropriately captioned, "I saw trees and the sun and a dog."

Ann Marie smiled as he talked, but her teeth were clenched and she squeezed his hand hard enough to cause pain. Finally, when the clock indicated he had ten minutes until what he'd told Ann Marie was a lunch with Harold, she said he'd better go. Harold was being really nice, and Farbman shouldn't keep him waiting. Farbman, who had told Ann Marie nothing of his and Harold's research efforts, felt an inward panic that Harold had spilled the beans. Nodding in agreement, he casually asked when she'd seen Harold.

She said Harold dropped by every morning without fail, and joked and flirted with her, which they both knew was the only way he could relate to women. But she liked it anyway. "You know how he always says I look like Jennifer O'Neil in *Summer of '42?*"

"Yes. It's his highest praise."

"Well, he told me I still looked like Jennifer O'Neil, only with a tube in her nose."

Farbman said he was right and kissed her again before leaving for his long walk through the maze of bleak corridors out of the hospital. He reflected on the unhappy truths he hadn't shared with Ann Marie about the kids. They were missing her terribly. While the hospital allowed children to visit, he and Ann Marie had agreed it would be better to wait until she was untubed and out of pain. Meanwhile, Farbman had not succeeded in keeping the kids' routines rolling as smoothly as he'd hoped. One morning earlier in the week he'd been surprised when both kids complained they had nothing to wear. He had checked their dresser drawers only the night before and they had been filled with neatly folded clothes. He checked again, first with Jennifer. He wasn't mistaken: there were a half dozen turtlenecks in a choice of colors.

"What about these?"

"I hate those. They kill. I can't breathe in them."

When he pointed out the pile of handsome wool sweaters to Jason, the reaction was no better.

"They're cactuses."

"Not this one. Feel it. And you can wear a long-sleeved shirt underneath."

"I'll be too hot. And besides they're really dorky. I'll look like a total dweeb."

"It's twenty degrees outside." Although he had marveled in the past at his son's fashionable predilection to bunch his socks just above his sneakers, completely indifferent to the six inches of snow outside, he found it hard to fathom that the only acceptable dress these days were soiled T-shirts and sweatshirts emblazoned with promotional messages worn with jeans and no hat and no gloves. Farbman finally gave up and sent them off to school with the prior day's Hard Rock Cafe and Rolling Stones shirts pulled from the hamper. But that night both children morosely reported being mocked by their classes' self-anointed wardrobe police for wearing the same clothes twice.

When Farbman pushed out the revolving front door of the hospital the red Porsche was right before him. Harold was putting the targa top under the hood.

"The three best pathologists who specialize in this tumor are an arrogant little shit named Brickner at Memorial, Richmond, who is head of the department at Yale, and Mullen, the most famous, who is at the Armed Forces Institute of Pathology. They will only read original slides so they have to be hand-carried to each one." He nodded toward the car. "They're in the box on the passenger seat. All of these guys are prima donnas, but Brickner is a friend of a friend of mine and he's agreed to look at them while we wait. Then we'll shoot up to New Haven where we'll have to leave them until Richmond can get to them. This will then give me a chance to find some military doc who can get them into Mullen, at which time I'll fly them down to Washington."

They tore up the F.D.R. Drive, Farbman holding the slides on his lap, Led Zeppelin playing loud enough to be heard on the passing tugboats. Then, as they dodged the traffic approaching the hospital complex, Harold turned down the volume to ask Farbman what he'd gotten out of the articles. He didn't look at Farbman, and his tone gave nothing away.

"If I got it right, not even ten percent of the stage threes make it five years, no matter what you do. With a lot of residual disease the survival figure for the stage threes is about twelve months—again, no matter what is done—but I am confused by all the variables and by the categories of subgroups and the different modes of treatment."

Harold parked in a No Standing Zone and told his friend to stay in the car and to consider this as he waited: Statistics have no application to the individual case.

"Meaning?" asked Farbman.

"Meaning," said Harold, "that it doesn't matter if ninety-eight percent die if you're one of the two percent who don't."

While he waited, Farbman used Harold's car phone to check in with Joy and to return calls. He had decided that no matter what, he would not abdicate his responsibilities to his clients or the firm. He feared losing his identity, as being seen as some kind of hyphenated entity: Farbman-with-the-ill-wife. First, Marucci; next he would be getting understanding looks and hushed expressions of sympathy from the gang at the courthouse. He began to appreciate Ann Marie's near violent insistence on anonymity—how illness stripped people of their privacy. And help, no matter how well-intentioned, was accepted at a price: an inevitable loss of dignity. Despite the conflicts caused by caring for Ann

Marie and the children, Farbman was determined to pull his weight at the office.

Darlene Perpiacere had come in for her interview and officially signed on as a customer of Farbman & Marucci. Joy had gotten the insert rates from the *Times* and told Marucci about Farbman's plan to advertise for more implant victims. Marucci was excited at the prospect. He had torn something about implants out of the paper he wanted to tell Farbman about.

Mironovic, who had found his wife starkers by the pool being oiled by the gardener's helpers, had sent in a new proposal. This one had shaded pie charts and present value analyses of alternative alimony buy-outs.

An enraged Rhonda Pond wanted her complaint amended. She was convinced that her onanist husband was having an affair since the level of her Nivea cream had not dropped appreciably in four weeks.

Ask Kleegel to draft the amendment, Farbman told Joy, and tell her we need a five grand refresher.

Elmo Blocker and his son had met Father Jim. The boy had brought along a huge crucifix which, on meeting Father Jim, had shed tears, and the boy also had shed tears and was now replacing his Penthouse pet poster with a blowup of the Shroud of Turin his father had given him. He had also apparently agreed to start attending a traditional Latin Mass held weekly in a Moose Lodge about an hour's drive out on the Island. Best of all, when Joy had informed Blocker of the trial notice just received from the court, he had replied that Father Jim had persuaded him to render up to Caesar. Farbman could start negotiating an agreement or prepare for trial just so long as he didn't concede she had a right to divorce. Farbman called Blocker immediately to ask if it were really true and to pry a large or two out of him as well.

"Yes," said Blocker, "it's true." Even in these decadent times there are still a handful, like this courageous priest he'd found out at the Moose Lodge, struggling to save the rest of us from the influence of secular humanism. "That's how I found him," Blocker explained, "he had an ad in *Newsday*—'Save your family from the influence of secular humanism.'"

"That's not what I meant," said Farbman.

"Oh," said Blocker, "you meant Father Jim, and was there a statue of Mary that poured tears?"

"I never doubted that. I want to know is it true you're ready to make a deal?"

"Absolutely, now my boy's turned around." Blocker was positively ebullient. "He told me if his mother refuses to drive him out to services, he'll stay over at my place and go to church with me. I told him that if he did that, I'd go to a later Mass so he could party Saturday nights and sleep in. She can have the house." His Christian spirit radiated through the telephone.

Farbman had never heard the man so elated, and certainly never so reasonable. The driver's door opened abruptly and Farbman signed off. Harold handed over the box of slides and slid behind the wheel with a dark scowl on his face. He dropped the Porsche into first and roared in front of a taxi, forcing it to slam on its brakes. The driver tailgated them honking belligerently. Harold waved in his rear-view mirror, then shot down a narrow lane that had opened to his right and, barely missing two women stepping into the crosswalk, made the left onto York Avenue just as the light turned red.

Brickner had turned out to be the obnoxious little prick he was reputed to be. He had flipped the slides under his scope, shrugged, and said "So?" implying that he had been insufficiently challenged. Harold said it was only with difficulty that he had refrained from punching his lights out. They could expect a report to follow. In the meantime Brickner was sure the tumor was no wildfire type, which is a big break, and he says the appendix tip is just endometriosis, not cancer.

Harold turned the volume up on a Z.Z. Top cassette, and they drove all the way to New Haven with no conversation except to decide on music selections. While Harold took the slides into Richmond, Farbman called Marucci to get the latest implant news.

"This is heavy," said Marucci. "The plastic surgeons have poured millions into a campaign to stop the F.D.A. from banning these implants. Women's health advocacy groups have filed claims with the F.T.C. against the plastic surgeons' groups, claiming that they have used false and misleading advertising. The F.D.A. is holding hearings, as is a congressional committee, and the plastic surgeons are rounding up women all over the country who love their silicone titties to be witnesses."

"Speaking of the F.D.A., get Kleegel to run down their 'Dear Doctors' and see what risks they were telling doctors to advise patients about."

Marucci said he was making a note, then asked Farbman if he was ready for this: there were two to three million women with implants. "Three hundred ten thousand of them are supposed to have developed enough stiffness to make them uncomfortable."

"Wow," said Farbman. "We better get a marketing plan together pronto. The big tort lawyers probably have runners out in all fifty states by now."

Marucci also told Farbman that Big's file had been delivered, and it seemed the violation was already determined, that Big by not answering had waived his right to a hearing. The court proceedings were to collect penalties only. They wouldn't even be permitted to put in a defense. Meanwhile the U.S.D.A. was going full steam to revoke Big's license and were relying heavily on this conviction by default to buttress their case.

"We'll move right away to set aside the default, and answer. At the same time we'll turn the agency's reliance on this violation against them and get a stay of the revocation proceedings until the trial is over—hopefully, in a month from never."

"It's scheduled in two weeks."

"Hey, we're new counsel coming in—the first adjournment should be a snap. After that we'll have to get creative, but there's something wrong if we can't get six months out of a system whose essence is inertia."

When Harold returned, he told Farbman that Richmond promised to look at them by the following day and messenger them back to Harold so he could take them to Bethesda the day after that. Farbman informed Harold of his plans to take on the implant establishment. "I'd go slow, if I were you. Capsules of scar tissue are a common systemic reaction. The claim that mammograms are obscured so that it interferes with breast cancer diagnosis is nonsense if you've got competent radiologists and technicians. And from what I've read there is still no research supporting the connection to immune diseases."

"Well," said Farbman, "there's obviously data supporting such a connection, but people are interpreting it differently."

"Of course, but understand that when a doctor reads the medical literature, he weighs the reported problems against his personal experience and the experience of the profession. He evaluates everything as a matter of proportionality—of risk and benefit—and that's how he should present it to the patient."

Farbman disagreed. "This is breast size, not cancer, we're talking about. How can the surgeon justify taking any significant risk when the purpose is purely cosmetic?"

Harold looked at Farbman incredulously. "You don't think a valid argument can be made that misshapen or inadequately developed breasts are a deformity, a disease with serious psychological effects—feelings of inadequacy, loss of normal self-image, and so on?" He had himself diagnosed such psychic damage when he had the good fortune of meeting a beautiful, flat-chested graphic designer. "Her sense of bosomal inadequacy caused her to overcompensate in a number of gratifying ways."

By the time they'd gotten back to the city, Harold had provided more details than Farbman wanted, along with his theories on human mating habits. "Woman, unlike man, wants to mate only after forming affectional bonds—a useful adaptive mechanism for preserving the human species. This, in turn, created the male's adaptive strategy of pretending to care."

Farbman picked up Jason and Jennifer at their friends' homes and took them for pizza. Jason had memorized all the presidents in order and would not stop challenging everyone within range to call out a number so he could shout out the name. Grover Cleveland, it turned out, was both the twenty-second and the twenty-fourth. While Farbman was not surprised to learn there were seven early presidents from Virginia, he doubted that Ann Marie knew there were seven presidents from Ohio. Jason made him promise to ask his mother tomorrow if she could name them. "Grant, Garfield, Harrison, McKinley, Taft." Farbman ticked them off on his fingers. "And who are the other two again?" he asked Jason. "Can we get gellati?" Jennifer interrupted. Farbman still hadn't adjusted to the town's ice cream parlor having become The International Cafe, or accepted his kids asking for pignoli cookies or raspberry sorbet. "You know, when I was your age—"

"We know," said both children together. "You only got Good Humors off a truck. Please, can we?" Jennifer said please, please, and Farbman figured they deserved it and said sure to a chorus of hurrays.

Walking in the house with their take-out, Farbman found a reminder he'd stuck on the fridge that it was parent-teacher conference week and he was scheduled to meet with Jason's teacher that evening. Knowing he couldn't get a sitter on short notice, he called the lonely woman he paid to walk the dog and she came right over.

"It really is a worldwide brotherhood of man," Morrie Beck, Sharon Beck's husband, declared to Farbman as he and the Becks waited outside their kids' classroom, examining the fourth grade posters on that theme. There were lots of multicolored folk standing on, beside, or holding hands around, lots of globes.

"I believe, Morrie," said Farbman, "that today one should speak in more gender-neutral terms. Perhaps 'the siblinghood of people.'"

"Ain't it the truth," said Morrie.

Sharon, who was clutching an armful of raccoon pelts, said, "While you two smartasses are making jokes, our kids and others like them all over the world are establishing new relationships." She turned to Farbman. "You know that Kimberly's sister, Laurel, is exploring the Amazon basin right now."

"I had no idea," said Farbman. "Tell me about it."

"Well, she spent two weeks hacking through the jungle, living off piranha—the group leader throws in a hand grenade and they float up—Laurel says the meat around the gills is very tasty. Then they met up with the Auca tribe—they were headhunters—they showed the kids how to make their own blowguns and darts. I told her, Laurel, no blowguns in this house. She said I was being ridiculous. I finally said okay to the blowgun—it's an artifact and frankly I've got a spot for it on the wall of the great room—you know over where Morrie keeps his beer stein collection—but no darts, I said. Well, you can't believe the argument.

You know Laurel, when she makes up her mind—"

Morrie jumped in. "I took the phone from Sharon and eventually got Laurel to compromise. We agreed on no darts with curare. I pointed out the liability issue. I mean, we're not just talking an eye—someone could die."

Farbman said he'd never heard of anything the like of it.

Sharon said that he should prepare himself. It's a different world than when they were young. This is what young people did today. Farbman knew the Jacobs, right? Sy, the lawyer? Their boy Lewis has been seal hunting with the Innuits in Alaska for most of the year.

"It's for college credit," said Morrie, adding that since he'd heard about the Jacobs' boy, it's like all he hears about are Inuits nowadays. "And the Aleuts—you notice on all the college applications how they're listed with the other minorities? So tell me, how come the Jews are never a minority? I mean they had quotas to keep us out when we were struggling immigrants, and now that we've finally made it to the point where our kids are advantaged enough to compete with the old-line families who get in no matter what, now they've got affirmative action quotas to keep us out."

"It's terrible," Sharon agreed. "The Chinese and Cambodians and what have you get all the top spots, which I don't care, mind you—I mean if a couple of boat people working twenty hours a day in a laundry or at a vegetable stand can raise their kid in a New York slum to get straight A's and 700s and play the cello, I say, more power. But I have a problem with pushing black people ahead who blame the Jews and the Koreans for the fact that they haven't been able to learn English in three hundred years."

Morrie looked both ways down the hallway, then leaned toward Farbman, lowering his voice. "You know, Dartmouth was so excited to find that black boy with 600s, what's his name, the basketball player, he's a junior at the high school. They flew him and his family up for an all-expense-paid weekend. Meanwhile, Harvard and Princeton had both already offered him free rides and probably a sports car and an over-paying job to go with it."

Farbman shook his head in seeming disbelief.

"So what are you going to do?" Morrie shrugged. "You spend all that money and time to find out what the colleges want, and you try and give it to them. Courses to raise their SAT scores; tutors for their grades. Develop their talent. They have no talent? Send them off to enrichment programs and exotic camps: And then, when you've groomed them like the winner at Westminster, some pound dog gets the prize."

The door to Jason's classroom opened.

"Mr. Farbman?"

Farbman took one of the undersized chairs at the blond wood table where the teacher, who gave her name as Ms. Bordnick, had established herself for the evening. She looked to be about eighteen with a smattering of zits on an otherwise smooth-complected face. She wore large horn-rimmed glasses and an earnest, carefully composed expression as she told Farbman she was sorry to hear from Jason that his mother's been in the hospital. "I hope she's doing better?"

"Thank you. She is. I'm sorry, I should have told you myself."

"Well, we do appreciate knowing when something's going on at home as significant as the mother's absence. It helps us to understand when the child's behavior changes. But I'm sure you've had your hands full."

Farbman shifted on the hard, too small chair. "Has Jason's behavior changed?"

"Actually, yes, it has." She opened a manila file folder with Jason's name on it, revealing a stack of graded tests and assignments. "His work has deteriorated and I think his peer relationships as well. Here—" She turned a slim black book around using two cardboard markers to conceal above and below the line on which Jason's grades were recorded. A couple of F's jumped out among some C's and a B in the most recently inscribed section. To the left, in the prior marking period, were the familiar A's and B's. "He's somewhat withdrawn. I don't see him hanging around with his usual crowd of boys. Today, he didn't even play kickball at lunch, which is one of his favorite activities. Do you know who he's playing with after school?"

"Of course." Farbman rattled off the names of the kids whose homes he'd picked Jason up or dropped him off at, adding that most recently he'd been spending a lot of time with a boy named Flaco, whom Farbman didn't know that well.

She nodded. "He's a new student. Joined us midterm when his family moved here from Texas, although I believe they are originally refugees from El Salvador. He's a nice boy who hasn't fully integrated yet. Interesting that Jason would seek him out at a time like this. Well, I wouldn't worry, I'm sure this is all just a temporary situation, nothing to be alarmed about. I'll keep an eye on him at my end and let you know if I see anything that I think requires an intervention."

Farbman thanked the young woman profusely for her attentiveness and concern but realized as he drove home that he was very much alarmed by what she'd told him. He wanted to rush upstairs to hold both of his children, but the sitter told him they were in bed so he had to content himself with kissing them as they slept and fooling with their covers. He sat in his study trying to work on the Blocker agreement but found he couldn't concentrate. He needed to talk to someone and dialed Leah before he could decide against it.

"You're still up—I was afraid to call at this hour."

"You're lucky you caught me. I was just running out."

"Out? It's almost eleven."

"I have a late date."

"Wow. I couldn't do it."

"Neither can I normally, but Larry's a young cardiologist with limited time off and I stood him up last Saturday because I went to bless the new moon."

"And you did this at what pagan shrine?"

"At B'nai Israel, my neighborhood shul. In the yard behind it to be precise."

"What, you sneaked in? Climbed the shulyard fence with a bunch of Druids?"

"No, you dolt, I walked out of the synagogue with the rest of the congregation during the service."

"Jews do that?"

"Some do."

"Why?"

"You're greeting God's presence. The moon, waxing and waning causes the ebb and flow of the oceans, making a visible example of nature's cycles. The rabbis described the dying and rebirth of the moon as a metaphor for the rise and fall of the fortunes of the Jewish people through history."

"Okay. But why do you go?"

It was an opportunity, Leah said, to reflect on her questions: who she was, how she stood in relation to others and to the world. "Going to services is sort of taking a consciousness break."

"How do you get from God and lunar tides to your life?"

She paused. "I think that when I greet the new moon I'm actually greeting my own life. Looking for my own renewal. Understand that I rarely come away from services with answers. Just a greater resolve to keep looking."

"For…?"

"Nothing much. How to live joyfully. Same thing you and everyone else wants, right?"

"Yeah, but it never occurred to me that moon worship would get me there."

She laughed. "It won't."

"You mean it only works for you?"

"Not me either."

"So what does?"

"Shucking unhealthy habits and self-limiting beliefs, say the wise ones. Trying to perform the daily grind like it's on-the-job training for living a happy life. Not dividing your life into 'life' and 'preparation for life.'"

"Isn't going out this late an unhealthy habit?"

"Yup, and I'm going to be even later if I don't get moving."

Farbman said he'd be quick, that he was calling because of another ebb tide in this Jew's fortunes. "Jason's failing and apparently feels so stigmatized by his mother's absence that he's made himself a social outcast."

Leah asked him to be a little more specific, so Farbman repeated what he'd been told by Jason's teacher. What's worse, the boy didn't even feel he could come to his father.

"Maybe," said Leah, "this is his way of letting you know he's upset. Have you considered approaching Jason and saying you understand he's worried? Have you told him what's going on?"

"I'm afraid if I tell him his mother's very ill, he'll ask if she's going to die." Farbman paused, choked up. An intercom buzzed in the background, and Leah said hang on. When she came back she said she was sorry but they could talk more tomorrow. "Take care of yourself," she said.

That's all I'd need, thought Farbman, one more person to take care of.

Elmo Blocker called to discuss Farbman's draft settlement agreement. He wanted to emphasize that it was not sufficient merely to indicate that their boy was to be reared Roman Catholic. In his mother's hands that ensured little. Hopefully, Blocker said to Farbman, you read my last letter. Of course Farbman had. Well, then you remember her subversive feminist literature. Catholic women should leave the communion because the Church won't "dialogue" with them about issues like abortion, contraception, ordaining females. Can you imagine "dialoguing" about sacred principles? Blocker clearly considered the question rhetorical.

Would talking really be so bad? I'm just asking, said Farbman.

What would be the point? What kind of church would it be then? What kind of faith would there be if we say that truth is whatever the most convincing argument says it is? A church for lawyers, maybe—nothing personal—but not one founded on the truth of God becoming man in Jesus Christ. You're Jewish, right? Try to picture what your religion would be if anyone could believe whatever he wanted and still be a member in good standing. (Farbman did and concluded it would be Judaism.) Everyone being his own pope or priest. "It's bad enough to see the Pope giving in to the pressures of fashion, letting girls assist at Mass and all."

"So, even Catholicism changes—"

"No, it's not a change. The rule is against women getting involved in stuff that requires ordination. The Holy Father has just made a new interpretation, is all. The rule stays. What she wants is to pick and choose, accept this part, reject that—cafeteria Catholicism. You can't have a religion like that. Especially not for kids. Leave them alone to make choices and you'll end up with nothing. Either you follow the rules or you're out of the game. Now, you've got to get all that into my agreement."

Farbman told Pittipaldi he was busting his hump to get a draft to her before their dinner the following week. He said he hoped she would work with him and let the religious provisions slide.

Pittipaldi said of course she had to look at the document, but she'd see what she could do. While she was pleased with Farbman's effort, she regretted that even if they had the agreement done before Thursday they couldn't really celebrate that night. It was going to have to be a quick meal and no more because her mother needed a lift home after her belly dancing class and she was her only option.

"Belly dancing?"

"Very popular—courses springing up all over the place," said Pittipaldi. "Mother and some of her friends signed up just as a lark at first—to get a little exercise, maybe to help wake up their husbands." Now they were really into it. They had discovered their bodies, these suburban matrons. They were remaking themselves, even to selecting exotic new names. "My mother calls herself 'Shalimar,'" said Pittipaldi.

Farbman rang off thinking about his own reinvention fantasies. He figured there was as good a chance of trading his sheepskin for sheep as remaking his marriage with abdominal gyrations and finger cymbals. But was change really needed for their marriage to work? When Farbman talked to Ann Marie in her hospital bed he always came away moved by the love they shared for Jason and Jennifer. Farbman understood he was seeing Ann Marie then not as wife, but as mother of his children; nonetheless, he thought, "I do not require happiness to live with her." He could do without sex and even without her friendship. I have a greater responsibility, he told himself, that I took on when I decided to have these children, than I do to my own gratification. And, no matter how miserable I may be, or for that matter the two of us together, I know that for the children divorce would not be an improvement.

Moreover, what exactly was the big sacrifice he was asking of himself? It wasn't as though Ann Marie had lost her looks, that she wasn't companionable, that she didn't appreciate his humor.

Still, looking at Ann Marie tubed up in her bed of pain, Farbman was moved to do something. He sought to manifest some willingness to change—if only to give Ann Marie hope. He wanted to take her purple and yellow, IV-bruised hand in his own, and tell her that they'd been fools, that perhaps it took something dreadful like this to make a person realize how much he had in his life, that as soon as she was up to it, he would arrange a trip for them, just the two of them, to some place romantic. When they returned, it would be to a new life together.

Of course, he couldn't simply move himself and his family to the farm he'd envisioned. At least not immediately. The transition would be too abrupt. Besides, Farbman knew it wasn't really farming that impelled him but a desire to live a life that was personally meaningful. No matter, he argued with himself, he needed to be in an environment in which he did not have to deal every day with corruption, venality, and greed.

Leah said the idea was not to disengage. "Become what you want the world to be." She said that was Gandhi's advice. Leah wasn't keen on the idea of monasticism, of permanent retreats of any kind.

How did Farbman want the world to be? He wanted people to behave rationally. To be decent in their dealings with one another. To find such people he was sure he'd have to relocate and take up a new profession. He'd need money until he could reestablish his family. More money meant more lawyering. He pulled out his cell phone and called Michael to see how his investment was prospering. Michael was clearly getting annoyed at the frequency of the calls.

"These units you and Marucci are holding are tickets on the train to financial independence. But you're like a kid who starts yelling "Are we there yet?" when you've just pulled out of the driveway."

"The construction's coming along?"

"No. I can't remember where we were at last time we spoke."

"You said the takeout financiers were somewhat concerned because of oil prices, but construction was moving ahead."

"Good memory. But I'm sure I didn't say construction was actually moving ahead because the construction lenders, as you know, wouldn't provide money to start building unless they were sure the permanent financing was in place."

"So no work's been started?"

"What are you talking about? Of course, it's started. The architectural, engineering, site plan, and environmental are all done. All government approvals—state and local—have been gotten. All the legal is done, and the contracts have been bid."

"Okay. When will they start digging?"

"Just as soon as the takeout money is in place. It was a group. One of the main bankers was that California life insurance company that was taken over by the regulators because some derivatives losses affected their net capital requirements. I'm sure you read about it. Anyway, the deal is too big for the other two to do by themselves so they're trying to get someone else to participate with them. These things happen. I'll keep you posted. But stop worrying; you're like an old lady. Let's talk about important things. How's Ann Marie?"

"Good."

"The kids?"

"Great."

"Great."

How Ann Marie really was became clearer two days later when Richmond's pathology report reached Twiford Potter. Harold got a copy and ran off an extra for Farbman. Richmond had found two primary sources for the cancer, graded one tumor a level higher than the other, wrote that he was "reluctant to interpret the multiple cystic glands in the obliterated tip of the appendix as metastatic carcinoma." Whether the cancer in the omentum was implanted directly, he said, the surgeon was in the best position to judge.

Harold then got Mullen to agree to review the slides. Harold had networked back to a med school acquaintance who hadn't been able to make it in private practice and had had the Navy activate his reserve commission. The guy was now a bird colonel doing research genetics in

Bethesda. To get Mullen's attention when he presented the slides, he'd worn a full uniform for the first time in five years.

Twiford Potter called Farbman directly and said let's get the show on the road. She needs chemo now.

Farbman said they were waiting for Mullen's report and still hadn't compared the efficacy of the available drug protocols. He also intimated he would be gathering other opinions.

"Ah, yes. Patient participation. The 'in' thing." Potter's displeasure was undisguised. "It seems you've got the New York disease, Mr. Farbman," said Potter, by which he referred to second-guessing a doctor's authority. Farbman heard the chide as "the Jewish disease," but it was the arrogance he found enraging.

Back at his office Farbman found three messages from Amber Fleischman. Joy reported that this good-paying client was very upset—she wanted her husband put out of the house immediately. Farbman returned her call at once, trying to imagine how violent or threatening the man must have become. Amber explained that it was his mere presence that was intolerable and that she was the only one of her divorcing girlfriends who still had a husband hanging around meddling in her life and she wanted him out. They made an appointment for the following day for what Farbman called a review but more accurately could have been termed an invention of the facts necessary to procure an order locking Seymour Fleischman out. It shouldn't be too difficult. Such husband-restraining orders were virtually automatic and were quickly becoming the most common form of spousal abuse between divorcing couples.

The following day Farbman was at his desk scanning his morning *Times*. Now that his mornings were spent dressing and feeding the children, making their lunches and driving them to school, there was no time to look at the paper until he reached his office.

Farbman's attention was arrested by photographs of beautiful women in religious garb, including one costumed as a nun in a habit with flesh-revealing cut-outs over her breasts and midriff; another in the black coat and huge hat of the Hasidic Jew with her hair done to suggest the peis, the earlocks of the ultraorthodox. He read that the oversized, bejeweled cross, strung on silk, chain or leather, and hanging either from the neck or the waist, was the definitive accessory for today's fashionable cassocks and monk's cape or even as a mix and match with Madonna-style underwear. That Calvin Klein was selling Hare Krishna slips and tank tops in orange transparencies, and Carolyne Roehm accessory rope belts and rosaries in choker, matinee and opera length. There were sets of interchangeable crosses, amulets and miniature reliquaries.

The designers said it was the look of the times. For in our post-Christian, secularized century people long for religious expression. What, they ask, is more today than religious and cultural diversity? (How about division and warfare? thought Farbman.)

The article suggested that while Catholics might not care about the Pope's views, they were as full of prideful identifications as the Jewish or Protestant or Muslim nonbelievers. People were nostalgic for the days when their religion was sufficiently concrete and iconized that they didn't disappear in a sea of ecumenical homogeneity, when they didn't have to focus so much on stuff like belief systems and behavior.

Farbman imagined how disgusted Blocker would be at such vulgar secularizing. Then, he acknowledged his own repugnance. These merchandisers, trivializing profound symbols for a buck, were shameful.

Could they get away with it, Farbman reflected, if the rest of the world hadn't lost its moral compass? He thought about the courts' recent declaration that the proof needed for criminal conviction—that is, beyond a reasonable doubt—could no longer be defined in terms of the centuries old standard of having the jurors hold a conviction to "a moral certainty" of the truth of the charge, because no one knew what a moral standard was today. Blocker's reactionary theology was laughable, but at what desecration would Farbman draw the line? Suppose they made tank tops and raincoats decorated with Holocaust stars of David, yellow stars with the word "Jude," embroidered in the center?

Marucci walked in to ask about the status of their investment with Michael. Farbman, who didn't have the heart to level with him, just answered by saying he'd spoken to Michael and he seemed to be on top of everything. Marucci said it didn't matter anyway he had a new moneymaker. Inspired by Peter Lynch's advice to look around you to see what to invest in, he had and saw lots of hungry, homeless people. In rural areas people were eating road kill. He'd read where over ten thousand deer and tens of thousands of smaller animals were killed by cars in New York State alone. His idea was to create a book of recipes for road kill that would be cooked on the car engine. He showed Farbman yellow-ruled legal sheets with names like "Datsun Deer" … "Carbureted Crow" … "Possum Porsche" … "Squirrel Sentra" …

Joy buzzed to say Amber Fleischman had arrived. Farbman spent the rest of the day with her, creating a domestic violence case which would enable her to throw her husband out of his home. Unfortunately the only known act of violence the man had committed was his unprovable reptilian assault on Turk Horowitz. He hadn't threatened Amber, hadn't even followed her around the house like other men pleading with their wives to be rational. The best she could come up with was his telling her on more than one occasion over the past year that she was not sexually attractive to him and that he didn't love her.

Farbman decided that it was a fair inference that these words were intended to demean and belittle Amber and that that could arguably constitute the infliction of emotional abuse because the drafters of the domestic violence statute included as prohibited behavior that which fell within the statute defining harassment. "Harassment," said New York State, was "repeatedly committed acts intended to alarm or seriously annoy." Since the initial application to the court was made without notice to her husband, and was one of hundreds of such one-sided requests to a backlogged judge, there was no problem getting the court to issue a temporary order. The police would have him out that evening. Then when the hearing was held, Farbman would just have to convince the judge that everything was fine with them separated, that they were going to be divorced soon anyway, and that the status quo should be maintained.

That evening, snug in his home, Farbman telephoned Ann Marie and learned that her bowels had returned to life. All tubes had been pulled. Two days later Farbman helped his wife from her hospital wheelchair into the car and brought her home under a rare sunny sky, acting as if their troubles were behind them. He did not mention and tried not to think about the last exasperated call from Twiford Potter a few hours earlier insisting that she start chemotherapy at once, but Farbman admitted to himself that he was running out of time.

THERAPIES

Farbman was reluctant to give up his new-found pleasure of mornings with the children and gladly continued their recent routine while Ann Marie was still too weak to resume household responsibilities. Jason would crack the egg and measure out oil and milk for the health food pancakes. Jennifer would set the table, starting with a can of pure maple syrup which she used to drown any nutrients, saying always, "Oops, I didn't mean to pour that much." Farbman would prepare the lunches: drawings on both bags, with a light shmeer bagel for Jason—cut into quarters in deference to his braces—fruit leather and pretzel sticks. For Jennifer, celery-less tuna salad, or string cheese and crackers. For both, apple juice and a plastic container of fresh fruit salad made like Grandma Bea's.

After dropping the kids at school, Farbman, already a daily visitor at the medical school library, now drove there first thing each morning, having decided to camp there until he figured out what to do. He collated the articles he'd been gathering on the trials of unpronounceable chemical compounds with twenty-letter names like hexamethylmelamine, cyclophosphamide, and cisdiammine-dichloroplatinum. In order to get apple-to-apple comparisons he bought graph paper and made up charts separating patients by staging and by type and grade of tumor as well as by how much tumor was left after their operations. Then he looked at the results of therapies with different drugs and with radiation.

He showed his notes to Harold. "Good start, but you're missing a key point here. What counts to the patient is not the response rates of the cancer to this or that combination of drugs but the number of complete remissions they get. What we're interested in is *survival.*"

Farbman, comprehending, moved his head.

"Then we want to consider the quality of life cost," said Harold. "These are highly toxic regimens and, as you read, they can induce an acute leukemia, which is too high a price to pay."

Harold added that what they needed was a good research oncologist to help them, and the next day he introduced Farbman to a quiet, round-faced young woman named Carla with granny glasses and a wart on her nose. Harold had invited her out for drinks at a hip grill in Chelsea. He and Farbman bought her beers and fawned over her shamelessly while she critiqued a given study's randomization and stratification factors. She told Farbman to forget about the twenty years of human interferon studies he had been reviewing. Although there had been success with some leukemias and lymphomas and a slowing of metastasis in osteogenic cancer, it held no promise here. Harold hugged her when after a week she brought them a lengthy charted analysis of the survival rates of all patients in the major treatment groups.

Each symbol, she explained over the bar noise, represented a time of death, each curve either complete, partial, or no response. Farbman could see clearly that only a tiny number of the little black dots and triangles made it past 24 months.

"Okay, Carla," Harold asked her, "how would you call it?"

"Well," she said, "if we're talking stage three with little residual disease, this"—she flipped through her papers and pointed to a column of figures in her table of treatment regimens—"is the most statistically significant difference by continuity corrected contingency chi-square test." Harold got up from his chair and stood behind Carla with a hand on her shoulder while he studied the data. She said it was obviously a riskier regimen, but this guy was really the only one getting results. Wilson, at M.D. Anderson, whose less toxic treatment Farbman had favored, she was sorry to report had just published a retraction. Finally, Harold nodded and told Farbman to write down the name of the doctor whose experiment it was.

That evening after the children were in bed Farbman told Ann Marie that, while she would probably do fine without it, to be on the safe side Twif and Harold felt she should take some drugs for a while. They were referring her to a doctor at New York Hospital named Arthur Leopold.

Arthur Leopold was shooting Ann Marie up with death-dealing chemicals. Or, to be precise, as he was injecting the cell-murdering drugs into her line—the line the doctor had just been forced to run because after a three-and-a-half hour wait the IV team still hadn't shown up. The doctor's hair had come undone from bending over. He had a long, hairpinned lock that he grew behind one ear and wound around his head like a turban to cover his baldness. He had to let go of the syringe with one hand to catch and repin it. "Whoops," he said. Embarrassed, he nonetheless smiled and joked, you got to be careful. "Real platinum in here, too expensive to spill."

"Could you tell me how long till the vomiting starts and my hair falls out?"

"It varies."

Leopold was vague in areas like his patients' despair (to which Farbman inferred after his first waiting room encounter with the doctor's wispy haired, yellowy, amputated clientele, he must have inured himself in order to function). Farbman had, therefore, searched out the social worker assigned to oncology and took Ann Marie to meet her after the diagnosis but before treatment. The young woman had sympathetic eyes, was knowledgeable and businesslike, and straight in her answers. Ann Marie declined with thanks her offer to join a support group of dying patients. All she wanted to know she said, was how many times would she throw up, and would her hair fall out all at once, or in clumps, or some other way?

The M.S.W. suggested twenty to thirty was about average although the bulk were mainly dry heaves—retching, you know. The hair loss would occur over time. Ann Marie would wake up and find loose hairs on her pillow. In her brush. In the sink. She said some people claimed pot or THC, its operative extract, helped; also sleeping with a hairnet.

Leopold had no THC to prescribe. Farbman got an ounce of Thai stick from Deborah Must who wouldn't take any money for it. Farbman removed five fat joints from his pocket and after twisting some loose ends laid them, along with a disposable lighter, within easy reach of Ann Marie. The doctor, about to speak, glanced into Farbman's eyes and apparently read something there which decided him against continuing.

Ann Marie squeezed Farbman's arm and looked into his eyes. At that moment he was flooded with memories of their shared history—of the innocence of their college courtship, Ann Marie's courage and decisiveness in leaving her family and faith, her Midwestern society and a host of more eligible men, to live with a New York Jew of dubious promise, and all that they had made of their lives since. Farbman felt tears pressing as he considered the love his wife had shown him. He was determined to demonstrate his love. To see her well.

"Go home to the children," she said. "I don't want you to stay." Farbman stared.

"I mean it. I don't want you here watching me retch."

"The children are okay They're with my parents."

"You know I do better by myself."

Illness, Farbman saw, served as an awful reminder that one is, finally, completely alone. Ann Marie had communicated that aloneness so fully that Farbman paused outside her door, overcome. He shut his eyes, leaned his forehead against the wall, and marveled at her courage.

Dr. Leopold caught Farbman waiting by the elevator and asked if he had a minute. After being assured that Farbman did matrimonial work, he averted his eyes, fingered the rope of hair coiled on his head, and allowed that he was a little distracted because his wife had recently left with their three children, and could he ask Farbman a question.

Farbman was pleased at this sudden elevation to the status of mutual professionalism, at the prospect of no longer having to play sycophant.

Leopold told Farbman that, as far as he was concerned, she could have the house and the kids so long as he could take them for fast food and to his parents on Sundays; and he was willing to share or, if worse came to worst, give up their Montauk place, although he'd bought the lot right behind the dunes before they were married and he'd personally designed the place and spent weekends selecting each board for his random-planked floor.

"So there's another woman," said Farbman, who had encountered such generosity before.

The doctor's eyes widened at the rapidity and accuracy of Farbman's diagnosis, but quickly added that it was not what Farbman thought. She was not younger or better looking, she just wanted him. Period. This was about values. The woman only had a Sears charge account. She didn't shop at Bloomingdales. She couldn't even pronounce Bendel's.

The problem was that he was too sensitive to continue watching his patients suffer and die. He had signed up for a residency in dermatology, which paid about a tenth of what he was making now, but at least he wouldn't have to confront despair on a daily basis. His wife, however, who had installed herself in an apartment in the West Village costing forty-five hundred a month without utilities, and enrolled the kids in private schools with college-sized tuitions, expected him to continue paying support at the same level.

Farbman said that Leopold's decision to change careers transformed his case from what Farbman would call legal flu into legal pneumonia. He suggested the doctor call for an appointment right away.

Outside the doors of the hospital, a man was handing out pamphlets, small newsprint booklets really, to passersby. Taking one, Farbman saw that it was a "Free Premier Issue of Miracle Healing and Spontaneous Remission." The publication declared it could conquer supposedly incurable cancer with simple procedures that unlocked the body's own natural healing. The course of the disease would be altered with powerful therapies, including thought-medicine techniques suppressed by the medical establishment.

Farbman flipped the pages while the world moved blurrily around him. If he subscribed now, he might be able to snatch himself and his loved ones from the jaws of death, disease, pain, and loss of function. He would have revealed to him ancient holistic techniques and an all-natural secret potion that rendered so-called incurable cancers harmless. He could cancel at any time and get his money back if not fully satisfied. He threw it in a trash can. Then reflecting as he walked down the block, he decided he did believe that how we think determines our health and well-being. On the other hand, he wasn't prepared to say that a person was responsible for his immune system not working because he didn't get his head together. He walked back and fished the pamphlet out of the trash.

He asked Leah if she thought the brain could be taught to transmit instructions to the body so it would release its own curative chemicals.

"Listen," she said, "I'm of the 'There are more things in heaven and earth, Horatio' school. I just read about serious scientific studies showing that people get better when they're prayed for—people who don't know that anyone's praying for them, who were in intensive care and randomly assigned to the people praying."

"C'mon," said Farbman.

"I'll get you the name of the book. Meanwhile, I'll keep praying for you all."

"Keep?"

"Sure."

"What's Larry the cardiologist think?"

"Never asked, why?"

"Just curious about a doctor's reaction is all."

"Well, Larry's history—I'm too involved with Lionel right now—but the book about healing prayer is written by a doctor."

"Lionel—?"

"I told you about him. The ethnologist from N.Y.U.? He wears silver amulets from Africa and fetish necklaces. Big split cowry shells. If you thought I had late dates with Larry—Lionel has me greeting the dawn doing aboriginal dances."

Harold, taking a close loss in the last racquetball game very poorly, scoffed at the notion of curative prayer. Everything was chemicals.

Human beings were just cauldrons of reacting chemicals. Medicine was biochemistry. Even human relationships were chemically based.

Farbman used a finger to wipe the dripping mixture of steam and sweat from his brow. "Don't you think that's a little extreme?"

"Hardly. We now know that falling in love is a state induced by neurotransmitters—dopamine and phenylthylamine. As anyone who's been in a long-term relationship can tell you, eventually the body stops producing enough of the stuff to keep you interested."

"So why do couples stay together?"

"It appears to be endorphins—you know, the feel-good juice your brain secretes after long runs or a few racquetball games. There is an inverse correlation between sexual desire and the level of endorphins your body produces. This keeps you from caring when you can't get it up anymore."

"The wonderful post-coital closeness? Just the oxytocin secreted during orgasm."

"Bullshit."

"Look at you. Who would have believed you were such a romantic. You can inject monkeys with oxytocin and watch them grab each other and snuggle up. Researchers have done it."

Whatever endorphins their workout had produced were neutralized by Harold's little talk on love and affection. Farbman was overcome by a foul mood he couldn't shake. It worsened over the weekend, and Monday morning he was a bear in the office. He demanded status reports on fifty matters. Joy ran back and forth with files—Farbman's and everyone else's—that Farbman inspected, cross-examined Marucci and the associates about, and dictated memos on.

Amber Fleischman had lined up family and friends who would testify as to her emotional sufferings from Seymour's presence in the house. He'd shortly be furnishing a new apartment.

The motion had been drafted to set aside Bigonocco's state court default and to stay the proceedings to revoke his U.S.D.A. license. And (Farbman was right) as new counsel the court had given them a sixty-day adjournment to learn the file. Big was very pleased.

The bad news was that their dream of scoring implant cases was in jeopardy. Deborah and Darlene were talking about dropping their foundation suits because their doctors didn't want to support the idea that their diseases were caused by the implants, pointing out that the women would lose their insurance coverage. Major medical didn't cover the complications of cosmetic surgery. Worse, they would not be able to get new insurance, either, with a recorded history of such problems.

Farbman said not to worry and not to stop working toward a potential class action. "Where is the research I asked Kleegel to do?"

Marucci called Kleegel into the room to give his report. Kleegel said that the F.D.A. originally estimated there were two million silicone implants out there. The A.M.A. and the manufacturers and the American Society of Plastic and Reconstructive Surgeons agreed with that number, but now the F.D.A. has said there are only half that number.

Farbman interrupted. "Look, we're operating on the assumption that we won't be able to connect a specific manufacturer to a specific implant and that ultimately we are going to have to try and impose liability on the basis of each manufacturer's respective market share—"

"I'm getting there," said Kleegel.

"No, you're there," said Farbman. "Just give us the answer."

Kleegel, reddened from the chastisement, flipped over several pages and read in a monotone that Bristol Myers Squibb says it has about two hundred thousand implants, which would amount, they believe, to ten percent of the market. Dow Corning says it has eight hundred thousand worldwide which, if the two million figure is right, would be more than a third. Menton Corporation says it has thirty percent, but they don't indicate how many women have them. He put the document on the edge of Farbman's desk and before exiting, suggested that Farbman might want to take a look at some of the other information it contained, even if he weren't interested at the moment.

Marucci asked Farbman what kind of hair he had up his ass. Kleegel was a good associate, but if Farbman continued to be that rough with him he was liable to go the way of Reilly.

Finally, there was a letter from Blocker.

Sunday
Returning without son
from God's house on
the Sabbath

Dear Lawyer Farbman,

For the sake of expediting the matter. And after telephoning and failing to reach my wife, my lifetime mate and our child. Who likewise failed
to appear for church despite the commitment of which you are aware.
After receiving your informative letter of two days hence advising of
court date before the Honorable Peter Lowenstein and acting immediately
thereupon. Especially focusing on the last paragraph which stretches from
page one to page two.

My memory is fairly cognizant on this considered crucial matter.
Already believed that said wife and son have already followed through
properly.

Early on while memories possibly retained more clarity. A particular
private investigation having even been suggested whose services I agreed
to pay were never stopped, and who will establish before the said Judge
Lowenstein such as is needed.

One 30 day month and three days ago I directly released to your
associate Kleegel a suggested name list who should be contacted. Inspiring
the fact that any delay would probably see all the witnesses back in out
of area places yet circumstances suggest no action was or has been or
may not be taken.

This letter and my prior one of two weeks hence and yours dated
immediately after my last which wife and son will receive copies. Relates
here and now that each should be guided immediately and accordingly as
to what must be done at this late but still not too late date.

For certainly we've (you and I have) tried to install the right lessons
and values and point in the right direction early on. And it remains only
to make it clear to the court.

Farbman understood completely. Blocker had signed the settlement agreement resolving every substantive matter in dispute between him and his wife so that the formal courtroom declaration was now all that stood between him and divorce and he was not about to go gently. He wanted the court to know that his yielding to temporal authority was an empty gesture, that, as far as he was concerned, the sacred bonds were indissolvable. The court and the rest of the world had to know what kind of woman Mrs. Blocker was, and he had lined up a dozen witnesses, none of whom had a single bit of relevant testimony to offer. Farbman believed he could convince Blocker to forego dragging the neighbors and parish priest in if he were allowed some opportunity for catharsis. But would Pittipaldi and the judge go along with it?

Farbman, crossing the midtown streets toward the Alibi, felt tired in his bones. He had a worrisome inability to focus. The noise of rush hour was strangely muted, the edges of everything around him—the people, the piles of restaurant garbage, the traffic, the blowing soot, the neon of the discount electronic stores, the blare of cheap merchandising—all blurred, all ugly. Why, he asked himself, was he there? On the other hand, was there anything uglier than the fact that he had left his wife in a hospital bed to puke her guts out while he went off to have dinner with another woman? No matter the motive that propelled him? He convinced himself it wasn't sex and in no event was he about to fake interest in order to circumvent what Harold had described as the female's atavistic need for a real relationship. Pittipaldi was certainly normative. She was married; her chest belonged in a sculpture gallery. He paused at the Alibi's entrance, his hand on the cold brass door pull, reflecting on how much he didn't want to do what he was doing. How much he wanted just to turn around and go home. He would do it. He would call and leave a message that he'd had an emergency. He could think of nothing in the world he desired at that moment so much as to be home preparing dinner for his children, and nothing he wanted less than to be involved in anything sordid with Pittipaldi. Well, he asked himself, who said he had to do anything more than get a quick bite, discuss how they would handle the Blocker divorce, exchange enough pleasantries to reassure themselves that their misunderstanding was behind them, and leave?

Pittipaldi was waiting for him like a contest prize behind the door when he opened it. She gave him a warm greeting, and Farbman took her hand when she extended it. She told the hostess she'd keep her coat with her. Farbman said he'd do the same, and they were led to an out-of-the-way table. Deborah Must appeared and without comment lit their candle and asked what they were drinking. Farbman, feeling his face flush, said he was surprised; he thought Deborah had Thursdays off. He introduced her to Pittipaldi as a client and friend, then Pittipaldi to Deborah as a competitor lawyer. The women showed their teeth to each other. Pittipaldi said she'd like a Lone Star long neck. Deborah said she thought she knew what Farbman wanted, would he like to try the newest designer water they'd got in, and he said sure, with lemon, not lime. Farbman was embarrassed at what Pittipaldi, from her quizzical look, must be thinking. She asked Deborah for menus, explaining their time constraints. Deborah dropped two menus and the wine list on their table and headed off to the bar.

Farbman caught himself as he was about to remark on Pittipaldi's cross as a fashion statement, recalling the porcelain pope and bleeding artifacts in her office. She was definitely not just accessorizing.

Deborah reappeared with their drinks. She said she wasn't pushing, but Pittipaldi did say she had an appointment to keep, right?

Pittipaldi opened her menu and said the veal scallopine marsala was appealing, but then again maybe she'd just have the chops broiled. What did he think?

Farbman said he knew too much about veal to eat it.

She ordered the penne in pesto and a tricolore, and Farbman said make it two. Deborah said she'd hurry it right along.

Pittipaldi filled her glass, and before the foam settled, started shredding the label with her thumbs. She said she didn't know where it came from, her habit of peeling the labels off beer bottles.

"Don't worry, sometimes a beer bottle is just a cigar."

"What is that supposed to mean?"

"A famous Freudian insight. It means there's nothing wrong with you."

"That's comforting."

Farbman thought of his children waiting to be picked up at friends' houses. He looked at his watch and saw a hurt expression appear in Pittipaldi's eyes. "Could we talk about the Blockers for a minute?" he asked.

"Their agreement's signed. It's done," said Pittipaldi.

"Exactly my point. So what harm is there if we let the guy spout off a little about his religious principles?"

Pittipaldi asked why they should reward neurosis. Farbman responded that they should not lose sight of the truth, that what they were going to do in that courtroom was wrong, even putting canon law and Blocker's rantings aside.

"Divorce is wrong?"

"Divorce is shredding our society. As terrible as it is for an unwilling spouse to be dragged into public scrutiny, it's been proved over and again that children are the real victims, that they suffer much worse than they would if left in an unhappy household with arguing parents. The legislature gave no thought to the so-called 'best interests' of children when they liberalized divorce laws. And it is these generations of scarred, parentally abandoned kids who are our future."

"You're suggesting we give up the matrimonial practice?"

"No," said Farbman, "just be honest about what we're doing: Not pretend we're above being reminded about the values we give lip service to."

To Farbman's relief, a different waitress brought their food and the three-foot pepper mill which she ground over everything before leaving. Pittipaldi picked up her fork and spoke before taking a bite.

"It's not about values. Blocker wants to humiliate his wife, and I won't allow it."

"Grace, he's a true believer—in this case, Catholic. He's bought it all—the rules, hierarchies, tithes, celestial intermediaries, chains of command, syllogistic proofs for God's existence. He's got a clear view of heaven and hell and a set of directions to each. I don't know what you believe—but even I, who believe none of it, have to credit the man's sincerity."

Pittipaldi said she'd think about it, but she'd like a change of subject while they ate. So they discussed movies and news and legal gossip with their pasta. When they were finished, Pittipaldi ordered a coffee, and Farbman excused himself to go to the toilet. On the way back he found Deborah and asked her for the check. Deborah said his lady friend had already taken care of it, adding, "it must be nice ..."

As they exited, Farbman asked where Pittipaldi had parked her car and she indicated the lot across the street. She said he didn't have to walk her to her car, but if he insisted she certainly wouldn't object. Farbman figured he'd been brusque enough already. Considering how she'd paid and how it was supposed to be a reconciliation, he certainly did not want to leave her with a bad taste. He said it was his pleasure. Pittipaldi took his arm as they crossed the street. I'm prepaid, she said, releasing him at the lot to lead the way down a narrow space between two parked cars. Then she made a right turn, down an aisle, Farbman looking around for her car as he followed, absurdly, he realized, as he had no idea what she drove. He decided, given her conventional lifestyle, it would be something practical and American, and felt smug as she stopped before a beat-up-looking Chevy sedan. Pittipaldi turned coquettishly toward Farbman, her back to the car, and smiled. Thank you, she said. Then she kissed him, pulling him by his coat lapels to her as she leaned back into the car so that Farbman, off balance, felt his body pressed full against hers. Pittipaldi's breasts could be felt through the fabric of both their coats, although her hands were against his chest. She crushed her lips against his, then tore them away in a gasp of passion, her head back, inviting him to her neck, which the astonished Farbman reflexively kissed. She murmured appreciatively, then pushed him gently from her only to grab him again, exactly as she'd done before and proceeded, rather unimaginatively he thought in the second he had to catch his breath, to pull him back on her in precisely the same fashion, repositioning her hands on his chest as before, and kissed him deeply. The difference this time was that, instead of passionately tearing her lips from him, she drew Farbman to her slowly with her open mouth, so that her head was already tilted well backward when she broke for air and offered her neck again. If that's what she wants, thought Farbman. Aroused, he kissed her neck on each side, eliciting soft, groaning sounds. Once again, Pittipaldi pushed Farbman off, exhaled hard, steadied herself, made a visible effort to get her emotions back under control.

"Go get your kids," she said. "I'll call you." She put her hand to his cheek and held it for an instant. Then she smiled and shoved it away in a mock blow that was full of affection.

"Do you think this is a good idea right now?"

"Don't worry," she answered. "Nothing will happen until the Blocker case is behind us."

The Blockers' uncontested divorce was to be put through before the Honorable Peter Lowenstein, a burned-out veteran of the Family Part. His courtroom was one of a number of converted windowless storage rooms in an annex building. Family cases did not require juries for resolution so they could be handled in smaller quarters; and since in the eyes of the judicial system the issues that divided families did not have the import of a rear-end collision, or a drug bust, the trappings were appropriately scaled down.

The storage room walls were entirely unadorned unless you counted the illuminated exit sign over the door and an electrical panel box that read "460 Volts Danger." The judge's bench was faced with cheap sheets of blond oak-veneer paneling. On the bench were a carafe of water, a box of tissues next to the witness box, and stacks of rubber-banded papers creating a barrier around the clerk.

The clerk, a grizzled gray-suited civil servant with a bird's nest of dingy hair, announced that the judge was coming out. He gestured toward a pair of formica-topped counsel tables with chrome legs and a King James Bible on each, and said, "Assume the position, counselors."

Before the Blockers could be heard, they and their counsel had to sit through a number of routine, self-styled, emergent applications. Two were from fathers deprived of weekend access to their kids. Farbman tried to amuse himself by reciting the litigants' lines in his head before they spoke, seeing how accurately he could predict the husbands' stories, the wives' excuses, how close he could come to verbatim words:

"They hate his girlfriend." "They'd rather be with their friends." "He just drops them at his parents' and goes off to play softball." "Am I supposed to push them screaming out the door?"

The fathers and their children were left to their midweek dinners. A domestic violence case followed and was quickly disposed of, Judge Lowenstein checking off the squares of the form lockout order as the woman, with no visible injury, began telling the story of a kicked-in bathroom door and offered as her sole evidence a snapshot of a broken door hinge. The clerk put a sticker on the Polaroid, gave her extra copies of the order for the police; and then it was the Blockers' turn.

The clerk asked Mr. and Mrs. Blocker to place their hands on their respective Bibles and if they swore to tell the truth, the whole truth, and nothing but. Mrs. Blocker, in a brown polyester pantsuit, said she did and Elmo said, "What happened to God, in 'So help me God'?" The clerk said God's not necessary anymore.

Mrs. Blocker testified to the elements of divorce and that she understood the terms of her agreement and that she had entered into it freely and voluntarily. Farbman then asked the carefully prepped Elmo only to admit that he had also entered into the agreement freely and voluntarily. Farbman said he would hand up the proposed form of judgment if the court would permit.

Lowenstein said just a minute and asked Blocker the final question in the litany that established the binding nature of the parties' agreement:

"Do you have any questions, Mr. Blocker, that you wish to put to counsel or the court?"

Farbman braced himself and glanced at Pittipaldi, who had gone rigid.

"Why, yes, I do, Your Honor."

Blocker stood, put on his magnifiers, shuffled a handful of papers, then started in. "Judge Lowenstein, I assume you are of the Jewish faith. I am sure that you have brought your children into your religious community, stood beside them as they recited as we Christians do: 'Holy, Holy, Holy is the Lord of Hosts', Sanctus, Sanctus, Sanctus, Kadosh, Kadosh, Kadosh, and that you, too, wanted them to proclaim the watchwords of your persuasion. (Blocker paused and glanced down at his notes.) 'Hear O Israel the Lord Our God, the LORD IS ONE,' and, to hear and heed the injunction 'to bind these words to your arms and wear them as forefrontlets between thine eyes, and attach them to your door-posts and your gates.' We must teach our children, Judge Lowenstein, at home and away, teach them Sabbath observance, teach them not to covet and lust. This is what my son must learn. Then will you eat to contentment and your animals will eat as well to contentment, and there will be sufficient rain in your fields."

"Mr. Blocker, I understand your son's mother is of the same faith."

Pittipaldi rose as if Farbman's hand had goosed her. "That's correct, Your Honor, Mrs. Blocker is Catholic, and she's been rearing the boy Catholic."

"Judge, a Catholic who's filed for divorce? Who's she kidding? That woman doesn't have a trace of spirituality. You're looking at a woman who prays to Mammon, who would have me work on Sunday so she could go away weekends."

Pittipaldi spoke right up. "This man turns down double-time work despite being in debt, gave his savings to the church when his family was sweltering without an air conditioner."

"Judge, the woman thinks I'm a dray horse."

Judge Lowenstein rapped his gavel twice. "Mr. Blocker, let me ask again. Do you have a question, yes or no?"

"Yes I do, Your Honor. I was trying to ask it when I was interrupted."

"Please ask it."

"Here's my question, Judge. How can we be divorced if this woman is a Catholic? Can you answer me that? The Holy Bible she swore on not a half hour ago says, right in Mark 10, Verse 12—Your Honor can look it up and charge me with perjury if I'm not right—'And if a woman shall put away her husband, and be married to another, she committeth adultery.' So if I'm right, would you explain that to me, Your Honor?"

"I'd have to be crazier than you to get married again." Mrs. Blocker leaned in front of the lawyers to yell at her husband. "And if I ever get that crazy, hopefully someone will shoot me!"

"You hear, Judge, how she derogates? If she talks like this in front of the court, can you imagine what she says behind my back to our son? Judge, now you can see why I have to have custody. Do you think this blaspheming adulteress is going to teach him Sanctus, Sanctus, Sanctus? You understand, Judge? Kadosh, Kadosh, Kadosh."

Lowenstein gavelled him down, called a recess, and left the bench. Mrs. Blocker yelled "See what you do," and Blocker yelled "What I do?" and their lawyers pulled them separately toward the exit.

They were driving home, Farbman and Ann Marie, after a Saturday night dinner she had been too nauseated to eat. They had dined with Harold and his latest, and Farbman had entertained them all with the story of the Blocker divorce and Elmo's courtroom purgation. Ann Marie pulled down the visor mirror to fix her hair only to have a large clump come out in her hand. She began to cry. Farbman, unsure what he could offer by way of comfort, said, "Thank God."

Ann Marie turned to him with a confused look.

"I was afraid it wasn't working."

Ann Marie nodded and wiped her eyes.

The next morning she had all her hair cut off. Leopold wrote a letter to the insurance company justifying a "cranial prosthesis." Ann Marie got the best wig made but then kept it mainly in her closet and took to wearing scarves. Farbman decided it wouldn't hurt if he, too, said a little prayer for her and maybe one for himself. Lying in bed listening to the air conditioner, Ann Marie burrowed beside him.

N.E.D.

Almost a year had passed since Ann Marie was knocked off her horse and into her medical nightmare. It ended as it began, with excruciating belly surgery. It was amazing to Farbman, his wife's capacity—in a larger sense, the human capacity—to endure and adapt. Between surgeries they lived their lives around her twenty-eight-day cycles of puking, ear-ringing chemotherapy. Ann Marie carried on—nauseated, shiny bald, near deaf and, because the drugs slaughtered her immune system, vulnerable to colds and flus nobody else got and that lingered for weeks on end. She confessed she was never quite sure who she was; but felt "just off, like misregistered printing." She detached herself from her poisoned body. Several nights she was awakened by the smell of her own innards.

The decision to proceed with the last operation on Ann Marie was made by default. Leopold had blasted his patient with an experimental three-month round of radiation on top of the chemo, and the lab results indicated that she'd had all she could take. Her body could absorb no more toxicity, so it was time for an exploratory surgery, a "look and see," a final insult. A specialist named Baraff opened her and took dozens of biopsies.

By the fifth day post-op, Farbman began calling Baraff's office for the report that would tell them into which statistical column Ann Marie would be tallied: Days and many calls later, the results came. "N.E.D."

"What's that?" Farbman asked the surgeon's receptionist, shaken by the ominous sounding acronym.

"Your wife," she explained, "is N.E.D."

"I'm sorry," said Farbman. "I don't know what that is, 'N.E.D.'"

"It's good. It means no evidence of disease."

"So what do we do now?"

"The doctor will talk to you. Basically nothing. She'll just be followed by her local oncologist with occasional checkups. But as far as we're concerned, she's cured."

The Farbmans were as terrifyingly adaptable as other humans; and despite a bunch of vacations there was no way out of the day-to-day. The dentist. The supermarket and mall. Jennifer had to go to Brownies, Jason to soccer, and Farbman to work. After a few symphonic chords, the music of their lives became once again like that of most marrieds: it lost its highs and lows and compressed like muzak, albeit in a minor key.

Of course, when they emerged from the cave into sunlight, when they discovered that some unseen authority had granted a reprieve and they were free, they were filled with appreciation. No longer would they take life or their relationship for granted. Farbman held Ann Marie to his chest, lips against her now crewcut hair. They whispered their vows to each other. They would not waste their allotted time in pettiness. They would cherish each other and every minute.

With her returned strength Ann Marie declared that even pushing a grocery cart possessed an exciting, life-affirming quality. But, given time, it became just shopping again. Likewise, packing the kids' lunches stopped being the privilege it had seemed when she first took the chore back from Farbman.

He, on the other hand, was surprised to discover that he didn't like giving up the childcare responsibilities. He returned to full-time work but now fought traffic to have an early dinner with the kids and saw to it that he sat with the children at breakfast.

Sex hadn't come back into his life, but Farbman was reconciled to living celibately. A friendship had evolved with Leah. They spoke almost daily. Farbman commiserated when she got honeymoon cystitis after a weekend with a new lover, or when a director failed to give her a role after five callbacks. Farbman was struck by the oddness of her knowing so many of his thoughts and feelings, of the everyday complications of his existence while occupying no literal space in his life.

Then, one day, they ran into each other on Forty-Sixth Street and for several awkward moments fumbled trying to make conversation. Leah said it felt like she'd encountered a member of her therapy group on the street, that she felt shy in public after all their telephone intimacy. Farbman said, "Let's walk a little."

They headed downtown, through the midtown bustle, around the sidewalk vendors, office boys smoking dope, speeding cyclists, Japanese businessmen, and taxis blocking crosswalks. They strolled through the perfumed gardens of the Sixth Avenue flower district and around the garment center men dragging pipe racks of clothes. In the Village, they stopped in a coffeehouse and shared a cannoli. Then they walked on through Chinatown's narrow streets and across the Brooklyn Bridge and back. Eventually they discovered themselves in Central Park, neither ready to call it quits, both prepared to walk so long as there was a path before them. Farbman knew it was time to stop and that he must not see her again.

Harold had become a constant presence in the Farbmans' lives. The whine of the Porsche engine on Sunday mornings announced his arrival with smoked fish and hot bagels from the city. When summer came, Harold sublet the spare bedroom in the Amagansett rental. Having a doctor around gave Farbman peace of mind, as well as needed cash. He had been spending without thought. Marucci had encouraged Farbman to overdraw his capital account at the firm—they had pried another hundred thousand dollars out of Worrad on the strength of the new work in process. Farbman used it for family trips on every school break, and to renovate the kitchen and bathrooms as Ann Marie had always wanted.

Harold said he was happy for the experience of domesticity. And while he claimed that being able to borrow Jennifer and the dog to troll the beach for women was payment enough, it was obvious to the Farbmans that their confirmed bachelor friend enjoyed being a surrogate parent as well.

Work hadn't changed. He and Marucci still eked and scratched, and if there wasn't enough to cover Farbman's draws, at least they held off creditors and covered payrolls, and they were confident that their day was coming. Deborah and Darlene had been convinced to hang in and Farbman's campaign had rounded up more than two dozen implant victims including a man who had bought leaking silicone calves. There were a number of heavy cases in the pipeline, one of which, the arm lost in Big's hock cutter, was shaping up as a seven-figure deal.

Janet Sodowick had survived her suicide attempt and Ida had resumed calling and writing with a new self-righteous fervor, regularly reminding Farbman that her fears for Janet were well-grounded, prefacing her pleas for assistance with "I know now you believe me when I tell you..." In fact, Farbman didn't believe her, but he took her calls anyway because if he couldn't do anything else he could at least make her feel better.

Using a variety of delaying tactics, both legal and otherwise, Farbman had managed to put off Big's violation hearing until the court finally lost patience and set the trial down peremptorily. The first adjournment had been before Passover, and the case had been carried through the High Holy Days. It would now be heard in a week, on Hashana Rabbah, which Leah said was a second shot at atonement. Farbman certainly hadn't done much with his first: on Yom Kippur he dropped the kids at the children's service for an hour while he took Ann Marie out to lunch; then later they all went to his Aunt Deena's house to break the fast. The legal stalls Farbman had used to avoid Big's trial—motions made to compel production of unneeded and often impossible-to-get discovery, motions to dismiss on abstruse and sometimes even invented legal theories, motions for reconsideration when the motions were denied, applications for leave to appeal on the denied motions for reconsideration—had run tens of thousands of dollars but they had kept Big in business.

That money was also life support for the firm of Farbman & Marucci. It was as though God had been eavesdropping on Farbman's conversations with Leah—conversations in which he had unthinkingly expressed his desire to live in a world in which people behaved with integrity and didn't spend every minute trying to get an edge over someone else—and had decided to punish Farbman by granting his wish with his own clients. Everyone, it seemed, was N.E.D.

It started with a young woman's call from, she said, a water stop on the pony express trail in Wyoming. She had consulted Farbman only two days earlier about signing a prenuptial agreement that had been prepared by her lover's lawyer. It was twenty-five convoluted pages and Farbman had just started what he figured would be at least a five thousand dollar rewrite. The woman said her fiancé and a long stretch of beautiful open range were waiting and wanted to know if she should sign the agreement. Farbman heard horses nickering in the background. The woman was planning on being married tomorrow, or today if they made it to a town with a justice of the peace. No, said Farbman, do not sign. The agreement appears to exclude as premarital assets more than your intended really has, limiting your interest in the future potential profits of this shared enterprise in a fashion that may prove inequitable. No provision has been made for allocation of expenses. There is no provision—

"Thank you," she interrupted, "but I have lived with this man and I have a good notion of what he has and what he is likely to generate within the next few years, and I think that whatever it may be, it's all his. I mean I'm going to be his wife, not his partner. I'm employed. I'm a self-sufficient human being. I intend to continue to support myself and to contribute my fair share to our joint expenses just as I have been doing for the last few years. So stop working, Mr. Farbman, and bill me for the time you've spent. I must go, I've got a long ride ahead."

No sooner had Farbman, still in a state of wonderment, returned to his office from telling Marucci of this remarkable client, than a young robbery defendant who had paid Farbman and Marucci a flat ten thousand dollar fee they had already spent and which they were going to earn with no real work by copping a plea, rejected the deal Farbman had just negotiated for him. The twenty-year-old thief—who had pulled himself up from a Bedford-Sty project to Phillips-Exeter, and then to Brown (where he was a junior)—was facing fifteen years on the robbery and ten for an unloaded gun. He sat behind the thick glass interview window in the jail basement and shook his head when Farbman excitedly reported he'd gotten the prosecutor to forget the gun and downgrade the robbery to larceny. "Your basic purse snatch," Farbman fairly shouted into the telephone. "Don't say no. They've agreed to recommend you be sentenced on a no-minimum basis to the reformatory so you can take classes. If you go to trial and you're convicted, you'll end up in prison with a definite minimum to serve. And, given your slight build and nice brown eyes, you are what the prison cons call fresh meat."

"Mr. Farbman," he asked, "how can a plea bargain not offend your sense of rightness? Either I did the crime and should be punished, or I didn't and shouldn't. Either the state can prove it beyond a reasonable doubt or it can't. No, Mr. Farbman, please try your case and, if you are not up to it, I'll find someone who is."

Within weeks of being lectured on the ethics of criminal procedure, Farbman received a sermon on fair play from an even less likely source: a cuckolded husband. The normally placid executive had erupted angrily when Farbman informed him of the extraordinary package he had won for him. "I didn't ask you to do that," said the man. "You were engaged to negotiate a fair agreement. The property split is lopsided in my favor, and you haven't adequately provided for her support." Not only did Farbman end up with a trivial fee on a large asset case full of potential for expensive acting out, he had to eat about five thousand dollars in time.

But nothing felt as bad as watching the evaporation of a clear liability wrongful death case that would have put a million in his pocket with no heavy lifting. The widow said there was plenty of insurance to cover their needs and she thought the money he'd get them would be tainted. She wouldn't want it, she said.

Farbman, who had resumed his telephone relationship with Leah, told her God was punishing him with a plague of moralism. "Bitter clients are just dropping the rope. If they can't persuade the other party to settle outside the judicial system, they capitulate."

"Why do you ascribe this to heavenly intervention? I can think of lots of good, down-to-earth reasons for avoiding legal battles."

"Of course," said Farbman. "Besides not giving up several years of their lives, they save enough in dollars and energy to go through college or start a business. But the emotional and financial tolls, the interminable delays, and the arbitrariness of the outcome have never before been enough to overcome the human need for revenge or satisfaction, or catharsis."

Blocker, for example, kept finding money to continue his crusade. Finally accepting that he would never win physical custody of his son, he applied to be designated the child's spiritual custodian. Farbman found some recent precedent involving interfaith divorces that seemed to give implicit recognition to the idea of religious custodianship. In those cases the courts had let an out-of-custody parent's religion control the child's upbringing at least where the parties had agreed to raise the child in that religion before the split-up. While distinguishable, the precedent was enough to keep the Blockers' legal forces engaged for another ten months and to force the court to examine what Elmo considered to be moral issues. And, finally, it appeared to have gotten Blocker what he wanted when Lowenstein declared that, for the year remaining until the boy turned eighteen, his father, after consultation with his mother, would have primacy in all decisions touching on the young man's Catholic upbringing. Pittipaldi forwarded the final court order with a neatly ambiguous handwritten note: "At long last we can move on."

Farbman did not have time to consider the implications of the note. He was preoccupied with beating Bigonocco's state violation. The case was to be tried before the Honorable Antonio Bongialine and a jury. His newly-elected Honor made the pretrial ruling that if Big had received proper notice of the violation and failed to contest it in a timely manner, then he'd waived his rights. The only issue to be determined, therefore, was whether Big had been properly served notice.

"If it please the court, before the jury comes in, I have an application that may save us considerable time." Riccardo Ezwipe, career

Assistant Attorney General, rose and handed Farbman and the judge a memorandum.

"What?" Farbman said. "Decide now and hold the hearing after?"

Bongialine rapped his gavel. "Mr. Farbman. You will address your comments to the court. Mr. Ezwipe, what is your application?"

"I have copies of the notices sent to Bigonocco Veal, each one of which is dated—"

"Which proves nothing since there is no evidence of receipt," Farbman interjected.

"Don't interrupt, Mr. Farbman, and sit down please. Continue, Mr. Ezwipe."

"Thank you, Your Honor. As our brief sets forth, there is a legal presumption that letters in the U.S. mails are delivered."

"Yes, it arises on deposit."

"Excuse me, Your Honor"—Farbman was on his feet again—"with all due respect, I wonder when it was that this court last mailed a letter."

"You're interrupting again, Mr. Farbman." Farbman sat down. "But the answer is this morning. And, Mr. Farbman, I would ask that you refrain from addressing this court with the prefatory phrase 'with all due respect' given that what follows invariably establishes that the speaker holds exactly the contrary view.

"Mr. Ezwipe, the point I believe Mr. Farbman is so anxious to make is that the presumption is rebuttable. So you prove the deposit, then it's his burden to adduce sufficient evidence to overcome the presumption. Now, let's get the jury in here and get going."

Mr. Ezwipe called Ms. Patricia Ratsthorpe, Head Supervisor in the Office of the Deputy Chief of Enforcement, signer of the violation notices, as his first witness. Ms. Ratsthorpe said the violation notices were mailed on the dates shown on the copies. Ezwipe smiled at the jury and sat down. Farbman was invited to cross-examine.

Farbman asked her for her title again and then asked for a description of her duties, which she was pleased to give at length.

"That's quite a bit of responsibility," Farbman noted, "all that supervision plus having to type and send all the mail out yourself."

"I have a secretary."

"Oh, you have a secretary. And she types and mails the letters, does she?"

"Yes."

"What is your secretary's name?"

"Ms. Rodriguez."

"Was Ms. Rodriguez your secretary, back then, when these notices were dated?"

"No, Mrs. Lipshultz."

"Did Mrs. Lipshultz type each letter for your signature?"

"No, there are too many, it would be impossible. She used xeroxed forms. She filled in the blanks."

"Then brought them to you for signature?"

"No, they were pre-signed on the form."

"Then she placed them in a U.S. mailbox?"

"No, in a bin for pickup by the mail boys—I mean, persons."

"And if not dropped, or lost, then the mail boys put them in the mail, correct?"

"Yes."

"Now important letters go certified, return receipt requested, right?"

"Objection!" shouted an indignant Ezwipe. "We don't have to prove receipt, just mailing. *Morris v. Worth Insurance:* the citation is in the state's brief."

Farbman sighed audibly, demonstrating for the jurors a wearied patience with his intemperate adversary. "Your Honor, Mr. Ezwipe's reliance on Morris is misplaced. That case involved the cancellation of an insurance policy for nonpayment of premium. Because the money wasn't paid, the insurance contract had been breached. The contract— the parties' agreement—provided for the cancellation notice by mailing. And they proved they had at least deposited the notice in the mails. Here we are dealing with a matter of state action, with a grave issue of constitutional dimension. The state with its awesome power seeks to take the private property of my client without a hearing, under a claim that he got fair notice and waived his rights, that taking his property now is consistent with due process of law."

Bongialine sustained the objection and reminded Farbman that his opportunity to make a speech came at the end of the case.

Farbman was impassioned in summation.

"Where is Mrs. Lipshultz? She is the true witness against my client. We have the right to confront her—to ask her—"Did you type this and put it in the bin? Did Carlos, the mail person, pick it up?" And to ask Carlos, "Did you have a little buzz on? Were you tossing the mail while you listened to hip-hop on your walkperson? Did you drop the mail in the wastebasket?"

He told the jurors that it was not Bigonocco Veal alone on trial here but all of our rights as free citizens of this great nation. Looking into the eyes of those African Americans, Hispanic and Asian faces, Farbman told them he was talking about their rights under the Constitution, under the Magna Carta—wrung by their ancestors from King John in the fields of Runnymede.

After a free lunch and a quick deliberation, the jury asked, Where was Mrs. Lipshultz, where was Carlos? And then, after further instruction, and another closeted half hour, announced they were hung.

Judge Bongialine was disgusted. "I hope you're satisfied, Mr. Farbman," he said. Then he announced that he was exercising the judicial prerogative of entering judgment as a matter of law, that indulging every reasonable inference from the defense proofs was not sufficient to overcome the presumption.

Farbman took it worse than Big, who just shrugged and said, "You done your best." All the way home Farbman tried not to think about the implications of the loss, of what Bigonocco's retainers meant to Farbman's livelihood. As he pulled in his driveway, he reminded himself that he had in his healthy wife and wholesome children something far more precious than cash flow.

Farbman entered through the garage, expecting to find dinner preparations in progress, already relishing his time with the children, found no one, and began hollering from room to room, finally returning perplexed to the kitchen. There he saw some eight-by-ten photos on the kitchen island that he was surprised he hadn't noticed the first time through. The black-and-white glossies were of a man and woman.

Picking up the closest Farbman was astonished to see the man was indisputably himself, pinning Grace Pittipaldi to her car. Pittipaldi's hands were pressed defensively at Farbman's chest, her head tilted away from his face, her face reflecting her struggle to avoid Farbman's advance. The other photos showed more of the same, except for the last, in which, finally released, Pittipaldi could be seen striking Farbman's face with her hand, forcefully enough to swivel his head. Farbman at last heard his family, their voices coming from outside, muffled through the glass patio door. Understanding now the rehearsed, unimaginative way in which Pittipaldi had led him through these embraces, Farbman marveled at her planning and effort in setting him up, at the depth of her antipathy to have gone through with it. But surely the very fact that she had photographic evidence demonstrated her obvious complicity and the falsity of the charge.

The photos were date marked, and there was no possibility that Ann Marie would not remember that she lay tormented in a hospital bed when they were taken.

Farbman looked for a return address on the manila envelope and found none; but the envelope had been clearly addressed to Ann Marie, and there was a typed note inside with the typed signature "Fredo Pittipaldi." The note was brief. The author identified himself as the husband of Grace who was, he told Ann Marie, an attorney acquaintance of her husband. Suspicious that his wife was seeing another man he had taken to following her with his camera. These pictures had been taken in the parking lot across from the Alibi restaurant on Forty-Fourth Street. He regretted having to cause Ann Marie distress, but—

Farbman dropped the photos, gulped some air. With clammy hands he slid the door aside and walked outside.

In the back yard, Ann Marie was on her knees, moaning. Tugging at his mother's left arm, Jason cried, "Please stop, Mommy, please, get up—" About fifteen feet away, Jennifer, her skinny arms squeezing a doll to her chest, rocked herself at heartbeat speed, and stared numbly.

Ann Marie didn't appear to see the children. Farbman concluded her mind had found an escape hatch, had gone somewhere and left behind her contorted face, her body rigid with tension. He was shamed by his wife's naked pain. After all she had endured, it was he who had made her suffer beyond tolerance. The enormity of Farbman's own pain was not, however, sufficient to dislodge him from the excruciating clarity of the scene.

Then she saw him. "Bastard! You fucking bastard," she snarled. "You treat me like dirt." Her fingers clawed up the lawn, and she began with both hands to mash clumps of sod and grass into her crewcut hair. Jennifer screamed. The dog who had been wagging his tail, running from person to person with a rubber toy in his mouth trying to entice someone to play, bolted at the sound of her voice and stared quizzically from a distance. Ann Marie's eyes, ablaze with madness and hate, were fixed on Farbman. "I am dirt now. Okay? Now leave me *alone*!" Jason tried to brush off the pieces of sod, but his mother kept yanking out handfuls and striking herself in the head with them. "Leave me alone!" she screamed. "What else do you want to do to me?" She struck herself harder and harder, the percussive thumps of her blows turning Farbman's stomach queasy. Jason stood to shield his mother and asked his father to go away. Ann Marie, her face blotched and smeared with shades of brown and green, began just socking herself repeatedly in the head with both fists. Farbman told the children to go inside, he'd take care of their mother. But Jennifer just cried harder and no one moved.

III

VINCERE AUT MORI

MENS REA

Farbman believed that, painful as it was, his marital crisis was a refiner's fire. Not only their love for Jason and Jennifer, but a shared history that included overcoming family rejection, financial stress, and Ann Marie's terrifying illness created a bond too profound to be broken. The adulterants would burn off and leave their relationship not only intact but purified.

Indeed, Farbman fantasized that this cloud of unhappiness would evaporate as quickly as it had descended upon them. He kept this idea to himself, allowing Ann Marie her anger, respecting her silences with him, appreciating her civility around the children. Then, one evening, overcome with remorse and a longing to undo the hurts, to toss out the baggage, he tried to express his feelings to Ann Marie. He said he was reminded of the way a friend had put it: you wake up one day and find this pile of shit that's built up in your relationship, and you just want to step around or walk out on—

"You're the pile of shit I'd like to walk out on," yelled Ann Marie, firing the night-table clock she had been setting straight at his head. Farbman ducked, and the clock shattered against the wall behind him.

"I hate you. I hate my life with you. My stomach turns when I think of it. How I let you give me cancer. Don't tell me about suffering in silence while you're getting advice from your, quote, friends. Why don't you go be with your friend and leave me and my kids alone."

Shaken, Farbman didn't protest—even knowing silence in the face of such accusation could legally be construed as admission. All he said was, These are my kids, too, and I'd run to Pago Pago before I'd let them be taken from me.

After that incident, Farbman bit his tongue for a few days. When he felt she was more receptive he attempted, with Marucci's assistance, to persuade her that he'd been framed. He was more or less successful. She accepted that he'd called the bluff of Pittipaldi's attempted extortion, but said she didn't understand the woman's motive to go after him to begin with. When Farbman pursued his fuzzy explanation, Ann Marie said she really wasn't interested, that all his good excuses didn't matter. No, whether Farbman did or didn't carry on with this woman was beside the point. The sad truth was that if it weren't her it would have been somebody else, and Ann Marie had no doubt that there had been others and would he please spare her the insult of a denial for, if there were not others, then Farbman was truly pathetic given how he behaved as if his wife were dead, or, at least, irrelevant.

"Ask anyone who knows you," she said. "You walk around with 'available' written all over your face."

Despite his confidence that everything would conclude happily with Ann Marie, he had begun a workout program which Farbman recognized was, at some precautionary level, preparation for bachelorhood. He had signed up with a distempered man named Lamont Johnson, who had hypertrophied pectorals you could rest beer cans on and abdominals that could clench and release quarters.

Lamont let Farbman know right from jump street that he wasn't into no bullshit, from which Farbman understood that he only trained clients who were motivated. Farbman wasn't about to challenge the man's authority. Lamont carried 235 pounds on a five-ten frame with five and a half percent body fat by galvanometric reading—six using skin calipers—either way about the same as a world-class marathoner or famine victim. When he demonstrated an exercise, Farbman could observe individual fibers of muscle contracting under a lattice of bulging veins. Lamont's body was an anatomical chart. The question Farbman kept asking himself was why he was selecting Lamont when there were at least a half dozen other trainers at his club he could have, including several hard-bodied women with big wholesome smiles whom he would see gently leading their clientele from machine to machine, chatting and laughing as they made cleavage-revealing bends to add and subtract plates.

Lamont believed in making even weight training aerobic. "The weights is secondary," said Lamont, "yo' heart and lungs is firstary." Once Farbman was huffing from a half hour ride on the bicycle to nowhere, Lamont moved him so fast from set to set that Farbman was perpetually sucking wind. His heart pounded. He could wring quarts of sweat from the three shirts he wore every session.

It was futile to count repetitions; Lamont told Farbman when he'd had enough, a determination he made entirely independent of numbers and of Farbman's twitching legs, his grunts and grimaces. ("Don' bother making them ugly faces, you still got ten more," he would say.) And on days when Farbman foolishly let it slip either that he felt tired or had been eating too much, or that he felt strong for that matter, Lamont would squinch his eyes and declare: "I got sumpin' fo' yo' ass," and Farbman would be introduced to a whole new way of brutalizing himself.

This was propitious conditioning, for Lamont wasn't the only one who had something in store for Farbman's unsuspecting ass.

Farbman spent his days trying himself in the court of his own conscience on Ann Marie's terrible indictment of causing her cancer as well as the lesser charge of being faithless. Anxious to own up, Farbman knew that Pittipaldi wasn't the issue, but his relationship with Leah was another matter. He could not deny her importance to him, the depth of the feelings they shared. If they weren't having sex, didn't he wish they were? Even though the law didn't punish forbidden thoughts without forbidden acts, wasn't he morally accountable for his inner life?

To Ann Marie's charge that he had caused her cancer Farbman pled guilty. He figured he had made her miserable in their marriage and that her unhappiness must have depressed her immune system and made her susceptible. Farbman had even raised the subject with Harold, who confirmed his fears. Harold explained that the reason married people live longer and healthier lives is because they're supportive, and that scientists recently found that key markers of immunological strength were lowered after couples had angry exchanges.

Then, after another sleep-deprived night, Farbman left his bedroom with Ninja stealth to telephone Leah in the diffused, blue-gray light of early morning.

"It's me. Can you talk?"

"I can listen."

Rain cascaded over the edge of a neglected gutter and splashed loudly in a puddle next to the house on its way through the basement wall into Jennifer's new playroom carpet.

Farbman took a breath. "Ann Marie says I gave her cancer."

"Damn," said Leah. And before Farbman could concur, she added, "My blanket is soaked. It must have been raining in all night." She asked Farbman to hold on while she closed the window. He could hear her noisy efforts, then the window bang shut. She picked up the receiver again. "Well, I'm awake now. So what do you say?"

"I think it's true," said Farbman.

"So tell me, how did you give it to her?"

"What do you mean?"

"I mean, did it go directly from you to her? Or from you to God to her?"

"You think this is funny?"

"Not at all. I feel for you. That's why I think it's important that you tell me exactly how you did it."

Farbman explained the science to her, and what Harold had said.

"Nice friend you got."

"He is. Harold just tells the truth."

"His truth. How about taking responsibility for one's own emotions? While it may be true that some personalities are cancer prone, can you accept that a given behavior by person 'A' does not cause an emotion in person 'B'? That person 'B' has a range of options in reacting—or not reacting—to what person 'A' does?"

"You're right," said Farbman, "I'm probably making too much of her comment."

"You know, sometimes you piss me off you get so dumb."

Farbman thanked Leah and they said good-bye. He reflected that her support was so important to him maybe she was, in a sense, what Lamont would call a firstary cause of the breakup.

Legalisms aside, Farbman considered whether he should be held morally accountable for his thoughts. Certainly Jesus would hold him accountable. How many times had Blocker quoted Farbman from the Sermon on the Mount? Not only, said Jesus, is it a sin to sneak off to a motel, you've sinned in the lusting alone. Not only can't you steal your neighbor's Porsche, you must not even covet it.

Judaism, on the other hand, as Leah pointed out, never punished thought alone—"what lawyers term the *mens rea*," Farbman interjected—only the forbidden act. "The flip side, however, is that you don't get credit for thinking good thoughts if you don't translate them into action," which was perhaps an even more central problem in their marriage.

The failure to make good on his intentions, was that not the true firstary cause of their coming apart? Yet, in retrospect, Farbman realized that it was his effort to reconcile that pushed Ann Marie into open warfare. He had committed the unpardonable, distinctly Jewish act of confronting an issue with her directly. This, despite the cautionary advice of his mother-in-law when she heard they were having some difficulties. "I just hope you're not talking about it," she said. There was nothing like bringing problems into the open to start a couple on the inexorable path of total misunderstanding and eventual breakup.

But it was a beautiful winter day less than a week later, with a rare warming sun and Farbman was overcome with the awareness that there were only so many such mornings in life, and he and Ann Marie were spending their time sunk in misery. And why should Jason and Jennifer grow up with their notion of love shaped by their parents' poor example? Why not, he thought, just be loving?

So it was that Farbman, blinded by the sun's light, and pressed on by a sense of waste and the desire to retrieve what they once had, threw caution aside and shared his insight with Ann Marie. What he got was her quick agreement that yes, life was, God knows, too short, and her promise not to spend another unhappy minute of it with Farbman.

It was Constable Wolchensko who delivered Ann Marie's opening salvo. Joy informed Farbman that Wolchensko was at the reception desk with papers he had to give to him personally, which Farbman immediately understood meant that he was being sued. Walking out, Farbman tried to imagine which creditor could have finally lost patience with his dilatory tactics, then considered the possibility that Marucci had stiffed yet another forwarding attorney out of his third.

Wolchensko had a bad cold. The stolid, rotund process server said he was sorry Farbman was having marital troubles. At this, Farbman saw the receptionist look up, and he knew that he might as well have had his divorce announced on the radio.

"You used to just serve the papers, now you read them, too?"

Wolchensko shrugged. "Hey, all's I said was I was sorry."

"Okay," said Farbman, "you're sorry. Just give 'em to me."

Wolchensko wiped his runny nose with the back of his hand but only after he'd dripped on the summons, leaving a wet splotch large enough, Farbman observed, to cover half of "Farbman" and the first letters of "Defendant."

Farbman walked into the men's room to read the paper. He skimmed the uncontrovertible facts—his marriage, the two issue born thereof, the length of their residence in the jurisdiction, that property both real and personal had been acquired during the coverture—and then turned to the averments, the *public* averments, of his marital misconduct. He wondered what Ann Marie could have come up with. While New York laws did not create much of an obstacle to divorce, for a fault ground you still had to allege some wrongdoing, no matter how subjectively the plaintiff was permitted to view it.

Composing such allegations sometimes required a bit of creativity on the lawyer's part. On the other hand, Ann Marie and her lawyer knew Farbman wouldn't contest the divorce and, more importantly, that he was an attorney who worked at the courthouse where any castigations would be read and circulated and where even the most innocuous grievances could give him a label that would haunt him forever. It was a balancing problem, such drafting: being delicate and professionally sensitive while still being legally sufficient. Farbman did not recall Ann Marie's lawyer, Byron Silverdorf—a rabid Wolverine whose bizarre lawyering had become so notorious a benchmark for sleazy litigating that other craven advocates were often compared in "Silverdorf units"— as a particularly skilled draftsman. But if he and Ann Marie erred, Farbman believed it would be on the side of restraint. Something like his failing her emotionally, he speculated.

What Ann Marie swore in lettered paragraphs was:

That virtually from the inception of their marriage Farbman had emotionally and physically abandoned her and their two children in order to spend his time socializing with friends, and pursuing adulterous relationships;

That Farbman had deserted her sexually, refusing to have conjugal relations with her unless aberrantly performed and then when she was stricken with cancer rejected her completely to her great humiliation and despair;

That he had coerced her into making unsound and speculative investments, which had brought about their financial ruination;

That he had threatened to take their children and flee beyond the jurisdiction of this court, specifically to the Island of Tutuila.

Wherefore Ann Marie demanded not only a divorce, alimony, child support, and a fair separation of their property, but that she have sole custody of their children, that Farbman be restrained from returning to the marital home or communicating with her about any matters unrelated to their children on sanction of incarceration, and that his visitation, once his passport was turned into the clerk of the court, be circumscribed or supervised. She also asked to resume the name Jamison.

Farbman booted a half-open stall door with every ounce of force he had in his body, making a huge, explosive bang and eliciting a scream from the unseen user of the adjacent toilet who wanted to know what the fuck his problem was.

Farbman did not say, but his problem was that he felt sick to his stomach and thought the top of his head was about to blow off. These were lies, all lies. How could Ann Marie have sworn to their truthfulness? Murder, assault, these were human responses anyone was capable of, but lying, like stealing, took a unique type. A man swore before God with his heart and soul. And with his balls: the root word for "testify" and its variants was "testes," from the Roman practice of having a man hold them when he swore. Ann Marie was kicking Farbman and the entire Western legal system right in the nuts.

He ran to find Marucci, who took one look at his partner's face and made an abrupt end to the call he was on.

Farbman tossed the divorce papers on Marucci's desk and walked to the window where he stared trembling, blindly, into the distance. "Do you believe Silverdorf? I'll get his ticket lifted. A lawyer's got an obligation to make some inquiry into the facts before he signs his name to a complaint."

"What are you saying," said Marucci, "that he didn't talk to Ann Marie?"

"No, but it's obvious that the allegations are all lies and that had he probed a little, he would have known it. Jesus, I've never even heard of Tutuila."

"It's in the South Pacific. Pago Pago is there."

"It is? Jesus, I don't fucking believe it."

"So, when are you going to tell me about the kinky sex. Let me guess—you're a cross-dresser, right? You like to put on heels, something flouncy—"

"Don't, Marucci."

"Hey, congratulations."

Farbman looked at him.

"You are now a full-fledged matrimonial litigant. Your wife has hired the Jewish equivalent of Mad Dog Cole and has demonstrated in the first fifteen minutes of your case that she lies better than you tell the truth and that she clearly intends to annihilate you. She's already got you half out of your mind. Listen to you muttering like some street-corner psychotic—which is to say like every other divorce client—about your spouse's rotten tactics and her lowlife lawyer.

In a matter of weeks, Farbman noted other lawyers' heads turning whenever he entered the back room of the Oyster Bar. Farbman started lunching elsewhere and began to dread courthouse appearances.

PAPERS

At first, like thousands of other spouses on the receiving end of a divorce, Farbman didn't want to accept that he was at war. He trailed Ann Marie around the house imploring her to consider the children and the terrible effects breaking up would have on them. She said, You should have thought of that. He explained to her back that she didn't know what she was doing hiring Silverdorf, who only poured gasoline on fires, who would waste all of their assets with his scorched earth methods, that they should sit down with a counselor.

"Counseling! Talk about waste."

"Then what about a mediator?"

"What chance would I have in mediation with you, a divorce lawyer?"

It took Marucci to point out that Ann Marie was simply declining to fight within his logic. Countering reason with emotion should have been a familiar tactic, he'd seen it enough in his clients' disputes: Blocker was skilled at the game; Mironovic's wife was a grandmaster.

While Farbman tried desperately to bring an implacable foe to the bargaining table, while he assessed and assumed blame and developed a methodology for settling their differences, Ann Marie was marshalling troops. She intuited the military adage that says talk logistics not strategy. While he was philosophizing about divorce and arguing for reason, Ann Marie was rifling through and photocopying his papers. Before hiring the lawyer she had hired a detective to procure Farbman's phone bills and credit card records. Not only did she engage Silverdorf, but she preemptively interviewed a dozen top litigators, paying each a consulting fee in order to preclude them from representing Farbman.

Farbman was not, however, without resources. To counter Silverdorf he hired a half-black, half-Jewish, Ferrari-driving legal thug known as Predacious Wolf. If looking British and thinking Yiddish meant success fifty years ago, Wolf had the combination for his generation. Jurors loved the street persona behind which he hid his Columbia Law Review credentials; judges deferred to him fearing allegations of discrimination if they treated him with their customary discourtesy; clients of all stripes stood in line for him. It took a non-refundable twenty-five grand to get his attention and his four-hundred-dollar hours ran up like gallons on a gas pump.

After interrupting the initial interview to take calls from a client, an adversary, and a scalper confirming center court seats for the Knicks' game that evening, Wolf told Farbman that he liked him and that it couldn't be much fun sitting on the other side of the desk. He knocked ten percent off his rate and said he would call Silverdorf right away to see if they couldn't move toward a quick and amicable resolution both sides could live with. Farbman nodded as though this wasn't exactly the same pap he fed his own clients.

Unfortunately, Wolf and Silverdorf played tag for three weeks and, by the time they hooked up, Ann Marie's first application had been filed and served. Farbman stopped work and spent days filling entire legal pads with longhand responses to her allegations which he sent off to his lawyer.

When Farbman received Wolf's version of Farbman's version of the facts, he was upset even before he read it. Farbman had asked that correspondence sent to his office be marked "personal, confidential" or else someone besides him might open it. Wolf had assured Farbman it would be done, and he had even called his secretary over the intercom to give her the instruction in Farbman's presence.

Nonetheless, they'd forgotten and there was the draft affidavit opened and lying on the top of Farbman's stack of mail, Joy having recognized the new priority classification.

The affidavit had been prepared in opposition to Ann Marie's motion that the court act immediately to grant a laundry list of gratuitous requests: to compel Farbman to pay or bring current "roof charges"—that is, the mortgage, local property taxes, utilities, and the like—and weekly child and spousal support through the probation department on a two-week warrant status; to restrain him from disposing of any assets until final hearing; to fix a schedule when he could visit with his children and enjoin him from conducting that visitation in the presence of unrelated members of the opposite sex; to require him to place his passport in the custody of the court; to restrain him from harassing Ann Marie; to have him advance ten thousand dollars to engage an accountant of Ann Marie's selection to audit his partnership books; and to pay twenty thousand to Ann Marie's lawyer so she could litigate on an equal footing with him.

The application itself was not unusual. Indeed, it was a routine instrument of debasement for any man naive enough to believe he could separate from his wife and still continue to be a father to his children, or be respected as the otherwise responsible provider he'd been to that point in his family's lives. Farbman had the same sort of boilerplate formatted in his computer.

But it had never occurred to him that his name might be typed into the blank fields. After all, he was not like the hundreds of men to whom he had, without a second thought, addressed the same motion. Farbman cherished his children. It had never occurred to him to do anything other than maintain his family. The notion of abandoning them or even of running away with them was so bizarre as to be unimaginable. He didn't harass Ann Marie, and being restrained would be a completely unnecessary humiliation. And paying thirty thousand in retainers for Ann Marie's professional fees—over and above the twenty thousand Farbman had to come up with for his lawyer—while expecting him to bring the household nut current was completely unrealistic. Ann Marie knew there was no way he could come up with that kind of money.

The voluminous affidavit filed by Ann Marie in support of her application was another story. Not routine at all but a uniquely crafted sixty-seven point justification of her position, in which each point was neatly arranged in a numbered paragraph under the appropriate heading: "Defendant's Diversion of Marital Assets"; "Defendant's Concealment of Income"; "The Threat of Domestic Violence." The listing was preceded by a lengthy introduction entitled "Background Facts." In this preamble was described, also in trenchant, numbered paragraphs, Ann Marie's history of their life together. In the same neutral manner in which she provided their demographics—ages, date of marriage, names and ages of children—she summed up what it was like being married to the brute: the loneliness she'd endured; the humiliations; the burden of all of the responsibilities of homemaking and child-rearing.

Farbman grew dizzy after two pages and had to close his eyes. He understood that people were messy. The law recognized patterns of normative conduct, but peoples' lives generally failed to fall into these patterns, and it was the lawyers' job to marshall the sloppy facts of reality into a legally sympathetic version. A trial, if prepared properly, was always a well-scripted morality play.

The rules of the game demanded that the facts be treated as sacred. But the law also recognized "facts" as events or things that only existed as they were ultimately determined by the arbiter: the judge or jury. Until then, each side was understood to have a view of things which was colored, subjective, biased. The law recognized long before art that the mere act of framing some discrete portion of the world—a pile of discarded clothes, a few flowers in a field, the edge of a rusted can—implied the imposition of some consciousness that necessarily altered reality. The system in which Farbman labored presupposed that there existed no absolute truth but only truth and countervailing truth: that justice depended on the friction of necessarily subjective advocates to produce something resembling the truth.

So how could Farbman have expected to read his own truth in Ann Marie's lawyer's reassembly of her view of things? How could he not have been prepared to see "facts and events" describing how he had always been an indifferent or absent or emotionally abusive parent and husband? an inconsistent, irregular provider?

That's what Wolf rhetorically demanded as Farbman paused in his raging telephone call. "Silverdorf's only doing what he always does and what you probably do yourself—he's taking advantage of his first opportunity to annihilate your character. He wants to let the court know who the bad guy is right off so that she'll hold some bias against you through the remainder of the case."

"What do you mean 'she?'" Farbman asked.

"Your case has been assigned to LaFarge."

"No, no!" cried Farbman. "You've got to get it away from her. 'A,' she's an unbeatable combination of stupidity and arrogance—vicious, ugly, explosive, and unstable. 'B,' she hates me. No, make that 'A.'"

"I already spoke to her law clerk, who, you will be pleased to know, has been asking me about job prospects at my firm, and had her ask LaFarge if she didn't think recusal was appropriate considering that you appear before her."

"And—?"

"She didn't. She said she would have your cases distributed to the other judges in the Family Part."

Wolf said he knew that Farbman wanted to stay in the house until an agreement was signed, but Silverdorf had called to ask if he wouldn't do the gentlemanly thing and get out now. Silverdorf would give him a signed non-abandonment clause and some generous visitation.

"Silverdorf is telling me to get out of my own house? That wharf rat is going to decide when I can see my kids? Tell him to go fuck himself!"

"I know how you feel," said Wolf, telling Farbman to hold on, yelling to his secretary that he'd be there in two minutes, "but what's the alternative? It's obvious you're being set up for a domestic violence claim. You'll end up tossed out with no notice, no chance to find a place, to get some furniture, or anything else except some personal effects, and, worst of all, with a limited visitation schedule that will quickly become the status quo and, after a few years of litigation, just ratified at the final hearing. The possibility of a real shared parenting arrangement will be shot."

Harold agreed. "Look at you," he said. "Our last match it was a pulled back. Today it's a crick in your neck. The one thing Reich taught us—"

"What Reich?"

"The lunatic with the Orgone box, not Theodore—that what's going on in your mind gets laid down in your muscles and nerves. You've got spasms. You want an infarct? Cancer?"

Farbman grimaced as he attempted a slow rotation of his head in each direction. He thought the steam was starting to work. He told Harold he'd had enough of people summing up his life.

"Don't your clients sum up their lives for you?"

"Sure," he said. "I'm not about to spend the rest of my life in a dark room with him and Brahms, one said recently. Another said, 'I married this slim woman I met on a beach and two years later it's like I'd pulled the plug on an inflatable life raft.'"

"Look," said Harold, "in the few years left before your body really starts to betray you, before you come to think of pleasure as just the absence of pain, you don't want to expend your life and whatever is left of your assets in this kind of fight."

"Jesus, Harold! You think I started this? That I'm the one who demanded Ann Marie get out of her home and give up her children."

"Your marriage is over. Are you planning on living together post-divorce? Greeting each other's Saturday night dates?"

"I'm not leaving until she agrees I'm an equal parent."

"Listen to me," Harold said. "This is not about the children. This is about who's right. It's about power. Ann Marie needs to feel in charge. Give her custody and you'll get more time with the kids than you want."

Farbman said Harold didn't know what the fuck he was talking about and that he should not presume to give advice in the non-chemical side of human relationships. But he thanked him anyway; all the urging to give in to Ann Marie and her lawyer's bullying had strengthened Farbman's resolve.

He went home and stayed there. His plan was to care for his children, counting on his presence to keep Ann Marie away much of the time. He called Marucci and informed him that he had ordered a fax and a direct line to the office. He would come in occasionally to get and return files, or they could be messengered. His priority was not letting Ann Marie out-position him in the custody fight and he'd schedule his work around that. He had signed on as an indoor soccer coach and would do Little League in the spring. Farbman would drop the kids at school in the morning and be there to pick them up when it let out. He'd been reconstructing on the calendar the days he'd prepared meals for the kids and was totaling them up so when the time came he'd blow her away with quantified, objective standards. What he needed now was a refresher five thousand for Wolf, five to retain mental health experts and about five more to clean up some old bills, including past due car and mortgage payments.

Marucci said all that was great but Farbman was needed at the firm. He did know what time of year it was, didn't he?

Because a menorah was getting equal billing with a nativity scene on the front lawn of the town hall, Farbman knew it was Hanukkah. While he wasn't clear on the Greek-Syrians or why their assault on the Jews was special, he did know that Hanukkah meant that the happy time of Christmas was coming soon. Christmas was joyous because carriers liked to clean up their reserves at year-end, which meant a lot of settled cases and a good first quarter cash flow. Juries were more likely to acquit and make larger awards to plaintiffs. Matrimonial clients spent thousands and thousands of dollars at Christmas break to fight over every minute of school recess visitation.

Marucci told Farbman they had a dozen cases on the trial list. As for money, forget it. They had to talk, said Marucci.

They would, promised Farbman. They'd have dinner next time he came in, probably in a couple of weeks when he had secured the home front. Right now he had to get Jennifer to gymnastics before her mother came home and took her.

Farbman had to get some money. He had avoided calling Michael for months, but the most recent bad news report from the Houston partnership offered an opportunity.

"Look, I just broke from a special situation meeting with our top analysts to take your call."

"Michael, you have a script in front of you—I just read that exact line in a *Journal* exposé on boiler-room tactics."

"Hey, you asshole, I've got a situation here that is incredible. I'm not officially allowed to offer it to you yet—"

"Then don't. Just send me some info when you've got it."

"I've got it, but we've isolated a timely situation here and it would be a shame not to act on it while we send things back and forth, you know."

"First let's talk about the one you already sold me. I just got the latest bulletin from the developer, and my impression is the thing is going nowhere. Can I assume you're going to refund the limited partners' contributions?"

"Wait, wait, hold on. First, there is every reason to believe the project will be completed. The developer is just reporting delays. The report sounded pessimistic, but that's only because some lawyer drafted it. You certainly know what legal bullshit's all about. Second, the initial financing was already spent on all the soft costs, which is why you now own a valuable piece of property, fully approved, completely designed, ready to be built."

"Good. Then you or your company can just buy our unit back."

"Well, we don't buy for our own account, but if you really want to sell—and I'm telling you you'd be making a big mistake—I'll put your unit on a list for sale."

"Do it. Yesterday."

"Okay. Okay. It's done. Ann Marie and the kids good?"

"Great."

"Great. By the way I understand you and cousin Leah have become friends." Farbman could see the smirk a thousand miles away.

"I talk to her now and then."

"That's not the way I hear it."

"Yeah? Well, I don't know what you hear and I'm not even sure what I'm hearing."

"Nothing," said Michael. "Lighten up."

"Get my money back."

"I'll do what I can."

One morning after Farbman had been home about two weeks, as he sat in the kitchen reviewing materials from an Effective Parenting course on the best way to stop sibling battles, he heard Ann Marie making repeated trips up and down the second floor hallway. Farbman went to investigate and found his closets and his dresser drawers had been emptied and his stuff piled on the guest room bed. He was at Ann Marie's closets without a second's hesitation. A moment later he was dumping armfuls of dresses, blouses, jeans, sweaters, and shoes over the bannister, making a satisfying heap in the center hall below. Then he pulled each of her bureau drawers out and watched their overturned contents fall the same fifteen feet.

When he was finished and there wasn't an uncovered square of marble, Ann Marie appeared with a Polaroid, informed him that the police were on their way, and began snapping shots from every angle.

Heart pounding, his head feverish with the dead-end effort to find a way to undo what he'd done, Farbman fled, cursing himself. He drove until he found himself at the deserted beach of a state park and sat in his car in the parking lot weighing the enormity of his blunder. After a while he paced the hard, flat sand, overcome again by the notion he had entered another world that had emerged between seconds.

Farbman finally decided he would return home at dinnertime; with the children there Ann Marie wouldn't make a scene. They would all fall back into the routine of homework and baths and bedtime readings, and he'd apologize afterwards and deliver the speech he'd spent the afternoon crafting in his head, about how he wanted to keep their marriage intact, but if she didn't, then he would like to separate in a way that let her realize her goals, allowed both of them some dignity and spared their children as much pain as possible.

The garage door opener didn't work. The back door was locked and bolted. Farbman rang the front doorbell and pounded on the door with his fist, pointing and yelling when Jennifer and Jason appeared at the window.

Two Rockville Centre squad cars were there in seconds. A moon-faced patrolman, who couldn't have been more than twenty, handed Farbman a restraining order. It allowed him to remove personal effects in the presence of the police. Clearly impatient, they told Farbman he had about ten minutes, but he could talk to a lawyer about how to get anything else he wanted. Farbman said he was a lawyer. They said, Well, then you know. Jennifer was crying. Jason asked if his dad were under arrest.

After tossing underwear, shirts, and toiletries into a suitcase, he hurried through the house, unable to decide what to take. An impulse sent him to the back of his study closet for a shoebox with childhood mementos; from his desk he took homemade Father's Day cards, a clay ashtray Jason made him at camp, and his passport, and from the dining room sideboard the plastic bag with his grandfather's tefillin. At the last instant he remembered to get a couple of suits.

An hour later he was sitting on a Holiday Inn bed examining his collection of bennies, clearies, cat's eyes, and aggies. He called Marucci, who had been trying to reach him all day. They had to sit down and talk. Farbman said he'd be either with Wolf or looking for a place the next day, but he'd meet Marucci after work at the Alibi.

Farbman was a half-hour late. Marucci had been early and was fortifying himself the whole time. Marucci excused himself as Farbman was getting seated, and after fifteen minutes a worried Farbman followed him into the men's room. He found him genuflecting before a toilet bowl that appeared to be filled with blood. Marucci reached hurriedly for the flush lever. Farbman tried to help him up, but Marucci yanked his arm away, saying he was fine.

Marucci walked unsteadily back to their table, where his mood seemed to lift. The waiter appeared, and Marucci said, "No more Bourbon. Get me something with cream in it. And Kahlua.

"Now, where were we? I believe I was breaking the news to you."

"What news?"

Marucci looked confused. "What I've been telling you. I can't take any more parenting. Look, I know it's not your fault you're so controlling. You mean well. It's just me. I've got to see what I can do on my own. You know. Don't look at me that way, like this is some kind of surprise. I never made a secret of it. I tried to give you my resignation numerous times in the past. You can't deny that." The coffee-colored drink was placed before him, and Marucci looked up. "Thank you, wait, wait," he shouted as the waiter started to leave. Marucci took a deep swallow. "Wonderful," he said. "Better bring another just like it."

"We're building something here, Marucci," Farbman interjected. "Together. A firm. I don't want to practice law without you."

"Hey," said Marucci, "You don't want to practice law, period. How many times have I heard you say you'd like to be a laborer, sweating in the sun, or freezing in the winter or whatever. Me, I've done that. My parents have done that and theirs before them. I'm thrilled to make money with pieces of paper. I like telling people I'm a lawyer."

"You're full of shit, Marucci. You're always talking about getting out just like me and every other trial lawyer. There's hardly a morning goes by you don't walk in and try to convince me with some get-rich-quick scheme so we can stop practicing."

"My schemes? Why don't we discuss how much you've given to your friend Michael we'll never see again."

"That's a major development in Houston. I don't think you want to make a comparison between that and unstainable neckties or eating road kill."

Marucci swallowed the rest of his drink and wiped his mouth with the back of his hand. "You'll do just fine without me."

"C'mon, Marucci, what's got into you?"

"No, no. No discussion. No convincing. I'm too easily swayed by you. It's done. I did it."

"Did what?"

"Broke up the partnership. Thank you," Marucci said to the waiter, picking up a fresh drink.

"What are you talking about? You're just withdrawing now."

"I rented new space, split up the assets—and the files, of course."

"How could you draft an agreement before we even discussed what's fair?"

"I didn't. I just separated our interests."

"You mean you've actually, *physically* moved stuff out of our offices?"

"Hey, you start raising your voice, I'm leaving," said Marucci, draining his glass.

"Okay," said Farbman, taking a deep breath. "Look, this isn't like walking out on your ex-wife—just run down to the corner for the paper and never come back. We're both on the lease. We're both on the note and the bank has a lien on everything, including our accounts receivable and work-in-process."

"Well, you're wrong. I've been to the bank, told them what's happening, and made a deal."

"Worrad made a deal with you without consulting me?"

"You betcha. In fact, Almighty Oz, Mr. Know-it-all, at the moment they only want to deal with me. They took a look at our last statement and saw how overdrawn your capital account is. If it weren't for me, they would have called the loan and moved to have a receiver appointed to liquidate the firm. This would include having our contingent fees deposited into an escrow to assure that the bank and our other creditors are paid off in an orderly fashion. I explained that you've basically been part-time because of Ann Marie's problems and they understood. But they only agreed not to pull the plug s'long as I am designated the partner in charge of the winding up and that a percentage of each fee goes off the top to reduce debt. The rest is divided so much for overhead and a fee for me for servicing the files and any profit left over would be split between us. But you don't actually take any cash until you've paid back your overdrawn capital.

"Also, did I say, they want you to sign a note to the firm for your overdraft so that the partnership balance sheet looks—I don't know—balanced, I guess."

"And how am I supposed to live, and my family, while everything is going to you and the bank, huh? You know what my support obligation is; you're the one keeps saying don't worry we'll cover it."

"Jesus, what do you think I am? First, you have your own files, all the hourly billed stuff, and I've got a plan to share work with you on some of the implant cases." Marucci stood up abruptly then, attempted to drink out of his already emptied glass, and stuck his hand out at Farbman. "I want us to still be friends when this is over. I value our friendship. I think this is the only way our friendship has a chance. I think maybe we got too close. It's hard to stay good friends when you get really close to someone. You know what I mean?" Marucci got teary. "Don't look at me like that. I know what you've done for me. I would never hurt you. I swear on the lives of my children."

Farbman hurried into the building and signed the lobby register, his heart sinking as the night security man asked if the movers had forgotten something. He braced himself as he entered the office. Nothing was there. In the evidence room there were only shelves, a few dust balls, and Munro's leg, propped up in a corner. Farbman knew what he'd find in the rest of the place, but he looked anyway, beginning with the file room. Except for about eight feet of red envelopes there were only expanses of empty lateral drawers. Farbman could have recited the names on the remaining files with his eyes closed: Janet Sodowick, Elmo Blocker (divorce, not the injury), Amber Fleischman, Rhonda Pond, and every other client to whom hours were owed. With Big's license taken, all income-generating matters or cases with potential were gone.

Joy had left a typed note on Farbman's chair advising him that they'd received a trial notice in the Fleischman case and that the file was prepped as he'd taught her. Witnesses had been notified, although she didn't know what to do about Turk Horowitz and figured Farbman would want to talk to him. Exhibits were pre-marked. If he had any questions she could be reached at Marucci's new office.

On Farbman's desk was a stack of photocopied form letters signed by Farbman and Marucci clients directing the transfer of their files to Marco Marucci. The clients had been asked to indicate their choices by marking 'x' in a box next to either his name or Marucci's. Farbman could hear Marucci's voice explaining, as he had to the bank, how with Farbman being only part-time because of his personal problems, how he, Marucci, would be assuming responsibility for that client's case. Farbman recalled how quickly and industriously his former partner had moved to assist him. How touched Farbman had been. How much peace of mind he had had knowing Marucci was taking care of all these matters.

LEFT BEHIND

Farbman awoke shaking with night terrors. For an instant he was uncertain where he was. Then a hole in the window shade allowed the neon light of the Cuban-Chinese diner across the street to dimly illuminate his room and Farbman recognized his new home: a cramped, furnished studio on Fifteenth Street with bad plumbing and an inoperable stove filled with roaches. The wallpaper was a faded turquoise, an underwater pattern of fish and seaweed. He spilled a Librium into his palm from the bedside bottle and swallowed it dry.

Farbman decided he had enough of a future to force himself out the door for a run. Despite the still desolate look of deep winter, Leah said Jews were celebrating the first rising of the sap, a holiday of trees. Farbman wanted to believe in a hidden stirring of life. He succeeded to the point of getting dressed and lacing his sneakers. Then he turned punitive and threw himself out into the dark, cold West Chelsea street. A wet snow was falling. Farbman had to place each step carefully as he ran downtown past the loading docks of the meat markets, past men huddled around ash can fires whose circumstances no longer seemed so far removed from his own.

Painful images pursued him as he ran. Jennifer now called herself "divorced." During her second grade play, she'd looked around for her father and waved and then, on the other side of the room, for her mother and waved again. Farbman could still feel that punch in the chest. Blocker'd sent him a newsletter with a quote from St. Augustine— "Nascimur inter faeces et urinae": "We are born between the feces and the urine." The point, apparently, was not to stay there.

Afterward, Farbman undid the three locks that barred his junkie neighbors from entering his apartment, peeled off his wet sweats, and put on dry ones, deciding to keep the momentum going and try a weight workout for the first time in weeks.

At the gym, Lamont recommended forgetting about other people. "I don't give them no free rent in my head," he said. The important thing, said Lamont, was to stay strong, eat right, maybe take multiplex vitamins. And first chance, try and get his wife to take him back, tell her whatever he did was stupid.

Lamont told Farbman about a friend with a nice wife and steady job who got bored and wanted action. "Pulled in some fly bitch from the projects who figured he didn't get much and his nose was open. They sleep together once and she starts calling him, even comes to the man's house and rings the bell. That's it for Ron-Earl. His wife puts him out the door and he's still trying to get back in. No man who's involved with a woman is in control. You know what I mean?"

Farbman did.

Lamont said Farbman obviously needed someone to push him. Farbman said he was going to go easy today because he was experiencing a loss of strength, but Lamont shook his head, explaining that he hadn't really lost it. "It's just that because you didn't do nothing for a few weeks the fibers figured they could kick back. They think it's vacation time and they can chill out. You got to wake them up and get them back to work. I got just the thing fo' yo' ass."

The long run and brutal exercise made Farbman feel almost good enough to face an empty office with little work and few prospects. After Farbman processed the mail—which consisted mainly of packing it up in a large envelope for forwarding to Marucci—Wolf telephoned with the elating news that he'd gotten Silverdorf and Ann Marie to agree to a four-way. Farbman breathed easier. An armistice was at hand.

A week later a detached Farbman poured himself tea at Silverdorf's glass conference table, trying to get Ann Marie to make eye contact and observing the mad posturing of the lawyers. He thought the only thing missing from this eight-hundred-dollar-an-hour tea party was the dormouse. Silverdorf and Wolf were truly a matched pair: from their exchanges of misstated facts to their winter tans. Neither tried to move toward agreement. Each created uncompromisable positions.

Farbman panicked as he saw the opportunity being lost and offered more than he could afford, more than a court would order. Wolf chastised him openly for proposing unrealistic commitments, while Silverdorf and Ann Marie rejected them out of hand. Wolf wrote figures on a pad. Farbman was so anxious he couldn't decipher them.

Silverdorf waved off Wolf's proposal for alimony for Ann Marie until she became self-sufficient.

"You think he owes her for life?" asked Wolf.

"And then some," said Silverdorf.

Wolf suggested they put support aside and tackle asset distribution, which should be easier since there was nothing to whack up. They had no cash. The equity in their home was gone. The law practice belonged to Marucci and the bank, and Ann Marie could have half of whatever was left to Farbman.

"Don't insult our intelligence," Silverdorf retorted, "with so obvious a scam. The practice just happens to break up within days of his leaving the house?"

"Marucci's like his brother," added Ann Marie. "Let's get out of here."

They did, and the discussion continued through the court.

"It's clear we can't settle without full-blown discovery," Silverdorf told the judge. Wolf protested, but LaFarge agreed. "Funny," the judge noted for the record "how such black clouds appear coincident with divorce." She added that she would be inclined to deal harshly with an attorney who fraudulently pauperized himself. She asked Silverdorf what he required to get started. He figured six thousand for the depositions of Farbman, Marucci, and the bankers; for document inspections by his accountant and himself, including a report, another five. LaFarge thought eleven thousand dollars reasonable and gave Farbman two weeks to fork it over, without prejudice to reallocation at final hearing. She hinted at the possibility of a bench warrant if Farbman didn't comply.

Farbman was frightened enough to ask his father for help. His father said, "I'm not interested." His parents loved Ann Marie. They did not want to be in the middle and he shouldn't try and involve them. As Farbman's hysteria enlarged he began making calls to Michael in which he implied that, if money were not forthcoming, claims might be filed with the N.A.S.D. and the S.E.C. The result was that the next time Ann Marie heard Farbman's voice she asked him how long he'd been seeing Leah. She said she was so pleased that now he could replace his convert with a real Jewess. "Wasn't Leah the pawned off ugly sister the Biblical Jacob first married?" she asked as she hung up.

Michael confirmed to Farbman that, yes, he'd told Ann Marie about Leah, that Farbman had no right to make him a co-complicitor. Farbman hung up vowing he'd see his college buddy in a federal pen on securities fraud.

Farbman opened the day's *Times*, punched the crease flat, and began angrily turning pages, breathing deeply, trying to calm himself and get the print to come into focus. Unfortunately, it was all too focused as Farbman read the lead article in the Metro section on Con Ed's settlement with the estate of a Queens woman who'd frozen to death when her heat was cut off. Marco Marucci, the attorney for the estate, said that the landlord, the 1891 Realty Corporation of Queens, had contributed to a settlement totaling seven hundred fifty thousand dollars. Herbert Rothbard, the sole shareholder of the corporation was a major contributor to the Mayor's reelection campaign. Neither Mr. Rothbard nor the mayor's office would comment.

Sitting there in his empty offices, staring at the now unambiguous fact of Marucci's betrayal, Farbman realized that what was galling him was not the theft of the practice, nor even the prolonged deceit that had made it possible, but the thought that henceforth he would be viewed as the left-behind partner, the Art Garfunkel, the Sonny Bono, of their legal duet. However, that was nothing when compared with having no money. No money to cover the mortgage or the taxes on income already spent, or for the camp deposits or the orthodontist.

He had a one-month-old dispossess notice from the landlord and a two-month-old telephone bill with a cutoff threat. Farbman went up and down his receivables list: A woman for whose business he had done a year's work, agreeing to forbear payment until she was established, was giving it up to marry and move to Chicago. Janet Sodowick's bill could only be paid out of the sale of the marital home which she refused to list and which would pass to her husband if she succeeded in killing herself before she was divorced. Bigonocco Veal had gone into liquidation, and, although Big promised to make good, his hands were tied. Amber Fleischman, whose trial was imminent, sent a check for half of what she owed and left the signature off. A lawyer named Rosenbluth who had given Farbman some work when he'd heard about Marucci's decampment had failed to pay for any of it. In response to Farbman's calls, he'd left a message that the work was for his clients, not him, and he'd be in touch when he returned from Antigua in two weeks.

At first, Marucci made sure Farbman survived by periodically sending small checks as the personal injury files he had taken turned over. Marucci allocated sixty to eighty percent—varying the percentage so it wouldn't appear to be the arbitrary figure it was—to Marucci's post-partnership efforts to get the case resolved. Then he would take half of the remainder and send it to the bank and split what was left with his old buddy. Thus, a ten thousand dollar fee would typically end up divided seven thousand seven hundred fifty to Marucci, one thousand five hundred to Worrad and seven hundred fifty to Farbman. Of that, pursuant to a recent LaFarge order, about six hundred dollars went directly from Marucci's account to Ann Marie and the kids.

Farbman marveled at how the formerly financially helpless Marucci was able to prepare the detailed breakdowns, the self-serving accountings, that accompanied each check. In this way it was made clear to Farbman how artfully he was being fucked.

When it came to the Fudgsicle, Farbman didn't even get a check with the accounting. Marucci contended that Farbman had done nothing to advance the case until after the partnership broke up. Then he explained that when he'd sent Farbman checks in the past, he had over-looked the fact that Farbman still hadn't restored his overdrawn capital account. Marucci was, conveniently, obliged to see Farbman's account restored under the terms of the deal Marucci had negotiated with the bank.

Farbman couldn't bring himself to call Worrad. He had already got-ten him to forbear calling Farbman's car loans with a promise that he would renew regular payments shortly. But now, two months and four payments after the promise, he had delivered only the ones due on Ann Marie's car. Repossession was definitely in order, and it happened. One morning as Farbman entered his garage, Luis, the little Bolivian atten-dant, invited Farbman into his booth. On the floor was a space heater, and on the wall were several pinups of women who would never need implants. Luis told Farbman that two very ugly men had come with a paper saying they could take his car. Luis had tried to call Farbman, then called the police, who looked at the paper and said to give the car to the ugly men.

Without his car, visitations became more difficult. On a couple of Sundays when Harold wasn't on call and didn't need the Porsche for his own recreation, he let Farbman borrow it. However, he let Farbman know he wasn't happy with the arrangement and proposed that Farbman get a rental on Harold's credit card, which Farbman declined to do.

Asking Ann Marie for help was like asking a Department of Motor Vehicle employee to make an exception. Picking Farbman up at the sta-tion and allowing him to visit in the house was completely out of the question since it violated the terms of the restraining order. How about letting him use her car for the day? A bad idea; it would cross the bound-ary of the businesslike relationship she was struggling to achieve with him.

So Farbman spent as much time as possible on the phone with Jason and Jennifer until Ann Marie put her foot down. He was abusing the privilege. He was tying up her line, interrupting their dinner, interfering with bedtime routines. Worse, she felt his regular discussions with the children were contrary to their best interests since they were reminded of his absence and saddened for a period of time after each call.

Moreover, they always asked to see their father over the weekends and were disappointed when he didn't appear.

Three days after the eleven grand was due and Silverdorf had called Wolf to say he was reluctantly going to have Farbman jailed, Farbman got Amber Fleischman in to prepare for trial and collected her eight thousand dollar balance plus three on account to cover the trial and sent it over to underwrite the legal assault on himself. Amber, when she got on the stand, ignored everything Farbman had taught her in hours of rehearsal, not only forgetting her carefully prepared lines but allowing Blechnicht, her husband's clumsy lawyer, to bait her into angry outbursts on cross-examination. Worse, when Farbman tried to protect her by interrupting to cue her with frivolous objections, she ignored him. The judge had decided to work an extra hour, and as they were nearing the end of the long day Farbman was worn out with the effort.

"Mrs. Fleischman," Blechnicht paused for a large, powering inhalation, "isn't it a fact that your foot went through the windshield not, as you just testified, because you were struggling to avoid being thrown out of a moving car by your husband, but because you were angry that he was driving a new Mercedes and you had to make do with a used Audi?"

"It was a BMW."

"A six-year-old BMW, wasn't it, and it embarrassed you—"

"I object." Farbman was on his feet. He knew he had to cut off this line before it got started. Mrs. Fleischman did deeply resent driving the used Beemer and wouldn't hesitate to let everyone know how she felt.

"—driving a car you considered ready for the ash heap."

"Again, I object." Farbman was about to state his grounds when the image of Ann Marie in the kitchen a few weeks before his eviction flashed before his eyes. She had struck him with a large bag of celery which he'd yanked from her hand; then she'd lifted the colander of draining just-boiled pasta from the sink and hurled it furiously. Farbman, not quick enough to block it all, had ended up picking fettuccine strands from his hair while Ann Marie had shrieked "I've got to get away this instant! I no longer know who I am!" She'd run to the garage, and, tires squealing, floored her Mercedes out of the driveway. Farbman forgot why he had risen, his fingertips probing his hair, mumbled never mind, and sat back down.

"Listen, there were springs coming through the seats. The tires were original, paper-thin, seventy-five thousand miles. He gives his wife—forget his wife—his first-born son to drive around in. We were black-listed from three car pools. No cassette. Mr. Fleischman over there, he had auto reverse, eight speakers, a six-pack compact disc player, equal-izers, amplifiers under the seats. The bastard had sub woofers."

Thrilled at the witness' concession, the lawyer nodded and smirked at the judge to make sure the point had registered. Presumably it had, because Farbman could see His Honor making a note. Blechnicht now turned to a new topic, striding dramatically to the evidence on the Clerk's desk. As he passed his counsel table, Farbman was at the nurses' station outside Ann Marie's hospital room, trying to cajole them into relieving his wife's pain.

"Mrs. Fleischman, calling your attention to exhibit 'P-2,' the gun which you allege that your husband placed to your left temple saying 'Fuck or die,' prior to his allegedly forcing himself on you sexually—isn't it a fact that the gun was and is totally inoperable and that you knew that, that you took that line from the script of your favorite X-rated movie 'Go Ahead Make Me In the Day,'—"

"Fuck her over," Ann Marie is screaming, meaning herself, on her knees in the dirt. A chainsaw starts up in a neighbor's yard smothering her words. Farbman can still lip-read the phrase "piece of shit" as she socks herself. "Wait," said Farbman, getting to his feet again.

"—and that this was all part of your sex play, that you were non-orgasmic except under simulated duress and that that is why you and your husband were seeing a counselor, and not as you testified because he made your three-year-old run sobbing around the yard as a target while your husband and his parents threw tennis balls at him?"

Farbman tells Jason not to look. Jennifer sneezes into her plate of runny eggs, and Jason begins yelling she is gross and won't eat his omelette. Jason has to be ordered to take a shower, then reminded after five minutes of listening to the water run to get into it. Farbman sits at the pine plank harvest table reading parenting instructions. Upstairs

Ann Marie is emptying closets and loading her camera.

"I said I object," yelled Farbman, "there's been no proof such an X-rated movie even exists."

Blechnicht rushed to his brief case. "I'll represent to the court that it does exist, that I have it reserved through tomorrow, and will play it at the beginning of Mr. Fleischman's case." He turned to the judge triumphantly waving a yellow paper. "I offer in evidence my paid rental reservation receipt from Go Go Video."

"Offer it on your case," said Farbman. "I value our friendship," Marucci is saying, slurring his words. His proffered hand shakes slightly from side to side. "I swear on the lives of my children," he says. Farbman closed his eyes tight and opened them.

The judge directed Mrs. Fleischman to answer.

Farbman asked if he could have a ten-minute recess. The judge noted they were nearly done for the day and that they could break when Mr. Blechnicht finished this line of inquiry.

"Tell it to the dead woodchuck, it doesn't work."

"Excuse me," asked Blechnicht.

"You want to come see the bones, the patches of hair still left, not six feet from the swimming pool. In front of our son I might add. Dig around for the slug, you can send it to ballistics."

"I wonder why you call me," says Harold to Farbman. It is their last conversation. He is disgusted that Farbman won't do what he says and give Ann Marie what she wants. Farbman perspires at what he senses is an implied threat to withdraw his friendship if Farbman doesn't acquiesce.

They stood adjourned, announced the judge. His clerk would advise them of his next free day. Farbman exited hurriedly. His cell phone didn't work in the building so he ran down the stairs to a phone booth. He had to talk to Harold. He was decompensating. He punched in Harold's numbers as fast as he could, feeling the fever rise in him, the pictures starting to flash again. Lamont lines up three sets of dumbbells each ten pounds heavier than the next. "Guess who's coming to dinner?" he asks Farbman. "Pain," he says, "Pain is coming to dinner." A recording informed Farbman that at the customer's request the number had been changed to unlisted. Farbman told himself to slow down, to take a deep breath. He took a breath and then another, which he held and released in a thin stream. He was sure he hadn't said anything so hurtful that Harold too was writing Farbman out of his life. Farbman reviewed their last, heated conversation in his mind. Harold had been pushing Farbman, as he always did, to give in to Ann Marie's demands, including sole custody of the children, telling Farbman to reexamine his motives for insisting on joint. In Harold's opinion Farbman was battling just as a matter of principle. He noted that Farbman hadn't cared to spend much time with his kids for years before Ann Marie was sick and questioned his sudden interest. He reiterated his theory that if Farbman yielded authority to Ann Marie that she would voluntarily grant him as much time as he could handle, maybe more. When Farbman asked what evidence he had for that view and tried to offer justifications for his own, his friend got really annoyed. Harold said he couldn't listen to lawyer bullshit anymore. Finally he said, "I don't know why you call me," and got off.

Farbman tried the number again and got the same recording. Farbman closed his eyes and let his head fall back against the metal wall. He could think of no one else he could call, no other place to be.

GOD'S SHAPE

At his apartment, Farbman took a Librium and four Advil and clambered under the covers in his dress shirt and underpants. He lay there shivering, unable to get up to look for another blanket. Over and over he reviewed what he'd said to Harold, trying to figure where he'd gone wrong. He decided he'd go to his office, if necessary, get an appointment, confess error, and say he was willing to let Ann Marie have what she wanted and move on with his life.

Around ten o'clock the phone rang and Farbman snatched up the receiver on the first ring.

It was Harold.

"Thank God," said Farbman, "I've been trying to get you. I really need to talk. I think I'm losing it. I was hallucinating in court. Why did you change your phone number?"

"I was being hassled by Birgitta is all. She won't accept that it's over. Here's my new number, get a pencil." Farbman copied it down, then started to launch into a description of the latest legal skirmish with Ann Marie and what countermove he planned.

Harold interrupted.

"Listen, I'm with her right now."

"Has something happened to her?"

"Don't worry, she's fine. We're at home."

"What do you mean *at home?* Whose home?" asked Farbman.

"Her home. Your home. Or both of yours. Whatever you call where you used to live. Where Annie and the children live."

"Annie? You call her *Annie?* You use a neutral article to describe my children?"

"Jesus. You're so touchy. I'll choose my words more carefully next time."

"Don't get me wrong, Harold," Farbman laughed, "I appreciate your conceding me some non-possessory interest in the house, but I pay too much child support not to have my paternity acknowledged."

Harold sighed. He said he was calling to explain that he felt he "needed to support Ann Marie and confirm the truth of her reality." Farbman said huh? and Harold went on to say that by this he meant that he had told her that Farbman had had a sexual relationship with Leah two years earlier. He added that he had come to realize from listening to Farbman's infuriated ranting about Ann Marie and her lawyer that it was Farbman who was the venomous hate-filled one, that he sensed there had been a change in Farbman's character—perhaps it was the influence of his profession—but that Ann Marie was still the same open, loving person he used to spend nights chatting with when they first met. The proof, said Harold, was in the two wonderful children she had raised.

Ann Marie also needed Harold's assistance, he felt, to help correct the imbalance in the legal process. She was clearly disadvantaged. She was vulnerable emotionally, physically, and financially, and if there was one thing he'd learned from Farbman it was how unfairly the weak got treated in this system.

Glandular alarms were going off in Farbman. He felt clammy, sweaty, and nauseated. He tried to say, gentling his voice, that Harold had got it all wrong.

Harold said it didn't matter. Farbman asked what did he mean it didn't matter?

Harold allowed a long two beats of silence before he spoke again.

"I've started courting Annie," he said. Then he waited while it registered.

"I can't believe this," said Farbman, "you call her *Annie*? For how long?"

"It's moved beyond movies and trips to ballgames and museums with the kids. We're at the point where it looks as though we'll end up in bed, and we agree you should know what's going on before it happens." Another pause. "I mean we've been friends for too long."

"I agree," said Farbman, "for much too long. Now get the fuck out of my house, and away from my kids and my wife, you hear me? Or I'll resect your liver with my fingers. I'll yank out your bowels and stomp on them."

Farbman was nervously thumbing magazines in Wolf's waiting room when his lawyer arrived the next morning. Wolf gave him immediate attention, inviting Farbman to tell his story while he walked Wolf to get his coffee and while Wolf gave instructions to his staff. Farbman finished his description of Harold's betrayal sitting in Wolf's office, Wolf leaning forward, his face reflected in the glossy burled walnut of his desktop. He said that if he were in Farbman's shoes he'd take his case to Vito Corleone.

Farbman said he didn't care about Harold but that he would not give up his children.

"Isn't it a little late for that?" replied Wolf. "You're so far behind the eight ball you've got no shot at custody even if you could raise the hundred grand you'd need for the fight."

"Just get a hearing for me before this gets any worse. Demand a transfer to me until trial." Wolf looked dubious. Farbman said, "C'mon, LaFarge has already restrained me from cohabitation in the children's presence. She's going to think this stinks even if she's not offended at how my communication is being cut off. Do it by order to show cause."

Farbman managed to get twenty five hundred dollars out of Rosenbluth, which he gave to Wolf, and ten days later on a damp, cold day he had his hearing.

Farbman parked a distance from the courthouse and hurried gloveless with two filled briefcases, shortcutting through a vacant lot.

There were remnants of snow on the ground and patches of ice in the street. Two enormous crows eating unidentifiable carrion screaked and cackled as he passed. A pack of wild dogs trotted up. One growled and Farbman froze until they circled and sniffed and moved on. Dumping his keys and change into the guard's basket preparatory to his electronic frisk, Farbman was aware that the unease triggered by the dogs was still with him. He went to review his testimony with Wolf and found him in the cafeteria having coffee with another attorney. When both of them finished telling their golf stories, and Wolf got a second cup to go, he and Farbman walked up to LaFarge's courtroom, Wolf telling Farbman to relax.

Ann Marie did not deny that Harold had slept over. She smiled artlessly at LaFarge as she explained that Harold had been a regular guest for years, that he shared their summer rental, that he was like an uncle to the children; his presence was a source of comfort and stability to them at this difficult time. Farbman, said Ann Marie, was certainly aware of this, and his application was a dishonest, desperate tactic. Of course, she had never discouraged Farbman's calls to the children—sadly such communication was about all they got from their father before, as well as after, the separation.

Harold took the stand and qualified himself as physician and life-long friend of the family. He was concerned first and foremost for the children and didn't want to take sides. But pressed to give his view as to the relative fitness of their parents he would have to say that whatever true nurture they received came from their mother. That is not to say that their father did not love them; it was that he just lacked the capacity to see them as developing human beings.

From the innumerable and intimate opportunities Harold had had to observe Farbman's parenting over the years, he would describe his friend at first as mainly absent from his children's lives, then uncomfortably and resentfully pressed into service for brief periods during Ann Marie's illness, and now competing for them as a prize of war. Farbman's caretaking style was totally authoritarian. He saw the children as little more than objects.

Harold said that they should not get him wrong. "I would never suggest that Jason and Jennifer would not benefit from a relationship with their father; however, it is their mother they need for their primary day-to-day caretaking." Moreover, said the doctor, he did not believe, at this particular point in time, that Farbman was in emotional control. "He feels victimized and doesn't hesitate to vent his rage. He has threatened me, and while I do not fear for my safety, the court apparently found there had been serious acting out with his wife, and I am concerned for the children's emotional and perhaps even their physical well-being if more than the current limited visitation is allowed."

Farbman felt himself liquify in the flames of his humiliation. He caught LaFarge studying him disdainfully. Ten feet to his left, Ann Marie wrote industriously in a loose-leaf binder, a small but distinctly rapturous upturn at the corner of her mouth. There was nothing left to Farbman. He experienced himself as ash or less, as having passed like something exposed to nuclear heat, instantaneously from solid matter to gas. He had moved beyond pain to relief, from confusion to clarity, marveling at his capacity for self-delusion, at his ability to have believed so utterly in a friendship that wasn't there.

Wolf made a good try at crossing Harold, hitting all the bases but never scoring. Wasn't it fair to say he was moving in on his best friend's wife? No, and for the record, they hadn't had much of anything between them but racquetball games for years, unless you counted free medical advice. Hadn't Farbman often expressed parental concerns, such as Jennifer's bedwetting, to Harold and asked his advice? Harold didn't recall that, but he did remember being asked about the risk of Farbman's having contracted a venereal disease when he returned from what he described as a religious retreat.

LaFarge, whom Farbman had observed correcting orders and reviewing correspondence and motions during his turn on the stand, said she was troubled by much of what she'd heard but concluded that her existing orders should remain unmodified for now. A week later Farbman received notice in a letter from Silverdorf to Wolf that Ann Marie was taking the children to Ohio for a "long-planned" family visit. They would be available for telephone communication between the hours of five and six p.m., Eastern Standard.

They weren't. Farbman either got the answering machine or was curtly informed by Ann Marie or his in-laws that they were otherwise occupied. Farbman instructed Wolf to apply for sanctions, but Wolf pointed out that he was talking like a client. Spend a couple of grand on an unprovable issue that would be moot when they returned? So Farbman elected to wait it out; but shortly before they were due back came the announcement that Ann Marie had found a job out there and that her parents had agreed to help with the kids while she was at work.

Farbman didn't need Wolf to tell him Ann Marie's application to relocate was a lock. Every appellate decision in the prior five years had, following a sanctimonious declaration that the children's interests were paramount, affirmed their mother's right to move them with her out of state, no matter how the children's access to their father would be jeopardized.

Nor did he need Wolf to tell him what happened to the recalcitrant fathers. After they, and often their parents as well, had been pauperized by legal and expert and transcript fees, the family's assets turned into file drawers of conflicting facts and accusations, into reams of unread briefs and certifications and reports, after they had tried their sixth or seventh lawyer and then attempted to carry on by themselves, they became crusaders, tub thumpers in their cause, derided as they raved at bored judges about the Constitution and the fundamental right to rear one's children. Once branded kooks they were whispered after in the hallways, tormented by judges and clerks, and denied any relief.

Farbman did not think he could endure such humiliation, so he decided just to go along. He would write letters on distinctive stationary, make up games and activities he and the children could play on the phone when he was able to get through. He would visit when he could.

Then one evening Jennifer told him: "Mommy says you made her sick. Mommy says you made her crazy. Mommy says the judge doesn't want you to see us because you'll make us sick and crazy, too. She says our names are Jamison now. Is yours Jamison, too, Daddy?"

When Farbman asked for Jason she said he was busy with a video game and refused to come to the phone; and Farbman knew that thenceforth life would be a matter of trying to get through each day. He understood at once his children would not be present at breakfasts or bedtimes, or birthdays; would not be there to receive his love or nurture. That he would never escape that hurt as he could not escape schoolyard noises or TV cartoons or well-meaning inquiries or the recountings of other parents. That he would carry the loss of his children as a chronic and ever-present pain, as people bear their swollen joints and ulcers, their secret wounds and shames, the amputation of a limb.

That night Farbman got into bed early but found he was too tired to get up the next morning.

In the hope of recovering his lost energy he retired earlier each night but woke each morning tireder. He had his remaining files delivered to Marucci and stopped going to the office. Logy when his eyes opened, he would turn on the TV and watch commercials, cartoons, twenty-second news bites, weather maps, and traffic patterns. When he couldn't take anymore of the vacuity of the newspeople he would throw the covers off and shuffle into the bathroom, avoiding the mirror.

He gave up on showering since he never went out. Every morning he would spread the daily newspapers flat on the bed and, cross-legged, read every article on every page. Periodically he would glance up at the inexorably advancing digits on the clock, correlating the numbers with memories of getting the children's breakfast, or inching along the L.I.E., or walking in to his office or the courthouse. He absorbed the details of the marriages and breakups of rock stars and congressmen, of celebrity blood clots and brawls. Protesters and supporters clashed at abortion centers, at gay rights rallies, at the annual slaughter of five thousand pigeons in Hegins, Pennsylvania. There were armed conflicts between nations, between races and religions, between haves and have nots. Bridges collapsed, gas mains exploded, fires consumed tenements, people died, and survivors were left homeless.

What was he supposed to do with this information? Treat it like his clients' gripes and unburdenings? Absorb it all till he bled from his palms like Blocker's Father Jim?

Every gray day Farbman studied the weather map. He calculated when the cold fronts and high and low pressure systems would arrive and then began to read the forecasts for foreign cities, the daily temperatures in Jerusalem, Moscow, Rome and Tokyo. He became concerned about thunderstorms in southeast Texas, drought in the Florida panhandle. He studied the nuances of investigations into financial scandals on Wall Street and in Japan, the charges brought by prosecutors in Osaka and Paris. He read Heloise's Hints for stretching gas mileage, and the views of Dear Abby and Dr. Brothers and Miss Manners. He noted where he could get three rooms of carpet for ninety-nine dollars and where he could go to get leg veins treated and chronic pain and depression relieved with acupuncture. He learned from his horoscope that this was his day in the sun. Make hay, it said. Review your investments. Why not, thought Farbman, and he dug through the week-old stack of mail and opened the latest form dispatch from Michael, the engineer of his train to economic freedom.

The tidings were somewhat less than glad; while foreclosure proceedings had been instituted, the banks were working with the developer to restructure the loan. Uncertain of the implications, Farbman decided he should discuss the situation with Nussbaum, his accountant.

Farbman had only gotten as far as saying he'd bought a unit in a syndicated partnership that owned some real estate in Houston when Nussbaum said he was sorry.

"What does that mean?" asked Farbman. He pictured the chubby little bean counter on the other end of the line, in his white-on-white shirt and navy suit with the heavy saddle of dandruff sitting on his shoulders, as if all of his innumerable regulatory worries had taken on substance and congealed into flakes.

"Everyone knows," said Nussbaum "that oil prices have pushed Houston real estate values into the toilet. If the property is worth less than the mortgage financing—and it probably is since these are very leveraged deals—foreclosure means real tsuris."

"Let me guess," said Farbman, "I lose my investment but can't deduct the loss."

"Worse," said Nussbaum. "Your cost basis is reduced by accumulated depreciation so you may have a gain for tax purposes. Meaning even though you aren't getting any cash back you have taxable income to the extent you've got a negative capital account."

"Are you saying the property can go at a loss and I pay taxes as if I had profit?"

"You got it. Phantom income is the term for this."

Farbman had his own term for it, but all he wanted to know was how to get around it. Could he pay with phantom money?

"The best way to avoid phantom income," Nussbaum explained, "is to die before the property is disposed of. This is because Congress allows the adjusted basis of the decedent to be stepped up to fair market value on death. And here's the best part. You can legally transfer the interest to whichever spouse is likely to predecease the other, provided you don't transfer within a year of death."

"Ann Marie's in remission," said Farbman.

"I don't know what to tell you then. Maybe we can generate some offsetting capital losses. You own any bad stock, for example?"

"No," said Farbman.

"Too bad," said the grim reckoner, "but perhaps we'll find something with an unrecognized loss."

My life, thought Farbman, but I recognize the loss all too clearly.

"You know," said Farbman, glancing back at the letter, "they're not actually foreclosing. The banks don't want the property so they're restructuring the deal."

"Worse," said Nussbaum.

"How could that be worse?"

"Any reduction," said Nussbaum, "in the mortgage obligation will be ordinary income to you and not capital gain."

Farbman thanked Nussbaum for not asking why Farbman didn't check with him before purchasing the unit, and got off the phone. He decided, on disconnecting, that a final exit before the loan was restructured was the most elegant solution from several points of view, besides gaining a stepped-up basis.

A week later, Farbman opened the newspaper and found a smiling Marucci staring back at him, posed against a wall of law books he still owed Farbman for. It was a lengthy article on breast implant litigation

featuring Marucci. It seemed that he'd received hundreds of calls weekly from women who wanted to file lawsuits, that he'd filed about two
hundred so far, all involving ruptured implants and some form of
autoimmune disease. "These women," said their self-anointed spokesper-
son, "are suffering from terrible, progressive, incurable illnesses and they
were never warned of such risks. Many of them wandered, sometimes
for years, from doctor to doctor, trying to find out why they were
exhausted, had swollen joints and sweats and rashes, and their hair was
falling out."

How many more generalized symptoms can you bait with? thought
Farbman.

Marucci also explained that since many women are uninsured and
unable to afford surgical removal, and since many lawyers won't take
such cases because of the limited recoveries, he, Marucci, knight exem-
plar, had filed a class action suit against the primary manufacturers for
reimbursement of the costs of both insertion and removal.

On the same page was a piece on the Dalai Lama. He was in New
York for a series of meetings with a Canadian Hasid, Rabbi Avrom
Sholem, to be held at the 92nd Street Y. The subject of their dialogue
was how Tibetan Buddhism could be preserved in its diaspora. In the
same article, the Dalai Lama—also known by such names as Holy Lord,
Gentle Glory, Eloquent, Compassionate, Learned Defender of the Faith
and Ocean of Wisdom—said that despite persecution and exile, his faith
in human nature had never been tested. His everyday conduct was driven by the motivation to help others. He laughed a lot. To relax he
enjoyed looking at gruesome pictures of World War II and what he
termed beautiful machines of violence. His daily meditation involved
preparation for death.

Farbman decided that even if he couldn't buy the Eloquent's view of
human nature, preparing for death made sense. He crammed the newspaper into a wastebasket and called the Hemlock Society, only to learn
that their instructional book for those seeking to make their quietus was
on back order. He was out of tranquilizers, didn't own a gun, and slicing
himself up or crashing a car had an element of gruesome uncertainty to
them. His self-loathing swelled as Farbman acknowledged that whatever

he knew came from a book, that he couldn't figure out how to kill himself without reading a manual.

Determined to try anyway, he marched into the bathroom and took out a new razor blade. He had his hands in the stained bowl considering whether he should begin with a nick when the phone rang. It was Leah. She wanted to let him know, in case he'd missed it, that Rabbi Sholem was in New York to meet with the Dalai Lama.

"I read the papers," said Farbman. He added he didn't see them having much in common.

"I do," she said. There were so many parallels between the contemporary Tibetan Buddhist experience and that of the Jews. Not only the analogy of Pharaonic enslavement in Egypt to the conditions of Tibetans living under Communist Chinese occupation, the proscriptions against their religion and culture, but the problem now, of survival in exile.

Leah said she was concerned about Farbman. "You stopped calling with no explanation. When I called your office they said you were no longer there. Are you all right?"

"Couldn't be better," said Farbman. "My wife took my children from me, and their minds and love for me as well. My partner—a man I considered my brother—stole the practice, my life work. Harold, my closest friend, betrayed me, fucked Ann Marie, and helped her take the children from me." Not only was he destitute and in debt, but Michael, her cousin, Farbman's longtime buddy, had ripped off the last bit of equity in his house and got the IRS on his case to boot.

Farbman assumed he would soon be visited with boils.

Leah was silent.

After a long minute Farbman said, "So? What do you think?"

To which she replied, in slow, deliberate words. "I think," she said, "that you must sit in the shit a little bit longer."

As Farbman started across Lexington Avenue an attractive, smiling woman emerged from the doorway of the 'Y' and started toward him, catching his eye. She paused as if about to ask him something, then, noticing the raw drizzly weather said, "aargh." Farbman continued toward her, not averting his gaze, not smiling back. "Uggh," she said, pulling her coat closer around her. Farbman considered the woman's communications until she turned and walked off. Then he charged up the steps into the lobby and to the auditorium at its rear.

Ignoring the large "Latecomers Will Be Seated at the Discretion of the Management" sign, Farbman pushed through the double doors in the wall of marble. Above was the gilded declaration that the hall was a gift to the memory of Henry Kaufman's wife, Theresa. Theresa? thought Farbman. An intermarriage that had apparently made it to the end.

Farbman could hear but not see His Holiness, the Dalai Lama, say in response to someone's question that it was better to prepare for death than to be surprised because one failed to make preparation. Then, he said, if there is no afterlife it doesn't matter. The crowd standing in the rear of the auditorium blocked the aisle and Farbman's view except for the names inscribed high above the proscenium—Dante, Goethe, Shakespeare, Jefferson, Isaiah, Moses, David.

He recognized Rabbi Sholem's voice. It was living life properly that prepared one for death, the rabbi said, "And that means repentance, teshuvah." There was an old joke, he said. "The rabbi instructs the disciple that he must repent on the last day of his life. And how will I know which that is? he asks. And the rabbi says, "Aha!" Farbman's thoughts were not on repentance at that moment but on trying to discern in the names on the wall common denominators besides maleness and historical prominence and whether the clue was in the order of placement, in the apposition of Shakespeare and Jefferson, Jefferson and Isaiah. Was there something prophetic in Jefferson's work? Something democratic in Isaiah's?

Farbman squeezed around the clot of people next to him and could see more names: Washington, David, Lincoln, and Beethoven. Where was Jesus? And Buddha? And Leah? Apparently not in his life till he stepped out of the shit pile. The crowd of standees was so thick Farbman could penetrate no deeper into the room. He tried to figure out how to get to the area around the platform where the speakers sat. To his left was another room that appeared to connect with the auditorium near the stage. He entered the room and discovered it was being set up with coffee urns and punch bowls, perhaps, he thought, with some diasporal donuts to follow. A sign offering infrared headphones with a credit card or a twenty dollar deposit made Farbman realize he had neither. He continued on his way and found that others had had the same idea and stood in a cluster, craning their heads in the doorway that connected with the front of the hall. They were straining for a glimpse, cupping their ears to pick up a snatch of transcendent dialogue. Farbman started to force his way through. He hadn't bathed any time within recall, and people moved aside even before they glanced at his wild-eyed, unshaved face. As he squeezed past the innermost onlookers, several gave him dirty looks, and one irritated man elbowed him hard in the side. "Very spiritual!" Farbman said, shouldering the man onto the toes of somebody who yelled "Ow."

Now, if the Tibetans were right, the reincarnated Buddha, the embodiment of perfect spiritual fulfillment, sat before Farbman in clear view. With him were about seven or eight monks in marine corps haircuts. All wore the same style maroon robe draped over the left shoulder and under the right, so that their left arms were covered and their right bared. All but two had steel-rimmed spectacles. The Dalai Lama's were a dark-tinted shade which gave him a somewhat hip, slightly gangsterish look. He was inclined forward, left hand under his chin, his right arm braced with the elbow up, hand gripping the end of the armrest. The Gentle Glory was smiling, his eyebrows arched wryly, his attention focussed utterly on the bearded man in the black suit and enormous fur hat. Farbman remembered the hat from their weekend in the woods. It was the hat that his ancestors had worn in nineteenth-century Poland. Haute couture nowadays. How absurd to be wearing it in this overheated room. How ridiculous and weighted down the bearded rabbi looked in contrast with the clean-shaved saffron-robed monks who leaned toward him at the same angle, expressing the same attentiveness as their master, but with not a hint of his levity.

The subject at hand was what lesson could be learned from the Jewish experience of almost two thousand years of exile. Farbman listened for a while as it was explained how the destruction of Jerusalem was kept in the forefront of Jewish ritual and as the Dalai Lama nodded along and confirmed his understanding that the secret of Jewish survival lay in the constant reminder "We have to return." But the Dalai Lama wanted to know about the spiritual side of Judaism, and the rabbi began talking of the Jewish inner experience, of the secret teachings of Kabbalah, and before long Sholem was discoursing on angels, saying something about Jewish angels and Tibetan angels, and, when the Dalai Lama asked what colors they were, Farbman could stomach it no more.

"Hold on," he yelled, "may I just say something here? It's one thing if you want to discuss some practical techniques for remembering, maybe holding Tibetan seders—once a year you eat like four cups of rice out of a special bowl and promise yourselves next year in Lhasa or Potocho—but you cannot seriously sit around while the world is falling apart contemplating what some overgrown Tinkerbell looks like."

Farbman pushing his way toward the stage was intercepted by three uniformed guards; one blocked his path, the other two each laid hold of an arm. His Holiness instructed his security to allow the man to come forward and make his contribution. Reluctantly the guard moved aside. Farbman pulled his arms free and stepped up to the microphone.

"In case you haven't read a newspaper, at this very moment people are dying, there's suffering everywhere, everywhere starvation and disease. On the doorstep of this building there is a consumptive woman shaking an empty cup at passersby. For all of you so self-absorbed you don't notice or can't figure out why these people are living in doorways and cardboard boxes, they write it on signs for you to read. 'Stricken by AIDS.' 'Viet Nam fodder.' 'No Work.'

"I know that the Buddha here thinks everyone is good. But everywhere I look human relationships are a disgrace. Parents deform their children. Partners stab their partners in the back. A man's oldest friend, a doctor, runs off with the man's wife. Everywhere priests lie down with evil under the sign of the dollar. And you—" he turned to Sholem "—sit here in that stupid hat talking about angels. I mean it's like a sauna up here under these lights, but you must give deference to the God who says Treblinka is fine, Auschwitz is fine, just don't tear your toilet paper on Saturdays. Eat the flesh of tortured animals so long as you don't have cream in your coffee when you do it. When it's freezing rain or maybe a blizzard on a Shabbos in February, you go to shul to pray to this almighty meshuguna, but God forbid you take the car. You must arrive frozen and drenched because God will not have an ignition spark on His Holy Day. Ocean dumping, yes. Genocide, yes. But no ignition sparks. Tens of thousands of people can die in mudslides and typhoons. Millions of innocent children abused and raped. I don't know how many women were mutilated today in Africa, how many folks around the globe—Tibetans included—were eradicated by their neighbors, how many consumers were cheated, how many voters defrauded by their own representatives, how many good men betrayed, and you're talking about angels and sweating to show respect to a God whose concern is ignition sparks? This is Judaism?" Farbman addressed the Dalai Lama again. "Surely the 'Ocean of Wisdom' can see the silliness, can see that malevolence and cruelty is the makeup of human beings."

The Gentle Glory smiled at Farbman. "Human nature is gentleness. I have complete faith in that nature, although there are many people acting against their natures, being false.

"I am sad when I see many people killed, or tortured, homeless and hungry. Sometimes even I am briefly irritated, but quickly I try to think at a deeper level."

"I give up," said Farbman. "But let me at least tell you something about this man's view of Judaism. The Jewish tradition, he says, is a game. Five thousand years of suffering and law-making, tailoring and TV shtick. Of relativity and communism, the money business and the shmata business. The invention of the Uzi and the unconscious, of one day a week off, and the atomic bomb and the bagel with a shmeer. All this plus sweet sixteen parties, polio vaccine, and rendered chicken fat on rye bread, he calls the big game of Jewing. And he and the other Hasids are the self-designated ball carriers in this game."

Farbman's voice had risen to an hysterical level. The guards hovered on each side of him.

The Dalai Lama was smiling, but Farbman couldn't read his eyes behind the dark glasses.

Abruptly the rabbi rose and gestured for Farbman to approach. He moved to give Farbman a hug, but Farbman fended him off. What kind of God could allow such awfulness? he demanded of Sholem.

"You've been reading MacLeish?" asked the rabbi. "Not that it's so bad. 'If God is God he is not good, if God is good he is not God,' etcetera. In fact, for Broadway, it's excellent."

Farbman began to weep, great wracking sobs, and the rabbi folded him into his fathering arms. "Oy, sha shtill, kinder. Be calm, child." He spoke into Farbman's ear. "Wipe your nose and I will tell you a great secret, all I have learned about God."

Sholem glanced over his shoulder at the assembled monks who were anxiously watching him, then lowered his voice to barely a whisper. "I don't want them to hear. If they knew what I'm going to tell you, it would travel like wildfire—the Hindus, the Muslims, to say nothing of the entire Christian world—the havoc it would wreak. I'm not talking just the collapse of financial markets, of governments, but of social contracts everywhere—"

"So what is it already?" yelled Farbman, pushing him away. "What, that God is dead? You're about fifty years too late with that news."

"Oy, such a smarty-pants. You want I should do this on one leg like the stooge demanded of Hillel? All right, but I'll need to balance, come close." Sholem held his left foot up and hopped with his back to the audience, until he stood facing the stage curtain, then he grabbed Farbman's arm to steady himself.

"God is made in man's image," he told Farbman. "Are you listening? We create God daily in the world by our actions. God as man's creation is the only explanation. God is our invention, He is our responsibility."

The rabbi, back on two feet, held the snuffling Farbman at arms' length. "What," he asked, "have you done to shape God recently?"

"Me? You're asking me what have I done to make God? What am I supposed to do?"

"You know what to do. It only remains for you to do it."

"Yeah," said Farbman. "Well, I'll tell you what I'm doing—I'm leaving." And he ran to make his escape.

Farbman asked Mr. Big if he might pay him a visit. Bigonocco suggested Farbman come for dinner the following evening. Farbman demurred.

The inevitable veal dish made acceptance an impossibility; he couldn't imagine an explanation that would wash given his career representation of the meat business. He told Big he didn't want to impose. Big said Rosalie loved to cook, they'd see him around seven.

At the door Farbman handed Big a hundred dollar bottle of Sassacaia, the most expensive Italian wine he could find. It represented the last of the week's piecework wage from Rosenbluth. Big complimented Farbman on his taste and extravagance and introduced him to Rosalie as the smartest lawyer he knew. Rosalie wore the black of the Sicilian countryside. Farbman decided she could have been pretty forty pounds ago.

After a covert inspection of the pasta fagioli for evidence of chicken stock, and a sly pick through the salad to ensure no ham among the radicchio, arugula, olives, peppers, and onions, Farbman was presented with rigatoni zingara, broccoli di rape, and eggplant carbonara, and he realized he was home free. He complimented the pasta sauce, and Rosalie said Big grew the peppers and tomatoes himself.

Big said, "Rosalie was all set to make her specialty, veal marsala, but I explained you was a vegetarian."

Farbman looked wonderingly at Big.

"I knew. I knew. You think I don't check on the people who work for me?"

They went in the other room for espresso and some of Rosalie's cheesecake. Big told Farbman he was sorry to learn of his misfortunes. Farbman said that he felt bad about what had happened to Big, that somehow he felt responsible for not beating the rap.

Big shrugged, said he shouldn't worry. He would do just fine and he knew Farbman had done everything he could. Big said Farbman really was a great lawyer and that he especially appreciated that he knew his job was representing a client. It don't matter if you're a vegetarian and he slaughters calves, or if he's some fucking rapist pervert, you do your job and do it the best you can. You were always there when I needed you, and when you done good for me, like you done many times, you didn't think you suddenly was my partner. You never asked to get paid any more than you was supposed to. And you never tried to run up hours or cheat me—I'm not saying nothing about Marucci now and that scam with the judge's payoff. Yeah, I knew about that, too. Now go ahead and ask. If it's sumpin I can do for you, I will."

Farbman took a sip of his espresso and said, "I've got an idea, a proposition sort of, only I don't have any cash."

"Well, I don't have no cash, neither—at least not where nobody can reach it. The business is still in bankruptcy. The calves and all the equipment at the veal farm went at auction," said Big.

"I know," said Farbman. "But if I remember correctly, only about half the property was titled in Bigonocco Veal, the corporation. That's the half the government put under."

"Yeah," said Big, "and it's so fucked up with tax liens and creditors' claims no one knows what will happen to it."

"So the land and buildings are left?"

Big said, "That's right." He had been smart enough to put two hundred fifty acres with the farmhouse, barns, and outbuildings in Rosalie's name some years back. "Like I told you, you don't need to worry about me. So what's your proposal?"

"I'd like the land and buildings."

"You got an idea to make us some money? Some development scheme?"

"No," said Farbman, "I don't even know when I'll make anything, if ever. And, if I do, the return to you would never justify the investment— all I could do is maybe buy you out at fair value, on terms. Nothing you couldn't do yourself."

"You want a deal you can just walk away from it?"

"Yes," said Farbman, "but with an option if it works."

Big paused. "Okay, think how you want it and draw up the papers." He smiled at that and then held out his hand. They shook on the deal, and Farbman knew he had something better than papers, that Bigonocco had finally entered into a binding contract.

HAVDALAH

The farmhouse, barns, and outbuildings sat about a quarter-mile in from the northern edge of the property alongside a trout-stocked section of the Muscanetcong River, which was the property's eastern boundary. Beginning at the narrow blacktop, a dirt and gravel access road ran along the riverbank, the bank cleared on this side of all but some enormous willows that overhung the swift, noisy water. Visitors confronted by the sweep of the bending river, the graceful, untidy willows and, in the distance, visible over the thicket and trees on the far bank, a pale, rounded range of mountains, would imagine themselves time-warped into an earlier century, even before they caught sight of the rolling hay fields and pastures, the grazing sheep and the two-hundred-year-old stone structures.

Farbman sat in his high-riding, cancerous, gray pickup, elbow out the window, his border collie, Kali, sitting erect and dignified on the passenger side of the cab. He waved as he passed the roadside stand at the entrance to his farm, pleased to see carrot-haired Derick the Orange busy with a line of cheese customers. Then he followed the puddled road up the river toward the house. His eye registered the tiny bit of a huge boulder still visible in the risen water, how fast the current swirled around it, propelling tree limbs like missiles. He noted a murkiness that meant that upstream they'd opened the reservoir sluice gate.

The wheels slipped on a mound of mixed three-quarter-inch stone and quarry dust. It had just been delivered, dropped without any special care while Farbman was out. He debated whether to ask Derick or Crazy Greyhound Willie, Farbman's most recent resident guest (named for the bus station where his babbling acquaintanceship was made), to drag it with the old John Deere. Or whether Farbman should rake it as he'd done many times before, when he himself was newly arrived—a refugee, without family or means—and had to restore the whole length of road by hand.

These days Farbman no longer had to struggle in pain to locate pockets of strength on which to draw. His hard-muscled body performed the tasks he assigned it like a humming machine, harmoniously, without demanding the attention of his consciousness. In fact, he thought of roadwork now as an indulgence, rewarding not only for its extreme physicality but for its opportunities for reflection. Raking stones had not only developed Farbman's back and biceps, but had helped him to resolve intrapsychic conflicts and to make early spiritual leaps.

It was while pushing and tugging a pile of rocks and dust one day that Farbman, sweating and squinting into an August sun, had stopped and made his first tries at not doing, but being. The art which he taught himself was how to step out of the moment into the flow of time, to take communion with, for example, a stand of oak trees or the dried earth, the baking heat, or the cooling stream on his toes.

And it was while he was raking stones that the heron first appeared—a Great Blue Heron taking off from the marsh on the far side of the river opposite the farmhouse. The shock of impossibility, the fearsome grace of the bird, had penetrated Farbman, who stood frozen in place, staring. In that instant he experienced prehistory, as one might standing on the lip of the Grand Canyon, or in a boat with a whale breaching only feet away. It was as if a pterodactyl had passed overhead.

Farbman had felt awe. He had felt love.

He backed the truck into a dirt-floored equipment shed, and Henderson, a wiry, blue-black man totally bald under a knit cap pulled down to his eyebrows, stepped from the shadows and opened Farbman's door.

"I'll unload," he said. "I.O. Ewe just lay down and started grunting. Water bag's not out yet but any moment. I put O Ewe Doll in a pen, too. She's been antsy for days and running off by herself. She's about ready."

"Twins or triplets you think?" asked Farbman.

"I.O. Ewe? She's big enough for three and grunting enough. But two will cause plenty of trouble with her small hips."

Farbman hurried down the hill toward the house. A couple of groundhogs dove for their hole as they caught sight of Kali, accelerating their way. Deer spoor was everywhere on the lawn. Even though Farbman left a section of corn for them they came into his garden anyway. Each night at dusk a herd emerged from the woods and grazed brazenly in his yard. They were a source of extreme pleasure to Farbman, as were the rest of his undomesticated co-tenants.

These included a pair of Canada geese who returned each spring to nest and then parade around the property with their goslings. A swan who floated up and down the river in a pattern of random appearances. There were bluebirds and red-wing blackbirds and crows who yelled at Farbman and who swaggered around as though the place were theirs alone. And swallows who swooped menacingly by Farbman in the twilight and dive-bombed the cats if either approached anywhere near their nest.

At the farmhouse Farbman trimmed his fingernails, scrubbed his hands and forearms, opened a scarred valise, and checked off its contents: clean rags, iodine, lubricant, thick twine he'd soaked in antiseptic, his lambing snare.

Farbman had first arrived after a big dump of late season snow. He'd slept on a two-hour bus ride from the derelict-filled Port Authority terminal on Forty-Second Street to the little Greyhound station that harbored only a half dozen homeless men and women, then cabbed with two cumbersome valises out to the farm. There he would find a furnished home and a Toyota pickup in the garage. He was dropped by the mailbox, the road invisible under glinting, unplowed, undulating snow, too risky for the taxi to attempt. Farbman in his street shoes stepped high, planted each leg with deliberation, up to a knee, then, in spots, to the groin. He shifted weight, his suitcases sinking in, pulling him backward, then the other soaked, freezing foot was raised and replanted. Breaking through the drifts encrusted with refrozen melt, he slowly made his way. A hundred miles across the Steppes of Asia. Across the frozen Antarctic. Through the waves of a solid white ocean to a new world. Against the farmhouse door the snow was chest high. Farbman attacked it for a bit with a fallen branch, then slogged around the garage looking for implements, huffing, overheated and sweating from the exertion. He found a piece of roofing slate and dug with both hands.

The sun was setting. The low light made the icicled trees glimmer as if electrified with ornamental bulbs. A plug was pulled somewhere, and the heat began to drain out of the world. Farbman's body shook with chill, and he began to move with a desperation, regretfully noting each lost ray of the dying sun. Then he was at the locks, then the knob, then inside. There was no wind but no immediate rush of warmth either.

Farbman pulled off his wet leather gloves, placed his reddened, dye-stained hand on icy pipes. There was a frozen block in the bottom of the toilet. In the sink, however, both faucets leaked steadily. Farbman turned each one. The hot produced hot water; the cold, cold. Thank you, thank you, he said to no one in particular, bent his head and slurped from the cold faucet. He was careful to leave both faucets running when he was finished. In the kitchen cabinets: lots of mouse droppings; two cans of black beans; a half jar of peanut butter; opened boxes of Captain Crunch and Shredded Wheat; two bottles of Louisiana Hot Sauce; a quart bottle half-filled with reconstituted lemon juice; assorted condiment jars highlighted on their greasy surfaces; loose packets of sugar substitute; most of a jar of decaf instant coffee and some tea bags. Farbman found the thermostat and thumbed the metal dial past ninety. Nothing. He continued to listen for the vibration of a motor, for some reassuring sound. Still nothing. There was a cast iron stove in the corner with browning newspapers piled next to it. Farbman ran outside and in the blue near-dark collected a few pieces of deadwood. He opened the flue and started a fire and then discovered under a tarp on a rear deck a stacked cord of wood. "Thank God," said Farbman aloud, sitting on the edge of a chair hugging himself, leaning into the radiating warmth, transfixed by the flames dancing behind the cloudy glass inset.

The next morning, Farbman, heartened by the first light's return of the world to him, said "Thank God" again. And he did it each reassuring morning each day thereafter.

On the sixth day, in the late afternoon, Farbman, who had eaten everything except the can of beans he was in the process of opening (when he'd finally cleared the garage doors he found the truck with no battery and two flat tires) was amazed to see a large oil truck with the words "A.A. Anthracite & Oil, There's No Fuel Like An Old Fuel" painted on the side pull up to his front door. A man with a wool knit cap jumped down, got his bearings, and marched in high boots deliberately over to a pile of snow and shoveled out a fill spout. Farbman, already in his coat and tasseled ski cap, ran out as the man was unwinding the hose.

"Who called you?" he asked.

"No one. You're on automatic delivery. Figure your use by degree days."

"Well, there's no heat anyway. Do you know how to start a furnace?"

"Sure, but you should wait for service, they're probably just backed up right now."

"I didn't call," said Farbman. "I don't have a phone."

The driver said his name was Henderson and he'd see what he could do. He found the problem in the furnace ignition but needed to get his tools. Also an electrical device for throwing a charge into the pipes to make them thaw. Henderson left and came back a few hours later with the equipment and a box of assorted doughnuts. He got the burner motor going right away, but the pipes could only be thawed a section at a time and it was two in the morning before the last piece of pipe turned hot to the touch and it was confirmed that none had burst. Meanwhile there was nothing to do in the silent house except talk and every now and then grip a pipe. Farbman heated water on the propane range and made coffee for Henderson and tea for himself.

Henderson volunteered that his wife had left him, run off to New York City for what she called a real life. That he didn't blame her, there wasn't much to do around here. Plus there were bad memories behind the fact that their little boy had died on his sixth birthday, choked on a balloon they couldn't get out of his throat. Rushed him to the emergency at County Hospital only minutes from where they lived, but they tried to fish it out with the wrong instrument. Pushed it in deeper, into a lung to where they needed to cut open his chest, but then it was too late.

Did he sue? asked Farbman.

Lots of people said he should've, but then he'd thought about it. All he'd get was money, right? And well, there's some money you don't want, you know?

Yeah, like just about every nickel Farbman had ever earned in his life, but he didn't say it.

So what did Farbman do?

Farbman said that he was, or anyway had been, a lawyer. That his wife, too, had run off with both his kids and that he thought he'd try his hand at farming. Sheep farming. He showed Henderson his dog-eared, underlined copy of *Raising Sheep the Modern Way.*

Henderson's parents had raised some goats but no sheep, but he figured Farbman should do well since there were a lot of Greeks in the area who would pay good dollars for spring lambs, especially if they could be slaughtered right on the premises.

Farbman explained he wasn't going to kill his animals, on or off the premises.

Henderson declared he never heard of no farmer who didn't kill his animals. Said it in a way that Farbman inferred the man thought he was some kind of half-baked, big-city crackpot with a few book-learned ideas that would enable him to succeed at farming about as well as he had succeeded in getting the heat on in his house.

Henderson wouldn't take any money for the doughnuts or for his help. He said to Farbman: "You're in the country now." He said he'd look in on Farbman from time to time to see how he was getting on. He wrote his number on the cover of Farbman's telephone book.

Henderson did return. Always with his tools, he worked side by side with Farbman, claiming that no thanks were due, he enjoyed the opportunity "to exchange profundities." Together they renovated the farmhouse. They tore out walls, and when they'd pried off the sheetrock, Henderson and he marveled over the half-tree timbers, the original horsehair and mud insulation, and in the later additions, the newspapers describing Roosevelt's anti-Depression projects. They thought about the former owners.

"Makes you realize that, no matter what they think they owned, all these folk was just tenants."

Farbman thought about the section of time he was renting and what he would do with it. He reflected that he had made his past life a commodity, selling his precious minutes, his tenths of hours to anyone who would buy. He considered in whose service he had put his mind and heart. "I was no better than a junkie turning tricks or marketing his blood," Farbman told Henderson.

Besides Henderson and the formerly homeless hands who helped him, there were not many humans in Farbman's life anymore. He and Leah had corresponded more or less regularly for some years, their friendship never diminishing despite the interruptions in contact, although she had never taken him up on his open invitation to visit. There were the people from whom he bought supplies or to whom he sold wool or cheese, or manure. Wholesalers mainly, since Farbman avoided the retail roadside trade whenever he could. There was Prudence Stockwell, the busy vet who had arms like a blacksmith and who helped out with abscesses and difficult lambings, and who kept Farbman apprised of the latest preventatives for ticks and wool maggots. There was his dentist, Dr. Dickstein, who taught Farbman extraction techniques so that Farbman could pull the remaining teeth on his old broken-mouthed sheep, allowing them to keep grazing once their gums toughened up. It was Dr. Dickstein whom Farbman eventually prevailed upon to make dentures for his ewes, extending their productive lives for years.

Although Farbman had never failed to send notes and cash to his children on birthdays and holidays, the gifts weren't acknowledged. On the other hand they weren't returned, either, which encouraged a spark of hope that in some way they'd still kept him in their lives. That hope was realized one day when a nearly unrecognizable Jason and Jennifer paid him an unannounced visit. His son was tall and sullen and costumed in biker's leather. Jennifer had rings through her eyebrow and nose, and a cigarette in her mouth. There was an upside-down cross depending from Jason's ear. Farbman welcomed them but was firm about the boom box and cassettes staying in their car.

"You lied. You cheated. You turned our mom into a battered woman," said Jason.

Jennifer said, "You deserted her for years before you actually abandoned us. She lay there night after night wondering why you didn't touch her, why you two had no sex for years, until she finally realized you'd been having one affair after another."

"You made her so depressed she got cancer. Then you shouted in her ears when they were ringing in pain from her chemotherapy."

From reading Sophocles and Freud, Farbman knew that even unalienated children grew up and killed their fathers; but he never expected it to be so painful. He stood before them and wept. Then he went off and dug postholes. As Farbman walked away, Henderson introduced himself to the gangsters and them to the concept that people who passed time at the farm were expected to contribute their labor. Jason said they were out of there. Farbman watched their car accelerate down the gravel drive, his wound reopened even before they were gone.

While there weren't a lot of humans in Farbman's life, there were plenty of animals, both wild and domesticated. Of the latter there were besides Kali, the collie, his suddenly appearing, roof-walking goats, Big Surprise and Little. There was the thoroughbred, Keats, retired from his track career, and his companion, Fanny, a gentle swayback gray mare Farbman took from a neighbor when he heard she was to be put down. There was his flock of chickens, including Henny Penny and Rooster Cogburn. Postmenopausal Henny Penny hadn't laid an egg in years, but she was his first hen and the lone survivor of a raccoon attack. Rooster Cogburn was the flock's caretaker and Farbman's alarm clock. There were Jake and

Elwood, the tiger-striped barn cats. And, of course, his sheep.

Farbman had begun his herd with a pair of heavy-fleece and milking sheep from Germany, Ewe de Cologne and Ram Beau, so that he could raise for cheese as well as wool, since he knew he would not raise for killing. As he worked to dismantle the veal stalls to create pens for his sheep and lambs, Farbman sensed the ghosts of that evil enterprise lurking everywhere. Indeed, the bucolic setting in which Big's factory farm had been situated brought to mind the remote pastures the Germans selected for mass exterminations. He considered the ground of the farm consecrated by the blood and pain of the calves who had lived out their brief lives in its barns until "harvested," as though those beautiful, sentient creatures, more intelligent than horses, were merely a field of corn.

Of course, the decision not to kill meant no more than subsistence for years, a period during which Farbman learned to economize and to salvage profit where he could. He promoted the sheep's high-quality manure and sold every bit that wasn't required to fertilize his own fields to local garden supply stores at a good price. He created a following of hand spinners who bought his entire wool production. He even took the waste wool from legs and belly, and treated and packaged it for home insulation.

When, some months after their first visit, the children returned, again unannounced, they ignored their father and spent their time with the animals. Farbman was willing to let it be the sheep or horses that drew them. Or the sweaty work; Henderson had had them feed the chickens and weed the pole beans and lettuce. In fact, before the day was out the kids had planted a big chunk of rolling hillside with the little strawberries the French call "fraise de bois." They didn't speak to their father before they left, but Farbman packed sandwiches for their trip and gave them to Henderson to deliver. On the bags in shaky outline were drawn a lamb for Jennifer, a ram for Jason. This time they waved good-bye, and they came back only a few weeks later and brought a friend and showed him around like the place was theirs.

Farbman scrubbed and prepared for delivery, closed the valise and with the bag in one hand and a bucket of hot water in the other—the doctor his parents had always wanted—started for the door, to his expectant patient. He paused to review the chores listed on the calendar and make sure they were covered: pick up molasses and grain (Henderson was unloading them now); install portable feeders; replace fencing in high pasture (he'd dug half the holes, left Greyhound Willie to do the rest); spread barn bedding/manure in garden.

Then he was out the door and on his way to the lambing barn. He spotted a strange car stopped where the road dipped and the swollen river had washed up and created a sizeable pond. The driver, a man, and the passenger, a woman, got out but were too distant for Farbman to recognize. Farbman, who didn't have time to waste speculating about who they were, figured if they really needed to see him they'd climb to the high ground and work their way around through the woods to the barns.

From what Henderson said, I.O. Ewe couldn't have been in labor an hour, yet she looked so tired that Farbman, who would normally wait up to two hours before intervening, decided to check her lambs' positions to see if she could use any help. He washed her and himself again, and with a lubricated hand felt gently around, trying to sort out legs.

One big hind leg tendon confronted Farbman immediately, then another. Then what appeared to be forelegs, but of which twin he hadn't a clue. Farbman tied strings to two front legs and followed them back to the body to confirm that they were attached to the same lamb.

He decided to deliver the breech baby first. He pushed the sibling part way back to get a little extra room, and began tugging, only to have the baby stick in his mother's narrow pelvis halfway out. He rocked him side to side as he pulled. Still no progress. Farbman, fearing he'd pinched the umbilical cord, started to perspire. If the lamb tried to breathe now it would suffocate in mucus.

Inhaling deeply, Farbman started to pull again, rotating the lamb as he pulled; suddenly its ribs appeared and with one quick tug he was out.

Farbman wiped its nose at once, then turned to the other. He positioned its head and legs, got his loop over the head, behind the ears, and gently pulled head and legs together until it was out. The lamb lay gurgling in the straw. Farbman seized its hind feet and stood, holding it until the fluid ran out the lungs; but still it didn't breathe.

He swung it in a circle, saying, "C'mon, buddy, c'mon." But it still failed to respond.

Then he knelt in straw beside the newly born but not-yet-alive lamb. He felt in the softness with his left hand for the heartbeat and with his right holding its wet head, gently breathed into its velvet mouth, praying its spirit would ignite. Nothing. He tried again. Still nothing. We're running out of time here, Bub. He picked up the lamb and carried it outside to the drinking trough and dunked it in the frigid water. There was an audible gasp as it started to breathe.

Farbman rushed back inside to dry the lamb and warm it up. I.O. Ewe lay there too tired even to lick off her other baby. Farbman placed them near her nose so she would identify them and bond, wiped their noses clean of mucus, rolled Momma on her side, and put them to the teat. He checked their eyelids for entropion, knotted and snipped their navel cords, dipped them in iodine, then sat back smiling on a bale of hay, savoring the moment.

"Thank you," he said to the still, odor-rich barn air, "for my lamb-caring life. For my place here among the ambling woodchucks and bramble-eating goats."

Not thanking anyone in particular. Not knowing then how to praise God for the fields and meadows, the lambs and the wind-riding hawks who threatened them, for the woodchucks and the heron who split the sky and arrested him in his work. Farbman felt like the simple boy of whom the rabbis spoke, whose prayer was no more than a loud blast of his horn, except that Farbman had no horn other than that which trumpeted in his head and his heart.

A movement glimpsed out of the corner of his eye. A murmur. Two figures not yet in focus. A woman stepping forward, beautiful, teary. A visceral pleasure, a sense of rightness in Farbman even before he thought *Leah*, even before she spoke his name.

"David," she said. "That was beautiful."

Farbman shook hands with Leah's companion, pleased at the effect of his calloused palm against the other man's softness. Sumner Gordon was

Leah's director, but it was apparent that their relationship was much more.

"Let me show you around," said Farbman. He called Kali to join them. Leah said, "I thought border collies all have four-letter names." So he spelled it, adding, "As in goddess of life."

The lambs bounded sillily by their grazing mothers. They were dressed in coats. Farbman explained it kept their fleece clean and the cold off their backs, increased the staple length of the wool, and made shearing easier.

"Do they have names?" asked Leah.

"Of course," said the proud shepherd. "Momma with the big lips over there is Ewe Bangi. The lady in perpetual motion up there on the hill is Ewe Biquitous. That's Ewenion Label over there, sister of Ewenion Made and Ewenion Shop. You'd think they'd hang together but they don't. Over by the apple trees I think I see Ewe Boat and Ewe F.O. The old lady with the torn blanket is Ewe Nit. Her daughters are Ewenit Price, Ewenit Rate, and Ewenit Vote—but they've all been so prolific I've taken to naming their daughters Ewenits one, two, three and so forth. I count them before sleep."

"Maybe your transformation is not as complete as I first thought," said Leah with a grin that was full of affection. "What about the dads?"

"The Ewenionists are all out of Ram Bunctious. Ewe Boat and I.O. Ewe, who just delivered, were both fathered by Ramschackle. Then there's Ramses, Rampage, Rambler, Ramjet, and Battering Ram. I've also acquired a new breeding pair, Wool Rogers and his wife Woolhelmina."

Yes, he sheared. It was a skill he learned right away, and in the early years to support himself he did the neighbors' flocks as well as his own. What he needed to master now was spinning so he could market directly to knitters. After he had the wool washed he sent it up to a mill in Vermont to be spun. Leah, too, it turned out, had always been interested in learning how to spin. Once for a school project she had gotten some lamb's wool and made felt by hand.

They walked under an endless sky. There were a few faint high clouds like trailing smoke. Farbman felt as though he were Prospero commanding his world: everyone appeared as if cued. The woodchucks ambled and dove for their holes when Kali charged. Keats came over to the fence, touched noses with Kali, then gave his head to Leah for petting. The river performed a medley of burbles and splashes and raced by in impressive torrents. Two huge trout leapt several feet into the air and, as Farbman and Leah and Sumner approached the house, the heron passed overhead, head cocked back, squawking loudly.

Sumner seated himself on a log left on the river bank and declared his intention "to listen to the water and the wind for a bit." They left him there, walking in silence until Farbman spoke.

"Your career is coming along then?"

"One day I got noticed in a showcase and then I was in my first Equity job—had a six-week run in Philadelphia but never made it to New York. The work just got better and better since then. I had a few lines in a John Sayles film last year and I'm about to go into rehearsal for a new Mamet play on Broadway. Sumner is really responsible; he matched me with material that better showed my range. He got important producers and agents in. He's very well connected. I mean he's very highly regarded. Rightfully. He's quite brilliant. Knowledgeable and intuitive."

Farbman nodded. "That's great," he said. "Because you know a lot of people have it in their heads but not in their hearts and guts. You're lucky."

"I know," she said. "It's a rare thing."

They walked along the river. Through fields and pastures. Walked and walked. Farbman told Leah about the good pasture and how he had run the goats with the sheep to clear the brush. How the goats ate the thorny brambles, the blackberry, and even saplings. That he could support four sheep on an acre. That he now had about a thousand sheep, that he also grew hay, which he fed them in winter with some grain that he bought. That he let them among his apple orchards and at the fallen fruit for extra nourishment.

They were really fragile creatures, sheep. Susceptible to innumerable diseases. Chased by a dog, they would suffer abortions and heart attacks as well as broken legs. He and his men fenced constantly. It was a problem, accommodating sheep and dogs in the same world. In this could be seen, said Farbman, an analogue to inter-nation strife. It was the basic problem of existential morality—the limits of one man's freedom when it ran afoul of the next man's.

"Have you and the dogs' owners worked out some solution?"

Not really, said Farbman. A group of sheep farmers had asked him to represent them at the county level and to try and get some protecting ordinances passed, but he'd turned them down.

Why so? Wasn't that exactly the kind of social contribution his legal skills were intended to make?

"I prefer, at this point in my life, just to improve my fencing."

"You're like Thomas Merton before he discovered that true spirituality is not lived in a Trappist monastery but requires involvement in the world." Although she spoke disapprovingly, she also seemed to Farbman to imply he was in an evolving state. That she could be interested in his future pleased him a lot.

A pair of cardinals spoke up as the couple passed by their tree, and Farbman said, "I'll second that."

"What did they say?" asked Leah, playing along.

"Pretty-pretty-pretty, sweet-sweet-sweet," said Farbman.

The field they were crossing climbed the side of a hill and at the top was a granite outcrop making a natural bench with a view over the farm and thickly wooded hills. They sat unspeaking and looked ahead of them.

Finally, Leah asked if he'd made his peace with Ann Marie. Most definitely, said Farbman. And, he added, with Marucci. And with Harold and Michael.

Was it a long time working through? Leah wanted to know.

"No. The decision to forgive happened in a single instant. There was this moment in which I recognized that the past was gone and the future was not here. That all I have is the present. That all I needed was the present.

"I was digging postholes, which means it was a typical day—posthole digging is an endless chore. The weather couldn't make up its mind. It was at war with itself—the sun fighting to come out, the rain falling so lightly the horses didn't stop grazing or the lambs stop playing." Farbman paused feeling the oak staves in his hands, the sensation of raising the digger, focusing its twin blades, held suspended in the air, then the satisfying bite as his shoulders, back, and arms drove them into the earth.

"I looked up and everything around me, the piney hills over there, the field, the barn, the white mare with her head up sniffing at the breeze, the river, the pile of posts and wire, everything had gone soft in the mist. I had this crazy feeling for the meadows and the grazing animals that I could only compare to the rush of emotion I used to feel watching Jason and Jennifer asleep when they were little. You know, overcome by their innocence, by the perfection of their being, by my will to protect and provide for them, by their trust in my ability to do that."

"Love," said Leah.

"Exactly. I came to recognize that I loved my lambs, I loved the earth and the cold wind and even the predator dogs, the foxes, and the raccoons against whom I had to protect my babies. I even loved the frost that attacked the crops.

"Eventually I came to love them, too—Marucci, Ann Marie, Michael."

"And the memories?"

"I have chosen the place and the time in which I live. Why shouldn't I also choose my memories? I hold onto the young, passionate Ann Marie—keep her forever on the softball field. I think of Marucci, still more brother than partner, standing with me back to back, taking on the world. I remember him and Michael and Harold as they were before their needs and urges conquered friendship and integrity."

The sun, dying, bled into the sky over the mountains. After a bit the sun was gone but there was still light. Leah explained that this was what cinematographers called 'the magic hour.' Farbman nodded in agreement and looked away so he wouldn't be caught staring. Finally Leah stood and said she'd better go find Sumner.

They made dinner. The glass doors were kept partly open so they could hear the river flowing by. A line of ribbons from county fairs and livestock shows moved softly in the breeze. The wood stove radiated coziness. Farbman's guests inspected his messy shelves stuffed with books on sheep and goat husbandry, with fencing and agricultural pamphlets. Sumner thumbed an old issue of the "National Lamb and Wool Grower." The house was built in the crook of the river and Farbman showed his guests a large window on the north side where you could look right into its flow. He told them that in the spring, after the snowmelt, the torrents came straight at you, shooting huge logs faster than stones from a slingshot, right from its violent heart. He said that even though his mind knew that the raging water would turn at the last instant, and that in two hundred years, the worst, bank-jumping flood tides had never even reached the basement, it still took all his courage to stand his ground. Leah gave a little shudder and said she'd like to be there next spring and see for herself. Farbman said she was welcome to, and they returned to dinner preparations.

Leah, directed to get a plastic container of Farbman's homemade pesto, found frozen colostrum instead. She shook her head at a refrigerator stuffed with sacks of seeds, grains, nuts, cheese, and marinating tofu all interspersed with bottles of antibiotics and lambs' milk.

After dinner Sumner played chess with Farbman. Leah opened the door of the woodstove, tilted her chair back, and watched the fire. When she pulled a knee up to her chin and flipped her hair to the side with her fingers, it cost Farbman the bishop that was the linchpin of his defense. Finally, Sumner said this was how he'd always wanted to live and that they'd better be leaving.

Farbman took the heavy big-beam flashlight and led them back through the woods. They listened to unseen creatures moving in the underbrush. In the clearing by the rental car, bats flashed by. Overhead, stars dazzled close enough to make the firmament seem reachable.

"Thank you," said Sumner.

"My pleasure." Farbman shook his hand, not hard. He turned to say good-bye to Leah. She was looking at Sumner.

"I'm not going back," she told him. Flat, informative. Sumner nodded as if this were old news. She turned to Farbman. "That is, if you'll let me stay."

There was an alligator slapping its tail around in Farbman's chest. He tried to rein in his thoughts as they exploded from some mental starting gate. "How do you know it's not just the night and the newborn lambs?"

Leah didn't answer. Before Farbman's mind could complete its whirring sort of the possibilities, she took his hand and pulled him toward home. They ascended the stairs to his bedroom without speaking and without letting go of their hands, Farbman trailing slightly behind, marveling at how so familiar a route could be leading him to someplace unknown, thanking God for bringing him to this moment. They separated only long enough to undress and slide under the covers where they met again and clung unmoving, in silence. Perfectly content, they lay like that, in silence, exchanging kisses, smoothing out their past, settling in. They savored each long moment, each vista on their way up the mountain, then they began to praise each other with their hands and eventually their bodies took over and soon they had to run to keep up.

Leah took the bus back to the city the next day to get her stuff and put things in order. Farbman set to work at once reorganizing his shelves and drawers, making space for her. Cleaning out his dresser he came across the cardboard box of memories that held his grandfather's tefill-in. He removed the hundred-year-old phylacteries from their plastic sandwich bag and untangled the still soft leather straps. One of the boxes was attached to what was clearly a head-sized band so he put it on. It was snug but it fit, although he could not figure out what to do with the two long leather cues that hung from the back of his head. The other box was attached to a strap he guessed was eight or nine feet long. He started to wrap his arm with it, first one way, then another, then gave up, feeling foolish. Maybe there was somebody Farbman could find who could show him how, if only, he thought, so that he would know in the unlikely event that his son should someday ask him.

The days waiting for Leah's return were anxious ones during which Farbman would stop dead in his tracks in the midst of some frenzied straightening up, panicked at the thought she had had a change of heart. But Leah did come back, arriving sundown on Friday in time to welcome their second Sabbath together. He watched her hands circling in the candlelight. And the following evening, after a holy day of love-making interrupted only by such necessary and excusable labors as feeding, milking, and birthing, the doors opened to the sound of owls and the river against the rocks, they made havdalah.

They raised their cups and blessed God, the creator of grapes.

They drew deep aromatic breaths over a box of rainwashed earth and blessed God, the creator of spices and the fragrance of growing things.

Then Leah held a candle aloft, and together they blessed God, the creator of the fire of creation and light.

Finally, hand in hand, alone in the warmth of burning logs, surrounded by blackness, by a society of animals, domestic and wild, alongside a pure rushing river, facing a future of labor and love, they recited: "Baruch atta adonai elohenu melech haolam … Blessed is our God, Lord of the Universe … hamavdil bein kodesh l'chol bein or l'choshech bein yisrael la amim bein yom hashvee l'shayshet yimay ham aahse … who separates sacred from profane, light from darkness, the House of Israel from other peoples, and the seventh day of rest from the six days of labor. Baruch atta adonai hamavdil bein kodesh l'chol … Blessed is the Lord who separates the sacred from the profane."